STEVE ALTEN

MEG

TSUNAMI BOOKS

Copyright ©2005 Steve Alten

ISBN: 0-9761659-1-0

Library of Congress Control Number: 2005903669

All rights reserved under all Copyright Conventions.

No part of this book may be reproduced, stored in a retrieval system, or transmitted by any means, electronic, mechanical, photocopying, recording, or otherwise, without written permission from the author.

Published in the United States by Tsunami Books, Mayfield Heights, Ohio

Submit all requests for reprinting to: Greenleaf Book Group LP, 4425 Mopac South, Suite 600, Longhorn Bldg., 3rd Floor, Austin, TX 78735, (512) 891-6100

Cover Design by Erik Hollander: www.erikART.com
Composition by Greenleaf Book Group LP

To personally contact the author or learn more about his novels, go to www.SteveAlten.com

For more information on Adopt-an-Author, go to www.AdoptAnAuthor.com

Printed in the United States of America

10 9 8 7 6 5 4 3 2

ACKNOWLEDGMENTS

It is with great pride and appreciation that I acknowledge those who contributed to the re-release of *MEG*. First and foremost, to my friend and business partner, Ed Davidson, whose support and guidance allowed me the freedom to spread my creative wings and whose business savvy made this all possible. And to the staff at Tsunami Books, especially CEO Bob Bellin, Leisa Coffman, and editor Jana Seely. And to Clint Greenleaf, Allison Pickett, Lari Bishop, Jay Hodges, Sheila Parr, and Tanya Hall.

Heartfelt thanks to literary manager Ken Atchity and his team at Atchity Entertainment International. And to Joel McKuin of Colden, McKuin & Frankel, and Matt Snyder at CAA.

A special thanks to my friend and movie producer Nick Nunziata, who personally hoisted this project on his shoulders and brought *MEG* out of extinction. And to the whole *MEG* Hollywood team, producers Larry Gordon and Lloyd Levin, Guillermo del Toro, and Ken Atchity, director Jan De Bont, and Shane Salerno . . . and especially to New Line Cinema's Toby Emmerich, Rolf Mitweg, Jeff Katz, and George Waud. You are my dream makers.

To my assistant, Leisa, for her talent and expertise in updating the www.SteveAlten.com Web site, as well as all her work in the Adopt-An-Author program, and to Erik Hollander, for his tremendous cover design and graphic artistry. Thanks also to Michelle Pryzstas at

Southeastern Business Solutions, and to Andrew Fox and Nimba Creations for their images.

Last, to my wife and partner, Kim, for all her support, to my parents for always being there, and to my readers: Thank you for your correspondence and contributions. Your comments are always a welcome treat, your input means so much, and you remain this author's greatest asset.

—Steve Alten, Ed.D.

To personally contact the author or learn more about his novels, go to www.SteveAlten.com

MEG is part of ADOPT-AN-AUTHOR,
a free nationwide program
for secondary school students and teachers.
For more information, go to
www.AdoptAnAuthor.com

This novel is dedicated to my father,

Lawrence Alten

Thanks, Dad . . .

AUTHOR'S NOTE

Not many people get a second chance in life . . .

In the summer of 1995, with aspirations of fame and fortune swirling in my head, I sat down at an old AT&T word processor and wrote *MEG*. Most of the manuscript was written from ten o'clock at night until three o'clock in the morning in my living room, a necessary sacrifice to keep my day job, the J-O-B. standing for "just over broke." Six months later I lucked into a literary agent, and inside of a year we had a development deal at Hollywood Pictures and a two-book deal with Bantam Doubleday.

Ah, the American dream . . .

A year later . . .

My second book was cancelled, the *MEG* movie rights reverted after changes at the studio, and I was looking for a new publisher and a new place to live.

In retrospect these setbacks probably saved my career, for they forced me to reevaluate my writing and pushed me to learn my craft in order to improve my storytelling with each novel. Ten years and seven novels later I'm proud to say that I'm still learning, but I'm no longer the same writer who penned *MEG*. And for that, I'm grateful.

Going back and revising *MEG* was something I've always wanted to do. After three *MEG* novels and a screenplay, I've come to know these characters quite well, and frankly, they deserved some spit and polish. My gratitude to Bantam for selling me back the rights to *MEG*, and to Tsunami Books for giving me this new opportunity.

This revision is for those loyal *MEG* fans: for standing by me, for opening their lives to me in e-mails, and for supporting my work.

—Steve Alten, Ed.D.

MEG

MEGALODON

From the moment the early morning fog had begun to lift, they sensed they were being watched. The herd of Shantungosaurus had been grazing along the misty shoreline all morning. Measuring more than forty feet from their duck-billed heads to the end of their tails, these reptiles, the largest of the hadrosaurs, gorged themselves on the abundant supply of kelp and seaweed that continued to wash up along the shoreline with the incoming tide. Every few moments, the hadrosaurs raised their heads like a herd of nervous deer, listening to the noises of the nearby forest. They watched the dark trees and thick vegetation for movement, ready to run at the first sign of approach.

Across the beach, hidden among the tall trees and thick undergrowth, a pair of red reptilian eyes followed the herd. The Tyrannosaurus rex, largest and most lethal of all terrestrial carnivores, towered twenty-two feet above the forest floor. Saliva oozed from the big male's mouth; its muscles quivered with adrenaline as it focused on two duckbills venturing out into the shallows, isolating themselves from the herd.

With a blood-curdling roar, the killer crashed from the trees, its eight tons pounding the sand and shaking the earth with every step. The duckbills momentarily froze, then rose on their hind legs and scattered in both directions along the beach.

The two hadrosaurs grazing in the surf saw the carnivore closing in on them, its jaws wide, fangs bared, its bone-chilling trumpet drowning the crash of the surf. Trapped, the pair turned and plunged into deeper water to escape. They strained their long necks forward and began to swim, their legs churning to keep their heads above water.

Driven by hunger, T. rex crashed through the surf after them. Far from buoyant, the killer waded into deeper waters, snapping its jaws, straining to shorten the distance. But as it neared its prey, the T. rex's clawed feet sank deep into the muddy sea floor, its weight driving it into the mire.

The hadrosaurs paddled in thirty feet of water, safe for the moment. But having escaped one predator, they now faced another.

The six-foot gray dorsal fin rose slowly from the sea, its unseen girth gliding silently across their path. If the T. rex was the most terrifying creature ever to walk the earth, then *Carcharodon megalodon* was easily lord and master of the sea. Sixty feet from its conical snout to the tip of its half-moon-shaped caudal fin, the shark moved effortlessly through its liquid domain, circling its outmatched prey. It could feel the racing heartbeats of the hadrosaurs and the heavier thumpa, thumpa of the T. rex, its ampullae of Lorenzini tuned in to the electrical impulses generated by the pounding organs. A line of neuro-senses along its flank registered each unique vibration in the water, while its directional nostrils tasted the scent of sweat and urine excreted from its floundering meal-to-be.

The pair of hadrosaurs were paralyzed in fear, their eyes following the unseen creature's sheer moving mass, which circled closer, creating a current of water that lifted and dragged the two reptiles into deeper waters. The sudden change panicked the duckbills, who quickly reversed direction, heading back toward the beach. They would take their chances with the Tyrannosaurus.

Thrashing and paddling frantically, they moved back into the shallows, feeling the mud swirling beneath their feet. T. rex, waiting in water up to its burly chest, let out a thundering growl, but could not advance, the predator struggling to keep from sinking farther into the soft sea floor.

The duckbills neared the reptile's snapping jaws, then suddenly broke formation, swimming in separate directions and passing within a few harrowing feet of the frustrated hunter. The T. rex lunged, snapping its terrible jaws, howling in rage at its fleeing prey. The duckbills never stopped, bounding through the smaller waves until they staggered onto the beach and collapsed on the warm sand, too exhausted to move.

Still sinking, the Tyrannosaurus had to struggle to keep its huge head only a few feet above water. Insane with rage, it lashed its tail wildly in an attempt to free one of its hind legs. Then, all at once, it stopped struggling and stared out to sea.

From the dark waters, a great dorsal fin was approaching, slicing through the fog.

The T. rex cocked its head and stood perfectly still, instincts telling it that it had wandered into the domain of a superior hunter. For the first and last time in its life, the Tyrannosaurus registered the acidic taste of fear.

The Tyrannosaurus felt the tug of current caused by thirty tons of circling mass. Its red eyes followed the gray dorsal fin until it finally disappeared beneath the murky waters.

T. rex growled quietly, searching through the haze. Leaning forward, it managed to free one of its thickly-muscled hind legs, then quickly freed the other.

On the beach, the hadrosaurs took notice and backed away—

—as the towering dorsal fin rose again from the mist, this time racing directly for the T. rex!

The reptile roared, accepting the challenge, its jaws snapping in anger.

The wake kept coming, the dorsal fin rising higher . . . higher, while underwater, the unseen assailant's head rotated slightly, its jaws hyperextending seconds before it slammed into the T. rex's soft midsection like a freight train striking a disabled SUV.

T. rex slammed backward through the ocean, its breath blasting out of its crushed lungs, an eruption of blood spewing from its open mouth seconds before its head disappeared beneath the waves. A moment later the dinosaur surfaced again, drowning in its own blood as its rib cage crumbled within the powerful jaws of its still-unseen killer, its gushing innards blocking its esophagus, strangling it to death.

Seconds later, the once-mighty land dweller vanished beneath a swirling pool of scarlet sea.

The hadrosaurs had watched the scene unfold, and were now whimpering and waiting, their bladders releasing in fear. Long moments passed, the sea remaining silent. The spell of the attack broken, the duckbills abandoned the beach, lumbering toward the trees to rejoin their herd.

An explosion of ocean sent their heads turning as the sixty-foot shark burst from the water, its enormous head and muscular upper torso quivering as it fought to remain suspended above the waves, the broken remains of its prey grasped within its terrible jaws. Then, in an incredible display of raw power, the Meg shook the reptile from side to side, allowing its massive rows of seven-inch serrated teeth ripped through gristle and bone, the action spraying pink froths and gouts of gore in every direction.

Finally *Carcharodon megalodon* crashed back into the sea, sending a great swell of water high into the morning air.

No other scavengers approached the Meg as it fed in the shallows. The predatory fish had no mate to share its kill with, no young to feed. A rogue hunter, territorial by nature, the Meg mated out of instinct and killed its young when it could, for the only challenge to its reign came from its own kind. An evolutionary marvel that had evolved over hundreds of millions of years, it would adapt and survive the natural catastrophes and climatic changes that caused the mass extinctions of the giant reptiles and countless prehistoric mammals. And while Megalodon's own numbers would eventually dwindle, some members of its species would manage to survive, isolated from the world of man in the perpetual darkness of the unexplored ocean depths . . .

THE PROFESSOR

"It was the ancient predecessor of our modern-day great white shark, only it was fifty to seventy-five feet in length, weighing close to seventy thousand pounds. Can you visualize that?"

Professor Jonas Taylor looked at his audience of just more than six hundred and paused for effect. "I find it hard to imagine myself sometimes, but we know for a fact this incredible monster did exist. Its head alone was probably as large as a Dodge Ram pickup. Its jaws could have engulfed and swallowed a dozen grown men whole. And I haven't even mentioned the teeth: razor-sharp, seven to eight inches long, each possessing the serrated edges of a stainless-steel steak knife."

The thirty-nine-year-old paleontologist knew he had his audience's attention, despite the fact that it had been years since his last public speaking engagement. Lecturing in front of a nearly sold-out crowd was not something Jonas had anticipated. He knew his theories were controversial, that there were as many critics in the audience as there were supporters. Still . . . just to be heard, to feel important again . . .

He loosened his collar and took a slow, deep breath, forcing himself to relax.

"Next slide, please. Ah, here we have an artist's rendition of a six-foot diver as compared with a sixteen-foot great white and our sixty-foot Megalodon. I think this gives you a fairly good idea why scientists refer to the species as the king of all predators."

Jonas reached for his bottle of water on the wooden podium, took a sip. "Fossilized Megalodon teeth found around the world tell us the species dominated the oceans for tens of millions of years, perhaps even longer. Who knows how old unfound Meg teeth buried in the depths might be? The big question is—why did the species die off at all. We know sharks survived the cataclysmic events that occurred about sixty-five and forty-five million years ago, events that wiped out most land animals and prehistoric species of fish. We know Megalodon's major food source—whales—was still quite abundant. In fact, we have Megalodon teeth that date back only a hundred thousand years. From a geological perspective, that's a tick of the clock, one that indicates our two species no doubt shared the planet at the same time, Homo sapiens dominating the land, Megalodon the sea. So, what happened?"

Jonas paused for effect, casually shuffling his cheat sheets on the wooden podium. "There it is, people, one of the great mysteries of the paleo-world. Of course, theories abound. Some so-called experts believe the staple of Megalodon's diet had once been large, slow-moving fish, and that the sharks couldn't adapt to the smaller, swifter species that exist today. Another theory is that falling ocean temperatures contributed to the creatures' demise."

An elderly man raised his hand emphatically from his seat in the first row, obviously wanting to be heard. Jonas recognized him, a former colleague at Scripps. A former critic.

"Professor Taylor, I think we'd like to hear your theory as to the disappearance of *Carcharodon megalodon.*"

Murmurs of approval followed. Jonas loosened his collar a bit more. He rarely wore suits, and this eighteen-year-old wool itched like hell.

"Those of you who know me or follow my work are aware of how my opinions often differ from those of most paleobiologists. Many in my field spend a great deal of time theorizing why a particular species no longer exists. I prefer to focus my energies on how a seemingly extinct species might still exist."

The elderly professor stood, readying his verbal assault. "Sir, are you saying you think *Carcharodon megalodon* may still be roaming the oceans?"

Jonas waited for quiet. "Not necessarily, Professor, I'm simply pointing out that, as scientists, we tend to take a rather short-sighted 'if we haven't seen it, it doesn't exist anymore' approach when it comes to declaring certain marine animals extinct. For instance, it wasn't long ago that scientists believed the coelacanth, a species of lobe-finned fish that thrived three hundred million years ago, had gone extinct over the last seventy million years. That so-called fact held up until 1938, when a fisherman hauled a living coelacanth out of the deep ocean waters off South Africa. Now scientists routinely observe these 'living fossils' in their natural habitat."

The elderly professor stood up again amid murmurs from the crowd.

"Professor Taylor, we're all familiar with the discovery of the coelacanth, but there's a big difference between a five-foot bottom-feeder and a sixty-foot predator!"

Jonas checked his watch, realizing he was running behind schedule. "Yes, I agree. My point was simply that I prefer to investigate the possibilities of a species' survival rather than add to the unproven conjecture regarding extinction among marine dwellers. Somehow, the scientific world has taken an 'it's dead until it shows itself' approach, and that simply doesn't work when it comes to fish."

"Then, again, sir, I ask for your opinion regarding Megalodon."

More murmurs.

Jonas wiped his brow; Maggie was going to kill him. "Okay, here it is: First, I disagree entirely with the theory regarding Megalodon being unable to catch quicker prey. We've learned the conical tail fin of the great white, the modern-day cousin of the Megalodon, is the most efficient design for propelling a body through water. As I've already stated, we know Megs existed as recently as a hundred thousand years ago. Then, as now, the predator would have had an abundant supply of slower-moving whales to feed upon.

"I do, however, agree that diminishing ocean temperatures would have affected these creatures, specifically their young, which would be more vulnerable to colder water. May I have the next slide, please? Sorry, one more."

A slide showing a series of maps of the changing planet over a three-hundred-million-year period appeared on the screen above his head. "As we can see, Earth's continental masses have shifted considerably over time." Jonas pointed to the center diagram. "This is how our planet looked about forty million years ago, during the Eocene. As we can see, the landmass that would become Antarctica separated from South America at about this time and drifted over the South Pole. When the continents shifted, they disrupted the transport of poleward oceanic heat, essentially replacing the heat-retaining water with heat-losing land. As the cooling progressed, the land accumulated snow and ice, which further lowered global temperatures and sea levels. As many of you know, the most important factor controlling the geographical distribution of a marine species is ocean temperature.

"Now, as the water temperatures dropped, the warmer tropical currents became top-heavy with salt and began running much deeper. Unlike air, salinity determines which currents run deeper, not temperature. In this example, the ocean temperatures were cooler along the shallower surface waters, with a tropical current, laden heavy with salt, running much deeper.

"Based on the locations of fossilized Megalodon teeth found in the rivers of South Carolina and other locations around the world, we know the sharks frequented shorelines, a fact most likely due to pregnant whales' preference for birthing their young in shallow-water lagoons. That's not to say the Megs didn't hunt in the open oceans. It simply means we have a tendency to draw conclusions based on the monsters behavior in the shallows.

"Now, about two million years ago, our planet's inhabitants had to deal with the effects of Earth's last major ice age. As you can see from this diagram, the deeper tropical currents that had provided a refuge for many marine species were suddenly cut off. As a result, a host of prehistoric fish, including generations of Megalodon young, died off in great numbers, unable to adapt to the extreme drops in oceanic temperatures."

The elderly professor called out from his seat. "So then, Taylor, you do believe that Megalodon became extinct as a result of climatic changes." The older man smiled, satisfied with himself.

"A decimated population doesn't necessarily equate to extinction. Remember, I said I prefer to theorize on how a species might still exist. About fifteen years ago, I was part of a scientific team that first studied deep-sea trenches. Deep-sea trenches form the hadal zone, an area of the Pacific Ocean about which scientists know virtually nothing. Deep-sea trenches form along the boundaries of two oceanic plates, where one plate melts back or subducts into the earth. Prior to 1977, scientists believed the abyss was actually barren; after all, how could life exist without light, or photosynthesis? When we actually bothered to take a look, we discovered hydrothermal vents—miniature volcanoes of life-giving chemicals—spewing mineral-rich waters at temperatures that often exceeded seven hundred degrees Fahrenheit. At some point, these minerals level off about a half-mile or so above the sea floor, creating a layer of insulation that keeps in the heat, forming what we now call a hydrothermal plume. In essence, you have an anomaly of nature, a tropical current of water—an oasis of life, if you will—running along the very bottom of the ocean in complete darkness. And these hydrothermal vents don't just spew hot water and minerals, they support life forms never before imagined . . . life forms whose food chain relies on chemosynthesis—chemicals in the water."

A middle-aged woman stood and asked excitedly, "Did you discover a Megalodon down there?"

Jonas forced a smile while he waited for the crowd's laughter to subside. "No, ma'am. But I'll show you something that was discovered in the abyss more than one hundred years ago that might be of interest." Jonas pulled out a glass case, roughly twice the size of a shoe box, from a shelf beneath the podium. "This is a fossilized tooth of *Carcharodon megalodon*. Scuba divers and beachcombers have turned up fossilized teeth like this by the thousands. Some are tens of millions of years old. This particular specimen is special because it's not very old. It was recovered in 1873 by the world's first true oceanic exploration vessel, the British HMS *Challenger*. Can you see these manganese nodules?" Jonas pointed to the black encrustations on the tooth. "Recent analysis of these manganese layers indicated the tooth's owner had been alive during the late Pleistocene or early Holocene period. In other words, this tooth is a mere ten thousand years old, and it was dredged from the deepest point on our planet, the Mariana Trench's Challenger Deep."

The crowd erupted.

"Professor! Professor Taylor!" All eyes turned to an Asian-American woman standing in the back of the auditorium. Jonas stared at her, caught off guard by her beauty. Somehow she looked familiar.

"Yes, go ahead," said Jonas, motioning for the audience to be quiet.

"Professor, are you saying that Megalodon may still exist in the depths of the Mariana Trench?" Silence took the room. It was the question the audience wanted answered.

"Theoretically, if members of the Megalodon species inhabited the waters of the Mariana Trench two million years ago, waters that maintain deep tropical plumes created and nourished by hydrothermal vents, then it's not beyond the realm of possibility that a branch of the species might have survived. The existence of this ten-thousand-year-old fossil certainly justifies the possibilities."

"What nonsense!" Mike "the Turk" Turzman, a popular local radio talk show host specializing in cryptozoology stood in the aisle, shaking his head. "There are no hydrothermal vents in the Mariana Trench. None!"

Jonas shook his head. He had heard excerpts of the Turk's recent interview with Richard Ellis, a painter and self-proclaimed expert on all things nautical who had lambasted Taylor's research. "Just for the record, Mr. Turzman, in 2003, the Ocean Exploration Ring of Fire Expedition surveyed more than fifty volcanoes along the Mariana Arc. Ten of these volcanoes had active hydrothermal systems. A follow-up expedition a year later found these hydrothermal systems were quite different from those found along the mid-Atlantic Ocean ridges, harboring all sorts of exotic life forms. So maybe the next time one of your guests decides to publicly critique my research over the airwaves, you'll do some fact checking of your own!"

A smattering of applause escorted "the Turk" back to his seat.

"Professor!" A middle-aged man with a young son sitting next to him raised his hand. "If these monsters still exist today, why haven't we seen them?"

"A good question," Jonas said, pausing as a beautiful blonde woman, tan and in her early thirties, strutted down the center aisle. Her classic topaz evening gown hugged a flawless figure, exposing athletic legs. Her male escort, also in his thirties, trailed behind, his long, dark hair slicked back into a tight ponytail, which contrasted with his conservative tuxedo. The pair took the two empty seats reserved in the front row.

Jonas composed himself, waiting for his wife and friend to be seated.

"Sorry. You asked why we haven't actually seen a Megalodon, assuming members of the species still exist. First, sharks that inhabit the midwaters and deepest realms of the ocean have no physical need to surface and flash us a telltale dorsal fin. Second, assuming a population of Megalodon did inhabit the waters of the Mariana Trench, it would have to be hard pressed to abandon that tropical bottom layer and its only known food source. The Challenger Deep is seven miles down. The water temperature above the warm layer is near freezing. The Meg might venture into that cold layer, ascending a mile or so at the most, but at some point, it would head back down to the warm layer again.

"Last, sharks are the one species that don't cooperate when it comes to leaving behind evidence they existed, especially those inhabiting the abyss. Unlike mammals, sharks do not float to the surface when they die, as their bodies are inherently heavier than seawater and contain no air sacs. Their skeletons are composed entirely of cartilage, so unlike dinosaurs and many species of bony fishes, there are no Megalodon bones to leave behind, only their gruesome, fossilized teeth."

Jonas caught Maggie's eye, her expression burning into his skull. "One . . . uh, other thing about the Mariana Trench. Man has only ventured down to the bottom twice, both expeditions occurring in 1960 and both times in bathyscaphes, essentially steel balls, hardly useful for exploration. In other words, we simply went straight down and back up again. The reality is, we've never come close to exploring the trench. In fact, we know more about distant galaxies than we do, a 1,550-mile-long, 40-mile-wide isolated section of the Pacific Ocean, seven miles down."

Jonas looked at Maggie and shrugged. She stood, pointing to her watch.

"You'll have to excuse me, ladies and gentlemen. This lecture has lasted a bit longer than expected and I'm due—"

"Excuse me, Taylor, one important question." It was the Asian-American woman again. She seemed perturbed. "Before you began studying these Megalodons, your career was focused entirely on piloting deep-sea submersibles. I'd like to know why, at the peak of your career, you suddenly quit."

Jonas was taken aback by the directness of the question. "First, I didn't quit, I retired. Second, my reasons are my own. Next question?" He searched the audience for another raised hand.

"Pretty young to retire, weren't you?" She was standing now, approaching from the center aisle. "Or maybe it was something else? You haven't been in a submersible for what? Seven years? Did you lose your nerve, Professor? Inquiring minds want to know."

The audience chuckled. No one was leaving—this was getting good.

Jonas felt trickles of sweat drip from his armpits. "What's your name, miss?"

"Tanaka. Terry Tanaka. I believe you know my father, Masao, CEO of the Tanaka Oceanographic Institute."

"Tanaka, of course. In fact, I think you and I met several years ago on a lecture circuit."

"That's right."

"Well, Terry Tanaka, since your inquiring mind insists on violating my privacy, let's just say, after a dozen years with the navy, I felt it was time to stop risking my life piloting deep-sea submersibles and join the academic circuit, researching prehistoric species like the Megalodon." Jonas collected his notes. "Now, if there are no other questions . . ."

"Dr. Taylor!" A balding man in his fifties, with tiny wire-rimmed glasses stood in the third row. He had bushy Andy Rooney-like elfin eyebrows and a tight, nervous grin. "Please, sir, one last question, if I may. As you mentioned, the two manned expeditions to the Mariana Trench occurred in 1960. But, Professor, isn't it true that there have been more recent descents into the Challenger Deep?"

Jonas stared at the man, red warning flags fluttering in his head. "I'm sorry?"

"Come now, Professor, you made several dives there yourself."

Jonas was silent. The audience began to murmur.

The man's bushy eyebrows raised, lifting his glasses. "Back in 1989, Professor. While you were still doing work for the navy?"

"I'm . . . not sure I understand." Jonas glanced at his wife like a condemned man.

Maggie looked away.

"You are Professor Jonas Taylor, aren't you?" The man smiled smugly as the audience broke into light laughter.

"Look, pal, I think you have your facts wrong, and I'm really running late. Drop me an e-mail or something. Oh . . . uh, thank you all for attending."

A smattering of applause trickled out amid murmurs from the crowd as Jonas Taylor stepped down from the podium. He was quickly approached by students with questions, scientists with theories of their own, and old colleagues desperate to say hello before he left. Jonas shook as many hands as he could, signed a few books, then apologized again for having to run.

The ponytailed man in the tuxedo squeezed his head through the swarming crowd. "Hey, J.T., the car's parked outside. Maggie says we need to leave now, bro."

Jonas nodded, finished signing a book for an admiring student, then hurried to the exit at the back of the auditorium where his wife was tapping her freshly pedicured toes, waiting impatiently.

As he reached the door, Jonas caught a glimpse of Terry Tanaka, looking at him from behind a sea of people. Her almond eyes seemed to burn into his as she mouthed the words, "We need to talk."

Jonas held up his watch and shrugged. He'd had enough of the verbal assaults for one night.

As if in response, his wife yelled through the exit door, "Jonas, let's go! Now!"

GOLDEN EAGLE

The limousine raced along the Coronado peninsula. Bud Harris was in back with Maggie, concluding a business transaction on his cell phone. Jonas sat across the aisle from Maggie, his back to the driver. He watched Bud absentmindedly finger his ponytail like a schoolgirl, then glanced over at Maggie. His wife of ten years looked very much at home on the wide leather seat, her slender legs crossed, a glass of champagne balanced in her fingertips. *She's grown used to his money*, Jonas thought. He allowed his mind to wander, imagining her in a bikini, tanning herself on Bud's yacht.

"You used to be afraid of the sun," he tossed out.

"What?"

"Your tan. You used to say you were afraid of skin cancer."

She stared at him. "I never said that. And it looks good on camera."

"What about your sister's melanoma—"

"Don't start with me, Jonas. I'm not in the mood. This is probably the biggest night of my career, and I had to practically drag you out of that lecture hall. You've known about this dinner for a month, and look at you—why the hell are you wearing that piece-of-shit suit? I should have tossed that in the Goodwill bin years ago."

"Hey, lighten up. This was my first time back on the lecture circuit in over two years, and you come prancing down the aisle like Madonna—"

"Whoa, guys, time-out!" Bud closed the cell phone. "Everybody take a breath and let's all just calm down. Maggie, this was a big night for Jonas too, maybe we should have just waited in the limo."

"A big night? Are you serious? Bud, do you know how long I've waited for this opportunity, how hard I had to work while I watched my husband flush his career down the toilet? Do you know how many times we've had to refinance the house, live off credit cards, all because Professor Jonas here insisted on studying dead animals for a living? Now it's my turn, and if he doesn't want to be here, that's fine by me. Let *him* wait in the limo. You'll escort me tonight."

"Oh, no, keep me out of this," said Bud.

Maggie frowned and looked out the window, the tension hanging in the air. After a few long minutes, Bud broke the silence. "Hey, uh, I spoke with Henderson. He thinks you're a shoo-in for the award. This really could be the turning point in your career, Maggie, assuming you win."

Maggie turned to face him, managing to avoid looking at her husband.

"I'll win," she said defiantly. "I know I'll win. Now pour me another drink."

Bud grinned, filled Maggie's glass, then offered the bottle to Jonas.

Jonas shook his head and sat back in his seat, staring absently out the window at the passing scenery, wondering who the blonde stranger was seated across from him.

Jonas Taylor had met Maggie Cobbs eleven years earlier in Massachusetts during his deep-sea pilot training at the Woods Hole Oceanographic Institute. Maggie had been in her senior year at Boston University, majoring in journalism. The petite blonde had at one time vigorously pursued a modeling career, but lacked the required height. Upon entering college, she had reset her sights on making it as a broadcast journalist.

Maggie had read about Jonas Taylor and his adventures aboard the *Alvin* submersible. She knew the former college football star was a celebrity in his own right and found him physically attractive. Under the guise of doing an article for the university press, she approached the naval commander for an exclusive interview.

Jonas Taylor was amazed that anyone like Maggie would be interested in deep-sea diving, or his own interests. His career had left him little time for a social life, and when the beautiful blonde showed signs of flirting, Jonas asked her out on a date. They hit it off almost immediately, and Jonas invited Maggie to the Galapagos Islands on spring break. She accompanied him on his last dive in the *Alvin* into the Galapagos Trench, and took up scuba at his urging.

Maggie was impressed by the influence Jonas wielded among his navy peers, and loved the excitement and adventure associated with ocean exploration. Ten months later they married and moved to California, where Jonas was preparing for a top-secret naval mission in the western Pacific.

For the small-town girl from New Jersey, California was the land of opportunity. She had always chased fame and the celebrity life, and quickly hired an agent to full-court press her pursuit of a career in the media. With Jonas's help, she was hired as a weekend correspondent at an ABC flagship station in San Diego.

And then disaster struck. For six months Jonas had been training to pilot a new deep-sea submersible. The target—the Mariana Trench. On his third dive in thirty-five thousand feet of water, the veteran pilot had panicked, surfacing the sub too quickly. Pipes had burst, causing pressurization problems that led to the deaths of the two naval scientists onboard. Jonas had survived—barely—only to learn his commanding officer blamed him for the incident. The official report called it "aberrations of the deep," and the event destroyed Jonas's career in the navy. Worse, it permanently scarred his psyche.

Maggie watched, helpless, as her husband floundered with bouts of depression. Months of psychiatric sessions followed—sessions that eventually refocused the once goal-oriented naval officer on another field—paleobiology. Jonas would earn his doctorate at

Scripps, while penning several books on the subject of extinction among deep-water species.

Without Jonas's naval income, Maggie's lifestyle quickly changed. The San Diego position turned out to be a dead-end job, and her life was suddenly thrust into that of the mundane.

Then, by chance, Jonas ran into Bud Harris, his former teammate at Penn State University. Harris, thirty at the time, had recently inherited his father's shipping business in San Diego. He and Jonas took in a few football games, but the paleobiologist was constantly doing research, leaving Maggie to entertain her husband's new best friend.

Bud used his father's connections to get Maggie part-time work as a writer for the *San Diego Register*. In turn, Maggie convinced her editor that Bud's shipping business would make an interesting article for the Sunday magazine. It was the excuse she needed to follow Bud around the harbor, with trips to his dock facilities in Long Beach, San Francisco, and Honolulu. She interviewed him on his yacht, sat in on board meetings, took a ride on his hovercraft, even spent afternoons learning how to sail.

The article she wrote became the *Register*'s cover story and made a local celebrity of the wild and woolly millionaire; his charter business boomed. Not one to forget a favor, Bud helped Maggie secure a weekend anchor spot with a local television station. Fred Henderson, the station manager, was a yachting partner of Bud's. Maggie started by doing two-minute fillers for the ten o'clock news, but it wasn't long before she maneuvered herself into a staff position, producing weekly features on California and the West Coast. While Jonas floundered as an author, Maggie Taylor was becoming a local celebrity.

Bud climbed out of the limo, extending a hand to Maggie. "Maybe I ought to get an award. Whaddya think, Maggie? Executive producer?"

"Not on your life," Maggie replied, handing her glass to the chauffeur. The alcohol had settled her down a bit. She smiled at Bud as they ascended the stairs of the Hotel del Coronado, Jonas lagging behind. "If they start giving you awards, there won't be any left for me."

They passed through the main entrance beneath a gold banner welcoming "The 15th Annual San Diego MEDIA Awards." Three enormous crystal chandeliers hung from the vaulted wooden ceiling of the Silver Strand Ballroom. A band played softly in the corner while well-heeled guests picked at hors d'oeuvres and sipped drinks, wandering among tables draped with white-and-gold tablecloths. Dinner would soon be served.

Jonas suddenly felt underdressed. Maggie had told him of the affair a month ago but had never mentioned it was black tie.

He recognized a few television people in the crowd, provincial stars from the local news. Harold Ray, the fifty-four-year-old co-anchor of Channel 9 Action News at Ten, smiled broadly as he said hello to Maggie.

Ray had helped secure network funding for Maggie's special about the effects of offshore oil drilling on whale migrations along the California coast, and now the piece was one of three competing for top honors in the "Environmental Issues Documentary" category.

"You just may take home the Eagle tonight, Maggs, Ray said, his eyes wandering toward her tantalizing cleavage.

"What makes you so sure?" she cooed back.

"For one thing, I'm married to one of the judges!" Harold said, laughing. Eyeing Bud's ponytail, he asked, "And this must be Jonas. Harold Ray—"

"Bud Harris, friend of the family," Bud replied, shaking his hand.

"Bud's my . . . executive producer," Maggie said, smiling. She glanced at Jonas. "This is Jonas."

"Sorry, big guy, honest mistake. Say, didn't we do a piece on you a couple years ago? Something about dinosaur bones in the Salton Sea?"

"You may have. There were a lot of newspeople out there. It was an unusual find—"

"Excuse me, Jonas," Maggie interrupted, "I'm just dying for a drink. Would you mind?"

Bud pointed a finger in the air. "Gin and tonic for me, J.T."

Jonas looked at Harold Ray.

"Nothing for me, Doc, I'm a presenter tonight. One more drink and I'll start making the news instead of reporting it."

Jonas forced a polite smile, then made his escape to the bar. The air was humid in the windowless ballroom, and Jonas's wool jacket felt prickly and hot. He asked for a beer, a glass of champagne, and a gin and tonic. The bartender pulled a bottle of Carta Blanca out of the ice. Jonas cooled his forehead with it and took a long draft.

He looked back at Maggie, who was still laughing with Bud and Harold.

"Another beer, sir?" The drinks were ready. Jonas looked at his bottle, suddenly realizing he had emptied it. "Give me one of those," he said, pointing at the gin.

"Me too," a voice said behind him. "With a lime."

Jonas turned. It was the balding man with the bushy eyebrows. He looked at Jonas, peering over his wire-rimmed bifocals with the same tight grin on his face. "Funny coincidence, meeting you here, Doc."

Jonas regarded him suspiciously. "Did you follow me here?"

"Hell no," the man replied, scooping up a handful of almonds from the bar. He gestured vaguely at the room. "I'm in the media."

The bartender handed Jonas his drink. "You here for an award?" Jonas asked skeptically.

"No, just an observer." He put out his hand. "David Adashek. *Science Journal.*"

Jonas shook his hand.

"I enjoyed your lecture tremendously. Fascinating stuff, about the Mega . . . What did you call it?"

Jonas sipped his drink, eyeing the reporter. "What is it you want?"

The man finished a mouthful of almonds, washing it down with a swig of his drink. "My sources tell me you made a series of dives for the navy in the Mariana Trench."

"Your sources tell you it was top secret?"

"So I heard. I also heard the navy was looking for a site to bury radioactive waste. That's a story I think my editors would have a great deal of interest in."

"Then you should pursue it, but not with me."

"Oh, I already have a source, a good one, too. Former navy guy, just like you." Adashek slipped another almond into his mouth, chewing it noisily like a stick of gum. "Funny thing, though. I interviewed the fellow about it four years ago. Couldn't get a word out of him. Then last week he calls out of the blue, says if I want to know what happened I ought to talk to you . . . Did I say something wrong, Doc?"

Jonas's brown eyes blazed at the shorter man. "Enjoy your dinner." He turned, walking back toward his table.

Adashek bit his lip, eyeing Jonas narrowly.

"Another drink, sir?" the bartender asked.

"Make it a double," Adashek said sharply, scooping up a handful of nuts.

From the other side of the room, a pair of dark almond eyes followed Jonas Taylor as he made his way across the ballroom, watching as he took a seat next to the blonde.

Four hours and a half-dozen drinks later, Jonas stared at the Golden Eagle now perched on the white tablecloth, a TV camera clutched in its claws. Maggie's whale film had beat out a Discovery Channel project on the Farallon Islands and a Greenpeace documentary on the Japanese whaling industry. His wife's acceptance speech had been largely a passionate "save the whales" plea. Her concern for the cetaceans' fate had inspired her to make the film, so she said. Jonas had wondered if he was the only one in the room who didn't believe a word she was saying.

Bud had passed out cigars. Harold Ray made a toast. Fred Henderson stopped by to offer his congratulations and say if he wasn't careful Maggie would get snapped up by a major station in Los Angeles. Maggie feigned disinterest. Jonas knew she'd heard the rumors . . . she had started many of them herself.

They were all dancing now. Maggie had taken Bud's hand and led him onto the floor, knowing Jonas wouldn't object. How could he? He didn't like to dance.

Jonas sat alone at the table, chewing the ice from his glass and trying to remember how many gins he'd downed in the last few hours. He felt tired, had a slight headache, and all signs pointed to a long evening still ahead. He got up and walked to the bar.

Harold Ray was there, picking up a bottle of wine and a pair of glasses.

"So how was Baja, Professor?"

Jonas wondered if the man was drunk. "Baja?"

"The cruise."

"What cruise?" He handed his glass to the bartender, nodded for a refill.

Ray laughed. "I warned her three days was no vacation. Look at you, you've already forgotten."

"Baja? You mean . . . last week." Then it hit him. The trip to San Francisco. The tan. *Bud Harris*.

"Too many margaritas, Professor?"

Jonas stared for a long moment at the glass in his hand, then scanned the dance floor for his wife. The band was playing "Crazy," the lights dimmed low, the couples dancing close. He located Maggie and Bud, clinging together like a pair of drunks. Bud's hands were caressing her back, working their way down. Jonas watched as Maggie absentmindedly repositioned his hands to her buttocks.

Blood rushed into Jonas's face, the veins in his neck throbbing. He slammed his drink down, then made his way awkwardly across the dance floor.

Oblivious, Maggie and Bud continued to grind their groins against one another, lost to the world.

Jonas tapped Bud on the shoulder. "Excuse me, pal, but I think that's my wife's ass in your hand."

Maggie and Bud stopped dancing, a look of apprehension coming over the millionaire's face. "Easy big guy, I was only—"

The right cross was a glancing blow, but still had enough force to send Bud crashing into another couple, then sprawling to the dance floor.

The band stopped playing.

The lights came up.

Maggie looked at Jonas, aghast. "Are you crazy?"

Jonas rubbed his sore knuckles. "Do me a favor, Maggie. Next time you take a cruise to Baja, don't come back." He turned and left the dance floor, the alcohol spinning the room as he strode toward the exit.

Jonas stepped out the front entrance and ripped off his tie. A uniformed bellboy asked him for his parking stub.

"I don't have a car."

"Would you like a taxi, then?"

"He doesn't need one. I'm his ride." Terry Tanaka stepped out the door behind him.

"Man, when it rains it pours. What is it you want, Tracy?"

"It's Terry, and we need to talk."

"You talk, I need to puke." He staggered down the block, searching for a trashcan, settling for the back of a dumpster.

Terry turned her back as he heaved his dinner. She searched her purse, then tossed him a pack of gum when he finished. "Now can we talk?"

"Look, Trixie . . ."

"Terry!"

Jonas sat on the curb and combed his fingers through his hair. His head was throbbing. "What is it you want?"

"Me following you here, it wasn't my idea. My father sent me."

Jonas glanced back at her. "Masao's an old friend. Find me on Monday, we'll talk. This isn't exactly a good time . . ."

"Ever hear of UNIS?"

"UNIS? Yeah, it's some kind of deep ROV, isn't it?"

"Unmanned Nautical Informational Submersible. UNIS. Our institute holds the patents. They're made for deep-water assignments, their hulls able to withstand 23,000 pounds per square inch of pressure."

"I'm happy for you. Now I need to find a cab and a bottle of aspirin."

She removed a manila envelope from her purse and shoved it in his face. "Look at this."

He opened the envelope and removed a black-and-white photograph taken underwater. The image was of a UNIS, lying on its side, its hull crushed almost beyond recognition.

Jonas looked back at the woman. "What the hell did this?"

UNIS

The Dodge Caravan sped along the rain-slick streets of San Diego, Terry at the wheel, challenging every yellow traffic light. Jonas laid back in the passenger seat, the window open, the cool breeze soothing his headache and sore knuckles. His eyes remained open and on the road—the woman's driving was making him nervous—but he kept studying the photograph in his mind.

Taken 35,000 feet beneath the surface of the western Pacific, the black-and-white photograph showed a spherical remote-sensing device resting near a dark canyon wall. Jonas was somewhat familiar with these remarkable robotic devices, having followed their development in science journals. He knew JAMSTEC, the Japan Marine Science and Technology Center, was involved with the Tanaka Institute in a joint project.

"My father agreed to deploy twenty-five UNIS robots into the Challenger Deep in exchange for financing for our whale lagoon in Monterey," Terry told him as they reached the freeway. "The UNIS array was designed to monitor tremors along a 125-mile stretch of the underwater canyon. Within days of the system's deployment, our surface ship, the *Kiku*, began receiving a steady stream of data, and seismologists on both sides of the Pacific were studying the information eagerly.

"Then something went wrong. Three weeks after the launch, one of the robots stopped transmitting data. A week later, two more units shut down. When another one stopped a few days after that, JAMSTEC cut off our funding, forcing my father to do something."

Terry looked at Jonas. "He sent my brother, D.J., down in the *Abyss Glider*."

"Alone?"

"D.J.'s the most experienced pilot we have, but I agree with you. In fact, I told Dad I should have gone with him in the second glider."

"You?"

Terry glared at him. "You have a problem with that? I happen to be a damn good pilot."

"I'm sure you are, but at thirty-five thousand feet? What's the deepest you've ever soloed?"

"I've hit sixteen thousand twice, no problem."

"Not bad," Jonas admitted.

"Not bad for a woman, you mean?"

"Easy, Gloria Steinem, I meant not bad for anyone. Very few humans have been down that deep."

She forced a smile. "Sorry. It gets frustrating, you know. Dad's strictly old-fashioned Japanese; his grandmother was a geisha. Woman are to be seen and not heard. It drives me crazy."

"Finish the story. What happened with D.J.? I assume he took this photo?"

"Yes. The photo came from his sub's video."

Jonas glanced again at the photograph. The titanium sphere had been cracked open, its tripod legs were mangled, a bolted bracket torn off. The hull itself looked battered beyond recognition.

Jonas studied the image. "Where's the sonar plate?"

"D.J. found it forty yards down-current. He hauled it up—it's at the Institute back in Monterey. That's why I tracked you down. My father needs you to take a look at it."

Jonas stared at her skeptically. "Why me?"

"He didn't say. You can fly up with me in the morning and ask him. I'm taking the Institute's plane back at eight."

Lost in thought, Jonas almost missed his driveway. "There—on the left."

She turned down the long, leaf-littered driveway, then parked in front of a handsome Spanish Colonial buried in foliage.

Terry switched off the engine. Jonas turned to her and narrowed his eyes. "Masao sent you all this way, just so I could render an opinion on scrap metal?"

"My father needs advice about redeploying along the Challenger Deep."

"You want my advice? Stay the hell out of the Mariana Trench. It's far too dangerous to be exploring, especially in a one-man submersible."

"Everything's dangerous to a man who's lost his nerve. D.J. and I are good pilots, we can handle this. What the hell happened to you anyway? I was only seventeen when we first met, but you were different. I still remember you turning me on with your piss-and-vinegar attitude."

Jonas blushed. "Shit happens when you grow old."

"You're not that old, but you're afraid. What are you so afraid of? A sixty-foot great white shark?"

"Maybe I'm afraid of Asian women with bad attitudes."

She smirked. "Let me tell you something. The data we collected during those first two weeks the UNIS array was functioning was invaluable. If the earthquake detection system works, it'll save thousands of lives. No one's asking you to dive the Challenger Deep, we simply want your opinion on why the UNIS was damaged. Is your schedule so damn busy that you can't take a day to fly up to the Institute? My father's asking for your help. Examine the sonar plate and review the video that my brother took and you'll be home to your darling wife by tomorrow night. We'll pay you for your time, and I'm sure Dad will even arrange a personal tour of our new whale lagoon."

Jonas took a breath. He considered Masao Tanaka a friend, a commodity he seemed to be running short of lately. "When would we leave?" he asked.

"Meet me tomorrow morning at the commuter airport, seven-thirty sharp."

"The commuter . . . we're taking one of those puddle jumpers?" Jonas swallowed hard.

"Relax. I know the pilot. See you in the morning."

Jonas exited the car and watched her drive away. "What the hell are you doing, J.T.?"

Jonas shut the door behind him and switched on the light, feeling for a moment like a stranger in his own home. The house was dead quiet. A trace of Maggie's perfume lingered in the air. *She won't be home until late,* he thought. *Ah, who are you kidding, she won't be home at all.*

He went into the kitchen, pulled a bottle of vodka from the cabinet, then changed his mind and turned on the coffeemaker. He replaced the filter and added some coffee, then filled the slot with water. He ran the faucet, sucked cold water from the spigot, and rinsed out his mouth.

For a long moment he stood at the sink, staring out the back window while the coffee brewed. It was dark out, all he could see was his reflection in the glass, all he could think of was a song from his navy days, the Talking Heads . . .

And you may tell yourself, this is not my beautiful house, and you may tell yourself, this is not my beautiful wife! Same as it ever was . . . Same as it ever was . . . Same as it ever was . . .

When the coffee was done, he grabbed a mug and the pot of coffee and went into his study.

Sanctuary. The one room in the house that was truly his own. The walls were covered with contour maps of the ocean's continental margins, mountain ranges, abyssal plains, and deep-sea trenches. Fossilized Megalodon teeth cluttered the shelves of a glass bookcase, sitting upright in their plastic support holders like small, lead-gray stalagmites. A framed photo of a great white shark hung above his desk, sent to him by Andrew Fox, son of Rodney, the famous Australian photographer who had nearly been bitten in two by a great white many years ago. Now the entire

Fox family made a living taking pictures of the very animal that had scarred Rodney for life . . . and had given him life.

Jonas set the coffee mug down beside his computer, then positioned himself at the keyboard. A set of jaws from a twelve-foot great white gaped at him from high above his monitor. He punched a few keys to access the Internet, then typed in the Web address of the Tanaka Oceanographic Institute.

Titanium. Even Jonas found it hard to believe.

NIGHT OWLS

Jonas gulped the hot coffee and waited for the Web site to upload. He typed in the word "UNIS."

UNIS
Unmanned Nautical Informational Submersible

Originally designed and developed in 1989 by Masao Tanaka, CEO of the Tanaka Oceanographic Institute, to study whale populations in the wild. Reconfigured in 1996 in conjunction with the Japan Marine Science and Technology Center (JAMSTEC) to record and track seismic disturbances along the deep-sea trenches.

Each UNIS system is composed of a three-inch-thick titanium outer shell. The unit is supported by three retractable legs and weighs 2,600 pounds. Each UNIS robot is designed to withstand pressures of 23,000 pounds per square inch. UNIS communicates information back to a surface ship by way of fiber-optic cable.

UNIS INSTRUMENTATION:
Electrical Fields
Mineral Deposits
Salinity
Seismic Equipment
Topography
Water Temperature

Jonas reviewed the engineering reports of the UNIS systems, impressed by the simplicity of the design. Positioned along a seismic fault line, their tripod legs burrowing deep into the ocean floor, the UNIS remotes could detect the telltale signs of an impending earthquake, providing, as Terry had said, an invaluable early warning system.

Southern Japan has the misfortune of being geographically located within a convergence zone of three major tectonic plates. Periodically, these plates grind against each other, generating about one-tenth of the world's annual earthquakes. One devastating Japanese quake in 1923 had killed more than 140,000 people.

In 1994, Masao Tanaka had been desperately seeking funds to complete his dream project, a monstrous man-made cetacean lagoon, or whale sanctuary. JAMSTEC had agreed to fund the entire project if the Tanaka Institute would complete the UNIS project. Now the system's breakdown was pushing the Tanaka Institute toward bankruptcy. Masao Tanaka was desperate; he needed Jonas's help.

Jonas took a long swig of coffee. *The Challenger Deep*, he thought to himself. Submarine experts referred to it as "hell's antechamber."

Jonas just called it "hell."

*   *   *

Twenty miles away, Terry Tanaka, freshly showered and wrapped in a hotel bath towel, sat on the edge of her queen-size bed at the Holiday Inn, her blood pressure still elevated. Jonas Taylor had really irked her. The man was obstinate, with strong chauvinistic ideas. Why her father had insisted their team seek his input was beyond her. Pulling out her briefcase, she decided to review the personnel file on Professor Jonas Taylor.

She knew the basics by heart. Educated at Penn State, advanced degrees from the University of California, San Diego, Scripps Institute of Oceanography, trained at the Woods Hole Oceanographic Institute. Author of three books on paleobiology. At one time, Jonas Taylor had been considered one of the most experienced submersible argonauts in the world. He had piloted the *Alvin* submersible seventeen times, leading multiple explorations to four different deep-sea trenches in the 1980s. And then, seven years ago, for some unknown reason, he had simply given it all up.

"Doesn't make sense," Terry said aloud. Thinking back to the lecture earlier that evening, she remembered the bushy-eyebrowed man who had practically accused Jonas of piloting an expedition into the Mariana Trench. Yet nothing in his personnel file indicated any trip to the western Pacific, let alone the Challenger Deep.

Terry put the file aside and powered up her laptop. She entered her personal code, then accessed the Institute's computers.

She punched in "Mariana Trench."

FILE NAME: MARIANA TRENCH

LOCATION:
Western Pacific Ocean, east of Philippines, close to island of Guam.

FACTS:
Deepest known depression on Earth. Measures 35,827 feet deep (10,920 m), over 1,550 miles long (2,500 km), averages 40 miles in width, making the trench the deepest abyss on the planet and the second longest. The deepest area of the Mariana Trench is called the Challenger Deep, named after the Challenger II expedition that discovered it in 1951. Note: A 1 kg weight dropped into the sea above the trench would require more than an hour of descent time just to reach bottom.

EXPLORATION (MANNED):
On January 23, 1960, the U.S. Navy bathyscaphe *Trieste* descended 35,800 feet (10,911 m), nearly touching the bottom of the Challenger Deep. On board were U.S. Navy Lt. Donald Walsh and Swiss oceanographer Jacques Piccard. In the same year, the French bathyscaphe *Archimede* completed a similar dive. In each case, the bathyscaphes simply descended and returned to the surface ship.

EXPLORATION (UNMANNED):
In 1993, the Japanese launched *Kaiko*, an unmanned robotic craft, which descended to 35,798 feet before

breaking down. In 1997, 25 UNIS robotic submersibles were successfully deployed by the Tanaka Oceanographic Institute along the Challenger Deep's seafloor.

Terry skimmed through the file. Nothing about Jonas Taylor here. She keyed in "Naval Exploration."

NAVAL EXPLORATION: (see) *TRIESTE*, **1960.**
SEACLIFF, **1990.**

Seacliff? Why hadn't the name appeared in the data above? She probed further.

SEACLIFF: **ACCESS DENIED.**
AUTHORIZED U.S. NAVAL PERSONNEL ONLY.

For several minutes, Terry attempted to gain access to the file, but it was hopeless. She signed off and closed the laptop, thinking back to the lecture. Her first meeting with Jonas Taylor had been ten years ago at a symposium held at her father's institute. Jonas had been invited to speak about his deep-sea dives aboard the *Alvin* submersible. At the time, Terry was fresh out of high school. She had worked closely with her father, organizing the symposium, coordinating travel and hotel arrangements for more than seventy scientists from around the world. She had booked Jonas's ticket and met him at the airport herself. She recalled developing a schoolgirl crush on the deep-sea pilot with the athletic build.

Terry looked at his picture again in her file. Tonight, Taylor had clearly lacked the confidence of their earlier meeting. He was still a physical specimen, possessing a handsome face, bearing a few more stress lines around the eyes. The dark brown hair was turning gray near the temples. Six foot one, she guessed, about 195. But something was missing on the inside.

What had happened to the man? And why had her father insisted on locating him? As far as Terry was concerned, Jonas Taylor's involvement was the last thing the UNIS project needed.

                    *   *   *

Jonas woke up on his office sofa, his wool suit jacket serving as his blanket. A dog was barking somewhere in the neighborhood. He squinted at the clock: 6:00 a.m. Computer printouts from the overflowing catch tray were scattered around him. He sat up slowly, his aching head pounding, his foot knocking over the half-empty coffeepot, staining the beige carpet brown. He rubbed his bloodshot eyes, then glanced at the computer. His screen saver was on. He tapped the mouse, revealing a diagram of the UNIS remote, glowing on screen. His memory came flooding back.

The dog stopped barking. The house seemed unusually quiet. Jonas got up, went into the hallway, and walked down to the master bedroom.

Maggie wasn't there. Their bed hadn't been touched.

MONTEREY

Terry spotted Jonas as he crossed the airport tarmac from the parking lot. She jogged out to meet him.

"Good morning, Professor" she said, just a little bit too loud. "How's your head?"

"Don't ask." He shifted his duffel bag to his other shoulder. "Talk softer, and stop calling me Professor. It's Jonas, or Taylor. Professor makes me feel old." He eyed the waiting plane. "Kind of small, isn't it?"

"Not for a Beechcraft."

The plane was a twin-turbo, with a whale logo and "TOI" painted on the fuselage. Jonas climbed aboard, tossed his bag behind him, then looked around. "Okay, where's the pilot?"

She gave him a mock salute.

"You? No way—"

"Hey, let's not start that shit again. I'm licensed and qualified, and if it makes you feel any better, I've been flying for six years."

Jonas nodded uneasily. It didn't make him feel better. It just made him feel old.

"Are you all right?" she asked as he fumbled with his seat belt. "You look a little pale."

Jonas nodded. "Low blood sugar."

"In back's a refrigerator, might be some apples. If you'd rather sit in back there's plenty of room to stretch out. Barf bags are in the side pocket." She smiled innocently.

"You're enjoying this."

"In all honesty, I never imagined an experienced deep-sea pilot like you would be so squeamish."

"Just fly the damn plane," he said, his eyes compulsively scanning the dials and meters on the control panel. The cockpit was a little tight, the copilot seat felt jammed up against the windshield.

"That's as far back as it goes," Terry told him as he searched for a lever to adjust the seat.

He swallowed dryly. "I need a glass of water."

She noticed his trembling hands. "In back."

Jonas got up and struggled into the rear compartment.

"There's beer in the fridge," she called out.

Jonas unzipped his duffel bag, found his dop kit, and took out an amber medicine bottle filled with small yellow pills.

Claustrophobia. His doctor had diagnosed the problem after the accident, a psychosomatic reaction to the stress he had endured. A deep-sea pilot with claustrophobia was as useless as a high diver with vertigo. The two just didn't mix.

Jonas chased down two of the pills with water from a paper cup. He stared at his trembling hand, crumpling the cup in his fist. He closed his eyes for a moment, then took a long, deep breath. When he slowly opened them and looked at the crinkled cup in the palm of his hand, he was no longer shaking.

"You okay?" Terry asked through the door of the cockpit.

Jonas looked up at her. "I told you, I'm fine."

*   *   *

The flight to Monterey lasted two and a half hours. The pills eventually took effect, allowing Jonas to relax. They were following the coastline north, flying over Big Sur, one of the most dramatic landscapes on the planet. For seventy-two miles violent Pacific waves crashed against the foot of the Santa Lucia Mountains, all bordered by California's scenic Highway 1, a mountainous roadway with harsh grades, twin bridges, and blind turns.

Terry spotted a pod of whales migrating south along the shore. "Grays," she said.

"Cruising to Baja," he mumbled, thinking of Maggie.

"Jonas, listen . . . about the lecture. I didn't mean to come off so harshly. It's just that Dad insisted I find you, and frankly, I didn't see the purpose of wasting your time. I mean, it's not like we need another submersible pilot."

"Good, because I wouldn't be interested."

"Good, because we don't need you!" She felt her blood beginning to boil again. "Maybe you could convince my father to allow me to follow D.J. down in the second *Abyss Glider*?"

"Pass." He gazed out his window.

"Why not?"

Jonas looked at the girl. "First, I've never seen you pilot a sub—"

"I'm piloting this plane!"

"It's totally different. You're dealing with harsh currents, water pressure—"

"Pressure? You want pressure? Hold on!" Terry pulled back on the wheel.

Jonas grabbed the dash in front of him as the Beechcraft rolled into a series of tight 360s, then dropped into a nauseating near-vertical nosedive.

The plane righted itself at 1,500 feet, as Jonas puked across the dashboard.

THE REPORTER

David Adashek adjusted his wire-rimmed bifocals, then knocked on the double doors of Suite 810. No reply. He knocked again, this time louder.

The door opened, revealing a groggy Maggie Taylor, wearing nothing but a white robe. It was untied, exposing one of her tan breasts.

"David? Christ, what time is it?"

"Almost noon. Rough night?"

She smiled, still half asleep. "Not as rough as my soon-to-be ex-husband's. Come in before someone sees you."

Adashek entered. She pointed to a pair of white sofas that faced a big-screen TV in the living area. "Sit."

"Where's Bud?"

Maggie curled up on the far sofa opposite Adashek. "He left about two hours ago. You did a nice job of harassing Jonas at the lecture."

"Is all this really necessary, Maggie? He seems like a decent enough guy—"

"So you marry him. After ten years, I've had enough."

"Why not just divorce him and get it over with?"

"It's not that simple. Now that I'm in the media's eye, my agent says we have to be very careful about the public's perception. Jonas still has a lot of friends in this town. He has to come off as a lunatic. People have to believe that his actions brought this divorce on. Last night was a good start."

"Okay, so what's next?"

"Where's Jonas now?"

Adashek pulled out his notes. "He went home with the Tanaka woman—"

"Jonas? With another woman?" Maggie laughed hysterically.

"It was innocent. Just a ride home from the awards. I followed him to the commuter airport earlier this morning. They're headed to Monterey. My guess is to that new whale lagoon the Tanaka Oceanographic Institute is constructing along the coast."

"Stay with him, and keep me informed. By the end of next week, I want you to go public with the navy story, emphasizing the fact that two of his crew were killed. Once the story hits, you'll do a follow-up interview with me, then I'll push for the divorce, public humiliation and all."

"You're the boss. Listen, if I'm going to be following Jonas, I'll need some more cash."

Maggie pulled a thick envelope out of her robe pocket. "Bud says to save the receipts."

Yeah, thought Adashek, *I'm sure he needs the write-off.*

LAGOON

"There it is." Terry pointed to the shoreline as they descended toward the sparkling Monterey Bay.

Jonas sipped the warm soda, his stomach still jumpy from Terry's little air show. His head pounded, and he had already made up his mind to leave immediately after meeting with Masao. As far as he was concerned, Terry Tanaka was the last pilot he'd ever recommend to descend to the bottom of the Challenger Deep.

Jonas looked down and to his right. An empty man-made lagoon stretched out like a giant bathtub on a ten-mile-square parcel of shoreline just south of Moss Landing. From the air it looked like an empty oval-shaped swimming pool. Lying parallel to the ocean, the structure was just over three-quarters of a mile in length and a quarter mile wide. It was eighty feet deep at its center, with walls two stories high and enormous acrylic windows along its southern border. A concrete canal at the far end of the lagoon ran west, connecting the man-made tank with the deep waters of the Pacific.

The lagoon held no water yet, only scaffolding. If and when it was ever finished, the massive steel doors located at the canal entrance would open and the lagoon would fill with seawater. It would be the largest man-made aquarium in the world.

"Impressive. If I hadn't seen it with my own eyes, I wouldn't have believed it," Jonas said as they prepared to land.

Terry nodded. "My father's dream. He designed it to be a living laboratory, a natural yet protective environment for its future inhabitants. Each winter tens of thousands of whales migrate along California's coastal waters to breed in the shallow lagoons around Baja."

Jonas rolled his eyes at the mention of Baja.

"Dad's thinking of ways we can coax a few females inside."

"Toss 'em some money, that should do it."

*   *   *

Twenty minutes later, Jonas found himself looking into the smiling eyes of the lagoon's owner.

"Taylor-san!" Masao Tanaka hustled over from his jeep to shake Jonas's hand. Tanaka had grayed since the last time Jonas had seen him, his goatee practically white, but the almond eyes were still full of life. "Let me look at you. Ah, you look like shit. Smell like it too! Hah. What's the matter? You don't like flying with my daughter?"

"No, as a matter of fact, I don't." Jonas gave the girl a look to kill.

Masao glanced at his daughter. "Terry?"

"His fault, Dad. It's not my problem if he can't handle the pressure. I'll be in the projection room." She walked off the tarmac, heading toward the three-story building at the end of the lagoon.

"My apologies, Taylor-san. Terry is very headstrong, she is somewhat of a free spirit. Is that the term? It is difficult raising a daughter without a female role model."

"Forget it. I really came up to see you and your whale lagoon. Looks amazing from up there."

"I'll give you a tour later. Come, we'll get you a fresh shirt. Then I want you to meet my chief engineer, Alphonse DeMarco. He is reviewing the video D.J. took in the trench. Jonas, I really need your input."

Jonas tossed his duffle bag in the back of the jeep and the two men climbed in.

*   *   *

A short while later, Jonas was cleaned up, wearing a new shirt, and seated in a projection room, the underwater video playing on a large screen. The image showed a spotlight cutting a beam through the clear, dark water. The wreckage of the UNIS loomed into view. It was lying on its side at the bottom of a canyon wall, wedged in between boulders and mud.

Alphonse DeMarco, a squat man carrying a wrestler's physique, stared at the monitor in the video-editing suite. "There it is. D.J. found it half-buried a hundred yards south of its original position."

Jonas rose from his seat and approached the screen. "What do you think happened?"

DeMarco watched the image change, the spotlight roaming over the scarred metal surface of the crushed submersible. "The simplest explanation's always the best. The robot got caught in a landslide."

"A landslide?"

"They're a frequent occurrence in the trench. Just look at all of those rocks."

Jonas walked to the table behind them. The retrieved half-shell of the sonar plate lay there like a severed piece of abstract sculpture. Jonas touched the torn edge of the metal dish. "The titanium casing's more than three-inches thick. I've seen the stress-test data—"

"The shell may have developed a crack on impact. The currents are incredibly strong."

"Is there any evidence—?"

"The UNIS recorded an increase in turbulence almost two minutes before we lost contact."

Jonas paused, then looked back at DeMarco. "What about the other damaged robots?"

"Both recorded similar changes in turbulence. If a landslide got this one, we can probably assume the same thing happened to the others."

Jonas turned toward the monitor. "You've lost four units," he said. "Isn't it pushing the limits of probability to say they've all been destroyed in landslides?"

DeMarco removed his glasses and rubbed his eyes. He'd had this argument with Masao more than once. "We knew the trenches were seismically active. Phone cables that cross other canyons are broken by landslides all the time. All this means is that the Mariana Trench is even more unstable than we expected."

"Changes in deep-sea currents often precede landslide activity," chimed in Terry.

"Jonas," said Masao, "this entire project depends on our ability to determine what happened to these robots and correct the situation immediately. We've located the last UNIS, the only one of the four not located directly along the canyon wall. I've decided we must retrieve this robot. My son . . . he cannot do the job alone. The job requires two subs working together: one to clear the debris and steady the UNIS while the second sub attaches the cable."

"I'm going, Dad," said Terry. "I've trained for this, I can get it done."

Masao was about to reply when Jonas yelled, "Stop the tape!" He pointed to the screen. "Go back," he called out to the projectionist. The image rewound. "Good, that's good. Let it play again from there."

They stared at the shifting image on the screen. The spotlight circled to the opposite side of the UNIS sphere, partially submerged in rocks and mud. The light shone into the debris near its base.

"There!" Jonas said. The projectionist froze the frame. Jonas pointed to a tiny white fragment wedged under the submersible. "Can you blow that up?"

The man punched some buttons and a square outline appeared on screen. Moving a joystick, he positioned the square around the object, then pulled it out so that it filled the entire screen.

The object appeared triangular and white, but fuzzy and unclear. Jonas stared at the screen. "It's a tooth," he stated.

DeMarco moved closer, scrutinizing the image. "A tooth? You're nuts."

"Al," commanded Masao. "Show the proper respect to our guest."

"Sorry, Mas, but what our professor here's saying is impossible. You see that?" He pointed to a bolt dangling from a steel strut. "That's a bolt holding one of the UNIS legs. It's three inches long." He pointed to the fuzzy white object below it. "That would mean that . . . thing . . . whatever it is, is at least seven, eight inches long."

He looked at Masao. "There's no creature on earth with teeth that big."

*   *   *

Masao held a photograph of the blown-up video frame in his hand as he, Jonas, and Terry followed the main interior corridor leading into the giant bowl-shaped arena that surrounded the Tanaka lagoon.

"Taylor-san, with all due respect, I don't see how this can be a tooth. It's too narrow—"

"The Meg's bottom teeth are narrow, they're used to puncture their prey to allow the top teeth to rip apart the meat."

"It's also white. There are no white Megalodon teeth."

"Mas, white indicates it's not a fossil, that the creature who owned it may still be alive. It's the reason we have to retrieve that tooth. It proves my theories."

Terry shook her head. "The Megalodon man here's letting his mind play games with his head, he's seeing only what he wants to see. There are no giant great white sharks in the trench. And even if there were, since when do sharks eat titanium robots?"

"They don't," Jonas snapped, "unless the titanium robots happen to be transmitting electrical signals, like your UNIS. Years ago, I was hired by AT&T to investigate problems they were having with a fiber-optic cable system they had just installed along the ocean floor, stretching from the eastern seaboard to the Canary Islands. The cable was laid in six thousand feet of water and was armored with stainless-steel mesh, yet the sharks still attacked it, tearing it up, costing the company millions of dollars in repairs. The sharks' ampullae of Lorenzini were attracted to the electronic booster signals originating in the fiber-optic bundles."

"Ampullae of who?"

"Lorenzini," Jonas shot back. "It's a cluster of sensory cells located along the underside of the shark's snout." Jonas stopped Masao. "Mas, I need D.J. to recover that tooth; it's very important to me."

"What about you, Jonas? Would you accompany my son in the second glider?"

Terry's almond eyes blazed. "No way! If anyone's going down with D.J., it'll be me!"

"Enough!" Masao looked at his daughter, the old man's eyes fierce. "I am here to show our guest the whale lagoon, this other matter shall be discussed at the proper time."

Terry waited for her father to move on, then glared back at Jonas. "This discussion isn't over."

They reached a ramp leading into the arena, following it into daylight.

The man-made lagoon was enormous, spread out before them like God's bathtub. Massive drains were set every forty feet, allowing circulation pumps to filter seawater. Fake rock formations situated along the bottom concealed acrylic windows accessible beneath the lagoon's basin. Thick two-story windows along the southern wall of the tank reminded Jonas of stadium skyboxes. The arena's bowl provided bench-style seating for 10,000, yet still allowed patrons to view the Pacific Ocean, sparkling just above the facility's western wall.

Jonas was awestruck by its immensity. "God, to see a pod of gray whales in here . . . you could watch them for days on end and not be bored."

Masao Tanaka stood in front of them proudly, a tight smile etched across his face. "We do nice work, eh, my friend?"

Jonas could only nod in agreement.

"This lagoon has been my dream since I was six years old. Forty million dollars, almost seven years of planning, four years of construction, Jonas. I did all I could, gave it everything I had."

He turned and faced them again, tears in his eyes. "It's too bad she is never gonna open."

MASAO

Jonas sat in the bamboo chair and gazed at the setting sun as it kissed the Pacific horizon. Masao Tanaka's home had been built into the Santa Lucia Mountains in California's Big Sur Valley. The cool ocean breeze and magnificent view were intoxicating, relaxing Jonas for the first time in as long as he could remember.

Despite his daughter's objections, Masao had invited Jonas to spend the night. Terry was in the kitchen at her father's request, preparing a plate of jumbo shrimp for the barbecue.

Masao emerged from the house, checked on the gas grill, then walked around the pool and took a seat next to Jonas.

"Terry says dinner will be ready soon. I hope you're hungry, Jonas. My daughter is a very good cook." He smiled.

Jonas looked at his friend. "I'm sure she is. I just might need a food taster to make sure she didn't drop arsenic into my serving."

Masao smiled, then shut his eyes and breathed deeply. "Jonas, you smell that ocean air? Makes you appreciate nature, eh?"

"Yes."

"My father . . . he was a fisherman. Back in Japan, he would take me out almost every morning. My mother, Kiku Tanaka, she died when I was only four. There was no one else to take care of me. Just my father.

"When I was six, we moved to America to live with relatives in San Francisco. Four months later, the Japanese attacked Pearl Harbor. All Asians were locked in detention camps. My father . . . he was a very proud man. He could never accept the fact that he was in a prison, unable to fish, unable to live his life. One morning, my father just decided to die. Left me all alone, locked in a prison in a foreign land, unable to speak or understand a word of English."

"I'm sorry. You must've been pretty scared."

Masao smiled. "Very scared. Then I saw my first whale. From the prison gates, I could see them leap. The humpbacks, they sang to me, kept me company at night, occupied my mind. My only friends." He closed his eyes for a moment, lost in the memory.

"You know, Taylor-san, Americans are funny people. One minute, you feel hated by them, the next loved. After eighteen months, I was released and adopted by an American couple, Jeffrey and Gay Gordon. I was very lucky. The Gordon family loved me, supported me, put me through school. But when I felt depressed, it was always my whales that kept me going."

"Now I understand why this project means so much to you."

"Hai. Learning about whales is very important. In many ways they are superior to man. But capturing and imprisoning them in small tanks, forcing them to perform stupid tricks so they can receive their rations of food, this is very cruel. This lagoon, it will allow me to study the whales in a natural setting. The lagoon will remain open so the whales can enter and exit of their own free will. No more small tanks. Having been locked up myself, I could never do that. Never."

"The lagoon will open, Masao. JAMSTEC won't hold the money back forever."

Masao shook his head. "Unless we can get the array working again, it is cancelled."

"What about finding another funding source?"

"I tried, but my net worth is too leveraged. No bank will support my dreams. Only JAMSTEC. But they don't care about building lagoons, they just want the UNIS array to monitor earthquakes. The Japanese government will not back down, there are careers at stake. We either fix the array or declare bankruptcy."

"You'll finish the lagoon, Masao. We'll figure out what happened."

"What do you think happened?" Masao's eyes blazed into Taylor's, searching for answers. "You really think it was a big shark?'

"Honestly, Masao, I don't know. DeMarco may be right. The UNIS robots could have anchored themselves too close to the canyon wall. But I can't imagine a boulder being able to crush titanium like that."

"Jonas, you and I are friends. I tell you my story, now you tell your old friend Tanaka the truth. What happened to you in the Mariana Trench?"

"What makes you think—"

Masao smiled knowingly. "We've known each other . . . what? Fifteen years? You lectured at my institute at least a dozen times. Now you underestimate me? I have contacts in the navy too, you know. I know what the navy says happened. Now I want to hear your side."

Jonas rubbed his eyes. "Okay, Masao, for some reason it seems the story's being leaked anyway. There were three of us who trained aboard the *Seacliff*, the navy's prototype for a new deepwater submersible. I was the pilot, the other two crewmen were scientists. We were measuring deep-sea currents in the trench to determine if plutonium rods from nuclear power plants could be safely buried within the Challenger Deep. At least that's what I was told."

Jonas closed his eyes. "I guess we were hovering about four thousand feet off the bottom, just above the warm layer's ceiling. It was my third descent in eight days, too much really, but I was the only qualified pilot. The scientists were busy conducting tests, they had just lowered a vacuum hose to the sea floor, collecting rock samples. I was looking out the porthole, staring down at this ceiling of swirling soot, when I thought I saw something circling just below the layer."

"What can you see in darkness?"

"I'm not sure, but it appeared to be glowing white, and it seemed very big. At first I thought it could be a whale, but I knew that was impossible. Then it just disappeared. I figured I had to be hallucinating."

"What happened next?"

"I . . . to tell you the truth, Masao, I'm not sure. I was so tired, could barely keep my eyes open . . . but suddenly I opened my eyes as this huge triangular head emerged out of the hydrothermal ceiling. It was monstrous, as big as a truck, its jaws filled with huge teeth. I don't remember much after that. They say I panicked, dropped every weight plate the sub had and rocketed toward the surface. We ascended way too fast, and something went wrong with the compression system. The two scientists died. I woke up in a hospital three days later . . . never knew what happened."

"And you think it was a Megalodon?"

"Mas, before this accident happened, I didn't even know what a Megalodon was. It was only after . . . it was after I saw a psychiatrist that I started piecing things together."

"But the monster . . . it never pursued you to the surface?"

"I don't know, apparently not. Like I said, I blacked out, but it could have overtaken us at any time. My guess is it wasn't interested in being in that cold layer, where the water temperature's barely above freezing."

"Two men died on your watch. Knowing the kind of man you are, that karma must have been hard to live with."

"Still is. Not a day goes by I don't think about it. I spent three weeks recovering in a naval hospital, then went through months of psychoanalysis. Not a fun time." Jonas looked to the horizon. "The truth is, it's been so long, I've begun to doubt my own memories of the event."

Masao sat back in his chair. "Jonas, I believe you saw something, but I don't think it was a monster. You know, D.J. tells me there are giant patches of tubeworms located all along the bottom. D.J. says these worms reflect light, glowing in the dark. You never did make it to the very bottom of the trench, did you?"

"No."

"D.J. made it. That boy loves deep-sea exploration, says it's like being in outer space. Jonas, I think what you saw was a patch of tubeworms. I think the currents pushed them in and out of your sight line, your submersible's exterior light catching their glow. That's why they seemed to disappear. Remember, you were exhausted, staring into the darkness. The navy worked you too hard, three dives in eight days is not safe. And now you've spent seven years of your life hypothesizing how these monsters may still be alive."

Jonas sat in silence and listened.

Masao placed his hand on Jonas's shoulder. "My friend, I need your help. And I think maybe it's time to face your fears. I want you to return to the Mariana Trench with D.J., but this time you'll make it all the way to the bottom. You'll see these patches of giant tubeworms for yourself. You were once a great pilot, and I know in my heart you still are. You can't live in fear your whole life."

"What about Terry? She wants to make the dive—"

"She's not ready. Too headstrong. No, I need you. And you need to do this, so that you can get on with your life."

Tears formed in Jonas's eyes. "Okay . . . I'll go back." He choked back a laugh. "Boy, your daughter is going to be pissed at me."

Masao smiled grimly. "My daughter will get her opportunities on other dives, but not in this hellhole."

"Agreed."

"Good. And when all of this is over, you will come work with me at the lagoon, okay?"

Jonas nodded. "We'll see."

THE *KIKU*

The American Airlines jumbo jet soared 36,000 feet above the blue carpet of the Pacific Ocean, five hours out of San Francisco.

Terry rose from her aisle seat and headed back toward the plane's restroom. Alphonse DeMarco, seated in the middle seat next to her, took advantage of her leave to stretch. In the window seat next to him sat Jonas Taylor, a briefcase-sized *Abyss Glider II* flight simulator on his lap.

Jonas had been at it for hours, maneuvering the two joysticks, trying to coordinate yaw and pitch with speed and stabilization. The AG II was a one-man, deep-sea submersible, the same model that had carried D.J. to the bottom of the Mariana Trench. Jonas would accompany him in a second sub to retrieve the damaged UNIS. He was already familiar with the basic design, having piloted the AG I, the sub's shallow-water predecessor, several years earlier. Now all he needed was to familiarize himself with the new deep-sea design. There'd be plenty of time for that. It was a twelve-hour flight across the Pacific to Guam, not counting a stopover in Honolulu for refueling.

Terry's attitude toward Jonas had gone from cold to ice. She was visibly hurt that her father had ignored her qualifications to back up D.J., and felt Jonas had lied to her about not being interested in piloting the sub in the Mariana Trench. She even refused to help train Jonas on the simulator.

The *Abyss Glider II* simulator used two computer joysticks to "steer" the submersible by simulating adjustment of its midwing and tail fins. Because most of the trip to the bottom was in complete darkness, the pilot had to learn to "fly blind and disoriented," navigating the craft to the bottom using readouts alone. For this reason, piloting with the simulator was very much like piloting the real thing. So similar, in fact, that Jonas had to stop working, close his eyes, and try to relax.

Staring out the window, he thought about his conversation with Masao Tanaka. It had never occurred to him that he could have been focused on tubeworms.

Riftia. Jonas had seen smaller varieties of the species growing in clusters around every hydrothermal vent he had ever explored. The tubeworms were a luminescent white, possessing neither mouths nor digestive organs. They relied on thick colonies of bacteria living inside their bodies. The worms supplied hydrogen sulfide, which they extracted from the sulfur-rich waters of the trench. The bacteria inside the worms used the hydrogen sulfide to make food for themselves and their host.

Prior to 1977, man believed life could not exist in the absence of light. Since humans need sunlight to exist, the assumption was that all lifeforms had to have it. It was the kind of logic that Jonas despised—logic brought about only by assumption, not actual research. Since no light could penetrate the deepest trenches of the sea, then photosynthesis could not exist, and life could never get a foothold in the abyss.

And then the *Alvin* submersible went down to the seafloor, and all the old textbooks were thrown out the window.

Jonas had seen it for himself. Colonies of hydrothermal vents supported a unique food chain by spewing searing-hot water and vast amounts of chemicals and mineral deposits out of cracks in the seabed. The high sulfur content, poisonous to most species, became food for a variety of deep-sea bacteria. The bacteria, in turn, were living inside worms and mollusks, breaking down other chemicals into usable food. The massive clumps of tubeworms also consumed the bacteria, and a variety of undiscovered species of fish ate the tubeworms.

The process was called chemosynthesis: bacteria receiving energy from chemicals rather than energy from the sun. Despite man's common beliefs, life flourished in the darkest, seemingly most uninhabitable location on the planet.

Now, twenty years after the discovery, scientists were theorizing that all life on our planet originated from these deep-sea vents.

D.J. had told Masao that the tubeworm clusters in the Challenger Deep often covered vast expanses along the bottom. It was possible, thought Jonas, that he had been staring at a worm cluster through the swirling debris of minerals, fallen asleep, then dreamed the triangular head.

The thought made Jonas ill. Two men had died for his mistake, two families shattered. At least the Megalodon defense had served to lessen his guilt. Coming to grips with this new evidence that he might have imagined the whole incident was not sitting well with his psyche.

One way or another, Jonas knew Masao was right; he had to face his fears and return to the trench. If a white Megalodon tooth could be found, it would justify seven years of research. If not, so be it. One way or the other, it was time to get on with his life.

*   *   *

Fifteen rows behind Jonas and DeMarco, David Adashek closed the hardback *Extinct Species of the Abyss* by Dr. Jonas Taylor. He removed his bifocals, positioned his pillow against the window, and fell asleep.

*   *   *

The navy helicopter flew low above the waves. The pilot glanced over his shoulder at Jonas and DeMarco. "She's just up ahead."

"About time," DeMarco said, turning to wake Terry. She'd been sleeping since they'd left the naval station in Guam.

Jonas trained his eyes on the horizon, a faint line separating the gray ocean from the gray sky. He couldn't see anything. *Maybe I should have slept*, he thought, rubbing his eyes. He was certainly tired enough. They'd been traveling for more than fifteen hours. Moments later he saw the ship, a flat speck quickly growing larger.

The *Kiku* was a decommissioned Oliver Hazard Perry–class guided missile frigate, disarmed and reconfigured for ocean research. The Tanaka Institute had purchased the 445-foot-long steel ship from the navy three years ago, rechristening it the *Kiku*, in honor of Masao's mother.

The frigate was perfect for deep-sea research. Removing the SAM missile launcher from her bow gave the crew plenty of deck space on which to work. Situated in the stern was a reinforced-steel winch and A-frame, designed to lift even the heaviest submersible into and out of the sea. Behind the winch was a massive spool containing more than seven miles of steel cable.

Forty feet of deck separated the winch from two hangars located in the stern. One held the twin pair of *Abyss Gliders*, the one-man submersibles that D.J. and Jonas would descend in; the other stored the ship's helicopter. Steel tracks embedded within the deck allowed the crafts to be rolled in and out of their respective hangars.

A pilothouse overlooked the bow from the second deck and contained the navigator's console board, which drove the two GE LM 2500 gas-turbine engines. A short corridor connected the pilothouse to the command information center (CIC). This once-secured room was always kept cool and dark, illuminated only by the soft blue overhead lights and the colorful computer console screens situated along the interior walls. The weapons stations, which had once controlled the frigate's SAM and harpoon missiles, antisub torpedoes, and a variety of other guns and countermeasures had been replaced with computers that now monitored the deployed UNIS systems, retrieving data from the robots implanted along the Challenger Deep seven miles below the ship.

The *Kiku*'s CIC also contained the hull-mounted Raytheon SQS-56 sonar and Raytheon SPS-49 radar systems, the exterior dishes of which could be seen rotating on two towers rising twenty-five feet above the upper deck. All of these systems were linked to a computer integration program that displayed the information across a dozen computer consoles.

Below the control deck were the galley and the crew quarters. The triple-stacked coffinlike bunks of the navy had been torn out, the interior reconfigured to accommodate more private quarters for the crew of thirty-two. Below this deck was the engine room and the main machinery that drove the twin-shaft propellers. As large as she was, the *Kiku* was a fast ship, capable of speeds up to twenty-nine knots.

As the helicopter approached the aft deck, Terry pressed her face to her window. She could see a young man in his early twenties standing on the main deck, waving. His body was lean and taut with muscles, his skin a deep Asian tan. Terry waved back excitedly. "D.J.," she said with a grin.

Terry's brother grabbed her bags the moment she stepped off the chopper.

He received his older sister's hug, then turned to Jonas. With their black hair, dark eyes, and bright smiles they almost looked like twins.

"D.J., this is Jonas Taylor," she said. "Don't call him Professor, it makes him feel old."

D.J. dropped the bags and shook Jonas's hand. "My sister's a pistol, huh?"

"A real delight."

"So," D.J. said, "I hear you're going to be descending with me into the Challenger Deep. Sure you're up to it?"

"I'll be fine," said Jonas, sensing D.J.'s competitive nature.

D.J. turned to Terry. "Does the doc here know Frank Heller's on board?"

Terry smiled coyly. "Gee, I don't know. Jonas, did Dad happen to mention that to you yesterday?"

Jonas felt the breath squeeze out of his chest. "Frank Heller's part of this expedition? No, your father definitely didn't mention that to me."

"I take it you two have a history?" asked D.J.

Jonas regained his composure. "Frank Heller was the physician in charge of a series of dives I piloted for the navy seven years ago."

"My guess is you two haven't kept in touch," Terry said, the sarcasm dripping.

"No. And if Masao had told me Heller was part of this mission, I doubt I would have come."

"Guess that's why Dad didn't mention it," chuckled D.J.

"If I had known, I would have told you myself," said Terry. "It's not too late to recall the chopper."

Jonas stared at Terry, his patience wearing thin. "I'm here. If Frank Heller has a problem with that, I guess he'll have to deal with it."

D.J. turned to DeMarco. "How'd he do with the simulator?"

"Not bad. Of course, the program lacks controls for the mechanical arm and escape pod."

"Plan on at least one practice run before we descend then," said D.J. "We'll give you a few hours to get your sea legs."

Jonas shrugged. "Whenever you're ready. Why don't you show me the *Gliders*."

As they approached the glider hangar, a large dark-skinned man in a red knit cap appeared on deck, accompanied by two Filipino crew members.

"Professor Taylor," D.J. said, "Leon Barre, the *Kiku*'s captain."

Jonas shook the French-Polynesian's hand, the man's calloused grip revealing the strength of an ox. A tiny silver cross dangled from his neck. "Welcome aboard," he said, his baritone voice booming. Barre tipped his hat to Terry. "Madam," he said reverently.

DeMarco slapped the big man's shoulder. "You putting on a little weight, Leon?"

Leon's face darkened. "The Thai woman, she fattens me like a pig."

DeMarco laughed, turning to Jonas. "The captain's wife's a hell of a cook. We could all use a little of that, Leon. We're starving."

The captain grunted an order to the Filipino sailor at his side. The sailor bowed, then rushed off toward the *Kiku*'s infrastructure. "We eat in an hour," the captain announced, then turned and left.

Jonas, D.J., DeMarco, and Terry walked across the wide deck to where the two *Abyss Glider* submersibles were perched on dry mounts.

D.J. beamed proudly. "So? What do you think?"

"Smaller than I remember."

"Like glass coffins," chimed in Terry.

Jonas ignored her. "I piloted the AG I in shallow waters. The AG II was still on the drawing board back then."

"Come on, Taylor," said DeMarco. "I'll give you the nickel tour."

The subs were ten feet long by four feet wide and resembled fat torpedoes with wings. They were one-man vessels, the pilot entering an internal Lexan-glass pod through a hatch in the tail section. Lying prone, the pilot used dual joysticks to "fly" the vessel. The clear nose cone allowed for 360 degrees of visibility.

"Lexan," said DeMarco, slapping his palm across one of the glider's nose cones. "This plastic's so strong, it's used as bulletproof glass in presidential limousines. The entire escape pod's made of the stuff. The AG I's were refitted with it several years ago."

Jonas inspected the plastic cone. "I don't remember escape pods being in the original design."

"They weren't," said D.J. "We added them after we realized they could make the craft neutrally buoyant.

The entire chamber's technically the escape pod. If the *Glider* gets into trouble, simply pull the lever located in a metal gear box along your right and the interior chamber will separate from the heavier tail and wing sections. It's like being in a buoyant bubble. You'll rise right to the top."

DeMarco frowned. "I'll give the tour, kid. After all, I did design the damn things."

D.J. smiled at the engineer. "Sorry."

DeMarco took center stage, obviously in his element. "The biggest challenge in deep-water exploration was to design and build a hull that's both buoyant and strong enough to withstand tremendous pressures. The other problem we had to deal with in getting to the bottom of the Challenger Deep was the length of time it takes for a submersible to travel seven miles straight down. The *Alvin*, the *French Nautile*, and the *Russian Mir I* and *II* are all bulky vessels that can only descend at a rate of fifty to one hundred feet per minute. At those speeds, it would take us well over five hours just to enter the trench."

"And," added D.J., "those subs can't even descend beyond twenty thousand feet."

"What about JAMSTEC's *Shinkai 6500*?" asked Jonas. "I thought she was designed to reach the bottom."

"The *Shinkai* was designed for a maximum depth of twenty-one thousand feet," corrected DeMarco. "You're thinking of JAMSTEC's latest unmanned sub, the *Kaiko*. Until D.J. piloted the AG II last week, the

Kaiko was the only vessel, manned or unmanned, to reenter the Challenger Deep since the *Trieste* in '60. She spent just over a half hour at a depth of 35,798 feet, two feet shy of the record, before suffering mechanical problems."

"Now the record's mine," said D.J. "Guess I'll be sharing it with you soon, Doc."

"Should've been me," mumbled Terry.

DeMarco ignored the siblings' comments. "Those other subs I mentioned have hulls made of a titanium alloy, similar to our UNIS systems. Half your power source is exhausted in just piloting the heavily weighted sub along the bottom, all so you can drop the weighted plates later to surface. The *Abyss Gliders* are made from a reinforced, positively buoyant ceramic capable of withstanding forces greater then twenty thousand pounds per square inch. With her maneuverable wings, she'll fly to the bottom at a rate of six hundred feet per minute and float back to the surface without the use of weights. Saves a ton of battery power."

Jonas nodded. "How will we bring the damaged UNIS to the surface?"

"Look beneath the belly of the sub," instructed D.J. "There's a retractable mechanical arm with a claw. The arm has a limited extension of about six feet directly in front of the nose cone. The claw was designed to gather specimens. When we make our descent, you'll take the lead. I'll follow in my sub, which will have a steel cable attached to my mechanical claw. The damaged UNIS has several eye bolts located along its outer casing. Once you clear the debris away from the UNIS, I'll attach the cable and the *Kiku's* winch will haul the unit back to the surface."

"Doesn't sound too bad."

"It's a walk in the park, but it's still a two-man job," said D.J. "I tried to attach the cable on my first descent, but there was too much debris covering the UNIS. I couldn't maintain the claw's grip on the steel cable and clear the rocks away. The currents are just too strong for one glider."

"Maybe you were nervous," added Terry.

"Bullshit," responded her brother.

"Come on, D.J.," Terry said, directing her comments at Jonas. "You told me it's kind of scary down there. It's not even the constant darkness. It's the claustrophobia, knowing that you're seven miles down, surrounded by thousands of pounds of pressure. One mistake, one crack in the hull, and your brains implode from the change in pressure." Terry glanced at Jonas, looking for a reaction.

"Ah, you're just jealous," said D.J. He looked to Jonas, his face full of animation. "Truth is, I loved it down there! What a rush, I can't wait to go back. I thought bungee jumping and parachuting were cool, but this beats the shit out of them."

Jonas stared at the young man, recognizing traits from his own youth. "You consider yourself an adrenaline junkie?"

D.J. calmed himself. "Me? No . . . I mean, yeah, I'm an adrenaline junkie, sure, but this is different. The

Challenger Deep . . . it's like being the first person to explore another planet. There are these huge black smokers everywhere, and the weirdest fish you ever saw. But why am I telling you? You've been on dozens of trench dives before."

Jonas tugged on one of the red vinyl flags with the Tanaka logo attached to the back of each sub. "I've piloted more than my share of dives into deep-sea trenches, but the Mariana Trench is a whole different ball game. I suggest leaving the cowboy stuff behind."

He looked back toward the *Kiku*'s infrastructure. "Where can I find Dr. Heller?"

D.J. threw a glance at his sister. "He's in the CIC, I think."

"Good. See you at dinner." Jonas turned and walked away.

Jonas followed a main corridor to a door labeled "Operations." He entered the dark chamber humming with computers, video monitors, and radar and sonar equipment.

A gaunt man with short-clipped gray hair and heavy, black-framed glasses was bent over a control panel, pecking at computer keys with his long fingers. He looked up at Jonas, his moist gray eyes swollen behind the thick lenses, then turned back to his computer, studying his monitor. "Another fishing expedition, Taylor?"

Jonas paused a moment before he answered. "That's not why I'm here, Frank."

"Why are you here?"

"Masao asked for my help."

"The Japanese have no sense of irony."

"Like it or not, we're going to have to work together, Frank. The only way to find out what's going on down there is to haul up the damaged UNIS. D.J. can't do it alone—"

"I know that!" Heller rose quickly and crossed the room to refill his coffee. "What I don't understand is why you should be the one to go with him."

"Because nobody else has been down there in the last thirty years."

"Oh yes they have," Heller said bitterly. "Only they died making the trip."

Jonas broke eye contact. "I want to talk to you about that. I . . ." Jonas searched for the right words. "Look, there hasn't been a day that's gone by in the last seven years that I haven't thought about the *Seacliff*. To be honest, I'm still not sure what happened. All I know is that I believed I saw something rise up from the bottom to attack our sub, and I reacted."

"Reacted? You panicked like an ensign on his first day at boot camp." Heller moved to Jonas, standing nose to nose. His eyes burned with hatred. "Maybe your little confession makes everything all right in your book, but it changes nothing with me. You were daydreaming, Taylor. You hallucinated, and instead of reasoning, you panicked. You killed two of our team. Mike Shaffer was my friend, I'm godfather to his kid. I live with your mistake every day."

"I'm sorry."

"Do you know what really ticks me off? You've spent the last seven years making a career of justifying the existence of this Megala-shark, substantiating your fabricated excuse so you wouldn't look so bad." Heller was shaking with emotion. He took a step back and leaned against his desk. "You make me ill, Taylor. Those men didn't deserve to die. Now here we are, seven years later, and you still can't face up to the truth."

"I don't know what the truth is, Frank. Maybe I dreamt it, maybe I was looking at a cluster of tubeworms. All I know is that I screwed up. Don't forget, I almost died down there myself. Now I've got to deal with this thing for the rest of my life."

"I'm not your priest, Taylor. I'm not here to take your confession or hear about your feelings of guilt."

"And what about your contribution to the accident?" Jonas yelled back. "You were the physician of record. You assured Danielson that I was medically fit to make a third dive. Three descents within eight days! Do you think that decision may have had anything to do with my ability to function?"

"Don't blame me for following orders!"

"Orders?" Jonas paced, his blood pressure simmering. "You said it yourself, wrote it on the official report: 'psychosis of the deep.' You and Danielson forced me to pilot those dives without sufficient rest, and then the two of you railroaded me, set me up to be the navy's fall guy . . . to cover your own asses."

"It was your fault!"

"Yes," whispered Jonas, "it was my piloting error, but I never would have been placed in that position without your involvement or Danielson's. Now I've decided to go back down, to finally face my fears, to figure out for myself what happened. Maybe it's time you faced up to your own responsibilities."

Jonas headed toward the door.

"Hold it, Taylor. Look, maybe you shouldn't have been in the trench on that third dive. Danielson was my commanding officer, but he was being pressured by the Pentagon. Still, I believed you were mentally fit. You were a damn good pilot once. But let's just make sure that the reason you're making this dive with D.J.

is to assist him and not to go off looking for some tooth."

Jonas opened the door, then turned to face Heller. "I know my responsibilities, Frank. I hope you remember yours."

Twenty minutes later, having showered and changed, Jonas entered the galley, where a dozen crewmen were noisily feasting on fried chicken and potatoes. He saw Terry seated next to D.J., the only vacant chair to her left.

"This seat taken?"

"Sit," she ordered.

He sat down, listening to D.J., who was involved in a heated debate with DeMarco and Captain Barre. Heller's absence was conspicuous.

"Doc!" D.J. sprayed half his mouthful of chicken out with the word. "You're just in time. You know that practice dive we had scheduled for tomorrow? Well, forget about it."

Jonas felt butterflies in his stomach. "What are you saying?"

Captain Barre turned to Jonas, swallowing a mouthful of food. "Storm front moving in from the east. No time for practice dives. If you're gonna descend this week, it's gonna be tomorrow, first light."

"Jonas, if you're not ready yet, I think you should be man enough to admit it and let me step in," interjected Terry.

"Nah, he'll be fine. Right, Doc?" said D.J., winking. "After all, you've been down to the Mariana Trench before."

"According to who?" Jonas felt the room go quiet, all eyes on him.

"Come on, Doc. It's all over the ship. Some reporter in Guam interviewed half the crew by radio an hour after you boarded."

"What? What reporter? How the hell—?" Jonas no longer felt hungry.

Terry nodded. "Same guy who was questioning you at the lecture. He claims two people died on the sub you were piloting. Told us you panicked because you hallucinated, claiming to have seen one of those Megalodons."

D.J. looked him squarely in the eye. "So, Doc, any of this true?"

The room was dead silent. Jonas pushed his tray away from him. "It's true. Only what this reporter left out is that I was exhausted at the time, having already completed two deep trench dives during the same week. I was pushed into service, okayed by the medical officer—your pal, Heller. To this day I'm not sure if what I saw was real or if I imagined it. But as far as tomorrow's dive's concerned, I made a commitment to your father to complete the mission and I intend to keep that commitment. I've piloted subs on more deep-sea missions than you've had birthdays, D.J., so if you have a problem with me escorting you down, then let's get it out on the table right now."

D.J. smiled nervously. "Hey, I've got no problem with you, so chill. Actually, Al and I were just talking about this giant prehistoric shark of yours. Al says that it would be impossible for a creature that size to exist in water pressures as great as those in the trench.

Now, me, I'm on your side. I say it's possible. Not that I believe your theory, 'cause I don't. But I've seen dozens of different species of fish down there. Now, if those little fish can withstand the water pressures, why couldn't this mega-shark, or whatever the hell you call it?" D.J. was grinning from ear to ear. Several crew members began snickering.

Jonas stood up to leave. "You'll excuse me. I think I've lost my appetite."

D.J. grabbed his arm. "No, wait, Doc, come on now. Tell me about this shark. I really want to know. After all, how will I recognize it if I see it tomorrow?"

"It'll be the big shark with the missing tooth!" blurted out Terry.

Laughter cascaded around them.

Jonas sat back down. "Okay, kid, you really want to know about these monsters, I'll tell you. The first thing you have to realize about sharks is that they've been around a lot longer than us, about four hundred million years. Compare that with humans, whose ancestors fell from the trees only about two million years ago. And of all the species of shark ever to have evolved, old Megalodon was the undisputed king. What little we know about these monsters is that nature endowed the creatures not just to survive but to dominate every ocean and marine species. So we're not just talking about a shark here, we're talking about a formidable killing machine, the apex predator of all time. Forget for a moment this species was a sixty-foot version of a great white shark. The Meg was a supreme hunter, endowed with size and senses that would put a nuclear submarine to shame. The creature possessed eight highly efficient sensory organs that could track you down from miles away. It could smell and taste you, sense the beating of your heart or the electrical impulses generated by your moving muscles. Piss or bleed in the water, and you might as well have lit up a flare. And if it ever got close enough to see you, then you were already dead."

Leon Barre chuckled. "Hey, how do you know all this shit about some dead fish nobody's ever seen?"

The room quieted once more, awaiting Jonas's response.

"For one thing, we have their fossilized teeth, which not only tells us about their enormous size but reveals certain things about their predatory tendencies. We also have fossilized evidence from the species they fed on."

"Go on about their senses," said D.J., now truly curious.

Jonas gathered his thoughts, noting that other members of the crew had grown silent, listening as well. "The Megalodon, just like its modern-day cousin the great white, possessed eight sensory organs that allowed it to search, detect, identify, and stalk its prey. Let's start with its most amazing sensory organ, called the ampullae of Lorenzini. Along the top and underside of the Meg's snout were tiny, jelly-filled capsules beneath the skin that could detect electrical discharges in the water. Let me put that in layman's terms. The Megalodon could detect the faint electrical field of its prey's beating heart or moving muscles miles away. That means if the Megalodon was circling our ship, it could still detect a whale calf in distress off the shoreline of Guam."

The room was silent now, all eyes focused on Jonas.

"Almost as amazing as the ampullae of Lorenzini was the Megalodon's sense of smell. Unlike man, the creature possessed directional nostrils, which could not only detect one part of blood or sweat or urine in a billion parts of water, but could also determine the exact location of the scent. That's why you see great whites swimming with a side-to-side motion of their heads. They're actually smelling the water in different directions. And a full-grown adult Megalodon's nostrils . . . they were probably the size of a grapefruit.

"Now we come to the monster's skin, a sensory organ and weapon combined in one. Running along either side of the Meg's flank was an organ we call the lateral line. Actually, the line is more of a canal that contains sensory cells called neuromasts. These neuromasts were able to detect the slightest vibrations in water, even the flutter of another fish's heartbeat. The skin itself was made up of denticles, which were essentially layered scales, sharp as scalpels. Rub your hand against the grain and your flesh would be sliced to ribbons."

Al DeMarco stood up. "You'll have to excuse me. I've got work to do."

"Ah, come on, Al," said D.J. lightheartedly. "There's no school tomorrow. We'll let you stay up late."

DeMarco gave D.J. a stern look. "Tomorrow happens to be a big day for all of us. I suggest we all get some rest."

"Al's right, D.J." agreed Jonas. "I've already mentioned the best parts anyway. But I'll answer your first question, about the shark's ability to deal with water pressure. Megalodon possessed an enormous liver that probably constituted one-fourth of its entire weight. Besides serving the creature's normal hepatic functions and storing fatty energy reserves, the liver would have allowed the Megalodon to adjust to any changes in water pressure, even at depths as great as those in the Challenger Deep."

"All right, Professor," said DeMarco, feeling baited, "let's assume, just for shits and giggles, that these Megalodon sharks do exist in the trench. Why haven't they surfaced? There's got to be a lot more food up here than down there."

"Conditioning. Above the warm bottom layer is six miles of freezing-cold water. Any Megalodon surviving in the trench did so because they were able to escape the colder waters above. The creatures would be conditioned over eons to remain in the depths. And there'd be no impetus to surface."

"Food's an impetus," said DeMarco, the cynicism rising in his voice. "What food source would be available in the Mariana Trench that could sustain a colony of predators the size of a sixty-foot great white?"

Jonas hesitated. "To be honest, I don't know. My assumption's always been that the Megalodon's food source would also have migrated to inhabit the deeper, warmer currents. Maybe that's what led them down there in the first place. Nature has a tendency to allow a species to adapt to certain limitations over millions of years. I think the trench waters, which maintain a much lower oxygen content than our surface waters, would effectively slow the creatures' metabolism down, greatly decreasing their appetites. Megalodons, being territorial predators, would probably thin out their numbers by devouring any weaker members of their own species. Every habitat has its food chain; the Challenger Deep is no exception."

"What nonsense," scoffed DeMarco. "We both know there's nothing inhabiting the Mariana Trench large enough to sustain even one Megalodon."

"How do you know?" Jonas retorted. "See, that closed-minded attitude is so typical. The very notion of a species existing in an unexplored environment like the Challenger Deep is impossible for you to comprehend simply because you haven't seen the species with your own eyes. It's far easier to criticize my theories than to consider the possibilities of existence. If you remember, it was only a short time ago that man refused to accept the notion that life could exist without photosynthesis, but it does. Who really knows what life forms inhabit the unexplored Challenger Deep? For your information, the unmanned submersible, *Kaiko*, recently recorded schools of unidentified fish inhabiting the deep waters of the Mariana Trench. We also know giant squids, measuring sixty feet and weighing a good ton, prefer the abyss. Surely these creatures would be adequate dining for a limited number of Megs. And what if other prehistoric species also managed to survive without our knowledge or blessings?"

DeMarco shook his head in disbelief. "Your theories are based on nothing but conjecture, fueled by your own vivid imagination, motivated by your guilt. I've had enough of this nonsense for one night." DeMarco headed out the door.

D.J. whistled. "Well Doc, personally I'm glad you just hallucinated these things," he said, winking at his sister. "Now all of us can sleep real good. G' night, Terry." D.J. kissed his sister and followed DeMarco out of the galley. Seconds later, their laughter could be heard down the corridor.

Jonas felt humiliated. He stood up, leaving his dinner plate on the table, and headed out on deck.

*   *   *

It was a calm sea, but clouds could be seen moving in from the east. Jonas watched the half-moon dance along the black surface of the Pacific. He thought about Maggie. Did he still love her? Did it really matter anymore? He gazed at the black water and felt the butterflies return, unaware that, one deck up, Frank Heller was watching.

*   *   *

Jonas awoke sometime before dawn. His cabin was pitch black, and for a moment he didn't know where he was. When he remembered, a shiver of fear flared in his gut. In a few hours he'd be in similar darkness with seven miles of frigid water over his head. He closed his eyes and tried to go back to sleep. He couldn't.

An hour later D.J. knocked on his door to wake him. It was time.

DESCENT

The dawn sky was a fierce tapestry of gray, gusting with thunderclouds that blew whitecaps across the roiling sea. Wind assaulted Jonas as he stepped out onto the main deck in his wetsuit. He had forced down a light breakfast of scrambled eggs and toast, needing to put something in his stomach before popping two of his yellow pills for the descent. In his left shoulder pouch were four more tablets. Despite the medication, he still felt anxious.

The *Kiku*'s crew were busy, half of them seeing to cables attached to the twin *Abyss Gliders*, others, in scuba gear, awaiting the release of the first submersible.

D.J.'s sub would be the first to go, its cocky young pilot giving last minute instructions to his older sister, who was wearing a matching wetsuit. Terry watched Jonas approach, never bothering to hide her disappointment. "So you decided to show."

"Give it a rest."

"I want to speak with you in private." She pulled him away from D.J. "Why are you doing this? Is it ego?"

"No. It's something I just have to do. A piece of me died down there, maybe this is the only way to make myself whole again."

"What if I paid you to sit this one out?"

Jonas shook his head, incredulous. "You want to bribe me to allow you to take my place?"

She nodded. "D.J. will go for it. No one else has to know."

"This is ridiculous. I'm going, that's all there is to it."

"Pack your little yellow pills, Dr. Feel Good?"

She grabbed his arm as he tried to walk away.

"D.J.'s my brother, Jonas. When our mother died, I practically raised him. So if you screw up down there . . . if anything happens to him, don't bother surfacing."

Without waiting for a reply, she turned her back, hugged D.J., then walked away.

Jonas shook his head. *J.T., you do have a way with women . . .*

D.J. waited until crewmen had attached the steel cable to his sub's claw. He waved to Jonas, then crawled through the rear hatch of his glider. Moments later, the big A-frame powered up, lifting the torpedo-shaped vessel off the deck, over the stern rail, and into the sea.

Alphonse DeMarco's booming voice faltered in the wind. "Let's go, Taylor, we're burning daylight."

As if we'll need it where we're going. Ducking down on all fours, Jonas climbed through the rear hatch of his submersible, straining his back as he sealed the Lexan pod behind him.

The interior of the pod was tight, the padding and shoulder harnesses smelling of new leather. Jonas realized the sub *was* new, and the sudden thought of taking an untested vessel seven miles below the surface only added to his angst.

He crawled forward, securing himself in the shoulder and waist harnesses. Mounted by his right shin was the sub's battery, and on the opposite side was the life-support system. Two joysticks attached to padded elbow rests were situated in front of his chest, the portside control operating thrust, the starboard control on his right designed to steer. Magnetic couplings were situated along the inside of the glass, securing the sub's wings and tail to the interior pod, allowing him the option of jettisoning the heavy exterior assemblies in an emergency. Below his belly was a storage area, holding flashlights, a pony bottle of air, a medical kit, a diving knife, and a diving mask.

Small LCD computer screens mounted on a low forward rise provided him with sonar, radio, and life-support readouts. As he ran through a quick check of his vitals, the sub suddenly lifted away from the deck, sending his equilibrium spinning.

Jonas's heart raced as the big winch hoisted the *Abyss Glider* beyond the *Kiku*'s rail, offering him a frightening view of the harsh Pacific. The A-frame lowered him to a team of divers, who were waiting in the fifteen-foot swells. For several harrowing minutes he held on, feeling seasick, as the incoming storm's fury lifted and dropped the buoyant submersible relentlessly. Outside the capsule, teams of frogmen were detaching harnesses and checking the wing assemblies. Finally, one of the divers knocked on the Lexan nose cone, giving the all-clear sign.

Jonas started the engine, pressed forward on the throttle, then adjusted the midwings, aiming his vessel underwater.

The glider responded at once, nose diving beneath the waves. The sensation of nausea immediately subsided, yielding to smooth sailing. Jonas noticed the sub felt much heavier, perhaps even sluggish compared with the lightweight AG I he had test-piloted years ago. Still, no other submersible could compare with the *Abyss Glider*'s sleek design.

Jonas followed the thick steel cable down another thirty feet before seeing D.J.'s sub. The radio crackled, the young pilot's voice filtering through.

"Age before beauty, Professor. You take the lead, I'm right behind you."

Walk in the park . . . Jonas moved the starboard joystick forward, sending his ten-foot glider into a steep forty-five-degree descent.

D.J. followed him down, the steel recovery cable in tow, the two subs looping downward in a slow spiraling pattern.

Within minutes the curtains of gray light faded to a deep shade of purple, followed by pitch blackness. Jonas checked his depth gauge: a mere 1,250 feet. He searched a pad of toggle switches on his right, located the exterior lights, and flicked them on.

A column of light illuminated a patch of sea below, scattering a school of fish. Descending into nothingness was disorienting, and Jonas wondered if he'd be better off just focusing on his LCD readout. He checked his depth gauge again: 2,352 feet. "Relax and breathe," he whispered to himself. "This is a marathon, not a sprint, J.T. You've got a long way to go."

"Everything all right, Taylor?" Dr. Heller's voice crackled over the radio with an air of insinuation. Jonas realized Frank was assigned to monitor the two pilots' vital signs. He must have noticed Jonas's heart rate increase on the console's cardiac monitor, his pulse recorded over a metallic band located on each of the joysticks' hand grips.

"Yeah . . . I'm fine."

"Good. Now you can switch off your exterior light, you're wasting battery power. Nothing to see down there anyway."

Jonas gritted his teeth, then flipped back the toggle switch, casting his existence into darkness, save for the soft orange glow from his forward console. He took a deep breath, trying to focus on the nothingness before him.

In the distance he saw a flash of light, followed by a dozen more. Soon the underworld was twinkling with ten thousand points of light. He had entered the twilight zone, the ocean's vast midwater region, the most inhabited domain on the planet.

The deeper he descended, the more curious the fish became. Schools of hatchet fish flew past his nose cone, staring at him with bulbous eyes, their narrow bodies blinking blue by means of light-producing photophores. The glider propelled past harvests of bioluminescent jellyfish, their transparent bodies filtering red in his sub's emergency keel light.

"Abyssopelagic animals," Jonas whispered to himself, reciting the technical name for these unique groups of fish, squid, and prawns. He watched as a four-foot gulper eel hovered in front of him, surfing on the nose cone's wake. Deciding to attack the larger sub, the eel spun around and opened its mouth, hyperextending and unhinging its jaws, revealing vicious rows of needle-sharp teeth. Jonas tapped the acrylic and the eel darted away.

To his left, a deep-sea anglerfish circled, an eerie light appearing over its mouth. The species possessed a rod fin that lit up like a lightning bug's tail. Small fish would mistake the light for food and swim straight toward it, right into the angler's wide-open mouth.

Even in the cold, perpetual darkness of the sea, nature had found a way to adapt.

Jonas hadn't noticed the cold creeping up on him. He glanced at his temperature gauge. Forty-two degrees outside. He adjusted the thermostat to heat the interior capsule.

The wave of panic happened without warning, jerking Jonas right off his stomach, causing him to slam his head against the ceiling of the pod. It was a desperate feeling, comparable to being buried alive in a coffin, unable to see, unable to escape. Sweat poured from his body, his breathing became erratic, and he found himself hyperventilating. He reached for two more pills, then, fearing an overdose, flicked on the exterior lights of the sub.

The beam revealed nothing but more blackness, but it served its purpose—to reorientate its pilot. Jonas took a breath, then wiped the sweat from his eyes. He turned down the heat, the cooler air helping.

D.J. was calling him over the radio. "What's with the light, Doc? We have strict orders."

"Just, uh . . . testing to make sure they still work. How're you doing back there?"

"Okay, I guess. This damn cable's all tangled around the mechanical arm. Kind of like my telephone cord gets."

"D.J., if it's a problem, we should head back—"

"I've got it under control. When we get to the bottom, I'll flip around a few dozen times and unwind." D.J. laughed at his own joke, but Jonas could hear the tension in the younger pilot's voice.

Jonas called up to DeMarco. "D.J. says his cable's twisting around the mechanical arm. Can you do anything topside to relieve some of the pressure?"

"Negative. D.J.'s got the problem under control. We'll monitor him. You concentrate on what you're doing, and turn off that damn light. DeMarco out."

Jonas hit the toggle switch again, then checked his depth gauge: 17,266 feet. They had been descending now for forty minutes, and were still only halfway to the bottom. He rubbed his eyes, then attempted to stretch his lower back within the tight leather harness.

The cramped capsule reminded Jonas of the time he had to submit to ninety minutes' worth of MRIs. The massive machine had been situated only inches above his head, the sword of Damocles waiting to crush his skull. Only the soft glow from the *Abyss Glider*'s control panel gave him a sense of direction, keeping him sane.

The Lexan pod creaked. The water pressure surrounding him was 8,000 pounds per square inch and rising. Jonas felt the telltale signs of claustrophobia creeping in again, his skin tingling, his face flushing. This time he fought the urge to flick on the 7,500-watt searchlight, focusing on his breathing. His eyes moved over the Lexan interior of the capsule, damp with condensation.

Why am I here?

Long minutes passed. The depth gauge numbers continued to mount: 23,850 . . . 28,400 . . . 30,560 . . . 31,200 . . . He stared out into the blackness, his hands trembling from nerves and fatigue. 33,120 . . . 34,000! He was now deeper than he'd ever gone before.

Jonas felt a slight trace of vertigo, which he hoped had more to do with the rich oxygen mixture in the submersible than with his medicine. His eyes moved from the inky water to the control panel readouts. The outside ocean temperature was thirty-six degrees . . . and rising!

D.J.'s voice shattered his thoughts. "Okay, Doc, turn on your exterior light, you should be able to see the hydrothermal ceiling."

Jonas complied, the light cannon piercing the darkness, illuminating a steaming, swirling, muddy layer of soot.

"Hang on, Doc, here's where it gets a bit rough."

The glider shook, jump-starting Jonas's heart. Lexan creaked, then the nose cone penetrated the mineral ceiling, the sweeping current slamming him sideways in his harness.

He began hyperventilating, the fear washing over him like a tsunami, his mind praying to his maker, begging for the ship's hull to maintain its integrity beneath the weight of the ocean's depths. *Please, Lord, don't let me die down here! Anywhere but here!*

And then he was through, piercing the crystal clear bottom waters as if entering the eye of a hurricane. Jonas opened his eyes wide, awestruck by the view. Below was a petrified forest of black smokers—towering chimneys of hardened mineral deposits, their open vents spewing thick brownish black clouds of superheated mineralized water into the abyss. Spread out along the sea floor surrounding these tall, skinny volcanoes were uncountable rows of giant albino clams, their white shells glowing as his heavenly light passed over them. Each was more than a foot in diameter, and there were thousands of them, lying in formation around the vents as if worshipping a god. The searchlight picked up movement along the bottom, and Jonas caught sight of vent crustaceans, albino lobsters, and albino crabs, all glowing in the darkness of the abyss, all completely blind.

D.J. was right. He had entered a different world.

THE BOTTOM

D.J.'s voice snapped him back to the reality of their mission. "Okay, Doc, I'm through. My glider has a tracking device that'll guide me to the UNIS, so follow me. It's gonna get very hot as we pass above those black smokers, so be careful. You catch a geyser of superheated water full on and it could melt the ceramic seals on your sub."

"Thanks for the warning." Jonas checked his digital temperature readout: 77 degrees Fahrenheit and still climbing as they descended toward the bottom. *How hot could it go? How much could the* Abyss Glider *handle?*

He followed D.J.'s submersible as it wove its way through the blackness, the trailing steel cable occasionally slapping against his nose cone. Water billowed up at them from below, heavy in sulfur, copper, iron, and other minerals that seeped out of the seabed's cracks.

Jonas maneuvered his sub between two of the smoking towers, his visibility virtually eliminated as he passed through the murk. His temperature gauge momentarily rocketed past 230 degrees, causing him to turn hard to port, grazing his left wing against the side of another black smoker.

As he descended beyond 35,000 feet, bizarre albino life forms came into view. Jonas knew that many species of fish living in the dark sea depths made their own light by means of chemicals called luciferins—a luminous bacteria that lived in their bodies. Nature had endowed the species with white skin and a luminescent glow to attract prey and locate each other.

Life. The amount and variety within the trenches had shocked scientists, who had incorrectly theorized that no life form could exist on the planet without sunlight. Jonas felt awed at being in the Challenger Deep. In the most desolate location on the planet, nature had found a way to allow life to not only exist, but to thrive.

A wave of trepidation washed over him with the thought.

What else is down here?

Jonas was overwhelmed by a sudden urge to locate the damaged UNIS, help secure the tow line, and get the hell out of Dodge.

The glider passed over massive clusters of tubeworms, flowing like clumps of spaghetti in the warm currents. Pure white and fluorescent, except for the tips, which were blood red. Twelve feet long, five inches thick, in groups too numerous to even approximate. The tubeworms fed on the bacteria in the water. In turn, eelpouts and other small fish fed off the tubeworms.

D.J.'s sub slowed up ahead. Jonas backed off, careful to maintain a safe distance. The two aquanauts wanted to remain within sight of one another, but didn't want Jonas to get caught in D.J.'s trailing cable.

D.J.'s voice crackled over the radio. "It's up ahead, steady on course one-five-zero."

Jonas followed D.J.'s sub along the 200-million-year-old sea floor, maneuvering just above a winding highway-sized gulley.

"Doc, I'm getting hit by strong currents, better hold on." As if on cue, Jonas felt his tail section begin wagging like a dog's tail. The submersible pitched, its engine fighting to maintain course and speed.

"There it is!" D.J. announced.

The shell of the destroyed UNIS looked like a piece of scrap metal buried beneath a ton of debris. D.J. positioned his sub well above the remains, shining his spotlight over it like a streetlamp. "It's all yours, Doc. Go ahead and survey the damage."

Jonas moved closer to the UNIS, floating into the light of D.J.'s sub. He aimed his own spotlight at the shattered hull and drifted past it to the other side. *Something's different*, he thought, looking at the debris around the base. *It's moved.*

"What do you think?" D.J. asked over the radio. "Another landslide?"

"Maybe, but that's not what destroyed this UNIS. There are no boulders large enough to leave these kind of indentations." Remembering the tooth, Jonas strained his eyes for a glimpse of something white. He inched the glider closer, aiming its light between rocks.

And there it was!

"D.J., I can't believe it! I think I've located that tooth!" Jonas could barely contain his excitement. He extended his sub's mechanical arm, aiming the claw above the eight-inch white triangular object. He felt contact! Carefully, he lifted the object out of the crevice.

D.J. was laughing hysterically over the radio. So were Terry and DeMarco.

Jonas looked at the object he had traveled seven miles down to obtain.

It was the remains of a dead albino starfish.

THE MALE

Terry, Frank Heller, and Alphonse DeMarco nearly fell out of their chairs in uncontrollable fits of laughter. Jonas could hear them over the radio, could feel his blood pressure rising. For a long moment, he seriously considered ramming his submersible into the canyon wall.

"I'm sorry for laughing, man," said D.J., "but you gotta admit, that was pretty funny. The thought of a killer starfish crushing the UNIS—"

"Enough already!"

"Okay, okay. Hey, wanna laugh at my stupidity? Take a look at my sub's mechanical arm."

Jonas looked up. The steel cable had wound in a dozen chaotic loops around the six-foot mechanical limb of D.J.'s sub, so much so that the arm was barely visible. "D.J., that's not funny. You've got a lot of untangling to do before you can free yourself to attach the line."

"I can handle it. You work on clearing that debris."

Jonas lowered the mechanical arm, trying to focus on the task at hand. He felt his blood boiling, beads of sweat dripping down his sides. Within minutes, he had managed to clear a third of the debris from the UNIS, exposing several intact eyebolts.

"Nice job, Doc." D.J. was slowly revolving the mechanical arm in tight counterclockwise circles. Gradually, the steel cable began freeing itself from around the extended appendage.

"You need some help?" asked Jonas.

"No, I'm fine. Stand by."

Jonas hovered the *Abyss Glider* twenty feet off the bottom. Masao had been right, all of them had. He had hallucinated, allowed his imagination to wander, violating a major rule of deep-sea exploration. One mistake, one simple loss of focus, had cost the lives of his crew and his reputation as a submersible pilot.

What was left for him now? Jonas thought about Maggie. She'll want a divorce, no doubt. Jonas was an embarrassment. She had turned to Bud Harris, his own friend, for love and support while Jonas had built his new career on a lie. His triumphant return to the Challenger Deep had merely served as a wake-up call. He had wasted seven years of his life, destroying his marriage in the process.

A starfish, for Christ's sake . . .

Blip.

The sound caught him off-guard. Jonas located his sonar. A red dot had appeared on the abyssal terrain, the source of the disturbance approaching fast.

Blip.

Blip, blip, blip . . .

Jonas felt his heart racing. Whatever it was, it was big!

"D.J., check your sonar!"

"My sonar? Whoa . . . what the hell is that?"

"DeMarco?"

Alphonse DeMarco had stopped laughing. "We see it too. Has D.J. attached the cable yet?"

Jonas looked up, where the sub's mechanical arm was twisting wildly, attempting to free the last loops. "Not yet. How big would you estimate this object to be?"

"Jonas, relax," shot back Terry. "We know what you're thinking. Heller says sonar's merely detecting a school of fish."

"Heller's a doctor, and not a very good one! Whatever this is, it's homing in on our location!"

Jonas took several deep breaths, forcing himself to think. *Homing in . . . it is homing in! Homing in on our vibrations!* "D.J., stop twisting!" commanded Jonas.

"Jonas, I'm nearly—"

"Shut down everything, all systems. Do it now!" Jonas shut off his sub's power, the 7,500-watt searchlight going dark. "D.J., if this object is a Megalodon, it's homing in on the vibrations and electrical impulses from our subs. Kill your power! Now, goddammit!"

D.J.'s heart raced. He stopped twisting the mechanical arm. "Al, what should I do?"

"Taylor's crazy. Attach the cable and get the hell out of there."

"D.J. . . ." Jonas stopped speaking, his eye catching a massive object circling less than five hundred yards away.

It was glowing.

D.J.'s searchlight flickered off, dropping a cloak of darkness around the two submersibles. Without the glow from his LCD monitor, Jonas couldn't even see his own hand in front of his face, but he could feel it shaking. He kept it close to the power switch for his own light.

Slowly, the circling object came into view, a vague, pale glow gliding back and forth through the overwhelming blackness. It was sizing them up, evaluating, as it moved silently a football-field length from their subs.

Jonas felt his throat constrict.

There was no doubt. He could see the conical snout, the thick triangular head, the crescent-moon tail. He estimated the Megalodon to be a good forty-five feet long and 40,000 pounds. Pure white, an albino ghost, just like the giant clams, just like the tubeworms.

The beast turned again, revealing a pair of claspers. . .

A male.

D.J.'s voice whispered across the radio. "Okay, Doc, I swear to you, I'm a believer. So what's your plan?"

"Stay calm. It's sizing us up. It's not sure we're edible. No movements, we have to be careful not to trigger a response."

"Taylor, report!" Heller's voice ripped through the capsule.

"Frank, shut up," whispered Jonas. "We're being watched."

"D.J.," Terry's voice whispered over the radio.

D.J. didn't respond. He was mesmerized by the frightening creature before him, paralyzed with fear.

Jonas knew they had only one chance; somehow they had to make it past the hydrothermal plume and back into the frigid open waters. The Meg wouldn't follow, at least he prayed it wouldn't.

It was getting warm. The powerless subs were drifting, the bottom currents pushing them toward a patch of vents. Dripping with sweat, Jonas watched as the glow of the male's hide grew larger. He caught a glimpse of a bluish-gray eye.

The monster turned. It was coming straight for them!

The massive creature loomed ghostlike in the pitch black.

Mouth agape—

Rows of jagged teeth!

Jonas ignited his sub's exterior light, blasting 7,500 watts into the creature's sensitive nocturnal eyes. The male whipped its head sideways, disappearing with a flicker of its tail into the darkness.

D.J. screamed over the radio. "Holy shit, Doc—"

The concussion wave hit them seconds later. D.J.'s glider twisted and spun, the steel cable going taut, preventing it from drifting farther. Untethered, Jonas's ship swept into the side of a black smoker, striking it tail-first, the impact crushing the sub's propeller shaft.

The Megalodon instinctively followed the movement, diving toward Jonas's crippled glider, now lying upside down and powerless against the base of the black smoker. Jonas opened his eyes as the approaching glow filled the capsule. The monster's thick white snout lifted, the upper jaw pushing forward—

—the triangular head darting away, avoiding his sub's beacon of light.

Jonas closed his eyes, fighting to catch a breath. For a millisecond he felt gratitude that his death would be delivered by the pressure change and not by the hideous teeth of the creature that now stalked him.

The male rushed him again, then broke once more from its frontal assault, whipping its girth in a tight circle that sent a current of water rushing at the downed *Abyss Glider*. The impact wave tossed the powerless submersible over and over again, sending it tumbling deeper into the ravine.

Jonas felt warm liquid ooze down his forehead seconds before he slipped into unconsciousness.

THE KILL

D.J. Tanaka accelerated his *Abyss Glider* into a steep seventy-degree climb. He ignored the constant barrage begging him to respond, choosing instead to focus on the race at hand. Blood pounded in his ears, but his hands were steady. He knew the stakes were high—life and death. The adrenaline junkie grinned.

He stole a quick glance over his left shoulder. The albino monster had banked sharply away from the sea floor and was now pursuing him like a guided missile. D.J. estimated he had a twelve-hundred-foot lead, the frigid waters still a good two to three thousand feet away.

It was going to be close.

His sonar beeped louder—

The depth gauge rose—

Sweat poured from his angular face—

"Come on, baby! Climb!"

The small glider burst through the thick ceiling of mineral and debris, whipped sideways as if caught by a tornado, then burst free into the frigid open waters.

D.J. looked back over his shoulder. The Megalodon was nowhere in sight. He checked his exterior temperature gauge. Fifty-two degrees and falling.

Made it . . .

The glow of the albino's hide registered in D.J.'s vision a split second before the gargantuan mouth exploded sideways into the submersible. Spinning upside down, D.J. tried to scream, the sickening crunch of ceramic and Lexan deafening his ears as his skull imploded, splattering his brains across the shattering cockpit glass.

*   *   *

The Megalodon snorted the warm blood into its nostrils, its entire sensory system quivering in delight. It rammed its snout farther into the tight chamber, unable to reach the remains of D.J. Tanaka's upper torso.

Clutching its crippled prey within its jaws, the male descended back into the warm currents, guarding its kill.

*   *   *

Jonas opened his eyes, though his sight refused to register in the pitch darkness. The submersible was bobbing, but he had no idea as to its orientation. A sharp pain shot up his leg. His foot was caught on something. He worked it loose and turned his body. A warm liquid drained into his eye. He wiped it away. Blood, he realized, though he could still not see his hand in front of his face.

How long had he been out?

The power had shut down, but the compartment was steaming hot. *I must be lying on the bottom, in that ravine*, Jonas thought. He reached out blindly, feeling for the controls, only to find he had slipped out of the pilot's harness and fallen to the other end of the capsule. He felt his way back into the cockpit and groped for the controls on the panel. He flipped the power switch, but nothing happened.

The AG II was dead, resting beneath 35,000 feet of water.

Above and outside the sub he saw something—a fraction of bioluminescent light refracted in the Plexiglas. Jonas pushed forward into the Lexan bubble, craning his neck upward.

In the distance he caught a fleeting glimpse of the male, swimming slowly toward the sea floor, a dark object dangling between its upper jaw and snout.

"D.J. . . ." The crippled submersible dangled from the predator's jaws, the steel cable still attached, the slack now looping and winding itself around the Megalodon's torso.

*   *   *

Frank Heller sat frozen in his chair. "We need to know what's going on down there," he said, pointing at the blank monitors.

Terry continued in vain to make radio contact. "D.J., can you hear me? D.J.!"

DeMarco was speaking rapidly with Captain Barre over an internal phone line. He and his crew were stationed in the stern, manning the A-frame's massive winch.

"Frank, Leon says there's movement registering on the steel cable. D.J.'s sub is still attached."

Heller jumped to his feet, moving to the TV monitor showing the winch on the stern deck. "Haul him up before he dies down there! If he's lost power, we're his only hope."

"What about Jonas?" Terry asked.

"We have no way of reaching him," DeMarco answered, "but we might be able to save your brother."

Heller leaned forward in his console and spoke into the mike. "Leon, you there?"

Leon Barre's voice boomed over the speaker. "Standing by!"

"Do it. Retract the cable!"

*   *   *

Jonas watched as the male passed directly overhead, its belly quivering as its jaws opened and closed. The ravenous predator continued to prod its snout into the remains of the submersible, but could not gain enough leverage to access the gushing meat wedged inside.

Jonas held his breath, praying the creature could not detect his presence, hoping beyond hope that it would not equate its last meal with his own powerless sub.

But the male was preoccupied, its attention fully focused on D.J.'s bloated remains, unaware that the steel cable looped around its torso was going taut, the slack being rapidly taken in from above.

Seconds later, the steel line bit into the monster's white hide, tearing into the shark's tender pectoral fins.

The cable's crushing embrace sent the male Megalodon into spasms. It spun its torso in a fit of rage, whipping its caudal fin to and fro in a futile attempt to free itself. The more it fought, the more entangled it became.

Jonas stared in helpless fascination as the Meg fought in vain, unable to release itself from the steel bonds. With its pectoral fins pinned to its side, it couldn't stabilize itself. Shaking its monstrous head from side to side, it released powerful concussion waves that rocked Jonas's sub.

After several minutes, the predator stopped thrashing, exhausted. Within the entanglement of steel cable, the only sign of life came from the occasional flutter of its gills. Slowly, the *Kiku's* winch began hauling the entrapped creature toward the frigid waters above.

The dying male thrashed again, its movements sending telltale signals of distress throughout the Challenger Deep.

Miles away, a much larger predator moved through the abyss, homing in on the vibrations.

THE FEMALE

It appeared out of nowhere, sweeping directly over Jonas, its deathly glow illuminating the black landscape like an enormous moon. Its sheer mass took several seconds to pass overhead. Until he caught sight of its towering tail fin, Jonas thought it might be some kind of submarine.

From the emergency light's glow along the bottom of his glider Jonas could see the underside of a triangular snout, followed by a hideous lower jaw. A collection of luminescent deep-sea remora that looked to be from another planet followed in tow. All had bioluminescent lures and needle-like teeth that jutted out from all conceivable angles. Some were squat with cactus-like protrusions, others long and eel-like, with crimson dorsal fins. A nasty half-moon-shaped bite scar ringed the underside of the Megalodon's left pectoral fin, followed by a protruding stomach that was clearly swollen pregnant. A pelvic fin passed, then the female's cloaca, its rim lacerated and scarred, confirming the identity of the monster as a very large female.

The female Megalodon was at least fifteen feet longer than its mate, weighing well over thirty tons. A casual slap of her caudal fin sent a concussion wave exploding against the damaged sub, lifting and pushing it farther down the gully. Jonas braced himself as the AG II skidded across the crevice and flipped twice before settling in another cloud of silt. He pressed his face to the nose cone and, as the muck settled, saw the female rise toward the male, which was still struggling to free itself from the steel cable.

The female circled warily, her nostrils inhaling the remnants of D.J.'s blood. Suddenly she turned, driving her hyperextended jaws around the soft underbelly of her former mate, the colossal impact driving the smaller Megalodon fifty feet upward. Rows of seven-inch serrated teeth ripped open the male's white hide, the female whipping its monstrous head left, then right, left then right . . . until it tore away a ten-ton mouthful of flesh, exposing the mortally wounded male's stomach and intestines.

The *Kiku's* winch bit into the slack, gaining momentum, pulling the cable upward even as the female chewed and swallowed.

Jonas panted as he watched the spectacle. The male's glow was diminishing as it rose, the female refusing to abandon her kill, circling after her suddenly animated prey. As if jolted by electricity she struck again, burying her snout deep within the gushing wound, her swollen white belly quivering in spasms as she gorged herself on huge chunks of flesh and entrails.

The male's body spasmed as it rose beyond the hydrothermal layer and into the cold. The female escorted it up, the hot blood of her mate bathing her in a soothing thick river of warmth as she rose out of the depths. She continued to feed, her murderous jaws entrenched deep within the wound, her teeth shredding the spleen and duodenum as hundreds of gallons of warm blood rushed into her open mouth and over her torso, protecting her from the cold.

Trapped in his sub, Jonas watched the thrashing white glow disappear overhead. Seconds later, the batteries supplying the emergency lights petered out, leaving the blackness of the canyon to close in around him.

* * *

Terry, DeMarco, and Heller ran out on deck, where the ship's medical team and at least a dozen other crew members peered over the railing, waiting for their missing comrade to surface.

Captain Barre stared at the iron O-ring that suspended the pulley from the steel frame of the winch. It was straining under the weight of its load, threatening to snap apart at any moment.

He pulled DeMarco aside. "Don't know what's on the other end of this," he said gravely, "but it sure as shit ain't just D.J.'s sub."

ESCAPE

Jonas huddled in the suffocating darkness. The downed submersible refused to settle in the current, and he registered every bump, every creak, every ambient sound of the Challenger Deep. He was beyond frightened, yet he knew he'd suffocate if he didn't act quickly. The wings of his sub had been mangled in the crash, and the engine was out of commission. It would be impossible to ascend with the dead weight of the mechanical end of the craft. He had to find the emergency lever and jettison the Lexan escape pod.

But if he jettisoned free and floated toward the surface, the movement could attract the female!

Where was she? Had she risen out of the abyss and into the midwaters? Or had she circled back, waiting for him even now?

Jonas was drenched in sweat, beginning to feel dizzy again. He couldn't be sure if it was from loss of blood or the steadily diminishing supply of air. Waves of panic, accelerated by the claustrophobia, rattled his nerves. Seven miles of ocean sat on top of him! Seven miles!

Gotta breathe . . . Gotta get outta here . . .

Enveloped in darkness, his fingers groped along the floor beneath his stomach, locating the small storage compartment. Jonas leaned backward, pulling open the hatch, straining to reach the spare tank of air. He unscrewed a valve and released a steady stream into the pod.

Choose:

Stay here and die in peace, or take a chance and try to make it out of the trench alive by activating the escape pod, floating free . . . except you'll be exposing yourself to the monster that might be circling out there, waiting to eat you!

He chose.

Rolling over, Jonas strapped himself back into the shoulder harness. Suspended upside down, he felt along his right side until he found the metal latch box.

Opened it. Gripped the emergency lever. Readied himself.

Jonas yanked back hard on the handle. A bright flash seared the darkness behind him, jolting him against the pilot's harness as the capsule exploded through the water and across the canyon floor. The noise and burst of light terrified him—it was an announcement to the denizens of the deep—a dinner bell to feed!

He held his breath, waiting to see the albino killer.

The escape pod leveled out, then floated topside, gathering speed as it rose.

Within minutes he had reached the silt-covered ceiling. The rapid current grabbed the pod and whipped it around on its perpetual merry-go-round of gravel and soot and sulfuric gases, refusing to let go, until Jonas thrust his back over and over again against the pod's ceiling, helping release the submersible from the torrent's death grip.

The Lexan pod floated free.

The internal temperature dropped quickly, plunging into the forties. It would be several hours before he reached the surface, and Jonas knew he had to concentrate on keeping warm. His clothes were soaked with perspiration. His teeth began to chatter.

Pulling himself into a fetal position, he closed his eyes and tried to remain calm.

* * *

The *Kiku*'s crew stood by the guardrail in the stern, watching the steel cable emerge yard by yard from the heavy sea, waiting and hoping for D.J.'s submersible to peek out from under, dragged upward by its mechanical arm.

Terry pressed her forehead to the cold rail and prayed.

Shouts caught her attention. She opened her eyes, crewmen pointing to the green surface waters as they began to bubble . . . gurgling with a bright pink froth. Seconds later, the enormous white head of the male Megalodon broke the surface, the crushed ceramic and Lexan pod of the mangled *Abyss Glider* wedged between its horrible open jaws.

Crewmen screamed! Terry felt herself swooning.

The creature kept rising, revealing its own ravaged remains. Wound steel cable held together hunks of partially eaten flesh, muscle, and internal organs. A long spinal column and rib cage was exposed, clear back to the intact crescent-shaped caudal fin, which dangled in the churning sea beneath it.

The shocked crew could only stare as the remains of the partially devoured pigmentless monster were hauled out of the water and dragged over the rail and across the broad deck of the ship. As the monster's head struck the deck, the bloated, nearly unrecognizable remains of D.J. Tanaka poured out over the planks.

Terry collapsed to her knees and fainted.

* * *

The escaped pod had been rising steadily in the darkness for hours. Loss of blood and the bitter cold were pushing Jonas deeper into a state of shock. His shivering had ceased, yielding to a loss of feeling in his toes and fingers, and still he could see nothing but pitch-black water above his head.

Hang on, J.T. It's just a walk in the park . . .

* * *

Frank Heller lowered his binoculars and scanned the seascape with his naked eye from the bridge of the *Kiku*. The two Zodiac motorized rafts continued expanding their perimeter search, the high seas and blistering rain from the arriving storm making it near-impossible to see, let alone spot a three-foot red flag.

"Storm's getting worse. Taylor's probably dead. We're wasting time and risking a dozen lives in these seas looking for a corpse."

DeMarco stood beside him at the rail. "Masao insists we continue the search. Those coast-guard choppers had better get here soon."

"Al, we can't wait any longer. Assuming Taylor wasn't killed by the Megalodon, then he's certainly died from exposure to the cold."

DeMarco turned to look for the hundredth time at the ravaged torso of the albino monster lying on the main deck. The science team was examining the carcass, taking measurements, shooting photos and video. "How many more of those things could be down there?"

Heller shrugged. "I don't know. What's important is that they're down there, and not up here."

* * *

Terry Tanaka stood at the bow of the yellow Zodiac as it bounded along the swells, desperately searching the valley of waves ahead of her for any sign of the missing *Abyss Glider*. Until she found it, there would be no time for grieving, no time for the pain gripping her heart. She had to locate Jonas while any chance still remained.

There were two divers in her boat, plus Leon Barre, who was steering from the rear of the Zodiac. "Terry, that's it! DeMarco's called the search."

"DeMarco's not in charge, I am. Circle back again!"

He shook his head, but complied.

"Wait!" Terry saw something disappear behind a swell ... a flicker of color. She pointed off the starboard bow. "There! Head over there."

The red vinyl flag was just visible over the crest of an incoming wave. Leon guided them to the capsule, which floated in the water. They could barely see

Jonas's body through the fogged surface of the Lexan escape pod.

"Is he alive?" Terry asked, as her divers readied their masks and flipped overboard.

She leaned over, waiting for an answer.

The pod was too heavy to lift from the water. Divers opened the rear hatch and reached in, grabbing Jonas by his legs. They hauled him out of the craft as it quickly filled with water and sank, disappearing beneath the waves.

One of the divers turned, signaling a thumbs-up. "Unconscious, but he's breathing!"

Terry lay back in the raft, tears of grief for her brother welling in her eyes.

HARBOR

Frank Heller couldn't figure out how the news had spread so quickly. It had taken less than three hours for the *Kiku* to reach the Aura Harbor naval base in Guam. Despite heavy winds and rain, two Japanese television crews and members of a local station were waiting for them on the dock, along with press reporters and photographers from the navy, the *Manila Times*, and the local *Guam Sentinel*. They surrounded Heller the moment he disembarked, bombarding him with questions about the giant shark, the dead pilot, and the surviving scientist who'd been airlifted ahead for medical treatment.

"Professor Taylor suffered a concussion and is being treated for hypothermia," Heller told them.

The cameramen trained their lenses on the ship's physician, but when the carcass of the Megalodon was hoisted off the *Kiku*'s main deck by crane, they scrambled for a shot.

An insistent young Japanese woman pressed her microphone at Heller. "Where will you take the shark?"

"It'll be stored in a refrigerated warehouse. The remains will eventually be taken to the Tanaka Oceanographic Institute."

"What happened to the creature? What killed it?"

"We're not certain at this point. The shark might have been ripped apart by the cable that entangled it, and drowned."

"It looks like it's been eaten," said a balding American with bushy eyebrows. "Is it possible another shark attacked this one?"

"It's possible, but—"

"Are you saying there are more of these monsters out there?"

"Did anyone see—?"

"Do you think—?"

Heller raised his hands. "One at a time." He nodded to a heavyset man from the Guam paper with his pen raised in the air.

"Our readers will want to know if it's safe to go boating?"

Heller spoke confidently. "Let me put your fears to rest. If there are any more of these sharks in the Mariana Trench, six miles of near-freezing water stands between them and us. Apparently, it's kept them trapped down there for at least two million years. It'll probably keep 'em down there a few million more."

"Dr. Heller?"

Heller turned. David Adashek stood before him. "Isn't Professor Taylor a marine paleobiologist?"

Heller glanced furtively at the crowd. "Yes. He has done some work—"

"More than some work. I understand he has a theory about these . . . dinosaur sharks. I believe they're called Megalodons?"

"Yes, well, I think I'll leave it to Dr. Taylor to explain his theories to you. Now if you don't mind, we've just lost a loved one, try to understand." Heller pushed through the crowd, ignoring the flurry of questions that followed him.

"Gangway!" came a thundering voice from behind. Leon Barre was supervising the transfer of the Megalodon carcass onto the dock, a massive boom raising it by its crescent-moon-shaped tail.

A photographer pushed to the front and shouted, "Captain, could we get your picture with the monster?"

Barre waved his arm at the crane operator, who stopped the boom. Momentum sent the Megalodon's head swaying to and fro, drenching the crowd with bloody seawater. Cameramen scrambled for an angle, but the carcass was so long it would not fit into the frame. Barre stood beside the giant head, but was clearly unnerved to be so close to the mouth. He gazed inside the lower jaw line at the teeth, the front row standing upright, another five to six rows of replacement teeth folded neatly behind them, back into the gum line. Feeling his knees go weak, the burly sea captain backed away.

"Smile, Captain," someone shouted.

Barre turned, staring grimly ahead. "Just take the damn picture and let me be."

THE *MAGNATE*

It was another gorgeous day in San Diego, the sky near cloudless, the temperature a balmy 78 degrees. San Diego's harbor was teeming with boaters, the catamarans racing beneath the Coronado Bay Bridge, the whale watchers moving farther out to sea, hoping to catch a close-up view of California's Gray Whales, twenty-five thousand of which were passing through San Diego's waters on their annual 7,000-mile migration from the Bering Sea to Baja California.

The 97-foot Abeking & Rasmusen super-yacht, *Magnate*, moved at a leisurely three knots, its course paralleling the San Diego skyline. A sleek fortress of fiberglass and steel, she was white with pine-green trim, possessing a 25-foot beam and 9.5-foot draft. Her twin 1200 horsepower engines could drive her through choppy seas at an easy twenty knots, her lush interior making the ride a pleasure in any weather.

Bud Harris had purchased the yacht from the owner of a struggling Arena League football franchise. He had gutted the insides, redoing everything in polished teak and mahogany, the walls and cabinets in a deep cherry wood. The floors were blue sapphire marble, the bay windows tinted, running floor to ceiling in the master suite, which was complete with a small gymnasium, home entertainment center, and a Jacuzzi.

Maggie Taylor was lying topless on the teakwood deck of the master suite's private sundeck, her oiled body glistening under the noon-day sun.

Bud watched her from his Jacuzzi, reading the *Los Angeles Times*. "You always said a tan looks good on camera."

Maggie shielded her eyes, squinting up at him. "This is for you, baby," she said with a smile. She rolled over on her stomach and watched a tiny television. "How about another drink? This is hard work."

"You got it." He climbed out of the tub, wrapped himself in a towel, and headed back inside the air-conditioned stateroom.

Moments later, Maggie screamed his name. He ran out on deck to find her sitting up, clutching a towel to her breasts, staring openmouthed at the TV. "I don't believe it!"

"What!?!" Bud hurried over, gazing at the TV. "Jesus . . . is that thing real?"

The Megalodon's head and fang-filled jaws filled the screen, its body dangling from the crane of the *Kiku*.

Bud leaned over and turned up the sound:

". . . experts believe could be the giant prehistoric shark, *Carcharodon megalodon*, ancestor of the modern-day great white. No one seems to know how the shark could have survived, but Dr. Taylor, who was injured in the capture, may be able to provide some answers. Taylor is recovering at the naval hospital in Guam.

"In China today, negotiations for a trade . . ."

"Dr. Taylor? Maggie, you think they mean Jonas?"

"Who the hell else could they mean?" She rushed into the master suite, Bud shouting after her, "Hey? Where're you going?"

"I need to call my office." She grabbed the phone, dialing frantically. Her assistant answered. "It's Maggie. Any messages?"

"Mr. Henderson called twice, and I've got a dozen messages from media outlets looking for a quote. Something about your husband. Oh, and a David Adashek's been trying to reach you all morning."

"The rest can wait, give me Adashek's number."

Maggie hung up, then dialed the overseas operator to connect her to Guam. Several minutes later, the line was ringing.

"Adashek."

"David, what the hell is happening?"

"Maggie? I've been trying to reach you all morning. Where are you?"

"Never mind that. I just saw the news report. Where did that shark come from? Where's Jonas? Has anyone spoken with him yet?"

"Slow down. Jonas is recovering in the Guam naval hospital. He's okay, but there's a guard posted at his door so no one can speak with him. The Megalodon's for real. Looks like you were wrong about your husband."

Maggie felt ill.

"Maggie, you still there?"

"Shut up, I'm trying to think."

"Maggie, this could be the story of the decade. Jonas is a major player, you could still get to him before anyone else."

"That's true."

"Be sure to ask him about the other shark."

Maggie's heart skipped a beat. "What other shark?"

"The one that ate the one that killed the Tanaka kid. Everybody's talking about it, but the Tanaka Institute's people are refusing to comment. Jonas is the only one who knows what happened down there. Maybe he'd talk to you?"

Maggie's mind raced. "Okay, okay, I'm coming to Guam. Now listen carefully: I want you to stay on the story. Try to find out what the authorities are going to do to locate this other shark."

"Maggie, they don't even know if it surfaced. The crew of the *Kiku* are swearing it never left the trench, they're claiming the thing's still trapped down there."

"Just stay on it, someone will talk. There's an extra grand in it for you if you can get me some inside dope about this second shark. I'll call you as soon as I land in Guam."

"You're the boss."

Maggie hung up. Bud was standing next to her. "So?"

"Bud, I need your help. Who do you know in Guam?"

RECOVERY

The navy MP on duty outside Jonas's room at the Aura naval hospital rose to attention as Terry approached the door.

"Sorry, ma'am. No press allowed."

"I'm not with the press. My name's Terry Tanaka. I was with—"

"Oh . . . excuse me." The MP stepped aside. "My apologies, ma'am. And . . . my condolences." He averted his eyes.

"Thank you," she said softly, entering Jonas's room.

Jonas lay in bed, facing the window. A gauze bandage was wrapped around his forehead, an IV dripping into his left arm. He turned toward Terry as she entered, his face pale.

"Terry? I'm sorry . . ." he rasped.

Terry nodded. "Are you all right?"

"I will be. Have you talked to your father?"

"He'll be here in the morning."

Jonas turned toward the window, unsure of what to say. "This is my fault, I should have never—"

"You tried to warn us. We just ridiculed you."

"I shouldn't have let D.J. go. I should have—"

"Stop it, Jonas," Terry snapped. "I can't deal with my own guilt, let alone yours. D.J. was an adult, and he certainly wasn't about to listen to you. He wanted to go, and so did I, despite your warnings. We're all devastated . . . in shock. I don't know what's going to happen next. I can't think that far ahead—" Tears flowed from her almond eyes.

"Take it easy." She sat down next to him on his bed, hugging him while she cried on his chest. Jonas smoothed her hair, trying to comfort her.

After a few minutes, she sat up and turned away from Jonas to wipe her eyes. "You're seeing me in rare form. I never cry."

"You don't always have to be so tough."

She smiled. "Yeah, I do. I told you, my mom died when I was very young. I've had to take care of Dad and D.J. all these years by myself."

"How's your dad doing?"

"He's a wreck. I need to get him through this. I don't even know what to do . . . Do you have a funeral? Should we cremate his remains?" The tears clouded in her eyes.

"Speak to DeMarco. Have him arrange a service."

"I just want this to be over. I want to get back to California."

Jonas looked at her a moment. "Terry, you need to know something. There were two Megs in the trench. The one that the *Kiku* hauled up, it was attacked by a larger female. She was rising with the carcass . . ."

"No, it's okay. Everyone on board was watching. Nothing else surfaced. Heller says the other creature, this female, couldn't survive the journey through the icy waters. You told us that yourself."

"Terry, listen to me." He tried to sit up, but the pain forced him down again. "The male's carcass . . . there was a lot of blood in the water. Megalodons are like great whites. They're not warm-blooded like mammals, but they are warm-bodied."

"What's your point?"

"When the *Kiku* began hauling up D.J.'s sub, the male became caught in the steel cable. I saw the larger Meg, the female . . . she was rising with the carcass, remaining within the warm-blood stream. I watched her disappear into the colder waters. I think the male's blood trail was keeping her warm."

"How do you know she didn't return to the trench?"

"I don't. But she wouldn't be so quick to abandon her kill. If the female remained within her dead mate's blood stream, she could have made it to the thermocline. She's much bigger than the male, sixty feet or more. A shark that size could probably cover the distance from the trench to the warmer surface waters in less than an hour."

"Jonas, the second shark never surfaced, just the remains of the first . . . and D.J."

She wiped back tears. "I have to go. Try to get some rest."

She squeezed his hand, then left the room.

NIGHT

Jonas awoke with a start. He was in the *Abyss Glider* capsule, bobbing along the surface of the western Pacific. Sunlight glared through the Plexiglas sphere, waves washing over the escape pod's acrylic dome.

The *Kiku* was gone.

I've been dreaming, he thought. *The hospital ... Terry ... all a dream.*

He stared at his hands, covered in dried blood. He felt the lump on his scalp.

How long have I been out? Hours? Days?

The water beneath him rippled with curtains of sunlight. He stared down into the deep blue sea, watching ... waiting for the Megalodon to appear.

He knew she was down there.

He knew she was coming.

The glow appeared first, then the snout, and that smile, the demonic grin. The albino predator rose majestically beneath him, her sinister mouth widening, her jaws opening, revealing her upper gum receding as her jawline and front row of serrated teeth jutted forward, hyperextending ... her widening mouth a black abyss—

"Ahhhh!"

Jonas awoke with a start. He was in bed, his pajamas bathed in sweat. He was alone in his hospital room. The digital clock read 12:06 a.m.

A dream. A nightmare.

He fell back on the damp sheets and stared at the moonlit ceiling, then forced a deep breath, exhaling slowly.

The fear was gone. Suddenly, he realized he felt better. The fever, the drugs . . . maybe it was the vindication. *I'm hungry*, he thought.

He got out of bed, put on a robe, and walked into the corridor. Empty. He heard the sound of a TV down the hall.

At the nursing station he found the MP sitting alone, his feet on a desk, his shirt open, downing a submarine sandwich while he watched the late news. The young man jumped when he sensed Jonas standing behind him.

"Mr. Taylor . . . you're up."

Jonas looked around. "Where's the nurse?"

"She stepped out for a minute, sir. I told her I'd . . . I'd cover for her." He stared at the bandage on Jonas's head. "You sure you ought to be out of bed, sir?"

"Where can I find something to eat?"

"Cafeteria's closed till six."

Jonas looked desperate.

"You can have some of this." He picked up another half of the bulging sandwich, and held it out for Jonas.

Jonas stared at it. "No, that's all right—"

"Go ahead. It's good stuff."

"All right, sure, thanks." Jonas took the sandwich and began to eat. He felt like he hadn't tasted food in days. "This is great," he said between bites.

"Italian subs are hard to come by out here," the young man said. "Only place I know is halfway around the island. Me and my buddies, we make the trip once a week, just to kind of remind us of home. I don't know why they don't open something closer to the base. Seems to me ..."

The kid continued talking, but Jonas wasn't listening. Something had caught his eye on the television. "Excuse me," Jonas said. "Can you turn that up?"

The MP stopped talking. "Sure." He raised the volume.

"... over forty pilot whales and two dozen dolphins beached themselves along Saipan's northern shore. Unfortunately, most of the mammals died before rescuers could push them back out to sea. In other news ..."

Jonas turned off the volume on the TV. "Saipan. That's in the middle of the northern Marianas, isn't it?"

"That's right, sir. Third island up the chain."

Jonas looked away, thinking.

"What is it, sir?" the MP asked.

Jonas looked at him. "Nothing. Thanks for the sandwich." He turned and headed back down the hall.

The MP watched Jonas hurry back to his room. "Sir," he called after him, "you sure you're all right?"

SURFACE

The 455-foot cargo ship, RMS *St. Columba*, pushed through the dark waters of the western Pacific, her mass displacing 7800 tons. The vessel had set sail from the United Kingdom two months earlier, making her way to South Africa, the Ascensions, and the Canary and St. Helena Islands before continuing her voyage along the Asian coast. While most of her gross tonnage was devoted to cargo, she also carried seventy-nine passengers, the majority of them boarding in Japan, bound for the Hawaiian Islands.

Twenty-year-old Tehdi Badaut stood on the bow of the main deck, watching the last remnants of day bleed into the western horizon. The French-Portuguese first officer had been assigned to oversee the transportation of six Arabian stallions, caged in pairs in specially built stalls that were mounted in the forward deck. Two of the horses were studs, worth a small fortune, the others all national and legion of honor winners.

Tehdi approached the first stall, offering a carrot to a three-year-old black mare. He enjoyed caring for the animals, and the truth was, there were worse duties on board. "How's my lady tonight? Bet you wish you could run around this ship, huh? I'd love to take you out of that cage, but I can't."

The mare shook its head, agitated.

"What? Suddenly you don't like my carrots?"

The other horses started bucking, too, prancing in tight circles, rising up on their hindquarters. Within minutes they were all snorting and bucking, bashing their frames against their wooden stalls.

The first officer pulled the radio from his back pocket. "It's Badaut, on the main deck, forward. Better send that horse trainer, something's wrong with the stallions."

*   *   *

The female moved effortlessly through the thermocline, its torpedo-shaped body gliding with slow, snake-like movements. The distinct rhythm of her movements was perpetrated by the creature's powerful swimming muscles, which attached internally to her cartilaginous vertebral column and externally to her thick skin. As her flank muscles contracted, the Megalodon's crescent-moon-shaped tail fin pulled in a rhythmic, undulating motion, propelling the monster forward. The immense tail, or caudal fin, gave the shark maximum thrust with minimal drag while maintaining a streamlined flow through the sea.

Stabilizing the 60-foot Megalodon's forward thrust were her fins: the enormous dorsal, situated atop her back like a seven-foot sail, and her pair of broad pectoral fins, which provided lift and balance, like the wings of a passenger airliner. A smaller pair of pelvic fins, a second dorsal, and a tiny anal fin rounded out the complement.

She was one of the last of her kind, and the first in more than 80,000 years to venture from the abyss. Hunger had driven her from her warm-water purgatory, and she had guarded her kill nearly to the surface, until the gray curtains of daylight had burned into her sensitive nocturnal eyes, forcing her retreat into the depths. She had remained there for several hours, circling in two thousand feet of water, her ampullae of Lorenzini teased by the electrical impulses emanating from the *Kiku*'s keel, which she perceived to be a larger challenger. When the *Kiku* had finally left (taking her kill with it) the female had followed it toward Guam, her primordial senses gradually becoming attuned to the magnetic variations in her new geography.

Although the Megalodon had no external ears, the female could "hear" sound waves as they struck sensory hair cells located in her inner ear. Carried by the auditory nerve, these signals not only alerted the predator to variations within her environment, but allowed her to track the precise direction the disturbances were originating from.

Unlike the trench, there were disturbances everywhere. The female could feel deep, tantalizing heartbeats coming from distant pods of whales, and she could sense a cacophony of sounds created by the splashing of dozens of breaching dolphins. More alien acoustics and electrical fields teased her senses . . . but she remained in the midwater realm, waiting until the painful ultraviolet rays had diminished before rising once more.

Hitching a ride on an upwelling of cold, nutrient-rich water, the gargantuan female ascended, the oxygen-rich surface waters continuing to stimulate her hunger.

*   *   *

The horse trainer, an attractive Floridian woman named Dawn Salone, watched helplessly as a half-Arabian pinto filly bashed its head against the wooden gate of its stable, the other horses following suit. "What the hell's spooking them? I've never seen anything like this."

"They're getting worse," said Tehdi. "Perhaps you should tranquilize them before they injure themselves. And those wooden gates . . . they won't hold up too much longer."

The moon peeked out from behind a cloud formation, casting its glow upon the Pacific—

—illuminating a seven-foot dorsal fin that had surfaced ten yards off the starboard beam.

The horses went into a frenzy, neighing and bucking, their coats lathered in sweat. A few of the taller stallions smashed their skulls against the fifteen-foot stable roofs.

Dawn had seen enough. "I'll get the tranquilizer gun, you stay with them." She headed aft, jogging along the starboard rail as she headed for the cargo ship's infrastructure—

—never noticing the 62,000-pound albino creature now gliding through a stream of surface refuse and human waste along the side of the steel vessel.

SAIPAN

Moonlight retreated behind a canopy of cirrus clouds. Small waves lapped along Saipan's deserted beaches. Somewhere at sea, a humpback moaned a distress call, the haunting siren blotted out by the thundering of steel propellers.

The landing struts of the two-passenger Guimbal G2 Cabri helicopter bounced twice upon the dirt runway before settling down. The pilot, retired navy captain James "Mac" Mackreides glanced over at his lone passenger, who looked a bit shaken after the forty-five-minute flight.

"You okay, J.T.?"

"Fine." Jonas took a deep breath as the chopper's rotary blades gradually slowed to a stop. They had landed on the perimeter of a makeshift airfield. A faded wooden sign read, "Welcome to Saipan."

"Yeah, well, you look like hell."

"Maybe it's because your flying hasn't improved since the navy discharged you."

"Hey, pal, I'm the only game in town, especially at three in the goddamn morning. What's so damn important anyway that you needed to fly out to this godforsaken island now?"

"You mentioned that fisherman friend of yours might know the location of a recent whale kill. I need to examine that carcass."

"Because of this mega-shark?"

"Megalodon, and yes."

"At this time of night? We really need to get you laid."

"Mac, this is important. Where's your friend?"

"First, he's not my friend, he's a business associate. Second, this is gonna cost me, which means it'll cost you double." Mac climbed down from his chopper.

Jonas followed suit. "So where is he? I thought he was supposed to meet us here?"

"He's a fisherman, shit for brains. They usually keep the fish near the water."

Jonas followed Mac down a path leading to the beach, the sounds of the crashing shoreline in the distance.

*   *   *

Jonas Taylor had met James Mackreides seven years earlier at a naval mental facility. Jonas had been ordered to spend ninety days in the psychiatric ward following the incident aboard the *Seacliff*. After two months of "help," the dishonorably discharged submersible pilot found himself in a state of deep depression, separated from Maggie, his career in ruins. Unable to leave the mental ward, he felt alone and betrayed.

Until he had met Mac.

James Mackreides lived to buck authority. Drafted and sent to fight in Vietnam when he was only eighteen, he was assigned to the 155th Assault Helicopter Corps, and was stationed in Cambodia, long before any U.S. armed forces were supposed to be in there. Mac was eventually forced to take over the team after six of their commanding officers were ambushed in a daring day raid. Trained by the navy to fly Cobras, Mac survived the insanity of Vietnam from that point on by deciding himself when, where, and if it was time for his team to wage war. If an assignment seemed ridiculous, he never questioned his orders, he just did something else. When ordered to bomb the Ho Chi Minh Trail, Mac would organize his troops for battle, then lead his squadron of choppers to a U.S. hospital, pick up a group of nurses, and spend the day on the beaches of Con Son Island. Later that night, he'd submit his report on the outstanding job his men did in "banging" the enemy. The navy never knew any better. On one such adventure, Mac's team landed one of their two-million-dollar helicopters in a delta, shot it to pieces, then blew it up with a claymore mine. Mac reported to his superiors that his squadron had been under heavy fire, but his men had heroically managed to hold their own against superior forces. For their bravery, the young captain and his men received Bronze Stars.

This was not to say that Mackreides's team didn't see their fair share of combat. Mac simply refused to risk the lives of his men if he determined certain actions to be senseless. Of course, to Mac, the entire Vietnam conflict was senseless.

After the war, Mackreides continued flying for the navy, if only because it opened up other avenues of free enterprise. With airships at his disposal, he could supply small-time operators from Guam to Hawaii with everything under the sun. This went on for two years, until another commanding officer finally got wise when he caught his enlisted men lining up for a Hawaiian "Lay" tour. Mac was charging two hundred dollars for thirty minutes in the back of his chopper with two Hawaiian prostitutes and a six-pack of beer.

The "flying bordello" incident earned Mackreides his discharge, a mandatory psychiatric evaluation, and an extended stay at the navy's mental institution. It was either that or military prison. Confined against his will, the rebel without a cause found himself suffocating, with no outlet to express his disdain for authority.

Then he met Jonas Taylor.

In Mac's professional opinion, Jonas was yet another victim of the military's blame game, the refusal of higher-ups to take responsibility for their actions. This made Taylor a kindred spirit of sorts, and Mackreides felt a moral obligation to help his new comrade-in-arms.

Mac decided the best remedy for his newfound buddy's depression was a road trip. Stealing the coast-guard's helicopter had been easy, landing it in the parking lot of Candlestick Park slightly more challenging. Getting into the 49ers-Cowboys game proved to be the toughest part. After watching the game in a skybox and partying till dawn, the two "madhouse cowboys" returned to the hospital the next evening by cab, drunk, stupid, and happy. The coast guard located the chopper two days later, parked at a body shop, a 49ers logo painted on either side of the cabin.

The two had remained close friends ever since.

*   *   *

The last boat anchored in the shallow water along the beach hardly looked seaworthy. Eighteen feet long, carrying a deep draft that left less than two feet of free board, the wooden vessel lay low in the water, its worn gray planks showing specks of red paint that dated back to the Korean war. Only one person was on board, a Filipino man in his late sixties, wearing a sweatshirt and jeans. He was busy repairing a crab trap hijacked from another islander.

Mac waved. "Felipe!"

The old man ignored him.

"Hey, Felipe, what's wrong?"

"What's wrong? You owe me money, that's what's wrong. You ask me for three girls, I get you three girls."

"Girls, Felipe. You sent me livestock. The fat broad weighed more than me, and the older one had no teeth."

"Ahh." The old man waved his hand at Mac. "This your friend?"

"Jonas Taylor." Jonas extended his hand.

Felipe ignored it. "Dead humpback floating two miles out. Cost you one hundred American. Cash up front."

Mac shook his head. "Fifty, which is worth more than your whole damn boat."

"Eighty. You take it or leave it."

"Fine." Jonas turned to his friend. "Mac, pay the man."

"What? You don't have any money?"

"You owe me twice that. Bail money? Mexico?"

"You remember that, huh?" Mac dug into his wallet, then tossed Felipe two twenty-dollar bills. "You'll get the rest if and when we make it back to the dock in one piece."

"Ahh."

Jonas and Mac climbed aboard.

*   *   *

Jonas knew he needed some kind of evidence to prove the female had surfaced. The numerous whale and dolphin beachings weren't enough, but if Felipe had seen a dead humpback and the female had killed it, then the oversized bite radius would be all the proof he needed.

It took twenty minutes to locate the dead whale.

"There she is," announced Felipe. "Now give me my money."

The bleeding whale carcass bobbed along the calm surface, its stench overpowering. There were no wounds appearing along its dorsal side, so Jonas grabbed an oar, using it to manipulate the bloated carcass, bobbing it up and down in an attempt to flip it over.

"Lose that oar, it cost you another twenty dollar!"

Mac rolled his eyes. "Okay, Jonas, now what?"

"I need to see the underside of this whale."

"Yeah? You planning on getting in?" Mac shined his light on the carcass. "Lots of blood in the water, you'd think there'd be sharks?"

Jonas stopped to think about that when something was illuminated in Mac's flashlight beam. "Mac, shine your light near that bleeding wound, that's it, right there."

The beacon settled on a triangular white object jammed into an exposed section of the whale's ribcage just below the waterline.

"Christ," said Jonas, "I think that's a tooth!"

"A tooth? How big did you say this megala thingy was?"

"Sixty feet." Jonas looked around the boat. "Mac, I need something to pry it out with."

"What am I? Mr. Goodwrench?" Mac opened a toolbox. Removed a hammer and handed it to Jonas. "And don't drop it, or Happy Harry here will charge me another twenty dollars."

Jonas leaned over the side, attempting to pry the tooth from the whale's rib using the back end of the hammer.

Mac grabbed the oar, assisting him.

The tooth flipped high into the air, Jonas leaning out and catching it—

—as an ivory-white jaw, as large as a double garage, gracefully broke the surface along either side of the whale's remains. Massive teeth, the uppers as wide as dinner plates, clamped down upon the dead humpback . . . and submerged, taking the entire bloated carcass with it.

Mac and Jonas stared at the surface, pie-eyed. Felipe crossed himself.

Seconds later, the whale carcass burst to the surface again, bobbing free.

"Okeydokey," Mac said. "That's all the proof I'll be needing."

Felipe backed toward the motor and gunned the engine. It flooded, coughing blue smoke, then died. Grabbing the hammer from Jonas, the Filipino tore off the engine's hood and proceeded to whack the motor with the hammer, the blows reverberating across the deck.

Jonas yelled, "Felipe . . . no!"

"Too late." Mac pointed to starboard where a stark-white dorsal fin was rising as the Meg surfaced, slowly circling the boat.

Jonas felt his throat constrict. "Leaving now would be a really good thing."

Mac moved toward the engine, pushing Felipe aside as he hurriedly checked the spark plugs. He tried the engine again. It spewed more smoke and died.

The dorsal fin changed course, moving slowly toward the boat. Underwater, the Meg's albino snout grazed the boat's keel, tasting it—

—jolting it with enough force to knock Jonas and Mac off their feet.

Felipe tripped over his crab trap and fell into the water.

Jonas grabbed the oar. Searched for Felipe—

—whose scream was suddenly cut off by an enormous splash.

For a long moment, Mac and Jonas just stared at the surface, waiting. Then Mac hurried back to the engine, grabbed Felipe's hammer, and started smashing it against the motor as he tried to turn it over—

Miraculously, it started!

Grabbing the wheel, he gunned the engine, veering them away from the carcass, steering them toward land.

The shoreline beckoned two miles away.

Mac looked at Jonas, visibly shaken. "Christ, that poor bastard—"

"Uh, Mac?" Jonas pointed behind them.

A twenty-foot-high wake was racing after the boat, an unseen luminous mass pushing it.

Mac zigged and zagged, but the wave continued closing the distance. "Okay, professor, I'm open to suggestions!"

"She's homing in on our engine."

"No shit? You went to college for that, did you?"

As they watched, the wake disappeared, the monster going deep.

"Thank God," said Mac.

Jonas looked around. "No, Mac . . . this isn't good. She'll come up from below."

"How do you know that?"

"Don't you ever watch *National Geographic*? It's what they do!"

They sideswiped a marker buoy, causing its bell to toll.

"Okay, Mac . . . radical idea time!"

*　　*　　*

The female circled in 350 feet of water, the annoying whine of the engine reverberating in her head. Sensing the challenge, refusing to share her kill, the agitated predator pumped its tail harder and charged the surface. Soulless gray-blue eyes rolled back an instant before—

Wa-boosh! The sea erupted as the Meg smashed straight up through the keel of Felipe's boat, splintering it into kindling.

The female flopped sideways back into the sea, debris raining everywhere. An eerie silence followed, save for the dull *gong* of the marker buoy's bell.

It tolled once more, then ceased midgong.

Having watched the demolition from a safe distance, Jonas and Mac, dripping wet and hugging the buoy, balanced on its steel frame. Jonas's right hand gripped the bell, silencing it.

Thirty feet below, the white glow passed beneath them, heading back out to sea.

THE MEETING

Terry Tanaka entered the Aura naval hospital and glanced at her watch—8:40 a.m. That gave her exactly twenty minutes to get Jonas to Commander McGovern's office, assuming he was in any condition to travel. She walked down the empty hallway, the navy MP no longer on duty. Jonas's door was ajar.

Inside, a woman with platinum blond hair was ransacking a chest of drawers. The bed was empty. Jonas was gone.

"Can I help you?" Terry asked.

Maggie jumped. "I'm . . . I'm looking for my husband."

"You won't find him in a drawer. Wait . . . you're Maggie?"

Maggie's eyes narrowed. "That's right, I'm *Mrs.* Taylor. Who the hell are you?"

"Terry Tanaka."

Maggie eyed her up and down. "Well, well . . ."

"I'm a friend. My brother . . . he was the one who was killed. I stopped by to drive Dr. Taylor to the naval base."

Maggie's disposition changed. "Sorry . . . about your brother. Did you say naval base? What does the navy want with Jonas?"

"There's a hearing . . . exactly what are you doing here?"

"My husband was nearly killed. Where else would I be but by his side?"

Terry frowned. "Not that it's any of my business, but—"

"—but you're right," said Maggie, "it's not your business. Anyway, since Jonas obviously isn't here, he must already be at the meeting, so maybe you can take me?"

*　　　*　　　*

The hearing at Guam's naval base took place in a refrigerated warehouse that had once been used to "hold" the bodies of deceased soldiers awaiting transport back to the States. Under three sets of mobile surgical lights lay the remains of the male Megalodon. Two Japanese men, scientists from JAMSTEC, were busy examining the enormous jaws of the ancient predator.

An MP handed Terry and Maggie each a lined coat as they entered the cooler.

A conference table and chairs had been set on the far side of the room. Frank Heller and Al DeMarco were consoling Masao, who wore dark sunglasses to obscure his red-rimmed eyes. Terry embraced her father, then introduced Maggie.

Commander Bryce McGovern, a silver-haired veteran of two wars, entered the warehouse, followed by an aide and a Frenchman in his late forties. "I'm Commander McGovern. This is Andre Dupont of the Cousteau Society."

"I'm Tanaka," Masao said. "My daughter, Terry."

The commander shook her hand. "We're all sorry about what happened to your brother. Mr. Tanaka, is everyone present?"

"Dr. Tsukamoto and Dr. Simidu have just arrived from the Japan Marine Science and Technology Center. But Jonas Taylor is not here. Apparently, he left the hospital late last night."

McGovern grimaced. "Our only real witness. Anyone know where the hell this guy went?"

Terry pointed to Maggie. "There's his wife. Ask her."

Maggie flashed a smile. "I'm sure Jonas will show up eventually. Studying these creatures was such a big part of our lives."

Terry rolled her eyes.

"Let's get started," said McGovern, taking his place at the head of the table. "If everyone can find seats . . . including the two gentlemen by the shark." The commander waited. "The Mariana Trench is under United States jurisdiction. As such, the United States Navy has assigned me to investigate the incident that occurred in the Challenger Deep. With all due respect to the bereaved, my rules are simple: I'm going to ask the questions and you people are going to give me the answers. First question," he pointed toward the Megalodon carcass, "would somebody please tell me what that thing is over there?"

Dr. Simidu, the younger of the two Japanese, was the first to speak. "Commander, JAMSTEC has examined the teeth of the creature and compared it with those of *Carcharodon carcharius*, the great white shark, and its extinct predecessor, *Carcharodon megalodon*." Simidu unfolded a towel, revealing one of the male Megalodon's teeth. "This is an upper tooth. As you can see, the tooth has a chevron, or scar, above the root, identifying it as a Megalodon. Its existence in the Mariana Trench is shocking, to say the least."

"Not to us, Dr. Simidu," replied Andre Dupont. "The disappearance of the Megalodon has always been a mystery, but the HMS *Challenger's* discovery in 1873 of several ten-thousand-year-old fossilized teeth dredged from the floor of the Mariana Trench made it clear that some members of the species may have survived."

McGovern paused, allowing his aide, a stenographer, to catch up. "Next question: How many more of these creatures are down there, and is there a danger to the local island population?"

"There's no danger." All heads turned to Frank Heller. "Commander, the shark you see here attacked and killed the pilot of one of our deep-sea submersibles, then apparently got itself entangled in our cable and was attacked by another one of its kind. These creatures have been trapped in a tropical layer at the bottom of the Mariana Trench for God knows how many millions of years. The only reason you even see this specimen before you is because we accidentally hauled it up to the surface."

"So you're telling me at least one more of these . . . these Megalodons exists, but it's trapped at the bottom of the trench."

"That's correct."

"You're wrong, Frank." Jonas entered from the rear door, followed by Mac, their clothing still damp. Jonas stopped as he laid eyes on his wife. "Maggie? What are you doing here?"

She looked up innocently. "I came as soon as I heard."

"Yeah, I'll bet you did."

"Dr. Taylor, I presume?" McGovern was losing patience.

"Yes, sir. And this is James Mackreides, a friend of mine."

McGovern's eyes blazed. "Yes, the captain and I know one another." He signaled to the MP. "Get these men some coats."

"There was a second shark, Commander, a female, much larger. She followed the male's blood trail out of the abyss. She's hunting in our surface waters as we speak."

Masao looked incredulous.

"It's true, Commander," said Mac, "and I've got the stained skivvies to prove it. Jonas, show him the tooth."

Jonas passed McGovern the tooth he had taken from the humpback whale's carcass. The commander compared it to the tooth Dr. Simidu had handed him. The female's dwarfed the male's!

Masao shook his head. "My God . . ."

"A predator that size in these coastal waters," McGovern said, "it'll be a human smorgasbord."

Dr. Simidu objected, "Megalodon hunted whales, Commander, not humans."

Mac mumbled to Jonas, "And the occasional fisherman."

McGovern massaged his brow, clearly out of his element. "Dr. Taylor, since you seem to be the closest thing to an expert on these creatures and you were present in the trench, perhaps you can tell me how this monster managed to surface. Dr. Heller seems convinced these creatures were trapped below six miles of frigid water."

"They were. But the first Meg, the male, was bleeding badly. The second, this female, was ascending within its dense blood stream. As I tried to explain yesterday to Terry, if the Megalodons are like their cousins, the great whites, their blood temperatures will be about twelve degrees higher than the surrounding ocean water, or, as in the case of the hydrothermal layer of the trench, about ninety-two degrees. The *Kiku* hauled the first Meg topside and the female followed her kill straight up to our warmer surface waters, protected by a river of hot blood streaming out of its mate."

"You keep referring to this second shark as a female," Andre Dupont interrupted. "How do you know for sure?"

"Because I saw her. She passed over my sub when I was in the trench. She's much larger than this first shark . . . and she's pregnant."

Conversations broke out across the conference table.

Mac looked at Jonas. "Good God, how the hell do you know she's pregnant? You do a gynecological exam down there?"

McGovern banged his palm on the table for quiet. "What else do we need to know about this . . . female?"

"Like its mate, it's totally white, actually bioluminescent when the light hits its hide. This is a common genetic adaptation to its deep-water environment, where no light exists. Its eyes will be extremely sensitive to light. Consequently, it won't surface during the day." He turned to Terry. "That's why no one on board the *Kiku* saw her rise. She would have stayed deep enough to avoid the light. And now that the shark has adapted to our surface waters, I think she's going to be very aggressive."

"Why do you say that?" Dr. Tsukamoto spoke for the first time.

"The deep waters of the Mariana Trench are poorly oxygenated compared to our surface waters. The higher the oxygen content, the more efficiently the Megalodon's system will function. In its new, highly oxygenated environment, the creature will be able to process and generate greater outputs of energy. In order to accommodate these increases in energy, the Meg will have to consume greater quantities of food. And, I don't need to tell you, sufficient food sources are readily available."

McGovern's face darkened. "Our coastal populations could be attacked."

"No, Commander, these creatures are too large to venture into shallow water. So far, the female has only attacked whales—"

"And D.J.!" Heller reminded him.

"That was an accident," Jonas retorted. "We shouldn't have been down there."

"And if this female eats a group of divers? Will you make the same excuse then?"

"There's another concern," said Masao. The room quieted. "This female's presence could potentially affect one of the whale migrations."

"Whale migrations?" McGovern looked perplexed.

"Hai. Whale migration patterns began millions of years ago. Some scientists theorize the mammals first migrated into colder polar waters not just to follow the food, but to escape Megalodon attacks. I'm not saying one creature could change the annual southern migrations now occurring along the coastlines, but even a slight change could create an ecological disaster. For instance, if the whale populations that currently inhabit the coastal waters off Hawaii were to suddenly flee to Japan's coastal waters in an attempt to avoid the Megalodon, the area's entire marine food chain would be affected. The additional presence of several thousand whales would cause an imbalance among those species that share the same diets as these mammals. The competition among marine life for plankton, krill, and shrimp could drastically reduce the populations among other species of fish. The inadequate food supply would change breeding patterns, severely affecting the fishing industry in that locale for years to come."

Dr. Simidu and Dr. Tsukamoto whispered to each other in Japanese.

McGovern stood up, thinking on his feet. "Let me be sure I'm understanding this situation correctly. Essentially, we have an aggressive sixty-foot version of a great white shark on the loose, a pregnant female, no less, whose mere presence could indirectly affect the fishing industry of some coastal nation. Does that about sum it up?"

Jonas nodded. "Yes, sir."

"So how do we deal with the situation?"

"Commander, why must you do anything?" Andre Dupont asked. "Since when does the United States Navy concern itself with the behavioral patterns of a fish?"

"And what if this 'fish' starts devouring small boats or scuba divers? What then, Mr. Dupont?"

"Dr. Taylor," said Dr. Tsukamoto, "if this creature's presence alters the migration patterns of whales around Japan, our entire fishing industry could suffer a major setback. Theoretically, JAMSTEC and the Tanaka Institute could be held legally responsible. The UNIS program has already been suspended, and we can't afford any more financial setbacks. JAMSTEC therefore officially recommends that this creature be found and destroyed."

McGovern nodded. "I happen to agree. I don't think nature intended to release these monsters from the abyss. That was your doing. Despite your assurances, I can't take the chance that this . . . female might venture into populated waters. And what if she has her pups along our coasts? Christ, we could be looking at dozens of these monsters in the next decade. What then?"

"There's no precedent for this," Dupont retorted. "At the very least, we're dealing with an endangered species, on the brink of extinction, at the most, the scientific find of the century. You declare war on this shark, and everyone from PETA to the Cousteau Society will be picketing your naval base starting tomorrow."

"Jonas," Masao was a voice of reason, "in your opinion, in which direction will this Megalodon head?"

"Difficult to predict. She'll follow the food, that's for sure. Problem is, there are four distinct whale migration patterns occurring at this time of year in this hemisphere. West toward the coast of Japan, east and west of the Hawaiian Islands, and farther east, along the coast of California. At this juncture, it appears the female's heading east, toward Hawaii. I'm guessing she'll continue east, eventually ending up in California waters . . . Wait a minute!"

"What is it, Taylor?" McGovern asked.

"Maybe there's another option. Masao, how close to completion is the Tanaka Lagoon?"

"Two weeks, but JAMSTEC cut off our funding. Jonas, you're not thinking of capturing this creature?"

"Why not? If the lagoon was designed to study whales in a natural environment, why couldn't we use it to capture the Meg?" Jonas turned to face the JAMSTEC directors. "Gentlemen, consider the opportunity we'd have to study this predator!"

"Tanaka-san," Dr. Simidu asked, "is this option feasible?"

"Simidu-san, hai, it is possible, assuming we can locate the female."

"Capture it?" Terry stood, furious. "Dad, what are you thinking? One of these monsters ate D.J. We're responsible for allowing this female to surface. We need to kill it before it hurts anyone else, or starts laying eggs, or having babies . . . or whatever the hell these things do to breed!"

Masao turned to his daughter, removing his sunglasses. "Kill? Is that what I've taught you? Do you know what this creature is, Terry? It is not a monster, it is a work of nature, the culmination of a billion years of evolution. Killing this majestic animal is out of the question. Its capture, however, would bring great honor, great meaning to D.J.'s death. It's what your brother would want."

"It's not what I want!" Terry stomped toward the exit and left, slamming the warehouse door behind her.

Maggie smiled. "Temperamental little thing, isn't she?"

The two representatives from JAMSTEC were talking rapidly in Japanese. Dr. Simidu turned to Masao, "Tanaka-san, I have the authority to release funding to your Institute, and would do so, if you really believe you can capture this female."

Masao looked to Jonas. "Taylor-san?"

"The lagoon would have to be finished quickly, the *Kiku* refitted. If we could locate the creature, perhaps we could tranquilize it, then drag it in using nets and inflatable buoys."

"Inflatable buoys . . ." Maggie was scribbling notes. "And why do you need them exactly?"

Jonas turned to his wife. "Unlike whales, sharks don't float. Being inherently heavier than seawater, if they stop swimming they'll sink. Once we tranquilize the female, she'll sink and drown unless we can keep water pumping through her gills."

Mac snickered. "Oh, is that all."

"Tanaka-san," said Dr. Tsukamoto, "you have lost a son to these creatures. With respect, if you so desire to capture this female, we will agree to underwrite the project and allow you to complete the lagoon. Of course, assuming you are successful, JAMSTEC will expect full access to the captured Megalodon, as well as our agreed-upon financial share of the lagoon's tourism trade."

Masao paused, tears welling in his eyes. "I think D.J. would have wanted this. My son dedicated his life to the advancement of science. The last thing he'd want would be for us to destroy this unique species. Jonas, will you help us capture the Megalodon?"

"Of course he will," said Maggie, jumping in.

"Hold it gentlemen . . . and lady," said McGovern, rejoining the conversation. "Mr. Tanaka, just so we understand each other, the navy cannot support any of these efforts. My recommendation to my commanding officer will be to use gunboats to patrol the island shorelines. Now, should you manage to capture the shark first, so be it. Personally, I hope you're successful. Officially, however, the navy cannot recognize this course of action as being a viable option." McGovern stood up again, signaling an end to the meeting.

"By the way, Dr. Taylor," the commander turned to face Jonas, "what makes you so sure this female will travel all the way to California's waters?"

"Because, Commander, as we speak, more than twenty thousand whales are migrating from the Bering Sea south toward the peninsula of Baja, Mexico, and the Megalodon can hear their beating hearts."

STRATEGY

The officer's galley onboard the *Kiku* had been converted into a war room. On one wall Jonas had attached a large map illustrating the migration patterns of the whales. Red pins indicated the locations where whale carcasses had recently been spotted by coast-guard helicopters. A pattern was becoming apparent: the female was heading away from Japan to the northeast, possibly toward the Hawaiian Islands.

Next to the whale map hung a large diagram illustrating the internal anatomy of the great white shark.

Jonas had convinced Masao to add Mac to the payroll, needing his skills as a helicopter pilot for night patrols. Then there was Maggie.

Maggie had pitched her TV station on filming the expedition, using their funding as a means to buy her way aboard. Jonas had mixed feelings about this, but tucked them away for the time being. He knew Masao needed the money to finance the Meg's capture. He also knew, at some point, he'd confront his wife about their marriage.

Terry and Masao filed into the galley, taking seats opposite DeMarco and Mac. Maggie and her cameraman, Fred Barch, sat in the back of the room. Frank Heller was the last to arrive.

Masao addressed the group, with Maggie's cameraman filming. "As you know, I've appointed Jonas to head this expedition. If there's anyone in the room who has a problem with that, speak now." He glanced at his daughter and Frank, neither of whom made eye contact. "Jonas?"

Jonas stood. "Before I review my plan to capture the female, it's important everyone knows exactly what we're dealing with." He pointed to the anatomical chart. "Megalodon's no ordinary predator. It's intelligent, it can sense vibrations in the water miles away, and it can detect the electrical impulses of its preys' beating hearts. Its nostrils are directional, allowing it to target one particle of blood or urine in billions of particles of seawater—"

"Yes, we know all this," Terry said. "We'll all make sure we use the bathroom before we hunt her down."

Jonas shot her a look, then walked to the back of the room to a pneumatic drill. Loosening its vise, he attached the female's tooth to the hammer end, then held up a square piece of 3-inch titanium from a UNIS robot. "Megalodon teeth are among the hardest substances ever created by nature. Each tooth is serrated, like a steak knife, designed to puncture whale bone."

Jonas positioned the titanium plate beneath the tooth, then flipped on the drill's power switch. When the air pressure indicator pointed to green, he hit the ON switch—

—the tooth instantly blasting through the titanium plate, its tip protruding from the other side. He powered off the machine and returned to his seat.

"That was 10,000 pounds per square inch of pressure. The female's jaw probably exerts twice that force. Now imagine a mouth the size of a small bus filled with hundreds of these teeth—a jaw big enough to swallow our mini-sub whole."

In the back of the room, Maggie's eyes widened as an idea came to her. "Jonas, let's say we wanted to film her capture underwater."

Terry scoffed. "Are you suicidal or just stupid?"

"I'm talking to my husband, sweetheart." She turned to Jonas. "How large would a shark cage have to be in order to prevent the Meg from swallowing it?"

Fred Barch stopped filming. "Hey, I'm not getting in any cage."

"A shark cage would be crushed," Jonas replied. "However a Lexan tube, say twelve feet in diameter and cylindrical, would be too large and slippery for the female to expand its jaws around."

"I'm still not getting in any tube," said the cameraman.

"I don't care about filming it," spat Terry, "I just want this monster captured before anyone else gets hurt."

Maggie ignored her, jotting down notes.

"And I want to know how you're going to find one fish in all that ocean," stated DeMarco.

Jonas pointed to the map. "These are the locations of the winter breeding grounds of whales currently migrating south from the Bering Sea. The Megalodon can detect the massive vibrations produced by whale populations to the east and west of Guam. Based on recent kills, she seems to be heading east, toward the pods moving along the coastal waters off Hawaii."

Jonas looked at Masao. "It's not going to be easy to locate her, but we know that her eyes are too sensitive to surface during the day. That means she'll do the majority of her hunting at night, attacking whales, forcing her close to the surface. Mac's helicopter has been equipped with a thermal imager and monitor, which will assist us in spotting both the Megalodon and the whale pods in the dark. I'll be riding shotgun, using a pair of night-vision binoculars. The Meg's hide is white, making her easier to locate, so that helps."

Jonas held up a homing dart the size of a cardboard paper towel roll. It was attached to an electronic device roughly the size of a pocket flashlight. "This transmitter dart fits into the barrel of a high-powered rifle. If we can inject the homing dart close to the Megalodon's heart, we'll not only be able to track her, we should also be able to monitor her pulse rate."

"What good will that do?" asked DeMarco.

"Once we tranquilize the Meg, knowing her heart rate could be vital to our own safety, as well as to the female's survival. The harpoons will contain a mixture of pentobarbital and ketamine. The pentobarbital will depress the Meg's cerebral oxygen consumption, which concerns me a bit. The ketamine is more of a nonbarbiturate general anesthetic. The Meg's heart should slow significantly once the combination of drugs take effect. I've estimated the dosages based on the female's size."

Heller looked up. "Those are some nasty drugs. Have you even considered the side effects?"

Jonas nodded. "The pentobarbital could cause some initial excitement in the Meg."

"What the hell does that mean?" asked DeMarco.

Mac slapped both palms on the table. "It means she's gonna be one mighty pissed off fish just before she goes into la-la land."

Masao looked at Jonas. "Once we tranquilize the creature, how will you drag it to the lagoon?"

"That's the tricky part. The harpoon gun will be positioned at the *Kiku*'s stern. We'll use the steel cable that's wrapped around the big winch as its line. The harpoon won't remain fastened very long in the Meg's hide, so it's important that we get the harness around her as quickly as possible. The harness itself is basically a thick two-hundred-foot fishing net with flotation buoys attached every twenty feet along its perimeter. The net should level her out and allow seawater to enter her mouth, forcing her gills to breathe. Once she's secured, it's just a matter of getting her into the lagoon."

Terry looked skeptical. "And how do you propose we secure the net around a thirty-ton sleeping shark?"

"Once she's asleep, I'll enter the water in the *Abyss Glider* and use the sub to align the net into position."

Terry looked at Jonas, incredulous. "You're going back in the water with that monster?

"We'll be monitoring the Megalodon's heart rate, and I'll be in constant communication with the *Kiku*.

If the Meg begins to wake, her pulse rate will increase rapidly as a warning. The AG I's a fast sub, I'll have no problems getting out of harm's way. Believe me, I have no desire to play hero. The Meg will be knocked out long before I enter the water in the glider."

Jonas looked over his team. "The female hasn't fed for seventy-two hours, so tonight could be the night. There's a sense of urgency here. First, the longer we take, the wider the search perimeter, the more ocean we're dealing with. Second, she's pregnant. We need to capture her before she births those pups.

"Better get some rest, it could be a long night."

* * *

The *Kiku* plowed east through the Pacific, the setting sun kissing the western horizon, painting the sky a golden hue.

Maggie stood at the stern rail, speaking on her cell phone with Bud. "Darling, did you get the equipment list I e-mailed you?"

"I got it," Bud said. "I also have an estimate of the bill. Do you have any idea how much this scheme of yours will cost?"

"The station will cover most of it, and you'll be co-producer of the number one newscast in all of California."

"Maggie, I don't know about this, is it really worth the risk?"

She saw Jonas approaching. "For the evening news anchor, you bet your ass. Order the equipment, I'll check back later. Gotta run."

Maggie hung up, then turned to Jonas, pouring on the charm. "So? How's it feel to be vindicated after all these years?"

"It doesn't change anything."

"Of course it does. It changes public perception. Trust me, perception's everything."

"Tell that to the families of those men who died."

"It was an accident, Jonas. Life goes on. Take my advice. Let yourself off the hook."

She gazed at the sunset. "So beautiful, isn't it? Reminds me a little of our honeymoon."

Jonas stared at her profile. "What happened to us, Maggie?"

"Jonas, we're so beyond this—"

"Just answer the question."

She turned to face him. "Okay, if you really need to know. The man I fell in love with was a cocky navy commander with an ambition that matched my own stride for stride. You knew you were the best, and that turned me on."

"And after the accident?"

"The Jonas Taylor who surfaced from the Mariana Trench just wasn't the same man I fell in love with."

"Shit happens, Maggie. People change."

She touched his cheek, her eyes all business. "I don't."

ATTACK

The full moon reflected off the windshield of the helicopter, illuminating the interior of the small compartment. Jonas was up front in the passenger seat, using the night vision binoculars. Seated in back directly behind him was Terry, who was holding the high-powered rifle and a backpack full of transmitter darts. If they could locate the Megalodon, it would be Terry's job to tag it, allowing the *Kiku* to track it and move closer.

Maggie was seated next to Terry, holding the heavy video camera mounted on a steady-cam. The chopper only held four passengers, and she was not about to allow Fred Barch to hog her glory.

Situated between Jonas and Mac was a monitor wired by cable to an Agema Thermovision 1000 infrared imager. Mounted below the helicopter was a small gyrostabilized platform that held the thermal imager pod in place. The thermal imager was designed to detect objects in the water by the electromagnetic radiation the object emitted. The internal temperature of a warm body would appear on the monitor as a hot spot against the image of the cold sea. The warm-blooded whales were easily detected; the Megalodon's internal temperature would be slightly cooler.

For nearly seven hours, Mac had flown his chopper along a thirty-mile perimeter of ocean, hovering two hundred feet above the black Pacific. They had located nearly a dozen pods of whales without seeing a trace of the Megalodon, and the initial excitement Jonas had felt was quickly fading into boredom as he realized just how difficult their task was going to be.

"This is crazy, Jonas," Mac shouted over his headphone's mouthpiece. "It's worse than looking for a needle in a haystack."

"How are we set for fuel?"

"Another fifteen minutes and we'll have to turn back."

Jonas refocused his ITT Night Mariner Gen III binoculars on the Pacific. The bifocal night glasses penetrated the dark, improving light amplification by using a coating of gallium arsenide on the photocathode of the intensifier, turning the black sea a pale shade of gray.

In the back seat, Maggie had drifted off to sleep. Terry watched her, then quietly opened her backpack on the floor and removed a 20 mm explosive . . . swapping it for the tracking device.

Jonas spotted another pod of whales. "Mac, eleven o'clock. Looks like humpbacks. Let's follow them a while, then we'll turn back."

"You're the boss." Mac changed course to intercept the pod.

Jonas was growing worried. With each hour that passed, the search perimeter extended an additional ten miles. Soon there would simply be too much ocean to cover, even with their sophisticated tracking equipment.

Exhausted, Jonas felt himself becoming mesmerized by the moonlight dancing across the ocean, barely noticing the white blur streak across his peripheral vision. The moon had illuminated something below the surface. For a moment it had seemed to glow.

"See something, J.T.?"

"Not sure." He focused on the whale pod, locating three spouts. "I can make out two bulls, a cow and her calf . . . no, make that two cows, five whales total. Get us on top of them, Mac."

The helicopter hovered above the pod, keeping pace as the whales changed direction, turning north.

Jonas searched the sea to the left and right of the pod. His heart jumped in his chest, "There!"

Behind the pod, a white glow appeared, streaking beneath the surface like a giant luminescent torpedo.

Maggie stirred. Terry leaned forward, staring at the monitor. "What is it? Is it the shark?"

"Affirmative."

"What's she doing?" Maggie asked, fixing the camera to her shoulder.

Jonas looked at Mac. "I think she's stalking the calf."

*   *   *

One hundred feet below the black Pacific, a deadly game of cat and mouse was taking place. The humpbacks had detected the hunter's presence miles back, the mammals altering their course repeatedly to avoid a confrontation. As the albino predator closed to intercept, the two cows moved to surround the calf, the larger bulls taking positions at the front and rear of the pod.

The Megalodon slowed, circling to the right of her quarry, sizing up her prey, marking the position of the calf. Faster than the whales, the female darted in and out, testing the reaction time of the two bulls.

As the shark crossed in front of the lead male, the forty-ton bull broke from the group and made a run at her. Although the humpback whale possessed baleen instead of teeth, it was still quite dangerous, able to ram the female with its enormous head. The male humpback's charge was sudden, but the Meg was far too quick, accelerating away from the bull, then returning in a wide arc.

*   *   *

"What do you see?"

Jonas was peering through the night glasses. "Looks like the lead bull is chasing the Megalodon away from the pod."

"Wait a minute, did you say the whale's chasing the Meg?" Maggie chuckled. "I thought this Megalodon of yours was supposed to be fearsome?"

"Sure, you can say that now," said Mac. "Try hanging from a buoy, you'll change your tune real fast."

Jonas turned to Terry. "You ready with that tracking dart?"

She nodded.

*   *   *

Once more the pod altered its course, this time heading southeast to lose the hunter. The Megalodon compensated, selecting an alternative course, targeting the massive bull guarding the rear. This angle presented a different problem for the shark, which instinctively feared the humpback's powerful fluke.

The Megalodon remained parallel with the bull, darting closer, pulling away, trying to entice it to leave the pod and attack. She grew bolder with each foray, snapping at the humpback, once even biting at its enormous right pectoral fin.

The bull finally turned upon the Meg, chasing it from the rest of the pod. Only this time the female retreated to the rear, distancing the bull from the safety of the pack.

As the male humpback turned to rejoin the others, the albino hunter circled back with a frightening burst of speed and launched her 62,000 pounds at the retreating humpback's exposed flank. Her open mouth latched onto the whale, her teeth puncturing blubber and muscle, her powerful jaws holding on.

The bull spasmed and writhed in agony, its wild contortions only serving to aid the Megalodon's serrated teeth, which sliced cleanly through the humpback's gushing grooves. An agonizing, high-pitched moan reverberated from the bleeding rorqual as the albino predator shook itself loose, choking down a 12,000-pound mouthful of blubber.

* * *

"What the hell was that?" yelled Mac

"I can't be sure," said Jonas, the night glasses pressed against his eyes, "but I think the Meg just attacked one of the bulls."

"The pod's moving off."

"Forget the pod, Mac. Stay with the wounded bull."

*   *   *

A river of hot blood gushed from the gaping wound as the crippled humpback feebly attempted to propel itself forward with its massive lateral flippers.

The Megalodon circled below its wounded prey, allowing it to settle before launching its second attack—this one even more devastating than the first.

Seizing the baleen-fringed edges of the dying creature's mouth within its seven-and-a-half inch fangs, the Meg ripped and tore apart an entire section of the humpback's throat, whipping its enormous head to and fro until a long strip of grooved hide and blubber peeled away from the mammal's body like husk from a ripe ear of corn.

Helpless and in agony, the tortured humpback slapped its fluke repeatedly along the bloody surface as it wailed a death song of warning to its fleeing pod.

The Megalodon circled deep again, waiting for its wounded prey to die. That's when the female's lateral line detected the heavy vibrations coming from the surface above.

*   *   *

Maggie aimed her camera out her portside window. "Jonas, can you describe what's happening down there for my viewers?"

"Hard to tell, there's so much blood in the water. What's your thermal imager picking up, Mac?"

"I can't see shit from shine-ola. The blood's spreading out over the surface so fast, it's camouflaging everything."

"Bring us closer," Maggie yelled.

Mac descended to fifty feet. "How's that?"

Maggie focused through her viewfinder. "I still don't see the Meg, just that damn whale."

Terry aimed the barrel of her rifle out the open section on the starboard side of the cockpit. She stood in her seat, looking down through the night scope. She could just make out the Megalodon's white hide, circling below the dying whale. Her finger slipped around the trigger. She took a breath . . . *this is for you, D.J.—*

—as the blur suddenly disappeared. "Damn fish . . . it just went deep again. Mac, we need to be lower."

Mac adjusted the airship's altitude, dropping another twenty feet.

Jonas's heart raced. "Something's not right. She wouldn't just go deep, not with her kill so close."

"Probably scared her off," said Maggie, shifting her angle to aim over Terry's shoulder. "Oh yeah, that's much better. God, look at that whale bleed. Now if only the guest of honor wasn't such a wimp."

Jonas felt sweat pouring down his face. "She has to sense the chopper's vibrations, I wonder if she perceives us as a threat? Mac, I've got a bad feeling about this. Take us higher."

"Higher? But I—"

"Goddamnit, Mac, higher—now!"

The sea exploded in a bloody froth as the Megalodon launched its girth out of the water at its challenger. The conical snout struck the thermal imager, shattering it on impact, the midair collision sending the chopper caroming sideways—

—swinging Jonas's cockpit door open, his right foot losing its grip on the floorboard as the G-force of the copter's roll pushed him out, only the seat belt keeping his body from falling into the night and down into the gaping mouth and exposed teeth—

—as Maggie and Terry wrestled for position, Terry's finger inadvertently pulling the rifle's trigger—

—the 20 mm shell rocketing past the Meg's left pectoral fin, exploding as it struck the surface below—

—the cabin spinning, Mac screaming, "Come on!" as he clutched his control stick with both hands, the ocean racing at him in his peripheral vision as he fought a thirty-degree down angle, until . . .

—the rotors finally caught air.

Mac pulled the chopper out of its nosedive, leveling off just above the waves. The veteran pilot groaned with relief as his airship soared above the Pacific and climbed, making its getaway.

"Gawd-damn, Jonas, I think I just shit my pants!"

Jonas fought to catch his breath. His limbs quivered, his voice abandoning him. After a good minute, he forced the words out of his parched throat. "She's . . . she's a lot bigger than I thought."

Terry gritted her teeth, saying nothing.

Maggie stared at her. "What was that explosion?"

"I wouldn't know."

"Bullshit!"

Jonas reached back and grabbed her backpack. Found two more 20mm shells. "Nice."

Mac shook his head. "We're low on fuel. I'll radio the *Kiku* to rendezvous. Hopefully we won't have to ditch."

The three passengers looked at him, the blood rushing from their faces.

Mac smiled to himself, not bothering to mention his reserve tank.

The *Kiku* was berthed next to the USS *John Hancock*, the 563-foot Spruance class destroyer that had arrived in port earlier that morning. Under pressure from animal rights activists, Commander McGovern had personally arranged the docking space for Masao Tanaka's vessel, while he secretly recruited a makeshift crew to report to Pearl Harbor for a "special assignment."

Captain Barre stood on the *Kiku's* stern deck, overseeing the installation of a harpoon gun behind the ship's massive A-frame. Jonas and Mac were with Alphonse DeMarco, watching the engineer check and recheck the battery system on the *Abyss Glider I*. The AG I was a smaller, sleeker version of the deep-sea sub Jonas had piloted in the Mariana Trench. Designed for speed, the one-man vessel was smaller in length and weighed a mere 462 pounds, with the majority of that weight located in the instrument panels in the Lexan nose cone.

"Looks like a miniature jet fighter," said Mac.

"Handles like one too," DeMarco grunted.

"Is this the same model the Tanaka kid was attacked in?"

"No," said Jonas, "the AG II was bigger, the hull thicker and much heavier."

"The AG I was its prototype," said DeMarco. "It was only designed for depths up to two thousand meters. This hull's made of pure aluminum oxide, extremely sturdy, but positively buoyant. My baby can move fast, turn on a dime, even leap straight out of the water."

"Yeah? Can it out-leap the monster we saw last night?" Mac asked.

Jonas looked at his friend. "It would take a rocket to out-jump that fish."

"A rocket? You've got one." DeMarco climbed through the rear hatch, then pointed to a lockbox on the left side of the pilot's control console. "See this lever? Turn it a half-click counterclockwise, then pull it toward you, and it'll ignite a small tank of hydrogen installed in the tail. Never used it to launch the AG straight out of the water, but it would free up the sub in case you ever got stuck in the muck at the bottom."

"How long a burn?"

"Hell, I don't know . . . fifteen, maybe twenty seconds tops. Once the sub's freed, she'll float topside anyway, assuming you've lost power." DeMarco inched his way out of the sub. "'Course, you already knew that."

"Hey, Jonas!" Mac was at the portside rail, pointing at two tugboats that were busy pushing an antiquated nuclear submarine into an empty berth. The black vessel looked familiar. A dozen crewmen stood on deck, proudly standing by with ropes to tie the ship off.

Jonas stared at the insignia SSN-571 as if seeing a ghost. "Son of a bitch, that's the *Nautilus*. I thought they put her out to pasture in Groton?"

Mac nodded. "It's McGovern. He's in way over his head, fighting a losing publicity battle with the animal rights lovers. Bottom line: If you're ordered to kill a fish, kill it with a legend. Navy vets love the *Nautilus*. So McGovern ordered her refit for one last sail into the sunset."

"Christ."

* * *

It was back on September 30, 1954, that the *Nautilus* became the U.S. Navy's first commissioned nuclear powered ship. The submarine would shatter all submerged speed and distance records and become the first vessel to travel beneath the ice floe to reach the geographic North Pole. After serving the navy for twenty-five years, the famous submarine was eventually decommissioned, but only after having logged nearly a half million miles at sea.

As Jonas watched, two officers showed themselves in the sub's conning tower. "Holy shit. It's Danielson. Can you believe this?"

"Your former CO? Yeah, I already knew. A friend stationed on Guam told me Danielson volunteered when he heard you were involved. In fact, it was his suggestion to McGovern to use that old tin can to go after the shark."

As the *Nautilus* passed the *Kiku*, United States Navy Captain (Ret.) Richard Danielson squinted in the sunlight, stealing a glance at his former deep-sea pilot.

"Hi, Dick, how's it hanging?" muttered Mac, a smile plastered on his face.

"He probably heard you."

"Hey, Danielson can kiss my big hairy ass. This guy destroyed your career, not that I give a shit about the navy, mind you. How many months did he stow you away in that loony bin before your ol' buddy Mac here saved your sorry butt? Two months?"

"Three. Probably would have been easier if I had just told those doctors I imagined the Meg. You know, psychosis of the deep, temporary insanity brought on by fatigue."

"Would have been a lie, pal."

"Yeah, well somehow I don't think Danielson volunteered so he could apologize to me in person. Megalodon or not, the guy blames me for killing two of his men."

"Hey, J.T., no living person on this planet would have done any different than you if they had seen what we saw coming at us last night. And I told that to Heller."

"What'd he say?"

"Heller's an asshole. If he'd have been with me in 'Nam, he'd have been a casualty of friendly fire." Mac looked toward the stern. "When's that big net of yours due to arrive?"

"This afternoon."

"Good. Hey, you should've heard the old man ripping Terry a new one. Man, was he pissed. Meanwhile, what the hell's going on with you and the old lady?"

"I don't know. I know she's screwing Bud, but . . . I guess a part of me still loves her."

Mac turned to his friend, looking like he just swallowed turpentine. "Jonas . . . Jonas, you hopeless sack of shit. What were the three rules I taught you about women?"

"I don't remember."

"Come on!"

"No glove, no love. Use lemon juice to check for open wounds—"

"And never marry a woman who can't name at least two of the five Marx Brothers. Maggie was no good from the get-go and I told you that when you married her! Women like Maggie, they play by a different set of rules. Let her go, move on. Let this prick Harris deal with her. Trust me, he'll be bankrupt within a year."

Jonas stared at the horizon, a line of storm clouds building in the distance.

"So between me and thee, you really think this shark of yours will end up in California waters? I mean, no pressure, J.T., but I could really use that bonus Tanaka's offering."

"I don't know. Maybe. The truth is, our window of opportunity's closing quickly. Tracking the Megalodon in coastal waters is one thing, locating her in open ocean . . . probably impossible."

"What about California?"

"If it happens, it could take weeks, maybe years. No one can predict what a predator like this will do." Jonas paused, pointing to the horizon. "Looks bad. What do you think?"

Mac looked to the west, where dark storm clouds had gathered. "No hunting by chopper tonight, I'd say."

Jonas nodded. "Hope the Meg agrees with you."

*   *   *

Frank Heller stood on the pier, watching two crewmen secure the submarine's thick white bow lines, carefully lining the slack up along the deck of the *Nautilus*. Moments later, Captain Richard Danielson emerged from the forward section of the hull. He smiled at Heller, slapping the "571" painted in white along the black conning tower.

"So, Frank, what do you think of my new command?"

Heller shook his head. "I'm just amazed this old barge still floats. Why the hell would McGovern assign a decommissioned sub to hunt down this shark?"

Danielson strode across the open gangway. "My idea. McGovern's in a tough position. The publicity's killing him. But the *Nautilus*, she's a different story. The public loves this old boat. She's like an aging war hero, going out with one last victory. McGovern went crazy for the idea—"

"I don't like it. You have no concept of what you're dealing with, skipper."

"I read the reports. Don't forget, I tracked Russian Alphas for five years. This mission's nothing. One tube in the water and this overgrown shark is fish food."

Frank was about to respond when he saw a tall officer exit the sub, a big smile planted on his face.

"Denny?"

"Hey, big brother!" Chief Engineer Dennis Heller came bounding down the ramp and bear-hugged Frank.

"Denny, what in the hell are you doing aboard this rusty tin can?"

Dennis glanced at Danielson. "I'm due to retire this year. Turns out I'm thirty hours shy on active duty. I figured, why not serve them aboard the *Nautilus* with my first CO. Besides, shore leave in Honolulu beats the hell out of Bayonne, New Jersey."

"Sorry to disappoint you, Chief," interrupted Danielson, "but all shore leaves are cancelled until we fry this Megala . . . whatever Taylor calls it. By the way, Frank, I saw him on board your boat this afternoon. Honestly, I can't stomach the man."

"Turns out he was right. Why not just leave it alone—"

"So he was right. His actions still killed two of my crew, or did you forget?"

"It's our fault too." Heller lowered his voice to his former commanding officer. "I should have never allowed you to talk me into pushing him on that last dive."

"He was fine—"

"He was fried! Taylor was one of the best deep-sea pilots in the business. And that mission had nothing to do with the navy, it was those neo-cons working the Pentagon who were pushing that whole energy agenda!"

"You're out of line, Doctor." Danielson's neck was turning red.

"Whoa, Frank, Captain, take it easy." Dennis moved between them. "Come on, Frank, I'll take you out for a quick bite. Skip, I'll be back at sixteen-thirty hours."

Danielson stood in silence as the two men headed into town, the first drops of rain echoing against the outer steel casing of the *Nautilus*.

JAWS, MAUI

The towering swells, driven by the impending storm, rolled onto the rocky beach, carrying large chunks of whale blubber and debris. The two-hundred-odd tourists didn't seem to mind. They'd been gathering all day to watch local surfers brave some of the most dangerous waves on the planet.

It takes a variety of conditions to form big waves, the two most important being the distance a wave travels over deep ocean, and the effect created when the wave hits shallow water. Monster waves at the Maui site known to surfers and wind surfers as "JAWS" occur about a dozen times a year, a result of the unique shape of the geography's underwater ridge and a dramatic depth change from 120 feet to just 30 feet as waves strike the shallows. When storm swells longer than 1,000 feet meet the underwater ridge, waves can rise as high as 70 feet, a condition that sends hard-core surfers flocking to Maui. Because the waves are moving so fast, Wave Runners must tow the surfers into the path of these giant swells, with rides lasting as long as thirty seconds . . . and wipeouts sometimes fatal.

The big name surfers had been at it all day, Laird Hamilton, Pete Cabrinha, Dave Kalama. Now, as the sun began to set, the youngsters moved in to try their luck. Eighteen-year-old Zach Richards had been cutting waves on Oahu's North Shore since he was twelve. His younger brother, Jim, had only recently begun training on the big waves, but he was more than game, especially with an audience of spectators and cameras.

Jim pulled on his black wet suit while Zach and his surfer buddies, Scott and Ryan, decided who would man the two Jet Skis. As he headed for the beach, he circled around a group of girls he knew from high school. His target, Maria McGuire, a knockout brunette, caught his eye and gave him a quick wave, jump-starting his heart—

—until he saw Michael Barnes, a twenty-two-year-old with a tattoo on every muscle, join his brother's group.

Surfing is a spiritual release, with everyone watching out for one another, especially when it comes to riding the big waves. Barnes was driven strictly by ego, which was why none of the big surfers on the island allowed him to join their group.

Jim watched Scott tow his brother out to the break-point, Ryan readying the second Wave Runner as Barnes approached. "She's out of your league, faggot."

"Huh?"

"Maria. Don't even bother." Barnes pushed him aside with his board, then jumped into the surf and paddled out to hitch a ride on Ryan's tow rig.

"Asshole . . ." For a moment Jim debated whether to go out. But Scott was on his way in with a tow, and Maria was watching, rooting him on.

There was no turning back. Bellying up on his board, he dove into the surf.

Ten minutes later, the three surfers and two Jet Skiers were waiting beyond the breakpoint for the next incoming set. They were a good half-mile out, in water more than 120-feet deep.

*   *   *

The female moved lazily along the sea floor, digesting the remains of her last meal. Nestled within her swollen oviduct were live young, each seven to twelve feet long, weighing upwards of a ton.

Almost two years had passed since the violent act of copulation that had impregnated the female. As embryos, her unborn pups had been sheathed in a protective, transparent capsule, nourished by an external placenta-like yolk sac attached to their gut. Over time these capsules had ruptured, exposing the developing Megalodon sharks to a womb whose liquified world was far different from the chemistry of the ocean. As the day of their birth rapidly approached, their mother's uterus steadily regulated its ion-water balance, preparing the unborn young for their emergence into the sea.

For all its life-giving chemicals, the depths of the Challenger Deep were not equipped to sustain a large colony of apex predators, so it was left to nature to balance the scales and thin the herd. Undernourished, the unborn Megs at first subsisted on ovulated, unfertilized eggs. But as they grew larger, the pups instinctively turned to cannibalism, the larger infants feeding upon their smaller, less fortunate siblings.

What had begun as a brood of seventeen was down to three.

For the big female, inhabiting the abyss meant longer gestation periods than her surface-breeding ancestors had to endure, her internal anatomy delaying contractions until her pups could achieve greater size. This evolutionary feature, designed to increase the pups' rate of survival in the wild, was taking a toll on their mother, forcing the female to expend greater amounts of energy during these final weeks of pregnancy.

Expending more energy meant an increase in feeding.

Since leaving her abyssal habitat, the female had attacked more than a dozen different whale pods. Most of these earlier assaults had failed, but the Meg was learning, having succeeded in her last three tries.

Failure or not, the whale pods around Hawaii were spooked by the hunter's presence. Haunting calls from the humpback and gray whales reverberated through miles of ocean. Almost as one, the pods began altering their migratory course, skirting west, away from the suddenly dangerous coastal waters of Hawaii. By morning of the third day, few whales could be found off the island chain.

The Megalodon sensed the departure of its prey, but did not give chase. Gliding effortlessly through the thermocline, the boundary between sun-warmed waters and the ocean depths, it headed toward the shallows, its senses enticed by a strange new stimulus.

*   *   *

Zach and Barnes lay prone on the Wave Runner's tow rigs, waiting impatiently for their first set of waves to arrive. The sun was going down, the air had turned chilly, and Barnes was losing his audience as the beachgoers, sensing the best action had passed, began heading in.

Scott was the first to register the arriving swells. "Here we go!"

The two Wave Runners took off with their surfers, leaving Zach behind.

The first wave struck the underwater ridge, rising majestically like a deep blue mountain. Zach was on the inside as the 28-footer broke from left to right. He was in a zone, a mind space where his only focus remained at the front of his board and a hundred feet down the line. Rooted within this tunnel vision, he never saw what was happening behind him.

Fifty feet to Zach's left, Barnes had just made his turn, pulling into the wave's tube, enjoying the beginning of what he knew would be an "insane" ride. For a quick second, he stole a glance toward the beach, hoping to see the brunette chick, his peripheral vision catching a bizarre wall of white water emerging on his right.

Barnes turned, never seeing the creature break through the wave—

—and surfed right into the open mouth of the Megalodon!

Momentum slingshot Barnes into darkness, sending him smashing headfirst into an arching wall of cartilage. He bounced across an undulating tongue as rows of

serrated white teeth gnashed his surfboard and tossed
him about, spraying him with splinters. Disoriented,
unable to catch a second to reason, Barnes's mind was
convinced he was underwater, being pummeled by the
wave's fury, the lacerations now flailing at his wet suit
and skin caused by the sharp ridges of coral along the
bottom, and not serrated white teeth. Dark sky became
incoming sea and now he really was underwater, holding
on, the mouth he believed to be the underbelly of the
wave opening and closing, searching for his flesh, a
hideous tongue pushing him towards chomping rows
of teeth . . . and suddenly, he knew!

Michael Barnes heard himself scream—

—as his existence was crushed into scarlet oblivion.

*   *   *

Ryan circled on his Wave Runner, searching for
Barnes. As the roar of the breaking wave passed, he
suddenly heard noise coming from the beach—high-
pitched screams of terror! He looked back, shocked
to see dozens of onlookers waving frantically at
him.

And then he saw the circling dorsal fin—as tall as
a small sailboat—and he gunned the engine, racing
toward shore.

*   *   *

Her appetite primed, the female circled the kill
zone, gnashing her teeth as she swam, searching the
area for vibrations. Beneath her thick skin, along her
lateral line, a canal extended the entire length of her
body. The upper section of this canal held sensory

cells called neuromasts. Mucus contained in the lower half of the canals transmitted vibrations from the seawater to these sensation cells, giving the predator a spectacular "vision" of her surroundings through echolocation. Somewhere close was more prey, and her senses were isolating it.

* * *

Jim Richards shivered from the cold, waiting for one of the Wave Runners to come back out and get him. The swells were pushing him closer to the breakpoint, but were still moving too fast to catch.

What the hell's taking them so long?

Something struck his leg, causing him to look down.

"Jesus." Small bits of bloody flesh clung to his surfboard. He felt vomit rising in his throat and swallowed hard to keep it down.

Then he spotted the dorsal fin. It was impossibly tall, growing taller . . . gliding straight for him! Jim pulled his legs onto his surfboard and froze, willing his muscles and nerves to be still, but looking down, he saw his board was quivering in the water.

The Megalodon rose to the surface, the sheer mass of its moving girth creating a current that towed the surfboard and its passenger sideways and out to sea. Beyond the dorsal, the upper section of a half-moon-shaped tail slashed back and forth along the surface. Stretching higher than Jim's head, it swatted past his face, missing him by mere inches.

Jim felt something lifting him. His heart fluttered, anticipating the bloody mouth and rows of fangs. But the shark was still swimming away from him; the pressure had been caused by a swell. The next waves were coming in, fast and furious, and he needed to catch one.

He turned around, the monster already a good sixty feet behind him.

Go!

Jim rolled onto his stomach and paddled, stroking as fast as he could, his pounding heart threatening to explode from his chest.

The Megalodon turned, zeroing in on these new vibrations. The female's peppered white snout broke the surface thirty feet behind him, snorting sea like a Brahma bull.

Jim slammed his face against the board, simultaneously gripping the outer edges with his ankles as he plunged his arms into the water, double-stroking furiously. He screamed as he registered the monster's breath along the soles of his bare feet, and then he fell over the edge of a cliff and screamed.

Jim plunged down the rolling mountain of water, popping up at the last moment on his exhausted legs, feet wide, crouching low. He reached back with his right hand, the 36-foot wave roaring at him like a tornado, its whitewater crest, twenty feet above his head, threatening to bury him in the sea floor.

Jim cut hard to his right as the Megalodon burst through the wave, missing him by two board lengths, its forward inertia sending it momentarily airborne. The surfer stole a quick glance, then dug in, refusing to be tossed, riding the wave out 50 yards . . . 100 . . . until he felt it dying, his hope dying with it.

The ride over, Jim sank onto his board, the shoreline a good seventy yards away.

The dorsal fin turned, racing for him!

He heard the outboard. Turned to see his brother on the Jet-Ski, waving frantically.

Jim dove into the water, swimming toward him.

Zach never slowed. With the monstrous shark less then twenty feet behind Jim, he cut across its path, racing by his brother, who leaped onto the Wave Runner's tow rig and held on.

The Wave Runner shot through the shallows and straight onto the beach, the delirious crowd chanting, "Jim, Jim, Jim . . ."

Zach leaped off the Wave Runner and hugged his brother, slapping him on the back, telling him what a great job he'd done. Jim was exhausted, shaking with fear, the burst of adrenaline nearly forcing him to puke. He caught himself as Maria appeared, a huge smile stretched across her face, tears in her brown eyes as she hugged him.

"Are you okay?" she asked. "You scared the shit out of me!"

Jim cleared his throat and took a breath. "Yeah . . . no problem." Then, seeing his opening, he gave Maria a crooked smile and said, "So, you doing anything tonight?"

BATTLE AT SEA

Moments after Jim Richards had been pulled from the surf, the coast-guard air rescue arrived, hovering two hundred feet above the breaking swells. Spotting the predator's glow, the chopper followed the female as she headed out to sea, radioing her position to the naval base at Pearl Harbor. Within minutes, both the *Nautilus* and the *Kiku* had put to sea, racing north past Mamala Bay. By the time the *Kiku* reached Kaena Point, the incoming storm had reached gale-force proportions, the raging night fully upon them.

Jonas and Terry were in the pilothouse as the door leading to the deck tore open against the howling wind. Mac slipped into the dry compartment, slamming the hatch closed behind him, his yellow slicker dripping all over the floor.

"Copter's secured. So's the net and harpoon gun. Captain says we're in for a rough one."

"This may be our only chance. If we don't at least tag the female before she heads into open water, we may lose her for good."

The three entered the CIC, where Masao was standing over a crewman seated at the sonar console. He looked grim. "The coast guard broke off its pursuit because of the weather." Masao turned to the crewman. "Anything on sonar yet, Pasquale?"

Without looking up, the technician shook his head. "Just the *Nautilus*." Everyone grabbed a console as a twenty-foot swell lifted and tossed the research vessel from one side to the other.

Captain Barre stood at the helm, his sea legs giving naturally with the roll of his vessel. "Hope nobody had a big dinner. This storm's gonna be a bitch."

* * *

Life on board the world's first nuclear-powered submarine was relatively calm as the ship entered Waimea Bay one hundred feet below the raging storm. Though refitted several times during its life span, the sub still possessed a single nuclear reactor that created the superheated steam necessary to power its twin turbines and two shafts. It was an antiquated system, far from battle-ready.

Commander Danielson, too, felt far from battle-ready, but the retired naval man was more than game. "Anything on the sonar, Ensign Raby?"

The sonar man was listening with his headphones while watching his console screen. The screen was designed to give a visual representation of the difference between the background noise and a particular bearing. Any object within range would appear as a light line against the green background. Because they were searching for a biologic, sonar was actively pinging the area every three minutes, Raby looking for return signals. "Lots of surface interference from the storm. Nothing else yet, sir."

"Very well, keep me informed. Chief of the Watch, what's our weapons status?"

Chief Engineer Dennis Heller, six years younger than his brother Frank, yet still one of the oldest members of the sub's makeshift crew, looked up from his console. "Two Mark 48 AD-CAP torpedoes ready to fire on your command, sir. Torpedoes set for close range, as per your orders. A bit tight, if you don't mind my saying, sir."

"Has to be, Chief. When sonar locates this monster, we'll need to be as close as possible to ensure an accurate solution."

"Captain Danielson!" The radioman leaned back from his console. "Sir, I'm receiving a distress call from a Japanese whaler. Hard to make out, but it sounds as if they're being attacked."

"Navigator, plot an intercept course, ten degrees up on the fair-weather planes. If this is our friend, I want to kill it and be back at Pearl in time for last call at Grady's."

*   *   *

The Japanese whaler rolled with the massive swells, rain and wind pelting her crew mercilessly. The vessel's hold was dangerously overloaded with its illegal catch: the carcasses of eight gray whales. Two more had been lashed to the port side of the ship with a cargo net.

A pair of lookouts held on to the main mast, disoriented by weather and darkness. The two sailors had been assigned the hazardous duty of making sure the valuable whale blubber remained firmly secured during the storm. Unfortunately for the exhausted men, their searchlight hardly penetrated the maelstrom. Sporadic flashes of lightning afforded them their only real vision of their precious cargo.

Flash. The ocean dropped from view as the ship rolled to starboard, the cargo net groaning with its keep. The sailors hung on as the poorly ballasted vessel rolled back to port.

Flash. The sea threatened to suck them under, the net actually disappearing momentarily beneath the waves.

Flash. The vessel rolled again to starboard, the net reappearing. The men gasped—a massive white triangular head had risen from the sea with the cargo!

Darkness. The whaler rolled, its lookouts blind in the storm. Silent seconds passed. Then, *flash*, a fork of lightning lit the sky and the horrible head reappeared, its mouth bristling razor-sharp teeth.

The crewmen screamed, but the storm muted the sound. The senior mate signaled to the other that he would find the captain.

Flash. The unimaginably large jaws were tearing at the carcass now, the head leaning sideways against the rolling vessel, its teeth gnashing at the whale blubber.

The ship rolled to starboard once more. The senior mate struggled to make it belowdecks, squeezing his eyes shut against the gale and holding tight to the rope ladder. He could lower himself only a rung at a time as the ship listed to port . . . and kept rolling! He opened his eyes, felt his stomach churn.

Flash. The sea kept coming, the triangular head gone. But something was pulling the ship onto its side and into the water.

*   *   *

"Captain, the whaler is two hundred yards ahead."

"Thank you, Chief. Take us to periscope depth."

"Periscope depth, aye, sir."

The sub rose as Danielson pressed his face against the rubber housing of the periscope and stared into darkness. The scope turned night into shades of green, but the storm and rolling waves severely reduced visibility.

Flash. The raging Pacific was illuminated, and for an instant Danielson caught the silhouette of the whaler lying on its side. "The whaler's sinking, contact the coast guard," he ordered. "Where's the nearest cutter?"

"Sir," responded the radioman, "the only surface ship within twenty miles is the *Kiku*."

"Skipper, there's something else out there, circling the whaler!"

*   *   *

Pasquale held the headset tightly against his ears, verifying the message once more. "Captain, we're receiving an emergency call from the *Nautilus*." All heads in the control room turned. "A Japanese whaler's down, twelve nautical miles to the east. They say there may be survivors in the water, but no other surface ships are in the area. They're requesting immediate assistance."

Masao looked at Jonas. "The Meg?"

"If it is, we don't have much time."

"Get us there quickly, Captain," ordered Masao.

*   *   *

The Japanese whaler lay on her port side, refusing to sink, instead rising and falling with the twenty-foot swells. Within the bowels of the vessel, eleven men struggled in darkness to escape a chamber of death in which they could not tell which way was up. The cold ocean hissed from all directions, battering the keel, searching for a way inside the battened-down ship.

Below the waves the Megalodon tore at the remains of the whale meat lashed to the cargo net. It was her physical presence, in great part, that supported the vessel from below, keeping the dying ship afloat.

The senior lookout had been thrown overboard when the ship had toppled. Somehow he had managed to climb back on board, and now he struggled to hold on. From within, he heard the screams of his shipmates. Kicking open one of the battened-down hatches, he shone his flashlight inside. Four crewmen crawled out from below, joining him on the tilting main deck.

*   *   *

"Skipper, I can hear shouts," said the sonar man. "There are men in the water."

"How far away is the *Kiku*?"

"Six minutes," Chief Heller called out.

Danielson tried to think. What could he do to distract the Megalodon, keep the monster from the survivors? "Chief, continuous pinging, loud as you can. Sonar, watch the creature, tell me what happens."

"Continuous ping, aye, sir."

Ping . . . ping . . . ping. The metallic gongs rattled through the hull of the *Nautilus*, the deep throb of the reverberations radiating acoustically through the seawater.

*   *   *

The deafening pings reached the female's lateral line in seconds. The dense sound waves overloaded her senses, sending her into a rage. An unknown creature was challenging the female for her kill. Abandoning the last scraps of whale meat entangled within the cargo net, the Megalodon circled below the sinking whaler, shook her throbbing head twice, then homed in on the source of the annoying sounds.

*   *   *

"Skipper, I've got a bearing on the biologic. Sixty meters and closing. You've definitely got its attention!"

"Forty meters and closing."

"Chief?"

"I've got a temporary solution, sir, but the explosion could harm the crew of that whaler."

"Twenty meters, sir!"

"Helm, change course to zero-two-five, twenty degrees down-angle on the planes, take us to eight hundred feet, make your speed fifteen knots. Let's see if she'll chase us, then put some ocean between this fish and that whaler."

The sub accelerated in a shallow descent, the Megalodon in pursuit. The female measured less than half the *Nautilus*'s length, and the submarine, at 3,000 tons, easily outweighed her. But the female was faster and could outmaneuver its adversary; moreover, no adult Megalodon would allow a challenge within its domain to go unanswered.

The female accelerated at the sub's steel hull like a berserk sixty-foot locomotive.

"Ten meters . . . brace for impact!" The sonar man ripped off his headset.

BOOM!

The *Nautilus* rolled sideways, several crewmen hurtling from their posts. The power died, darkness enveloping the crew, as steel plates groaned all around them. Red emergency lights flickered on, but the engines had stopped, and the sub now drifted, listing at a forty-five-degree angle.

The Megalodon circled, carefully measuring her challenge. The collision had caused a painful throbbing in her snout. The female shook her head, several broken teeth falling out. In time they would be replaced by those lying beneath them in reserve.

Captain Danielson felt warmth seep into his right eye. "All stations report!" he yelled, wiping the blood from his forehead.

Chief Heller was the first to call out. "Engine room reports flooding in three compartments, sir. Reactor is off-line."

"Radiation?"

"No leaks found."

"Batteries?"

"Batteries appear functional and are on-line, Captain, but the stern planes are not responding. We got hit just above the keel."

"Son of a bitch." Danielson was fuming . . . how could he have allowed a fish to cripple his boat! "Where's the creature now?"

"Circling, sir. Very close," reported sonar.

"Captain," said the chief. "Damage control says one screw is out, the other should be on-line within ten minutes. Emergency batteries only, sir."

"Torpedoes?"

"Still ready, sir."

"Flood torpedo tubes one and two sonar, I want a firing solution."

The hull plates groaned . . . followed by a bizarre scratching sound.

Danielson looked around, baffled. "Raby, what the hell is that noise?"

"Sir?" the sonar man looked pale. "I think the Megalodon's attempting to bite through our hull."

* * *

The *Kiku* arrived at the last known coordinates of the whaler, but without the support of the Meg, pushing from below, the ship had gone under without a fight.

Jonas and Heller, dressed in life jackets and secured to the ship by lines around their waists, stood at the bow. Heller guided the searchlight. Jonas held the rifle loaded with the tracking dart in one hand, a life ring in his other. The *Kiku* rose wildly and fell. Swells crashed over her bow, threatening to send both men into the sea.

"There!" Jonas pointed to starboard. Two men clung to what was left of the whaler's mast.

Heller aimed the light, then called Barre on his walkie-talkie. The bow swung hard to starboard.

Jonas handed the rifle to Heller, held on to the rail, and threw the life ring toward the men. With the sea breaking in peaks and valleys and the *Kiku* bucking Jonas like a wild bronco, he could not tell whether the men could even see the flotation device, let alone reach it.

"Forget it, Taylor!" Heller yelled. "You'll never reach them!"

Jonas continued scanning the water as the bow dropped thirty feet, another swell rising ten yards away. They rose again and Jonas saw the light flash on the men. One was waving.

"Tie me off!" Jonas screamed.

"What?"

As the bow dropped, Jonas placed one foot onto the rail. When it rose again, he leaped into the maelstrom with all his might. Propelled by the rising deck, he launched into the air, falling beyond the next incoming swell.

Cold water shocked his body, driving the breath from his chest, sapping his strength. He rose with the next wave but was unable to see anything, then swam as hard as he could in the direction he prayed was correct.

Without warning, Jonas found himself falling into a valley between two swells. Swimming was not an option: he was being hurled up and down mountains of water. And then his head smashed into a hard object, blacking his vision.

* * *

The Meg couldn't tell if the creature was alive, its piercing vibrations having ceased. Her taste buds in her rostrum told her the strange fish was inedible. Still, she circled again, occasionally attempting to bite down upon the object, but the creature was simply too large.

And then the Meg detected familiar vibrations along the surface. *Prey . . .*

* * *

"It's moving off, skipper! She's heading back to the surface."

"Engines back on-line, Captain," reported Chief Heller. As if in response, the *Nautilus* leveled out.

"That's my girl. Helm, bring us around, make your course zero-five-zero, up ten degrees on the planes, take us to four hundred feet. Chief, I want a firing solution on that monster. On my command, start pinging again. When she descends to attack, we'll hit her with both torpedoes!"

Heller looked worried. "Sir, engineering warns the ship can't withstand another collision. I strongly suggest we return to Pearl and—"

"Negative, Mr. Heller. We end this now."

* * *

A hand grabbed Jonas by his collar and hung on. The senior lookout pulled Jonas onto the fallen mast and sputtered something in Japanese, obviously grateful. Jonas tried to look around. The second sailor was gone. He felt a strong tug on his waist—Heller and his men were pulling him back.

"Hold on!" Taylor grabbed the sailor from around his waist, and the two were dragged backward along the surface toward the *Kiku*.

*   *   *

The Meg locked in on the vibrations and circled its prey—

—as the pinging began anew. The female could smell blood, but the aggressive challenge of the vibrations overwhelmed her hunger. She wheeled around in a fluid motion, a white blur on course with its challenger.

*   *   *

"Six hundred meters and closing quickly, Captain," called out the sonar operator.

"Chief Heller, do we have a firing solution?"

"Aye, sir!"

"On my command . . ."

"Three hundred meters . . ."

"Steady, gentlemen."

"One hundred and fifty meters!"

"Let her come . . ."

"Skipper, course change!" Sonar looked up, frantic. "Sir, I lost her!"

Danielson ran to the console, sweat and blood dripping down his face. "What happened?"

Sonar was bent over, cupping his ears, trying to hear. "Sir, she went deep. I can barely hear her. . . . Wait . . . Oh shit, she's below us!"

"Full speed ahead!" ordered Danielson.

The crippled submarine lurched forward, struggling to reach a speed above ten knots. The Megalodon rose from below, homing again on what it perceived to be the creature's tail. Her snout impacted the steel plates at thirty knots, puncturing the already buckling hull. This time the casing gave, spreading a gap between the steel plates, venting the engine room to the sea.

The collision ruptured the submarine's aft ballast tanks. As the keel of the *Nautilus* filled with seawater, the crew's environment shifted to a forty-five-degree tilt. The engine room was hardest hit. Assistant Engineer David Freeman tumbled backward in the dark. His head slammed hard against a control panel, knocking him unconscious. Lieutenant Artie Krawitz found himself pinned under a collapsed bulkhead, his left ankle shattered. As the engine room filled with water, he managed to free himself and crawl upward into the next compartment, sealing the watertight door seconds before the sea could rush in.

"Damage report!" commanded Danielson.

"Engine room's flooded," Heller reported. "Sir, I can't raise—"

A loud wail, followed by flashing red sirens cut the chief engineer off.

"Core breach!" he yelled. "Someone's got to shut it down!"

"Helm, high-pressure air into the ballast tanks, put us on the ceiling. Heller, get down to the reactor room—"

"On my way!"

The *Nautilus* rose, still listing to starboard as she climbed toward the surface.

Heller ran through a maze of chaos. In every compartment, crew members attempted to staunch the flow of seawater spraying from a thousand leaks. At least half of the electrical consoles looked down.

Outside the engine room, Lieutenant Krawitz was frantically throwing switches, shutting down the nuclear reactor.

Heller joined him, shutting off the alarm. "Report, Lieutenant."

"Four dead in here, a whole section of pipe collapsed on impact. Everyone and everything aft of the engine room is underwater."

"Radiation?"

The officer looked at his friend of ten years. "Denny, this ship's over forty years old. We've lost the integrity of the hull, the steel plates are falling off like shingles. We'll drown before any radiation kills us."

* * *

Jonas was hauled onto the *Kiku*'s main deck and then dragged into the pilothouse. A moment later, Frank Heller and his men returned with the Japanese seaman.

"Taylor, are you insane?" screamed Heller.

"Frank, quiet," said DeMarco. "We're receiving a distress call from the *Nautilus*."

Heller strode into the command center. "A distress call?"

Bob Pasquale cupped his ears, trying to hear. "They're surfacing. No power. They need our assistance immediately!"

Captain Barre barked orders to change course. The *Kiku* turned, fighting against the relentless swells.

* * *

David Freeman had regained consciousness, his face pressed hard against the watertight door where a small pocket of air remained. The chamber was bathed in red emergency lighting. Blood gushed from his forehead.

As the *Nautilus* rose, debris began seeping out of the gap in the hull and into the Pacific. The Megalodon rose with the sub, snapping its jaws at anything that moved. The predator smelled Freeman's blood.

Driving her enormous head into the opening, the Meg separated the already loose steel plates, enlarging the gap in the hull significantly. Her white glow illuminated the flooded compartment, catching the engineer's attention. Holding his breath, he ducked underwater, looked down . . . and gulped a mouthful of seawater! The monster's ten-foot-wide jaws opened and closed below him, the upper jaw pushing forward and away from the creature's head like something out of a 3-D horror film.

The hideous triangular teeth were now less than five feet away. Freeman felt his body being sucked into the vortex. He surfaced. Tore at the door, his screams muffled by the rising sea. Unable to escape, he chose an alternative death, ducking his head underwater, inhaling the salt water deep into his lungs, struggling to kill himself before the mouthful of teeth could reach him.

The female inhaled the heaving body into her mouth, crushing and swallowing it in one gulp. The warm blood sent her into a renewed frenzy. She shook her head, freeing herself from the opening, then circled the *Nautilus* again as it burst through the surface.

* * *

"Abandon ship! All hands, abandon ship!" Captain Danielson barked his orders as the *Nautilus* tossed hard to starboard against the incoming swells.

Three hatches exploded open, water pouring into the hull, pink phosphorescent flares piercing the blackness. Three yellow rafts inflated instantaneously and were lashed to the side of the boat. Survivors rushed to board, struggling to maintain their balance against the raging sea. The *Kiku* was close, her spotlight now guiding the rafts.

Danielson was in the last life raft. Bolts of lightning lit the seascape as he looked back at the *Nautilus*. Within seconds, the submarine was overcome by the sea. Her once-mighty bow rose out of the ocean, then another swell drove the ship toward her final resting place at the bottom of the Pacific.

Flash. The first raft reached the *Kiku*. Fifteen men scrambled up a cargo net draped along her starboard side. A swell slammed against the ship, lifting it, then dropping it thirty feet.

Flash. The force of the wave had tossed some of Danielson's crew back into the sea. Like insects they scrambled to reach the net, climbing once again.

Jonas aimed the spotlight into the swell, locating a seaman. It was Dennis Heller. Frank saw his younger brother struggling to stay afloat less than fifteen feet from the *Kiku*'s cargo net.

Frank tossed a ring buoy to his brother as the second raft closed in from behind. Dennis grabbed at the life preserver and held on as his brother pulled him toward the *Kiku*. The crew from the second raft were already scaling the cargo net, the last group now within ten feet of the ship.

Dennis reached the net and began climbing. He was halfway up when his shipmates from the third raft joined him.

Frank Heller lay prone on deck beneath the starboard rail, one hand holding the metal pipe, the other extending toward his brother, now only two body-lengths away. "Denny, give me your hand!" They touched momentarily—

—as a rogue wave rolled over the starboard deck, battering the ship.

Flash. The white monster appeared from out of the swell, grasping Dennis Heller in its jaws. Frank froze in place, unable to react as the tip of the snout passed less than a foot from his face. The Meg seemed to hang in midair, suspended in time. And then the creature slid back into the sea, dragging Dennis Heller backward with her.

"No, no, noooo!" Frank screeched at empty sea, waiting for the creature to return with his brother.

Danielson and the others were still holding onto the net, having witnessed the scene. Petrified, they climbed for their lives with reckless abandon.

The Meg rose again, the bloody remains of Dennis Heller still shredded within its front row of teeth. Danielson turned and screamed, flattening himself against the cargo net.

Jonas spun the searchlight's beam toward the Meg with his left hand as he raised the rifle with his right. He was close, a mere thirty feet. Without aiming, he pulled the trigger.

The homing dart exploded out of the barrel, burying itself within the creature's thick white hide as the barbed device attached itself firmly behind the female's right pectoral fin.

The searchlight's powerful beam blazed into the right eye of the nocturnal predator, burning the sensitive ocular tissue like a laser. The pain sent the monster reeling backward into the sea, repelling her attack only feet from Danielson.

The skipper and his men collapsed onto the deck and were pulled, one by one, inside the shelter of the pilothouse. Jonas grabbed Frank, tugging him backward, but he refused to let go of the rail.

"You're dead, monster, you hear me!?!" Heller screamed into the night, his words deadened by the wind. "You're fucking dead!"

OPENING DAY

The crowd of nearly six hundred invited guests milled about the southern end of the arena, waiting for the ceremony to begin. Two weeks had passed since the disaster at sea. Nine members of the *Nautilus*'s crew had perished, as had fourteen from the Japanese whaler. A ceremony honoring the dead had taken place at Pearl Harbor. Two days later, Captain Richard Danielson retired from the navy.

Commander Bryce McGovern was on the hot seat. Who had authorized the United States Navy to hunt the Megalodon? Why had McGovern selected the *Nautilus* to complete the mission, knowing the decommissioned submarine was far from battle-worthy? The families of the deceased were outraged, and an internal investigation was ordered. Many believed Commander McGovern would be the next naval officer to be "retired."

Frank Heller was a raging bull. His brother Dennis had been his only family, and Heller's hatred for the Megalodon was all-consuming. He informed Masao he was through, stating that he had his own plans for the "white devil." After the ceremony in Oahu, he flew home to California, and no one had heard from him since.

Maggie broke the story about the Tanaka Institute's plans to capture the Megalodon. From that moment on, the hunt for the Megalodon had turned into a media circus. JAMSTEC was secretly delighted at the publicity, as it stood to share in the proceeds from Tanaka Lagoon. Construction crews had worked around the clock to complete the facility.

Now everyone wanted to know one thing: when would the guest of honor arrive?

The *Nautilus* controversy kept the governor of California, as well as other politicians, away from the lagoon's opening ceremony. The networks had no such fear, and were there en masse. CNN's Rudi Bakhtiar interviewed Masao, while Maggie waited in the wings, growling about "sloppy seconds."

"Mr. Tanaka, it's been weeks since the Megalodon was last seen, with many experts believing the creature has returned to deep water. What are the Institute's plans?"

"We still believe she'll migrate east. As long as we're funded, we'll continue the search."

"And the homing device?"

"Unfortunately, it may have failed. Either that, or the creature managed to tear it loose."

"A lot of people have died, including your own son, who you'll be honoring in a few minutes. If you could turn back time, what would you have done differently?"

"You cannot control karma, it is either good or bad. Our mission in the trench was honorable, our karma bad. Perhaps it will change, I don't know."

The news reporter turned to face the camera. "And so the Tanaka Lagoon opens. The real question now—where is its 62,000-pound guest of honor? In Monterey, Rudi Bakhtiar, CNN Headline News."

Masao stepped to the podium. Above his head, a banner read: D.J. TANAKA LAGOON.

"Colleagues and guests, on behalf of the people of California, I dedicate this research facility to my son, D.J. Tanaka."

At the far end of the access canal, a pair of King Kong–size, steel doors cracked open and the Pacific rushed in, filling the world's largest swimming pool.

Jonas stood next to Mac on the lower observation deck, watching the water level rise three feet a minute. *Fourteen days, and still no sign of the female.* For six consecutive nights following the attack on the *Nautilus*, he and Mac had flown over Hawaii's coastal waters in search of the Meg. The homing device had worked, allowing the copter to track the predator as it headed east, the *Kiku* always trailing close behind. But the female, perhaps still in pain, refused to surface, remaining deep. And then, on the seventh day, the signal had simply disappeared.

The *Kiku* and its helicopter circled the area over the next forty-eight hours, unable to relocate the signal. Frustrated, Jonas finally recommended to Masao that the *Kiku* should return to Monterey, hoping the Megalodon might head for the California coastline and the thousands of migrating whales. Now, almost a week later, there was still no sign of the female.

Where had she gone?

NETWORK

Maggie felt her blood pressure rising as she waited impatiently for Fred Henderson to get off his phone. Finally, she stood over her producer's desk and snatched the receiver out of his hand. "He'll have to call you back," she said into the mouthpiece, and hung up.

"Maggie, what the hell do you think you're doing? That was an important call—"

"Important my ass, you were talking to your accountant."

"All right, you have my undivided attention, Speak."

"You cancelled my expense account, and my cameraman. Why?"

"Why?" The station manager put his feet up on his desk. "Why do you think? You've been at this a month. So far, I've seen footage of bleeding whales, dying whales, dead whales, and your husband—or ex-husband, whatever he is—lecturing about how mean this shark is. This morning you gave us footage of an empty aquarium. What I don't have is footage of the goddamn shark."

"What if I got you underwater footage of the Meg, I mean the real McCoy, scary as hell."

"I'm listening."

"At some point, the female's bound to show up where Jonas predicted. What if I was there, waiting for it . . . in a shark cage."

"You're nuts."

"Just listen to what I have to say." For the next thirty minutes, she briefed her station manager about her plan to film the Megalodon.

Henderson leaned back in his leather chair. "You've got balls, lady, I'll say that for you. But how can we be sure that your husband really knows where this monster's headed?"

"Listen, Fred, if there's one subject my soon-to-be ex knows about, it's these damn sharks. Christ, he's spent more time studying them over the last seven years than he has with me. This is the biggest story to hit this century, and I'll give you footage that will rocket this station to the top. This is Pulitzer stuff."

Henderson was sold. "Tell me what you need."

*   *   *

Bud was reading the paper when Maggie rapped on the back window of the limousine an hour later. When he unlocked the door, she ripped it open, climbed onto his lap, and planted a huge kiss on his lips.

"We got it, Bud! He loves it! The network agreed to back me on everything!" She kissed him again, pushing her tongue into his mouth, then came up for air and leaned her forehead against his.

"Bud," she whispered, "this is really the one, the story that makes me an international star. And you'll be there with me. Bud Harris, executive producer. Right now, though, I really need your help."

Bud smiled, enjoying the con. "Okay, darling, just tell me what you need."

"For starters, we'll need the *Magnate*. And a skeleton crew. I've already spoken with three cameramen and a sound guy who have underwater experience. We'll all be meeting on board the *Magnate* in the morning. When will my equipment arrive?"

"Tomorrow. We'll pick it up on our way back to San Diego."

"Not San Diego, Bud. Our target's the Red Triangle."

THE CANYON

Situated less than two hundred yards offshore from the Tanaka Lagoon's western wall lay the deep waters of the Monterey Bay Canyon, an anomaly of underwater geology, its dynamic incision along the California coastline rivaling the size and shape of the Grand Canyon.

Created by the subduction of the North American plate over millions of years, the massive underwater gorge traverses over sixty miles of sea floor, plunging more than a mile below the ocean's surface. There, the canyon meets the ocean bottom, eventually dropping another 12,000 feet in depth. Originally located in the vicinity of Santa Barbara, the entire Monterey Bay region was pushed ninety miles northward over millions of years, carried along the San Andreas fault zone on a section of granite rock known as the Salinian Block. The canyon itself is a confluence of varying formations; steep and narrow in some places, as wide as a Himalayan valley in others. Sheer vertical walls can drop two miles to a sediment-buried sea floor that dates back to the Pleistocene. Closer to shore, twisting chasms, some as deep as 6,000 feet, reach out from the main artery of the crevice like fingers of a groping hand.

* * *

The female moved through the pitch-black mid-waters of the Monterey Bay Canyon, following the steep walls of the C-shaped crevasse. Millions of years ago, this same California coastline had been a favorite habitat of the Megalodon's ancestors . . . until the tropical seas had turned cold and the whales had altered their migration pattern. Having lost the staple of their diet, the apex predators eventually disappeared, "starved into extinction," according to the so-called experts.

Having been blinded in her left eye, the Megalodon had fled the waters off the Hawaiian Islands and come upon a warm undercurrent flowing southeast along the equator.

Riding the river of water just as a Boeing 747 rides an airstream, the female had traveled across the Pacific Ocean, arriving in the tropical waters off the Galapagos Islands. From there, she had migrated north along the coast of Central America, hunting gray whales and their newborn calves.

And then, as she approached the waters off Baja, her senses had become overwhelmed by the pounding of tens of thousands of beating hearts and moving muscles. The female changed course, following the coastline north, eventually ending up in the Monterey Bay Canyon.

Something seemed familiar. Perhaps it was the hydrothermal vents or the steep canyon walls. Territorial by nature, the sixty-foot female claimed the area as her own, an expanse of ocean awarded by her mere presence as its supreme hunter. Her senses indicated there were no other adult Megalodons in the area to challenge her rule. The territory therefore became hers to defend.

The female had not eaten in days, preparing for the labor of birthing her pups. Driven by hunger, her senses quickly targeted the closest available prey. For three hours, the predator had been stalking the blue whale and its calf, moving 2,300 feet directly beneath them, shadowing them in the darkness. The female waited to attack, refusing to venture into the daylight.

Nightfall was coming . . .

RED TRIANGLE

The Ana Nuevo and Farallon Islands are a series of windswept rocks situated twenty-six miles west of San Francisco's Golden Gate Bridge. These are jagged landscapes, uninhabited by people, dominated by one mammal—the northern elephant seal.

Reaching lengths of more than fifteen feet and weighing 6,000 pounds, the northern elephant seal is the largest pinniped in the world and the most sexually dimorphic, with an alpha male bull mating with as many as four dozen females. Pelagic, they spend most of their time underwater and can hold their breath on a single dive for well over an hour. Winter months are spent onshore at rookeries where they mate, birth, and fight for dominance. But each spring and summer, they return to the Farallons where they lay about the rocky beaches, playing, sleeping, and molting.

The presence of these massive creatures entice another species to visit the remote island chain: *Carcharodon carcharius*, the great white shark. The seals are the predator's favorite delicacy, and the sharks circle these islands en masse, giving this expanse of deadly sea the nickname the Red Triangle.

* * *

Anchored in six hundred feet of water, the super yacht, *Magnate*, reflected the last golden flecks of sunlight. On her main deck, a weary crew of cameramen and technicians watched as thousands of California seals and sea lions stretched out upon the rocky, uninhabited landmass, barking and flopping against one another.

Of all the documented attacks by great whites worldwide, more than half occurred in the Red Triangle. If Jonas's prediction proved accurate, Maggie reasoned that the Megalodon, like its modern-day cousin, would be drawn to the area to feast on elephant seals. For days her film crew had waited impatiently for the creature to show. Underwater video cameras, audio equipment, and special underwater lights littered the ship's deck, along with cigarette butts and candy wrappers. A community laundry line had been hung along the upper deck, dangling sweatshirts and towels.

Now the long hours of boredom, sun, and the occasional nausea associated with seasickness had finally gotten to the crew. And yet even these conditions would have been tolerable had it not been for the overwhelming stench that hung thick in the chilly Northern California air.

Trailing the yacht on a thirty-foot steel cable floated the rotting carcass of a male humpback whale. The pungent smell seemed to hover over the *Magnate* as if to mark the crime, for killing a whale in the Monterey Bay National Marine Sanctuary was indeed a criminal act. No matter: with his financial influence, Bud had made a deal with two local fishermen to locate and deliver a whale carcass to their location, no questions asked. But now, after nearly thirty-eight hours of the wicked stench, the *Magnate*'s crew were ready to mutiny.

"Maggs, listen to me," begged her director, Perry Meth, "give us a break here. Twelve hours of shore leave, that's all I'm asking. It could be weeks, months before this Megalodon even ventures into these waters. All of us need a break, even a fresh shower would be heaven. Just get us off this smelly barge."

"Perry, listen to me. This is the story of the decade, and I'm not about to blow it because you and your cronies feel the need to get drunk in some sleazy hotel bar."

"That's not fair—"

"No, what's not fair is that it's my ass on the line. Do you have any idea how difficult it was to organize all this? The cameras? The shark tube? Not to mention that hunk of whale blubber floating behind us?"

"Speaking of that, whatever happened to your campaign for protecting the whales? I would have sworn that was you I saw onstage accepting a Golden Eagle on behalf of the Save the Whales Foundation."

"Grow up, Perry, I didn't kill the damn thing, I'm just using it as bait. I mean, cut me some slack. There are thousands of them migrating along the coast." She tossed her blonde hair, causing strands of it to stick to her oiled bare shoulders.

Perry lowered his voice. "The crew's not happy about all this; they feel you're grasping at straws. Honestly, what're the chances of the Megalodon actually showing up in the Red Triangle? No one's even reported seeing the fish in weeks."

"The Meg will show, believe me, and we'll be the ones to get the footage."

"In what, that hunk of plastic?" He pointed to the ten-foot-high Lexan shark tube, which stood upright on the main deck, rigged to a winch. "Christ, Maggie, you'd have to be suicidal—"

"That hunk of plastic is three-inch-thick bullet-proof Plexiglas. Its diameter is too wide for the Meg to get its mouth around it." Maggie laughed. "I'll probably be safer in there than you guys will be on the *Magnate*."

"There's a comforting thought."

Maggie ran her fingers across her director's sweaty chest. She knew Bud was still in bed, sleeping off another hangover. "Perry, you and I have worked very hard together on these projects. Hell, look how much good our whale documentary did for those beasts."

He smirked. "Tell that to your dead humpback."

"Forget that already. Think big! I thought you wanted to direct movies?"

"I do."

"Then see this project for what it is, a door-opener into Hollywood, the story that puts us both on top. How does executive producer sound to you?"

Perry thought for a moment, then smiled. "It's a start."

"It's yours. Now, can we forget about the dead whale for a moment?"

"I guess so. But listen, as your executive producer I highly recommend we do something to create a little diversion, because your film crew's losing patience."

"I agree, and I've got an idea. I've been wanting to do a test run on the shark tube. What do you say we get it into the water and I'll shoot some footage this evening."

"Hmmm, now that's not a bad idea. That'll give me a chance to position the underwater lights." He smiled. "Maybe you'll be able to get some nice footage of a great white. That alone might be worth a few minutes on the weekend wrap-up."

Maggie shook her head. "See, that's your problem—you think way too small."

Bending over to pick up her wet suit, her sweatshirt rolled up, rewarding Perry with a glimpse of her tanned, thonged behind. "One last thing. Do me a favor and don't mention anything to Bud about being my executive producer." She smiled sweetly. "He gets jealous."

LIFE AND DEATH

The ghostly mass of the albino predator ascended effortlessly toward the surface. Darkness had fallen, it was time to feed.

The hunter quickly closed the distance to the calf. The mother blue stopped feeding, detecting the danger approaching rapidly from behind. She rose to the surface and forcefully nudged her young to remain in tight formation. Mother and offspring propelled their bodies faster, the Megalodon circling below, waiting for an opportunity to seize the calf.

The female darted closer, snapping at the blue whale's small pectoral fins, each feint designed to force the adult away from its offspring.

The mother whale charged, momentarily abandoning her calf.

The Meg circled back quickly, its jaws opening to seize the calf—

—when suddenly she was seized by muscle cramps that sent her arching in an uncontrollable spasm.

The female abandoned her prey, descending rapidly to the canyon floor. Her muscular body quivered with contortions, forcing her to swim in tight circles. Finally, with a mighty shudder that shook her entire girth, a fully developed Megalodon pup emerged from its mother's left oviduct.

It was a female, pure white and eleven feet long, already weighing 1,900 pounds. The teeth were smaller but sharper than its mother's. With its senses fully developed, the newborn was fully capable of hunting and surviving on its own. It hovered momentarily, icy-blue eyes focused on the adult, instinct warning the pup of imminent danger. With a burst of speed, it glided south along the canyon floor.

Still circling in convulsions, the female shuddered again, expelling a second pup, tail-first, out of its womb. This time a male, slightly smaller than its sibling by three feet. The pup shot past its mother, barely avoiding a mortal, reflexive bite from the jaws of its cold, uncaring parent.

Minutes passed. Then, with one last convulsion, the Meg birthed her final pup in a cloud of blood and embryonic fluid. The runt of the litter, a seven-and-a-half-foot male, twisted out of its mother's orifice and twirled toward the bottom, righted itself, then shook its head to clear its vision.

With a flick of her powerful caudal fin, the Meg pounced upon the runt from behind, severing its entire caudal fin and genitals as she snapped her jaws shut around its lower torso. Convulsing wildly, trailing a stream of blood, the dying pup writhed to the bottom.

Giving chase, mom finished off her newborn in one last bite.

The Megalodon hovered near the bottom, exhausted from the efforts of labor. Opening her mouth, she allowed the canyon's current to circulate through her mouth, causing her gill slits to flutter as she breathed. Water passed in and out of her nostril passages, feeding information to her brain. It moved along the underside of her snout, plugging her in to the faint electrical fields generated by the swimming muscles and beating hearts of her quarry. It ran along her lateral line, stimulating her neuromast cells, allowing her to "feel" the ocean's currents and the presence of solid objects within her environment.

The female heard every sound, registered every movement, tasted every trail, and saw every sight, for *Carcharodon megalodon* did not just move through the sea, the sea moved through the Megalodon.

Slowly, the creature's head rotated from side to side, her nostrils flaring, channeling water. The predator was homing in on an intoxicating scent.

Needing to feed, she swung her caudal fin back and forth, regaining her momentum, gliding over the canyon floor, heading north—

—passing within thirty feet of the concrete canal entrance that connected the Tanaka Lagoon with the Pacific Ocean.

VISITORS

They came without warning, their presence energizing the yacht's disgruntled crew. Captain Talbott spotted the lead-gray dorsal fin first, slicing through the dark waters of the Pacific twenty feet off the *Magnate*'s starboard bow. Within minutes, two more fins appeared, cutting back and forth through the slick of blood seeping out of the dead whale.

Perry Meth found Maggie already dressed in her white wet suit, ready for the night's dive.

"Okay, Maggie, you wanted some action. How about a test dive with three great whites?"

Maggie felt her heart race. "Sure, sounds like fun. Is everyone ready?"

"Both remotes are in the water, underwater lights are on, and the plastic tube's all set."

"Where's Bud?"

"Still asleep."

"Good. He's been on the rag about this whole trip. Now remember, when you start filming, I want it to look like I'm all alone in the water with the sharks. How much cable's attached to my tube?"

Perry thought. "Maybe two hundred feet. We'll keep you within seventy to maintain the light."

"Then I'm ready," she announced. "Grab my camera, I want to be in the water before Bud wakes up."

She followed him to the main deck. The crew had already lowered the Lexan shark cylinder over the side. The container had been custom-made for Maggie from a design originally developed in Australia. Unlike a steel-mesh shark cage, the shark tube could not be bitten or bent, save for its buoyancy tanks, attached to its top hatch. It would maintain positive buoyancy forty feet below the surface, affording its diver an unobstructed view of the underwater domain. A steel cable served as a leash, running from the top of the cylinder to a winch on board the *Magnate*.

Secured to the yacht's keel were two remote-operated underwater cameras attached to monitors on deck. While Maggie was in the tube filming, the crew would be filming Maggie. If the lighting worked properly, the shark tube would remain invisible in the water, giving the terrifying appearance of seeing the diver exposed and alone in the water among the circling sharks.

Maggie positioned her face mask, checking to make sure she was receiving an adequate supply of air. She had been diving for ten years now, though rarely at night. The practice would do her good.

Two crewmen helped her down the ladder. The *Magnate* had eight feet of freeboard and she climbed down carefully, balancing on the bobbing cylinder's buoyancy tanks. Perry handed her a flipper, then the other, then climbed halfway down the ladder to hand her the thirty-seven–pound underwater camera. He waited while she fixed her dive mask to her face. It was a bulky contraption that wrapped around her chin, allowing her to breath through her nose and mouth at once, and communicate via a speaker and headphone embedded in the mask.

"You ready?"

She nodded and took a quick glance around to confirm the location of her subjects. Satisfied she was not about to be attacked, Maggie squatted on the edge of the tube, lowered herself into the water and into the tube, pulling the hatch door closed above her.

She sank into the center of the plastic tube, treading water. The current was moving away from the yacht. Perry instructed his team to release steel cable, the underwater cameras focusing on the tube as it sank beneath the keel and drifted out to sea.

"Stu, how're your remotes functioning?"

Chief technician Stuart Schwartz looked up from his dual monitors. "Remote A's a little sluggish, but we'll get by. Remote B's perfect. I can zoom right up on her. Too bad she didn't wear her thong."

The sound woman, Stuart's wife, Abby, slapped him from behind. "Focus on your job."

* * *

Maggie shivered from the potent combination of adrenaline and fifty-eight-degree water. Her world was now shades of grays and blacks, visibility poor. She could see the *Magnate*'s keel in the distance and wondered how she looked.

"Hello? Can you guys hear me?"

"Loud and clear," reported Abby, her voice filtered.

Maggie looked around. Moments later, the first predator entered her arena.

It was a male, seventeen feet from snout to tail, weighing a full ton. Its head and dorsal surface were lead gray, blending perfectly with the water. It circled the plastic tube warily, and Maggie rotated to compensate.

Her eyes detected movement from below as a fifteen-foot female rose out of the shadows, catching the newswoman totally off guard. Forgetting she was in a protective tube, she panicked, frantically kicking her fins in an effort to get away. The shark's snout banged into the bottom of the tube just as Maggie's head collided with the sealed hatch above. She smiled in relief and embarrassment at her own stupidity.

Stuart Schwartz was also smiling. The footage looked incredible, and scary as hell. Maggie appeared totally alone in the water with the three killers. The *Magnate*'s artificial lights were just bright enough to highlight Maggie's white dive suit. The effect was perfect. Viewers would not be able to detect the protective tube.

"Perry, this is great stuff," he announced. "Our audience'll be squirming in their seats. I gotta admit it, Maggie really has a knack for the work."

Perry stood behind Stuart, watching the monitor focused on the humpback carcass. One of the sharks had bitten onto the waterlogged remains and was tearing away a mouthful.

"Film everything, Stu. Maybe we'll be able to convince her to quit before this Megalodon actually shows up."

But Perry had a hard time believing that himself.

*   *   *

The helicopter soared over the breathtaking California coastline, the Pacific crashing into the cliffs below.

Jonas held the night binoculars with two hands, steadying them against the herky-jerky motion of the helicopter. A new thermal imager had been purchased to replace the damaged unit, but after three weeks without a Megalodon sighting, it was the last money JAMSTEC would be laying out for the expedition.

Mac followed the coastline south, hovering at an altitude of two hundred feet. Terry was in back, the rifle balanced upright between her legs. Her presence on the chopper had been at the insistence of her father. But Masao had no control over her attitude, "So, Jonas, where's the bitch now?"

"My opinion? I think she's in California waters."

"I meant your wife."

Mac snickered.

"Is there a problem between you two?"

"Terry doesn't trust her."

"Shut up, Mac."

Mac continued, "It's a female thing. Women sense deception like a Meg smells blood. That's why they're so good at it."

"It wasn't Maggie who snuck that live round on-board the chopper," Jonas said, accusingly.

"So I want that monster dead. Sue me!"

"That's not what your father wants."

"My father's head's in the clouds. As for your ex, I know women like her. She'll lie, cheat, and steal to get what she wants. But don't worry, because it's obvious she doesn't want you!"

Mac whistled.

Jonas and Terry turned simultaneously and said, "Shut up, Mac."

They rode for several minutes in silence. On the thermal imager's monitor, pods of whales continued their migration south along the coastline.

"Mac, I can't recall ever seeing so many whales in one place," said Jonas, attempting to make conversation.

"Who cares?" Mac stared at Jonas with a burnt-out look. "We're wasting our time. That fish of yours could be a million miles from here."

Jonas turned back to face the ocean. He knew Mac was thinking about calling it quits, and would have days ago if it hadn't been for their friendship. He couldn't blame him. Money was tight and paychecks were being held. If the female had been feeding in these waters, there would've been traces of whale carcasses washing ashore. None had been reported.

Mac's right, Jonas thought to himself, and for the first time in years, he felt truly alone. *How many years of my life have I wasted chasing this monster? What do I have to show for it? A marriage that fell apart years ago, a struggle to make ends meet . . .*

"Hey!" Terry pointed to the yellow-red blurs of heat—whales—on the monitor.

"Whales. So?"

"Follow the line," she said, pointing to a section of pods that were breaking formation. "See? They're changing course. Don't you get it? They were all heading south, but these pods here, they're veering sharply to the west."

Jonas turned Mac. "She's right. They're changing course to avoid something."

Mac shook his head. "You two are grasping at straws. I say we land in San Francisco, then hit Chinatown for some dim sum . . . your treat."

"Mac . . . please?"

Mac looked down again at the thermal imager. If the Meg was heading north along the coast, it would be logical for the pods to avoid her.

"Okay, J.T., one last time." The helicopter banked sharply to starboard, changing course.

* * *

Maggie checked her camera. She had plenty of film left but only another twenty minutes of air. The shark tube had drifted beneath the humpback carcass, allowing for a spectacular view. But Maggie knew footage of great whites feeding had become commonplace. She was after much more.

I'm wasting film, she thought. She turned to signal the *Magnate* to pull her in, then noticed something very troublesome.

The three great whites had all vanished.

* * *

Bud Harris kicked the silk sheets off his naked body and reached for the bottle of Jack Daniel's. Empty.

"Damnit!" He sat up, his head pounding. It had been two days and still he couldn't get rid of the nagging sinus headache. "It's that damn whale," he said aloud. "The smell's killing me."

Bud staggered to the bathroom, picked up the bottle of aspirin, struggling to get the childproof cap lined up correctly. "Screw it," he yelled, tossing the bottle into the empty toilet. He looked at himself in the mirror. "You're miserable, Bud Harris," he said to his reflection. "You're too rich to be miserable. Why do you let her talk you into these things? Well, enough's enough!" He slipped on a crushed velvet sweat suit and docksiders, then left his master suite and headed down the circular stairwell to the main deck.

"Where's Maggie?" he demanded.

Abby Schwartz sat on deck, monitoring the audio track. "She's in the tube. We're getting some great footage."

"Where's that director guy?"

Perry looked up. "Right here, Bud. What do you need? I'm kind of busy."

"Pack up, we're leaving!"

Perry and Abby looked at one another. "Maybe you ought to speak with Maggie—"

"Maggie doesn't own this yacht, I do." He grabbed the makeshift laundry line and tore it down. "This isn't the USS *Minnow*! Now where's Maggie?"

"Take a look." Perry pointed to the row of monitors.

"Christ . . ." A smile broke on Bud's face. "That looks pretty cool."

"Hey!" Stu Schwartz held up his hand. "Something's happening out there. My light meter just jumped. It's getting brighter."

*   *   *

Maggie saw the glow first, illuminating what remained of the humpback carcass. Then the head appeared, as big as her mother's mobile home and totally white. She felt her heart pounding in her ears, unable to comprehend the size of the creature that was casually approaching the bait. The snout rubbed against the offering first, tasting it. Then the jaws opened. The first bite was a nibble, the second took her breath away—as the jaws opened into a tunnel, slamming down on a three-ton chunk of blubber.

The mammoth head shook itself loose from its meal, sending a flurry of blubber shards swirling in all directions. As the monster chewed, the movement of its powerful jaws sent quivers down its six gill slits, reverberating the loose flesh along its stomach.

Maggie felt herself drifting to the bottom of the shark tube, unable to move. She was in awe of this magnificent creature, its power, its nobility and grace. She raised her camera slowly, afraid she might alert the creature.

*   *   *

"Christ, pull her back in!" Bud ordered.

"Are you crazy? This is what we came here for!" Perry was excited. The whole crew was excited . . . or scared. "What a monster! Goddamn, this is amazing footage!"

"Pull her back in now, Meth," Bud warned, "or you'll be joining her."

Bud's crew closed ranks around him. The boss meant business.

"Okay, okay, but she's gonna be mighty pissed off." The director signaled to his assistant, who activated the winch.

The steel cable snapped to attention as it began dragging the shark cylinder through the water.

*   *   *

The Meg stopped feeding, her senses alerted to the sudden movement. Being plastic, the shark tube had not given off any electronic vibrations, and so the predator had ignored it. Now the big female abandoned the carcass, sculling forward to examine this new stimuli.

Maggie's heart fluttered as the tube jerked backward through the water, the Megalodon keeping pace. "Hey? What the hell are you assholes doing?"

Bud's voice came over her headpiece, filtered. "Maggie, you okay?"

"Bud Harris, if you have any desire to touch my naked body again, you'd better stop what you're doing. Now!"

The Meg rubbed its snout along the curvature of the shark tube, confused. It's head swayed, allowing it to focus on her with its good eye.

Christ, it sees me . . .

The tube stopped moving.

The Meg's enormous mouth opened and closed, almost as if it was speaking to her. Then its jaws opened wider, exposing its frightening front rows of teeth, which attempted to bite down upon the cylinder.

The smooth plastic surface slid harmlessly away.

Maggie smiled. "What's wrong, gorgeous? Too big for ya?" Regaining her swagger, she repositioned the camera, filming down the shark's cavernous gullet. "Can you say Academy Award?"

Applause filtered through her headpiece.

Maggie held up her hand, acknowledging the crew's appreciation.

The Megalodon turned and disappeared into the darkness. Maggie caught a flicker of its caudal fin on film before it vanished into the lead-gray periphery. She took a breath, all smiles.

*   *   *

"It moved off," confirmed Perry.

"Thank Christ," said Bud. "Okay, get her out of there before it comes back."

"Ohhhh shit!" yelled Stu, who impulsively backed away from the monitors.

The Meg had circled. It was accelerating at the tube.

*   *   *

Maggie screamed, her air tank banging against the back of the tube as the 62,000-pound monster bull-rushed the cylinder, rotating its hyperextended jaws. The impact sent Maggie's face mask smashing into the interior forward wall of the tube, her head spinning from a concussion wave that would have shattered her skull had she not been underwater.

The cylinder was driven backwards. It smashed against the *Magnate*'s keel, shattering cameras and lights, giving the enraged Megalodon enough leverage to wrap its mouth around its elusive prey, the tips of a few of its teeth catching onto the cylinder's drainage holes.

The Meg had established a grip, although, try as it might, the creature could not generate enough leverage with its jaws to crush the maddeningly wide tube.

Frustrated, the beast drove its kill to the surface, the plastic cylinder still locked sideways in its bite. Swimming away from the *Magnate*, which it perceived as another challenger, it plowed the tube ahead of its open mouth, creating a twenty-foot wake along the surface.

The spool of steel cable unwound ten feet a second, then the entire assembly was wrenched away from the decking. It smashed through the mahogany guard rail and splashed into the sea.

The Megalodon's upper torso rose vertically out of the Pacific, then, in an unfathomable display of brute strength, it lifted the Lexan tube above the waves and, as if in slow motion, shook it back and forth, left, then right, water streaming out of the tube's vent holes.

Maggie couldn't hold on, flopping one way, then the next, her air tank denting, the cylinder gathering speed as its weight grew lighter, its contents draining, each collision bringing her closer to unconsciousness.

The effort of supporting the shark tube and its passenger quickly wore down the Megalodon. The female released her death grip on the cylinder, circling it as it sank slowly beneath the waves.

CAT AND MOUSE

The helicopter roared over the Farallon Islands, approaching the luxury yacht anchored just off the jagged southern coastline.

Jonas looked through the night binoculars, zooming in on the deck of the ship. "Wait a minute . . . I know that yacht. That's the *Magnate*! Bud Harris's ship!"

"The guy banging your wife?" Mac circled the yacht. "Let's see if we can take out his satellite dish with my tool chest."

Jonas pulled the glasses away from his face. "Something's going on down there, the crew's in a panic."

* * *

Chaos reigned on board the *Magnate*. Captain Talbott had started the engines, then shut them down, afraid the noise would attract the Meg. Perry was excited, yelling orders to cameramen to climb to the highest point of the yacht to film. Bud was in a state of shock, watching by the starboard rail, helpless, as Stuart and Abby continued to try to communicate by radio with Maggie.

When the helicopter appeared, Bud had panicked, thinking it was the coast guard, afraid the authorities had come to arrest him because of the humpback carcass.

"Bud!" Captain Talbott yelled from the pilothouse, "some guy in that helicopter wants to speak with you. Says his name is Jonas."

"Jonas?" Bud ran to into the control room and snatched the radio. "Jonas, it's not my fault. You know Maggie, she does whatever she wants!"

"Bud, calm down," commanded Jonas. "What're you talking about?"

"The Meg. It took her. She's trapped in that damn shark tube. It wasn't my fault!"

*   *   *

Mac circled overhead. Terry spotted the Megalodon. She was circling in fifty feet of water, three hundred yards off the *Magnate*'s bow.

Jonas focused with the night glasses. He could just make out Maggie's white wet suit. "I think I see her. Bud, how much air's left in her tank?"

Perry Meth's voice filtered over the radio. "No more than five minutes. If you guys can distract the Meg, we could get her out of there!"

Jonas tried to think. What would draw the monster's attention away from Maggie? The copter? Then Jonas noticed the yellow Zodiac on the *Magnate*'s deck.

"Bud, the Zodiac, get it ready to launch," ordered Jonas. "I'm coming aboard."

*   *   *

Maggie fought to stay awake. Everything hurt, but the pain was good, it kept her conscious. Her face mask had a hairline crack and was leaking seawater into her eyes. The earpiece was buzzing with static. Her ears were ringing, and it hurt to breathe. The Megalodon continued circling counterclockwise, watching her with its one functional basketball-size gray eye. The glow from its hide cast an eerie light, illuminating Maggie's wet suit. She checked her air supply again: down to three minutes.

I've gotta make a break for it, she told herself, but refused to uncurl from her ball.

*   *   *

Jonas hung on a cable from the chopper's winch, a radio transmitter and receiver around his neck. "Remember, Mac," he yelled, "wait until I say before you hit her with the beam. Once I'm in the boat, I'll need you to tell me where the Meg is."

Terry squeezed out his door next to him. "I'm coming, too!

"Forget it," Jonas yelled, "it's too dangerous."

"You want to rescue Maggie, fine, but I'm still after that shark!" Terry pointed the transmitter rifle at his face. "It's a female thing. Slide over!"

Jonas allowed her to share the harness.

Mac's voice called out, "For the record, are you guys doing this outta love, greed, or because you two can't resist being morons?"

"Does it matter?"

"Just wanted to know what to say at the funeral."

Mac activated the winch, lowering them to the *Magnate*.

Stu and Perry secured them by the waist as they dropped to the main deck. Bud pointed to the starboard rail. "Zodiac's in the water. What do you want us to do?"

"We'll distract the Meg. Once she follows, get your yacht over to Maggie's location and get her the hell out of there, fast."

Jonas and Terry climbed over the rail, lowering themselves by aluminum ladder to the awaiting yellow motorized raft. Jonas started the engine, looking up at Bud.

"Wait for Mac to signal you that the Meg has moved off. Then get Maggie, okay?"

Bud nodded in agreement.

Abby appeared at the rail. She tossed Jonas a headset. "We've reestablished contact with Maggie."

Jonas gunned the engine. The rubber raft skimmed across the surface, its engine a high-pitched whine. He shouted over the headset, "Maggie, can you hear me?"

"Jonas? Is that you?"

"Hang in there, baby, we'll lead the Meg away. How deep are you?"

"I don't know, maybe ninety feet! Jonas, hurry, my mask cracked, the pressure's unbearable, and I'm almost out of air.

Terry tried her headset. "Mac, can you hear me?"

The helicopter was hovering a hundred feet above the Zodiac. "Barely. The Meg hears your engine! She stopped circling . . . she's rising! Hard to starboard!"

Terry yelled at Jonas, "Hard to starboard!"

Jonas veered hard to his right as the Meg surfaced, its jaws snapping, just missing the boat. He headed for the nearest Farallon island, the albino dorsal fin right behind them its presence sending elephant seals leaping out of the water onto the rocks.

* * *

The *Magnate* sprang to life, her twin engines growling as they pushed the yacht ahead. Maggie was already out of the cylinder. She released her weight belt, grabbed the underwater camera, and allowed her buoyant tanks to carry her to the surface, careful to exhale slowly.

* * *

"Jonas, move! Zigzag or something!" Terry yelled, as the creature's snout collided with the back of the Zodiac.

"Hold on!

Jonas zigzagged, then circled around a rock formation, nearly shredding the raft's skin on its jagged surface.

Terry looked around. The fin was gone. "Mac, where is she?"

"She went deep! I lost her!"

* * *

Maggie's heart pounded in her ears as she rose through the dark sea. Her head broke the surface and she exhaled, then gasped a few quick breaths. The *Magnate* was bearing down on her and she waved. The ship slowed. She leaped for an aluminum ladder, grabbed hold of a rung, but it was too slick and she fell away.

The yacht stopped. She swam to it, smiling to cheers from her production crew.

"Way to go, champ," yelled Perry.

"Maggie, get in the goddamn boat!" screamed Bud.

Exhausted, she released the heavy air tanks, allowing them to fall off her shoulders, then climbed the aluminum ladder, a rung at a time, her left hand still holding the heavy underwater camera.

Bud was hanging over the side, reaching down. "Damnit, Maggie, come on!"

Maggie felt a wave of dizziness. "If you want to help, take the goddamn camera!" She swung it toward him with her last bit of energy.

Bud grabbed the dripping case, hefting it over the rail to Abby, who caught it in both hands . . . then screamed!

Maggie was rising—but from within the creature's mouth! The Megalodon's upper torso continued moving higher, past the starboard rail, the crewmen screaming, backing away—

—as Maggie, barely conscious, imagined a warm scarlet blanket was being wrapped around her waist, protecting her against the painful cold.

The albino monster slipped back into the sea, tightening its grip around her torso, its teeth puncturing her white wet suit, turning it crimson, while crushing her ribcage, collapsing a lung.

She managed a final rasp before her head submerged.

Bud was hyperventilating, his limbs no longer his to control. The keel's underwater lights were on, illuminating the monster's head. Looking down, he couldn't move, staring at the face of a devil that stared back at him, hovering ten feet underwater. The creature appeared to be smiling, while Maggie, wedged in its mouth, thrashed about, screaming in silence as she drowned in its grasp. The ungodly beast seemed to be toying with her. Blood poured from his lover's open mouth and she convulsed one last time—

—as the shark turned an eye on Bud. The hideous mouth opened wide, creating a vacuum that sucked Maggie into its black vortex and out of sight, expelling a car-size burp of air and blood.

Bud shook. Unable to move, he closed his eyes and waited to die.

The monster rose again for its next meal, its jaws open.

The bolt of light from the helicopter smashed through the darkness as if guided by the hand of God. It burned into the Meg's one good eye, blinding the creature, sending a white-hot wave of stabbing pain into the optic lobe. Its massive head whipped sideways, bashing against the *Magnate*—

—as Terry fired the transmitter dart from the Zodiac's bow at point-blank range.

The dart pierced the creature's right flank as it slammed back into the water, the tremendous wake flipping the Zodiac, tossing Jonas and Terry overboard. They surfaced, climbing quickly up the aluminum ladder and over the crushed mahogany rail.

His world spinning out of control, Jonas Taylor collapsed to the deck and vomited.

MORNING, MOURNING

There was no moon, no stars. Not a wave stirred. Bud stood at the rail and waited, the underwater lights of the *Magnate* illuminating the yacht's hull and surrounding sea. And then the whispers came, tickling his ear.

"Bud? . . . Baby, where are you?"

"Maggie? Maggie, is that you?" Bud leaned over the rail, searching the black sea.

"Bud, my love, please help me," the whispers cooed into his ear.

"Oh God, Maggie, where are you?" Hot tears rolled down his cheeks. He watched a droplet fall into the ocean.

Bud waited until he felt its aura rising. Then he saw the glow, followed by the snout, still hovering below the surface. The jaws yawned opened, revealing icy cold blackness. The words came again, tearing at his heart . . . "Bud, please, I don't want to die."

"Maggie!"

Bud shot up in bed, tearing loose his IV. The nurse ran in, followed by an orderly, who grabbed his arm. "It's okay, Mr. Harris," she soothed. "It's okay." The orderly strapped him down, bound his wrists and ankles, as the nurse shot a syringe of sedative into his IV drip.

Bud fell backward in slow motion onto the *Magnate*'s deck. He watched the sky, helpless, as the gray haze of dawn approached.

*   *   *

Jonas awoke in the *Abyss Glider*. The sky was blue, the sea below the Lexan pod a mouse gray. Three-foot swells bobbed the AG I up and down along the surface.

He saw the swimmer approach. Recognized the black hair, almond eyes. It was D.J.

The powerless sub's heavy nose cone dropped, inverting him, forcing him to stare into the depths. Jonas hung suspended upside down, waiting for D.J. to pull him out. He looked below into the mist and waited.

The surreal glow appeared.

"D.J., you'd better hurry."

The sinister mouth widened, revealing rows of teeth. The half-moon tail wagged faster, propelling the shark closer.

"C'mon, kid." Jonas turned. But it wasn't D.J.—D.J. was dead. It was Terry!

"Terry, get away!"

She smiled, waving at Jonas, swimming closer.

The monster's mouth opened wider, revealing hideous pink gums . . .

"No!"

*   *   *

The heavy pounding on his front door woke him. "Terry?"

Three more knocks.

Jonas rolled off the sofa, spilling the remains of the half-empty bottle of Jack Daniel's on the carpet.

Staggering, he opened the door, daylight burning into his eyes.

"Masao?"

"Taylor-san, let me in."

Jonas stood aside.

"I have been trying to reach you all morning. You have coffee?" Masao went into the kitchen.

"Upper shelf, I think. What time is it?"

"Three-twenty. No more alcohol, okay? It'll rot your liver." Masao made coffee, handed a cup to Jonas. "I am truly sorry about your wife. She died a noble death, doing what she believed in."

"Death is death." Jonas shook his head, taking a seat at the kitchen table. "I'm sorry, Masao, I can't do this anymore."

"Can't? What can't you do?"

"There's been too much death. Let the authorities handle the Meg."

Masao sat down. "Authorities? I thought you were the authority? Jonas, we have a responsibility. I feel it. I know you do as well." Tanaka looked into Jonas's eyes, bloodshot and exhausted. "A tired mind should not make decisions, but we are running out of time."

"I already made my decision. I'm through."

"Hmm. Taylor-san, you are familiar with Sun Tzu?"

"No."

"Sun Tzu was a great warrior, he wrote *The Art of War* more than twenty-five hundred years ago. He said, 'If you know neither the enemy nor yourself, you will succumb in every battle. If you know yourself but not the enemy, for every victory gained you will also suffer a defeat. But if you know the enemy and know yourself, you need not fear the result of a hundred battles.' Do you understand?"

"I don't know, Masao. I can't think right now."

Masao placed his hand on Jonas's shoulder. "Jonas, who knows this creature better than you?"

"This is different."

Masao shook his head. "The enemy is the enemy." He stood. "But, if you will not face our foe, then I suppose my daughter will." He headed for the front door.

"Terry?" Jonas stood. "Masao, wait—"

"Terry can pilot the AG I. My daughter knows her responsibility. She is not afraid."

"Forget it then, I'm going!"

"No, my friend. As you say, this is different. D.J.'s death must not be a meaningless one. The Tanaka clan will finish this business ourselves."

"Five minutes . . . give me five minutes to get dressed." Jonas ran into the bedroom.

Masao smiled to himself and turned on the television.

Channel 9 Action News was showing Maggie's underwater footage taken from the Lexan cylinder.

". . . and shot this amazing film moments before she died in the creature's jaws. Maggie Taylor gave her life to her profession, leaving these incredible scenes as her lasting legacy. A public service will be held on Thursday, and Channel 9 will be presenting a two-hour special tonight at eight honoring Mrs. Taylor.

"In a related story, a federal judge ruled today that the Megalodon has officially been listed as a protected species of the Monterey Bay National Marine Sanctuary. We bring you live to the steps of the Federal Court Building."

Masao turned up the volume.

"Here he comes . . . Mr. Dupont, Mr. Dupont, were you surprised today how quickly the judge ruled in favor of protecting the Megalodon, especially in light of the recent attacks?"

Andre Dupont of the Cousteau Society stood next to his attorney, several microphones pressed to his face. "No, we weren't surprised. The Monterey Sanctuary is a federally protected marine park designed to protect all species, from the smallest otter to the largest whale. There are other marine predators in the park—orcas, great whites. Each year, we see isolated attacks by great white sharks on divers or surfers, but these are isolated attacks only. Studies have shown that the great white sometimes mistakes a surfer for a seal. Humans are not the staple of the great white's diet, and we certainly are not the preferred food source of the sixty-foot Megalodon. Of greater importance will be our effort to immediately place *Carcharodon megalodon* on the endangered species list so it is protected in international waters as well."

"Mr. Dupont, what is the Cousteau Society's opinion of the Tanaka Institute's plan to capture the Megalodon?"

"We believe all creatures have a right to exist in their natural habitat. However, in this case, we are dealing with a species that nature may have never intended to interact with man. The Tanaka Lagoon is certainly large enough to accommodate a creature of this size, therefore we agree it might be best if the Megalodon was captured."

The Channel 9 anchor reappeared.

"We had our field reporter, David Adashek, conduct an unofficial street poll to see what the public's opinion is. David?"

"Trudy, opinions seem to favor capturing the monster that destroyed the lives of so many, including my close friend Maggie Taylor. Personally, I feel the creature is a menace, and I've spoken to several biologists who concur it's not unfeasible the shark may have acquired a taste for humans. If true, we can expect more gruesome deaths, especially in light of today's federal court ruling. This is David Adashek reporting, Channel 9 News."

* * *

Jonas was watching the same report from the television in his master bedroom. He stared at David Adashek, his heart racing as he realized Maggie had set him up that night at Scripps. "God, Maggie, what did I ever do to make you so bitter?"

But Jonas knew in his heart: the long hours, the traveling, the nights spent alone in his study, writing his books. Tears rolled down his cheeks. "I really am sorry, Maggie, so sorry." At that moment, Jonas felt more love for his wife than he had in the last two years.

He washed his face, then grabbed his duffel bag and shoved a few days' worth of clothing inside. He pulled out his workout bag, already loaded with his wet suit. Jonas looked inside, verifying that his good-luck charm was packed. He took a moment to examine the blackened seven-inch fossil, as wide and as large as the palm of his hand. He felt its sharp serrated edges as he ran the tooth across his fingers.

He replaced the tooth in its leather pouch, dropped it in the gym bag, then slung the duffle over his shoulder.

He looked in the mirror. "Okay, J.T., time to get on with your life."

When he walked out the front door, Masao Tanaka was waiting.

WHALE WATCHERS

For two long days and nights, the *Kiku*, her helicopter, and three coast-guard cutters cruised the Monterey Bay National Marine Sanctuary, attempting to locate the homing signal of the transmitter. The device implanted in the hide of the Megalodon possessed a range of up to twelve miles, gaining strength as the receiver got closer. But after searching four hundred nautical miles of ocean, no signal could be detected.

Hundreds of whales continued migrating south through the sanctuary without any noticeable changes in activity among the pods. On the third day, the coast guard gave up the search, theorizing that either the Megalodon had left California waters or the transmitter had malfunctioned.

Two more days passed, and even the crew of the *Kiku* began to lose hope.

* * *

Rick and Naomi Morton were celebrating their tenth anniversary in San Francisco, glad to have escaped the cold weather of Pittsburgh and their three children. They had never actually seen a real whale, so the idea of spending the day whale watching seemed exciting. Wearing only a lightweight windbreaker ("It's California, how cold can it be?") and loaded with camcorder, binoculars, and his trusty 35 mm, Rick followed his wife on board *Captain Jack's Whale Watcher*, a forty-two-foot sightseeing boat docked at the Monterey Bay wharf. The couple found an empty spot on a bench along the stern, then huddled, freezing, with the twenty-seven other passengers. The boat chugged ahead, its exhaust choking those passengers seated behind the pilothouse.

The presence of the Megalodon had initially hurt business among Monterey's whale-watching boats. But the tourists gradually returned, mostly because the predator had not been seen in almost a week, and surfaced only at night. For their part, tour-boat operators cancelled all sunset excursions rather than risk a confrontation with the creature.

Twenty minutes and two cups of hot chocolate later, a deckhand announced over a crackling speaker, "Welcome aboard *Captain Jack's Whale Watcher*. You folks are in for a real treat today. The humpbacks have been putting on a great show all morning, so get those camcorders ready."

Moments later, "Folks, this is really exciting! On our port, or left side, is an unusually large pod of orca." Everyone moved to the port side, cameras poised. "Orca, also known as killer whales, are extremely intelligent hunters, able to kill whales many times larger than themselves. Looks like we're catching this pod in the middle of a hunt."

Rick focused his binoculars on the pack of towering black dorsal fins moving parallel to the boat, now less than two hundred yards away. There were at least thirty orca, a dozen converging on a smaller object, the rest racing along the perimeter for their turn at the prey. Rick watched, fascinated by the battle tactics.

And then he saw what looked like an albino shark, its three-foot dorsal fin half bitten and bleeding as the wolf pack tore at its hide.

*   *   *

The male Megalodon pup raced along the surface, prevented from submerging by the much larger predators below. The pod of orca had tracked the male as it hunted along the Farallon Islands. Being rogue hunters, Megalodon had only one natural enemy beside their own kind—orca. The whales, swarming pack hunters, could take an adult Megalodon down, if they could keep the shark from going deep. In ancient seas, a confrontation between a pod of orca and an adult Megalodon was a rarity, the two formidable species usually avoiding one another . . . but the rules of engagement changed when it came to Megalodon young.

With frightening speed and power, the orca males, each as least twice as large as their battered adversary, snapped at the pup, preferring to ride it to exhaustion than kill it outright. Eventually they'd take turns flipping its broken carcass high into the air, making a sport of the demise of the would-be future king of Monterey Bay.

*   *   *

Bud Harris gathered his belongings and stuffed them into a brown paper bag provided by the orderly. Unshaven, badly in need of a shower, the once-proud entrepreneur had been reduced to a feeble shell of his former self. Deeply depressed after having witnessed his lover's death, Bud was also suffering from exhaustion brought on by a lack of REM sleep. Memories of his awful experience were now manifesting themselves in his subconscious mind in the form of night terrors. More frightening than the worst nightmare, the night terrors were violent, surreal dreams of death. For the last five nights, Bud had let out bloodcurdling cries that rocked the west wing of the hospital's fourth floor. Even after the frantic nurses had managed to wake him, he would still be screaming, blindly flinging his fists into the air. After the second episode, orderlies had to strap his wrists and ankles to the bed while he slept.

Bud Harris no longer cared whether he lived or died. He felt alone and in pain, uninterested in eating and afraid to sleep. Extremely worried, his doctors wanted to bring in a psychiatrist. Bud wasn't interested.

The nurse arrived to escort her patient out of the hospital with the traditional wheelchair ride. "Mr. Harris, is anyone meeting you downstairs?"

"No."

Two men strode up to the nurse.

"We're here to meet Mr. Harris."

Bud looked up at them. "Who the hell are you?"

"Frank Heller. This is my associate, Richard Danielson." Heller held out his hand.

Bud ignored it. "Danielson? You're the asshole who got all those navy guys killed going after the shark. Should have killed it when you had the chance." Bud stood, walking away from the wheelchair and the two men. "I'll find my own way out."

"That's why we're here," Heller said, following him down the corridor. "My brother, Dennis, was butchered by the same monster that killed Maggie Taylor."

"Yeah? Well, I'm sorry for your loss, now if you'll excuse me . . ."

"Hold it," said Danielson. "This thing has killed a lot of people. We thought you'd want to be involved in a little payback." Danielson looked at Heller. "Maybe we were wrong."

The thought of killing the Megalodon seemed to set off a spark in Bud. He focused his eyes on Danielson for the first time. "Okay, I'm in. What is it you need? Money? Weapons?"

"Your boat."

"My boat." Bud shook his head. "That's how I got into this mess in the first place."

*   *   *

The gray whale's head remained out of the water, allowing passengers to reach over the rail and touch it.

"Wow! Rick, did you get that one on tape?" asked Naomi. "I touched its barnacle . . . eww."

"Got it."

"Get some more still shots, okay?"

"Naomi, I've got two full rolls already. Give it a rest."

The whale submerged. The passengers reloaded their cameras and waited.

The patch of sea began swirling, then pooled a dark red.

"Hey . . . is that blood?"

A member of the crew leaned over to get a better look. "Hell if it ain't."

Naomi turned to Rick, "Does that mean yes or no?"

"It's rising again, get your cameras ready!" Twenty camcorders rose in unison.

The gray whale surfaced, then rolled over on its side. A few tourists reached overboard to touch it—

—when the torso rotated again, revealing a gushing wound the size of a sand trap.

The passengers stared, mesmerized . . . until a monstrous set of jaws broke the surface along either side of the dead whale, giving it a vicious shake before dragging it underwater.

Passengers screamed and backed away. The crewman ran into the pilothouse. Seconds later, the engines caught, the boat veering away.

Fifty feet below, the predator registered the sudden electrical discharge.

*   *   *

The *Kiku* was eight miles due west of the Tanaka Institute, most of her crew still asleep from the previous night's patrol. Terry Tanaka, wearing a sweatshirt, shorts, and sunglasses, lay on a lounge chair on the uppermost open deck, facing the sun.

Jonas joined her. "Aren't you cold?"

She smiled. "It's warm in the sun. You should try it. You'd look good with a tan."

"Yeah. I think when this is all over, I'll take a vacation, get away somewhere. Maybe a tropical island."

"Take me with you."

Jonas wasn't sure if she was being serious or sarcastic. "Where would you want to go?"

"Tahiti. Bora Bora. At this point, I'd settle for the Jersey Shore."

"Not me. No more settling in my life. Bora Bora it is."

"It's expensive," she said. "We'd have to share a room."

"They have waterfront bungalows, some actually on stilts in the middle of the bay. On second thought, I think we should stick to the beach."

"Agreed."

"Jonas Taylor, report to the CIC immediately." Masao's voice squawked over the metal speaker, sounding urgent.

They hurried down the stairwell together, entering the command information center.

Masao was waiting. "Coast guard just picked up a distress call from a whale-watching boat not far from here."

"The female? In broad daylight? How—"The answer popped into Jonas's head almost as quickly as he said it. "She's blind, we must've permanently blinded her! Christ, how could I have been so stupid?"

"The monster's blind?" asked Terry. "That's a good thing, right?"

"Not if she's surfacing in the day. A Megalodon losing its sight's a lot different than you or me going blind. She has other sensory organs that are used to guide her in the darkness. No, I'd say things just got worse."

"Masao, I've got her tracking device on sonar," announced Pasquale. "Faint, but it's her. She's four miles due north, steady on course zero-three-zero."

Captain Barre adjusted their course and speed.

Terry turned to Jonas, "Here comes your flyboy."

Mac came stumbling in, still half asleep.

"Mac, we've located the Meg. You ready to go?" asked Jonas.

Mac rubbed his eyes. "Sure, just give me thirty seconds to pour some coffee into my eyes."

"Jonas, Alphonse, get to your stations," ordered Masao. "Mac—"

"I'm leaving, I'm leaving." Mac headed out through the pilothouse. Moments later, the helicopter lifted off the deck of the *Kiku*.

* * *

For the whale watchers, the safety of land was still a good two miles away. With no sign of the Megalodon, talk had shifted from the terrifying experience to whether they would be receiving a refund.

WHUMPPP!

The collision knocked Naomi off her bench. Passengers screamed. Naomi grabbed Rick's arm and held on, her nails digging into his flesh.

The female had tasted her prey, pushing her snout hard against the keel of the moving boat. Her senses told her this was not food. Satisfied, the Meg circled back to guard the remains of her kill.

Having seen the footage of the Megalodon on television, realizing this same creature was now attacking his boat, the captain of the whaler grabbed the wheel and began zigzagging. The boat's bow slammed back and forth against the sea's three-foot swells.

The Megalodon slowed. These new vibrations were different, the creature wounded. Instinct took over, and the female banked sharply, rising to the surface as she homed in once more.

* * *

"Jonas, you read me?"

"Go ahead, Mac," yelled Jonas into the walkie-talkie. He and DeMarco were positioned at the *Kiku*'s stern, ready at the deck-mounted harpoon gun.

"I'm about two hundred feet above the whale-watching boat. Hard to see anything because of the reflection. Stand by, I'm coming around." Mac turned the airship, facing south. "And thar she blows!"

"Where?"

"Right behind the whale watcher's keel. Christ, she's gotta be twice the size of that boat, and she's coming in fast! Damn tourists, don't they know not to feed the animals?"

The *Kiku* was bearing down on the tour boat's wake, coming up along its portside beam, attempting to bring its stern and harpoon gun ahead of the transom to give Jonas a clear shot.

Jonas spun the harpoon gun counterclockwise on its base and focused through its sight. The *Kiku*'s main deck towered twenty-five feet higher than the smaller boat. He released the safety just as the whale watcher began zigzagging again.

"Mac, where is she, I still can't see her?"

"Starboard side of the whaler's transom and she's coming up fast! Wait, you'll see her fin!"

*   *   *

The tourists were standing, dumbfounded by the sudden appearance of a navy frigate, more stunned by its close maneuvers. The *Kiku*'s bow wake was pummeling the tour boat as it attempted to position itself alongside the smaller boat.

Rick Morton stood by the transom, fighting with his wife to release his arm so he could film the passing ship. "Naomi, let go!" She released his arm as the boat zigzagged again.

As he lifted the camcorder, a different object appeared in his eyepiece.

Naomi screamed. The whale-watching boat shuddered, its rear end dropping down into the water, sending waves over the deck.

The Megalodon's head was resting on its side, its sheer weight sinking the stern as its jaws gnawed the wooden transom.

Rick slid down the sudden slope, his forehead colliding with the tip of the predator's snout. Naomi grabbed her husband and dragged him away. Rick hugged her tightly, closing his eyes.

Jonas fired.

The harpoon exploded out of the cannon, trailing smoke and steel cable. The projectile struck home, burying itself four feet deep into the Megalodon's thick hide, inches from the dorsal fin.

The monster spasmed. Arching its back, it whipped its head sideways and submerged, jerking the steel line faster than its spool could unravel slack.

The *Kiku* lurched hard to starboard, smashing into the whale-watcher. DeMarco flipped backward over the guardrail, Jonas lunging after him, catching his right ankle with both hands just before he disappeared over the side. He held on, feeling his own feet slide out from beneath him before two crewmen helped haul DeMarco back on deck.

The engineer's face was flushed purple, his eyes bugged out. "Goddamn." He coughed. "I owe you."

WHOMP!

The Meg rammed the *Kiku*'s keel, the force of the blow bending steel plates, sending Jonas, DeMarco, and the two crewmen flopping to the deck.

*   *   *

"Hard to port," growled Captain Barre, picking himself up off the control-room floor. "Masao, when the hell's this shark gonna fall asleep?"

"Just lead it away from that tour boat!"

*   *   *

Hovering two hundred feet above the Pacific, Mac watched the *Kiku* change course and race to open waters. The enraged Megalodon submerged, running deep before circling back to ram the ship again.

As Mac watched, the ship shuddered behind another devastating blow. "Je-sus. Jonas, you guys okay down there?"

"We're taking a beating. What's it look like to you?"

"Looks like I'm flying home alone. What happened to those drugs of yours?"

"My guess would be a bad reaction. Stand by!"

Jonas ran into the control room.

Terry was watching the cardiac monitor. "I think she's OD'-ing! Her pulse just rocketed from seventy-seven to two hundred and twelve beats per minute."

"Hold on," yelled Pasquale, "she's breaching again!"

Wa-BOOM!! The *Kiku* shuddered, the impact sending books and charts flying.

"She's gonna tear my ship apart!" yelled Barre, grabbing his ringing phone. "Captain here!"

"Engine room! Captain, another blow like that last one and we'll be swimming home."

"If it's leaking plug it, if it don't work fix it!" Barre slammed the receiver down, then turned to Jonas. "Well Mr. Scientist?"

*   *   *

The Megalodon's brain was on fire, her blood boiling, her heart racing out of control. The predator's sensory system was overloaded by the madness brought on by the overdose of pentobarbital. Unable to reason, the female simply followed her instinct: attack her enemy.

Plunging to a depth of fifteen hundred feet, the Meg spun around and raced to the surface. The crescent tail whipped back and forth, the monster a white blur streaking upward. Homing in on the vibrations of the *Kiku*'s propellers echoing in her brain, the Megalodon rammed the source again, smashing the forward compartment of the ship's keel.

This time, the force of the blow knocked the giant predator senseless, stymieing her heart rate long enough for the pentobarbital and ketamine to take hold, shutting down the creature's central nervous system.

* * *

"Heart rate's plummeting!" yelled Terry. "One-fifty . . . one hundred . . . stabilizing at eighty-three beats per minute."

"We don't have much time." Jonas picked up the receiver of the internal phone.

"Al, take up the slack and release the net. I'm on my way!"

Terry grabbed his arm. "How can you be sure?"

He looked her in the eye. "I'll be fine. But I need your help."

She followed him out onto the deck.

* * *

The female was losing feeling in her tail. She slowed, barely moving, hovering almost twelve hundred feet beneath the *Kiku*.

DeMarco and his assistant, Wade Maller, stood at the stern, watching the *Kiku*'s winch gather in steel cable.

"Wade, half-speed when you reach a thousand feet," instructed DeMarco. "Once we feel resistance on the line, secure the winch at five hundred feet and we'll tow this bitch in." He turned to see Jonas in his wet suit, preparing to crawl in the rear hatch of the *Abyss Glider*, the sub already secured in its saddle.

"Jonas, wait!" Terry moved close, pulling him toward her, whispering in his ear. "Don't forget about Bora Bora."

Jonas smiled as the butterflies in his stomach teased at his groin. "Just get the suntan oil ready." He crawled into the submersible, lying prone in its one-man chamber, inching forward until he could strap himself into the shoulder rig.

In one steady motion, the sub was lifted away from the deck, swung over the starboard rail, and lowered into the Pacific.

He allowed the glider to sink, clearing the saddle before starting the engine. The sub leaped forward, into the vast blue world.

"Taylor-san, can you hear me?" Masao's voice filtered over his radio.

"Yes, Masao, loud and clear. I'm at five hundred feet. Visibility's good."

"Can you see the Meg?"

Jonas's eyes followed the cable down, straining to see. Something was below. He could see a slight glow, but not as big as he expected. "Stand by." Jonas accelerated the submersible, descending at a forty-five-degree angle. He felt the interior temperature drop and checked the depth gauge again. Eight hundred sixty feet.

Then he saw the Meg.

She was suspended face-up, her tail dropping out of sight below her unmoving girth. With no water able to enter her mouth, her gills could not function.

She was drowning.

"Masao, the Meg's out cold, she's not breathing. You've got to tow her immediately. Do you copy?"

"Hai. Stand by." The *Kiku*'s engines restarted with a metallic, grinding sound. The line grew taut, and the Megalodon jerked upward at the sub, the sudden movement nearly stopping Jonas's heart. He circled the glider around her quickly, watching as she leveled off.

Moving closer, he drew the submersible parallel with the Megalodon's gills, focusing his attention on the six 15-foot long vertical slits. They were closed, inactive.

Christ, how do you resuscitate a shark?

Open her mouth!

He raced ahead to her lower jaw, which was clamped shut.

J.T., you are one insane asshole . . .

Aiming the Lexan nose cone at the powerful muscle surrounding the shark's mandible, he accelerated, ramming the impinged joint.

The lower jaw dropped. Seawater rushed in.

Seconds later, the gills began to flutter.

He beamed proudly. "Now don't make me do CPR."

"Good job, Taylor-san!"

"Thanks. Masao, have DeMarco take in another three hundred feet of cable so I can secure her in the netting."

Moments passed, the Meg rising slowly, pulled from above by the winch. Jonas followed her up, marveling at the size of the creature, her beauty, her savage grace. The paleobiologist found himself appreciating the Megalodon for what it was, a product of evolution, perfected by nature over hundreds of millions of years. She was the true master of the ocean, perhaps the last of her kind, and Jonas felt glad they were saving rather than destroying her.

The Meg stopped rising at two hundred and thirty feet. Jonas continued to the surface, circling until he had located the marker buoy signifying the towing end of the net. Extending the glider's retractable arm, he snatched the marker with the claw on the first try, then submerged, dragging the heavy netting straight down on a ninety-degree descent, stretching out the rolled-up slack.

The harness was a weighted cargo net, designed to sink uniformly in order to haul in tuna. Jonas had ordered flotation buoys attached along its perimeter. The inflatable devices were designed to be operated from the *Kiku*. In this way, the Megalodon could be released safely once secured inside the lagoon, with the net simply dropping away as the devices were deflated.

Jonas brought the AG I to eight hundred feet, moving well below the dormant monster. Satisfied, he raced beyond the Meg's lifeless caudal fin. "Masao, I'm in position. Inflate the harness."

"Stand by." Slowly, the net's perimeter buoys sprang to life, conforming the suddenly buoyant net to the contours of the Megalodon. The 62,000-pound monster rose, tension releasing from the harpoon.

"That's good, that's enough," yelled Jonas. "I think we're home!" He descended past the half-moon tail, feeling cocky. Moved past the belly—

"Whoa!"

Jonas circled back and hovered. Something was different. "Oh, shit. Masao, we've got a problem. The female gave birth!"

"Taylor-san, are you certain?"

"Unless she went on a crash diet, yeah. Stand by with the glider's saddle, I'm coming aboard."

"Taylor-san, before you surface, Captain Barre requests that you check the damage to the ship's keel."

"On my way." Jonas accelerated past the captive female, moving the clanging hull of the *Kiku*.

"Oh . . . Christ."

"I counted seven bent plates, at least three of which were taking on water," Jonas explained. "They're right on the seam, no way you can seal them. The starboard shaft's completely bent, it won't turn at all. The portside shaft's turning, but it's also damaged, making a helluva noise. Rev her any faster than six to seven knots and she'll tear loose."

"Will we sink?" Masao asked Captain Barre. The ship had taken on a tremendous amount of water, her draft had increased thirty percent, her decks now listing at a fifteen-degree angle to starboard.

"Sink? Yes. Maybe not tonight, who knows, maybe not tomorrow. We sealed off the forward compartment, but she's still takin' on water from other areas."

"How long until we arrive at the lagoon?" asked DeMarco.

"Pulling that monster out there, that's a lot of drag, lots of work for one screw. It's just after seven. I say we make it back tomorrow morning, just after dawn."

DeMarco looked at Barre, then back at Jonas. "Christ, Jonas, will the Meg stay unconscious that long?"

"I hate to add to all the uncertainty, but honestly, I don't know. There's no way of telling. I gave her what I thought was a sufficient dosage to keep her under twelve to sixteen hours."

"Taylor-san, can we inject her again?" asked Masao. "Maybe wait until dawn?"

"She'll die," said Jonas matter-of-factly. "You can't keep an animal this size under for so long without permanent damage to her nervous system. She'll need to come around and breathe on her own or she'll never regain consciousness."

Masao scratched his head, unsure. "Not many options. Captain, how many crew members do you need to run the ship? Maybe we evacuate some of the men now—"

"No. With the damage to the screw and the sea knocking on the door, I need every hand I've got, plus some. We leave this ship, we're all gonna leave together."

"Masao, let me make a suggestion," offered Jonas. "The cardiac monitor should warn us if the Meg's coming around. But just in case, let me go back down in the AG I before dawn and keep vigil. If she appears to be waking up, we'll release the line and get out of here. If we're not already in the lagoon, we'll be damn close. Without the additional weight of the Meg, we should be able to make it in fairly quickly."

"What happens when the Megalodon wakes up?" asked Masao.

"She'll have a bad hangover, probably be a little irritable. I wouldn't be surprised if she followed us right into the lagoon."

"More like chased us in," added DeMarco.

Masao thought it over. "Okay, Taylor-san, you take the glider out in the early morning and keep an eye on our fish. DeMarco, you have first watch on the cardiac monitor. I'll relieve you at midnight. Any changes, we call Jonas right away." Masao stopped, listening to the thunder rumbling in the distance. "That a storm moving in?"

Mac entered the CIC, having just refueled his chopper. "Not thunder, Masao. That's the sound of helicopters. News choppers, five of 'em to be exact, and there's more coming. I'd say it's gonna be mighty crowded around here by dawn."

*   *   *

Frank Heller paused from his work, looking up at the television screen for the fourth time in the last hour to watch the latest news update:

". . . two hundred feet below us, lying in a comatose state is the sixty-foot prehistoric Megalodon, a monster responsible for at least a dozen deaths over the last thirty days. From our view, you can clearly see the creature's snowy-white hide, its skin glowing under the reflection of the full moon.

"At her present course and speed, the heavily damaged *Kiku* is expected to reach the entrance of the Tanaka Lagoon sometime before dawn. Channel 9 News will be keeping a vigil all night, bringing you the latest on this breaking story. This is Michelle Prystas, Action News, reporting live from the . . ."

"Turn it off already, Frank," yelled Danielson. They were aboard the *Magnate*, assembling a homemade depth charge in the yacht's exercise room. Danielson was hard at work, installing the fuse to the four-by-two-foot steel barrel. "Haven't you had enough? You've been watching the same story all night."

"You asked me to find out how deep the Meg is," Heller said in his defense. "Did you expect me to swim out with a tape measure? From the camera angle, I'd guess she's about one hundred and fifty to two hundred feet down. What kind of kill zone you rigging that charge with?"

"Enough to fry that fish and the rest of her kind. I've added extra amatol, which is rather primitive but highly explosive. The challenge will be getting close enough to make an accurate drop. We'll have to rely on Harris for that. Where the hell is he anyway?"

"Up on deck. Did you hear the guy screaming in his sleep?"

"Half of San Francisco heard him. I'll tell you something, Frank, I haven't been sleeping well myself."

"Relax, skipper, after tomorrow, you'll be sleeping like a baby."

*   *   *

Bud Harris was at the starboard rail, staring at the reflection of moon on the black sea. The *Magnate* was anchored three hundred yards south of the Tanaka Lagoon, and in the lunar light, Bud could just make out the white concrete wall of the huge canal entrance.

"Maggie . . ." Bud drained his beer as he watched small wakes lap at the hull. "Look what you've got me into. Hanging out with a bunch of navy bozos, playing war against some freakin' fish."

Bud tossed the empty can in the water. Opened another. "Ahh, Maggs. Why couldn't you have just dropped the stupid camera?" Hot tears rolled down his cheeks. "Well, don't worry, your man's gonna kill that monster and cut out its eyes." He turned, staggering past the grand spiral staircase to one of the guestrooms. Bud found he could no longer sleep in the yacht's master suite. Maggie's perfume still lingered, her presence too vivid. When the mission was over, he planned to sell the yacht and move back East.

Collapsing onto the queen-size bed, he passed out.

*   *   *

The three-foot albino-white dorsal fin cut the surface, circling the discarded aluminum can as it sank into the black waters of the sanctuary.

DECISIONS

The *Kiku* crawled across the Pacific, escorted by the circling helicopters. Terry stood by the stern rail, staring at the soft white glow reflecting in the moonlight. Her hand caressed the switch controlling the air pressure feeding the net's inflatable buoys.

"Be easy to do, wouldn't it?"

Terry turned, surprised to find Jonas watching her.

"Release the net and she drowns. Been thinking about it myself. But it's not what he'd want."

"Maybe it's what I want."

"Then do it."

Terry fingered the controls. Her hand quivered.

Jonas placed his hand over hers. "It won't bring him back."

"And Maggie? What about her? We could do it for both of them."

"D.J. made his own decisions, so did Maggie. Sometimes decisions involve risk. Seven years ago, I allowed fear and guilt to rule my life. That was a mistake, one of many I've made. Your father made a mistake, too, but he's a good man. Give up now, and it'll destroy him."

Her eyes teared up. "My mother's death forced him to give up his dreams. I finally realized completing that stupid whale lagoon was the only thing keeping him going."

She turned to face him and wept. Jonas hugged her to his chest.

*   *   *

Jonas opened his eyes, his internal alarm clock going off moments before his watch. It was still dark, and he was in the lounge chair with Terry snuggled against his chest under the wool blanket, keeping him warm. Gently, he stroked her soft hair with his callused fingertips.

She stirred. "Go back to sleep," she mumbled.

"I can't. It's time."

She opened her eyes, twisting around to face him. She stretched, her arm reaching around his neck, hugging him. "I'm too cozy to move, Jonas. Let's sleep another five minutes."

"I can't. Sorry."

"Am I rushing things? I am . . . I'm sorry. I just thought—"

"It's not that. My relationship with Maggie ended years ago, I was just too preoccupied to notice." He smiled, thinking of Mac.

"What?" She teased at his hair. "Come on!"

"Can you name any of the Marx Brothers? Three would be great. Even two—"

"Marx Brothers? I don't know? Karl?"

"No, Karl was—"

She buried her mouth against his, stifling the retort.

*   *   *

DeMarco paced around the *Abyss Glider*, checking his watch again. *Where was the man?* The eastern sky was already turning gray, the media helicopters still buzzing overhead.

"Damn press," he muttered.

Terry walked by, smiling. "Morning, Al."

"Where the hell is Jonas?"

"He's coming."

Jonas hustled out of the *Kiku*'s infrastructure, zipping up his wet suit. "Sorry. Forgot my good luck charm." He held up the fossilized Meg tooth, black with age, but still extremely sharp, at least seven inches long.

DeMarco shook his head. "Ever hear of a rabbit's foot?"

Jonas winked at Terry, fighting to take his eyes off her. For the first time in as long as he could remember, he felt happy. He crawled inside the glider, allowing DeMarco to seal the hatch closed.

Five minutes later, the *Abyss Glider* slipped out of its saddle and descended into the gray sea.

Jonas flicked on the exterior light, descending below the *Kiku*'s keel, circling for a quick inspection. It looked worse, the ship sitting lower in the water, listing hard to one side. He accelerated past the slowly churning screw, then dropped to three hundred feet, approaching the dormant creature from its left flank.

The Megalodon's glow illuminated the dark sea for fifty yards in all directions. Schools of fish darted back and forth along her hide, jellyfish caught within the netting. Jonas turned his exterior light off. Banking in a tight circle, he maneuvered the AG I next to the creature's head, the cranium measuring nearly three times the length of the sub.

The mouth was agape, water passing through. Jonas hovered close to the Meg's right eye, the pupil involuntarily rolled backward in the monster's head. It was a natural response, the Meg's brain automatically repositioning the now-useless organ for its own protection.

"Jonas!"

His heart jumped from his chest, his harness pulling hard against his shoulders.

"Damnit, Terry, you scared the hell out of me."

He could hear her laughing through the radio. "Sorry. Hey, we're still steady at eighty-five beats per minute. How's the Meg?"

"Sleeping like a baby. How close are we to the lagoon?"

"Less than four miles. Barre says another two hours, tops. Hey, you're about to miss a gorgeous sunrise."

Jonas smiled. "Sounds like the beginning of a great day."

DAWN

They had been waiting all night, anchored close to shore, a pilgrimage gathered as if summoned by the creature itself. Some were scientists, but most were tourists and thrill seekers, apprehensive yet prepared to face the risks in order to be part of history. Their transports varied in size, from Wave Runners to yachts, from small outboards to larger fishing trawlers. Every whale-watching company within a fifty-mile radius was represented, their rates sufficiently inflated for the event. More than three hundred camcorders, batteries charged and cassettes loaded, stood ready.

Andre Dupont leaned against the rail of the forty-eight-foot fishing trawler, watching through binoculars as the gray haze of the winter sky grew lighter across the horizon. He could just make out the bow of the *Kiku*, still a good two miles northwest of the canal entrance. He walked back toward the cabin.

"Etienne, she's close now," Dupont whispered to his assistant. "How far out will our captain bring us?"

His assistant, Etienne, shook his head. "Sorry, Andre. He refuses to leave the shallows with the monster so close. He won't risk the boat. Family business, n'est-ce pas?"

"Oui. I do not blame the man." Dupont looked around in all directions, the morning light revealing several hundred boats. The Frenchman shook his head. "I fear that our other friends will probably not be as cautious."

* * *

Frank Heller sat in the *Magnate's* bridge, watching the *Kiku* crawl at its agonizingly slow pace through a pair of high-powered binoculars. He shared none of Andre Dupont's exhilaration, only rage. In his shirt pocket was a photo of his brother and his brother's family. The side of his neck felt tight, throbbing with his rising anger. He imagined himself sitting down with his two nephews one day in the near-future, describing how he had killed the monster that took their daddy. The thought strengthened his resolve.

"It's time, Mr. Harris," he said, not looking away from the horizon.

Bud engaged the throttle. The *Magnate's* twin engines jumped to life, pushing the yacht toward their destiny.

* * *

Dawn's first light filtered curtains of gray down through the depths. Jonas watched as the creature's entire torso became visible, a lethal dirigible being led toward its new hangar. He brought the AG I's Lexan nose cone within five feet of the female's right eye, the blue-gray pupil still rolled back in its head, the light exposing a bloodshot white-yellow membrane.

"Jonas?" Terry's voice crackled over the radio. "I think something's happening with the Meg. Her pulse has been climbing steadily. It's at eighty-seven, flirting with ninety. I think she's rousing herself, trying to come out of it."

"Jonas, DeMarco here. I've reloaded the harpoon gun as per Masao's latest orders. If your monster wakes up before we enter the lagoon, I'm injecting it again, whether you like it or not. Consider yourself warned."

Jonas thought about arguing, but changed his mind. DeMarco was right. If the Meg regained consciousness before the *Kiku* could get her safely in the lagoon, the ship and its entire crew would be in danger. He stared at the creature's open jaws. Coursing through its DNA was four hundred million years of instinct. The predator would not think or choose; she would only react, each cell attuned to her environment, every response preconditioned. Nature itself had decided that the species would dominate the oceans, commanding it to perpetually hunt and make babies in order to survive.

Jonas whispered, "We should have left you alone."

"Jonas!" Terry's voice pierced his thought. "Didn't you hear me?"

"Sorry, I—"

"Your friend's yacht's bearing down on us! Five hundred yards and closing fast!"

"The *Magnate*? What's Bud doing?"

*   *   *

DeMarco focused his binoculars on the yacht, his line of sight finally drifting back toward the activity in the stern. Two men, supporting a steel drum, were balancing their cargo on the transom.

"What the hell?" swore the engineer.

Three hundred yards. Two hundred . . . and then DeMarco caught a face . . . Heller! He refocused on the steel drum and realized—

"Jonas!" DeMarco snatched the mike out of Terry's hand. "It's a depth charge, they're coming right at you! Get deep!"

*   *   *

Jonas leaned hard on the joystick, circled right, then rolled the sub beneath the Megalodon's massive pectoral fin and dived.

*   *   *

Mac pulled back on the joystick, the helicopter leaping off the *Kiku*'s listing deck. Circling the airship hard to his left, he raced to intercept the incoming yacht as if leading an air assault on a North Vietnamese patrol boat.

Bud looked up as the helicopter appeared out of nowhere, bearing down on his bridge on a head-on collision course. The millionaire screamed, yanking the wheel hard to port seconds before the platform supporting the chopper's thermal imager smashed into the *Magnate*'s radar antenna, ripping it off of its aluminum base.

Debris exploded across the deck, the air raining shrapnel. Reacting as if a grenade had just gone off above their heads, Danielson and Heller dove for cover, abandoning the depth charge. The maneuver left the five-hundred-pound explosive teetering precariously on the transom. As the yacht veered hard to port, the steel drum rolled over the transom and plunged into the ocean. Seawater rushed into the canister's six holes, filling the pistol chamber, sinking the bomb.

Cursing, Heller sat up, looking back in time to see the helicopter bank sharply, nose-dive toward the ocean, then level out. This time, it would make its run from the stern.

"Lunatic!"

"The charge!" screamed Danielson, "Get down!"

* * *

Mac pushed down on the joystick, yelling into the wind, "Mac attack!" a smile fixed on his face.

Wa-BOOM!!

The underwater blast sent a geyser of sea rocketing skyward, catching the pilot off-guard. He yanked desperately on the joystick as the tail of his copter swung out from behind him, his landing gear smashing into the upper deck of the *Magnate*, tearing the roof off the luxurious stateroom, shearing the bottom off his helicopter.

The airship spun out of control, the blades unable to regain draft.

Before Mac could react, the copter slammed sideways into the ocean.

* * *

At three hundred and twelve feet, the depth charge's spring had released, thrusting the percussion detonator against the primer. The crude weapon had imploded, then exploded with a flash and subsonic boom. Although the lethal radius of the bomb measured only twenty-five feet, the resulting shock wave was devastating.

The invisible force of current caught the *Abyss Glider* broadside, rolling the winged craft over and over again. Jonas pitched hard against the Lexan cone, cracking his head against the curved windshield, nearly knocking himself out.

*   *   *

Aboard the *Kiku*, lights shattered and bodies flew as the ship's fittings loosened with the blast. Captain Barre yelled at his exhausted crew to seal off the engine room, but the roar of the media helicopters drowned out his voice.

Terry Tanaka knelt on deck, her first thoughts of Jonas. She located the radio transmitter and yelled, "Jonas! Jonas, come in, please!"

Static.

"Al, I'm not getting a signal."

"Terry . . ." Masao stumbled toward them, his head soaked in blood. He collapsed before she could reach him.

"Call the doctor!" she screamed, pressing her palm to his fractured skull.

*   *   *

The chilly Pacific snapped Mac to attention. He opened his eyes, startled to find himself submerged upside down and underwater, sinking fast. Forcing himself to remain calm, he located the shoulder harness release and ducked out of the cockpit's open side door, kicking toward the surface.

*   *   *

Jonas waited until the aftereffects of the shock wave subsided, then attempted to roll the submersible right-side up. The power was dead. He swore to himself, then began rolling hard against the interior, gradually gaining enough momentum to rotate the sub right-side up. As he completed the maneuver, he could feel the natural buoyancy of the sub taking over as it gradually began to rise, tail-first, the heavier nose cone dropping.

"Terry, come in." The radio, like everything else on the sub, was dead.

A glow loomed on his right, lighting up the interior. Jonas turned to find himself hovering within three feet of the female's basketball-size pupil.

The blue-gray eye was open. Though blind, it stared directly at Jonas.

The Megalodon was awake.

CHAOS

Bud Harris dragged himself off the polished marble floor, unsure of what had just taken place. The *Magnate* was drifting, her twin engines down. He glanced out the tinted glass in time to see the helicopter's blades slip beneath the waves.

"Hope you die," he muttered, then pressed the "on" switch, attempting to restart the engines.

Nothing happened.

"Danielson, Heller! Where the hell are you morons?" Bud headed out on deck, locating the two men standing by the transom.

"Well? Is the monster dead?"

Danielson and Heller looked at one another. "Yeah, it's gotta be," said Danielson, not sounding very sure of himself.

"You don't seem certain."

"We had to release the charge a little early when that chopper attacked," answered Heller. "We should really get out of here."

"Well, boys, that's gonna be a bit of a problem," said Bud. "The engines are dead. Your damn explosive apparently loosened something, and I'm not exactly a licensed mechanic."

"Christ, we're stuck out here with that monster?" Heller shook his head, his jaws locked tight.

"Frank, it's dead. Trust me," said Danielson. "We'll be watching it float belly-up any second now."

Heller looked at his former CO. "Dick, it's a shark. It's not going to float. If it's really dead, it'll sink to the bottom."

They turned in unison, a splashing sound to their left. A hand appeared at the ladder, followed by Mac, who dragged himself, dripping wet, on board the *Magnate*.

"Beautiful morning, isn't it, assholes?" he said, collapsing on a deck chair.

*　　*　　*

Jonas lay on his stomach, head down, his claustrophobia causing shortness of breath. The lifeless *Abyss Glider*'s left midwing had caught on the cargo net, keeping the sub eye level with the Megalodon. Jonas watched in fascination and horror as the female's blue-gray eye continued focusing involuntarily on the tiny submersible.

She's blind, but she still knows I'm here. Don't move. Don't even breathe.

The caudal fin animated, swishing in labored, side-to-side movements, propelling the predator slowly forward. The gill slits towered into view, passing quickly. And then the prominent snout suddenly whipped back and forth, freeing the AG I's wing from the net as the most frightening animal on the planet became cognizant of its surroundings.

The submersible continued to rise tail-first. Jonas looked down, watching the Megalodon lurch forward, but the cargo net ensnarled her pectoral fins, the harpoon restricting her movement. Enraged, she rolled once, then twice, twisting and tangling herself tighter in the trap.

The AG I tossed backward in the Meg's wake. With no means of control, Jonas spun away, losing sight of the creature. Then, as the sub's nose cone drifted downward, he caught a glimpse of the furious creature, completely entwined from her gill slits to her pelvic fin in the cargo net.

"Good . . . she's going to drown," he whispered to himself.

*   *   *

The myriad boaters anchored outside the Tanaka Lagoon had witnessed the super-yacht break from the group to rendezvous with the incoming guest of honor. They had seen the helicopter loop downward to intercept the vessel, only to end up crashing into the sea as the depth charge had detonated. Now, the onlookers grew anxious, wondering if the explosion had killed the creature they had paid good money to see. Almost as one, several dozen of the larger fishing boats and tours grew daring, gradually moving toward the listless *Kiku*, intent on filming the creature, dead or alive.

Nine media helicopters were hovering, continually shifting positions in their attempt to gain better camera angles. The underwater explosion created a new twist on the story. The networks ordered their helicopter crews to lower altitudes in order to assess whether the Megalodon had survived.

David Adashek was in the back of the Channel 9 Action News copter, straining to see over his cameraman's shoulder. The creature's white hide was visible, but whether the shark was dead or alive was impossible to ascertain. The pilot tapped his arm, motioning him to look down.

Racing toward the Megalodon was a flotilla of pleasure boats.

*　　　*　　　*

From the tip of her snout to the edge of her caudal fin, the Megalodon's skin contained fine, toothlike prickles called dermal denticles, literally "skin teeth." Sharp and sandpaper-like in texture, the denticles were another in the predator's arsenal of natural weapons. As the female twisted insanely within the cargo net, the dermal denticles sawed through the rope, slicing it to ribbons.

Jonas watched the female shake free from her bonds. His pulse pounded in his throat as she turned in his direction, jaws slack, triangular teeth splayed. Desperate, Jonas tried the power switch again—still dead—as the monster propelled itself past him and toward the surface.

*　　　*　　　*

Bud and Mac had gone below to the engine room, leaving Danielson and Heller on deck. Frank was leaning across the transom, staring into the green water, when the white mass materialized below.

"Oh, Christ . . ."

WHOMP! The stern exploded beneath his feet, fiberglass splintering in a thousand directions as Danielson and Heller fell backward onto the tilting deck.

*   *   *

DeMarco manned the harpoon gun, training the barrel on his target. He released the safety as the Meg surfaced. He watched as she swam upside down below the waterline, a river of sea passing into her mouth as she exposed her glistening white belly to the world.

It was too good a target to pass up.

DeMarco aimed, pulled the trigger . . .

Click.

"Goddamnit!" The explosion had jammed the gun's inner chamber.

The entire crew was on deck, frantically donning orange life vests.

In the control room, the ship's physician tended to Masao, still unconscious. Terry and Pasquale stood over them.

"He's fractured his skull," said the doctor. "We need to get him to a hospital as soon as possible."

She could hear the swarm of media copters hovering above. "Pasquale, get on the radio, try to get one of those news choppers to land on the *Kiku*. Tell 'em we have a serious injury. Doc, stay with my father. I'll be right back."

She ran out of the CIC, making her way to the hangar deck.

*   *   *

David Adashek saw her waving emphatically on the helo-deck. "Hey, I know that girl, that's Tanaka's daughter. Look's like an emergency. Captain, can you land this bird on the *Kiku's* deck?"

"What for?"

"Stand by!" the cameraman yelled. "My producer's screaming at me to get close-ups of the Meg. He'll have my balls for breakfast if you land on that ship."

"Are you crazy?" David said, "The Meg's attacking the ship."

"All the more reason why we're not landing."

"Hey," said the pilot, "I'm getting a distress call from the *Kiku*. They're requesting we transport an injured man to shore. Radioman says it's Masao Tanaka. Looks serious."

"Land the copter," ordered Adashek.

The cameraman looked at him with a scowl. "Blow me."

Adashek ripped the camera from the man's grip, holding it out his open door. "Choose now. We land or I feed this to the Meg."

Moments later, the helicopter touched down on the *Kiku's* tilting deck.

*   *   *

The Megalodon circled beneath the *Kiku*. The ship's exposed metal hull, immersed in seawater, generated galvanic currents—electrical impulses that stimulated the female's ampullae of Lorenzini like fingernails on a chalkboard, driving her to attack.

Sweating profusely, Jonas could feel his claustrophobia building as he strained to reach the battery connections at the rear of his sub. Blindly, he groped at the terminals inside the rear panels, searching in vain for a loose connection.

A sudden current twisted the AG I around and upward, giving Jonas an unobstructed view of a scene that sent pangs of fear through his heart: the Megalodon was pushing her snout inside the venting keel of the *Kiku*!

*　　*　　*

The *Kiku*'s crew gathered around the news chopper, each man hoping for a ride.

Leon Barre pushed his way through the crowd. "Get Masao aboard that chopper. We don't need his blood in the water!"

The pilot of the news copter looked at Adashek and the cameraman. "Okay, boys, someone has to give up his seat for the old man. Which one of you is going to play the hero?"

The cameraman looked at Adashek with an evil grin. "Hope you can swim, tough guy."

David felt butterflies in his stomach as he exited the safety of the chopper, allowing the doctor and Terry Tanaka to load Masao on board. Moments later, he stood on the lopsided deck, his heart in his mouth as the helicopter flew off toward the mainland.

Nice job, dickhead. You're supposed to be reporting the news, not making it.

*　　*　　*

Crumpled against the mahogany rail, Richard Danielson stood painfully, grabbed Heller beneath his armpits, and hoisted him to his feet. "Frank, we're sinking!"

"No shit." Heller looked around. "Where are Harris and Mac?"

"Probably dead. If so, they're lucky."

"The Zodiac!" Heller pointed at the motorized raft. "Give me a hand."

The two men released the catches to the pulleys supporting the bulky raft. It dropped to the surface with a *splat*.

"You first, Frank."

Heller hesitated, then swung his leg over the rail. Danielson followed him in.

The outboard whined to life. Heller gunned the throttle, sending the raft's lightweight bow lifting away from the sea as the Zodiac skimmed over the waves, accelerating toward land and the pack of oncoming boats.

"Frank, watch out!"

With little room to maneuver, Heller was forced to veer around the first wave of boats.

The second wave's wake flipped the off-balanced Zodiac upside down.

Danielson and Heller were thrown headfirst into the Pacific, surfacing in the path of still more pleasure craft.

One hundred yards to the west, the Megalodon rose straight out of the Pacific, attempting to snatch one of the low-flying helicopters. The monster's heart-stopping appearance started a chain reaction. Two of the incoming fishing boats veered sharply into adjacent vessels, creating two separate pile-ups. Chaos reigned among the other craft as the rules of boating were tossed aside for self-preservation. Screams rent the air as weekend captains frantically tried to turn back, only to crash into the unwitting boaters behind them.

Circling in a tight formation forty feet above the melee, the pilots of the eight news copters panicked, realizing for the first time how massive the Megalodon actually was. Their first reaction was to achieve a safer altitude. Eight joysticks were simultaneously yanked backward, eight sets of rotors climbing toward the same airspace.

The pilots were so frightened of the monster below they completely ignored the danger above. Two copters rose at intersecting angles, their rotors slashing into one another, igniting a cataclysm. Flying shrapnel ricocheted into the paths of the other helicopter blades. In a matter of seconds, all eight choppers either had careened sideways against another airship or had been hit with shrapnel, causing their rotors to shatter. Matching fireballs exploded upward two at a time, raining metal, gasoline, and human body parts across the crowded sea.

Swimming fifty feet below the carnage, the predator circled slowly, snapping at the sinking debris, attempting to isolate food with her powerful senses.

Danielson swam toward the nearest pleasure craft, a thirty-two-foot speedboat overloaded with seven passengers and a golden retriever. The sleek boat had stalled, blocking traffic. He tried pulling himself aboard, but couldn't reach high enough. The preoccupied passengers didn't see him, nor could they hear his pleas for help over the fireballs and thunder of the choppers. Then he saw the ladder behind the transom and kicked toward it.

The attack came without warning, dragging Danielson underwater by his legs. He struggled in time to catch the ladder in a death grip, registering the feel of the sun-warmed aluminum, refusing to let go. The Megalodon's teeth severed both legs at the knees and Danielson slipped out of the monster's mouth, blood pouring from both open wounds.

Danielson screamed, still dangling from the ladder. Now the passengers in the stern heard him, several reaching for him, pulling him up by his wrists—

—as the Meg's head appeared behind the boat.

Terrified, the passengers released Danielson—

—the Meg snatching him as he slipped overboard. Tossing his mangled body into the air above her open mouth, the shark snatched its prey as a dog might catch a biscuit.

The monster slipped back beneath the waves before the first screams from the petrified witnesses could be uttered.

FEEDING FRENZY

The once-mighty United States Navy frigate dipped sideways, the *Kiku*'s waterlogged hull finally pulling her beneath the waves. The twenty-three crew members, packed into two lifeboats, rowed desperately to escape the swirling currents of the sinking vessel that seemed to reach for them from below. The outboard motors were not used—in fear that they might alert the monster.

Leon Barre, tears in his eyes, watched as the bow of his command slid silently into the Pacific. Terry Tanaka scanned the surf for any sign of Jonas or his *Abyss Glider*. David Adashek was visibly shaking, praying quietly, as were many of the crew. Next to him, crouched at the ready, DeMarco waited for the albino monster to reappear, a loaded Colt .45 shaking in his hand.

Captain Barre stood above the rowers, scanning the tangle of boats and helicopter wreckage a half mile away. "Son of a bitch," he swore aloud. "Do we start the motors or wait?" He looked into the eyes of his men, seeing their fear. "DeMarco?"

"After seeing that carnage, I have to believe those ships have the Meg's attention."

"How fast can these boats move?"

"Overloaded like we are, maybe it'd take us fifteen, twenty minutes to make land." The men looked up at him, nodding their heads.

"Wait." Terry looked to each man as she spoke, "Jonas said this creature can feel the vibrations of the engines. I think we should wait, let the Megalodon clear the area."

"And what if she doesn't?" asked Wade Maller. "I've got a wife and kids who'd like to see me again!"

Another crewmen spoke out. "You expect us to just sit here and wait to get eaten alive?"

DeMarco held up his hands. He looked at Terry. "Jonas is dead, and the rest of us might wind up the same way if we do nothing."

Murmurs of agreement. In the distance they could hear an occasional scream.

Terry felt a lump in her throat. She tried to swallow, holding back tears.

Jonas was either injured or dead, and they were going to leave him. She stared ahead, watching as a cigarette speedboat rose from the water and flipped. More screams tore the air. Terry realized they had no choice.

Both engines jumped to life, Leon Barre's boat taking the lead, heading south to skirt around the chaos ahead.

*　　　*　　　*

Frank Heller had managed to swim to one of the boats. Exhausted and frightened beyond reason, he remained in the water, clinging to the side of a fishing trawler's tuna net, eyes closed, waiting for death.

Minutes passed.

"Hey!"

Frank opened his eyes. A muscular black man was leaning overboard. "This ain't no time to be taking a dip, old man. Get your ass in the boat." A large hand grabbed a hold of Heller's life vest and dragged him out of the water.

* * *

Bud Harris slogged chest-deep in seawater in the flooding engine room of his yacht. The chopper pilot who had caused this mess was trying to get the engine to start.

"No good, she's dead."

"Then so are you."

Bud trudged up the stairs to the next deck.

Mac searched for the pumps. Flipped the toggle switch. The motors churned, vibrating the entire vessel as seawater was expelled overboard. He clicked the pumps off. "Way too noisy."

He left the engine room, finding his way to the pilothouse. Activating the radio, he sent a mayday call to the coast guard.

Bud entered the chamber. In one hand was an unopened bottle of Jack Daniel's, in the other, a .44 Magnum.

Mac saw the gun and chuckled. "Hey, Dirty Harry, you gonna kill the shark with that?"

Bud pointed the gun at Mac's head. "No, flyboy, but I may just kill you."

* * *

The powerless *Abyss Glider* bobbed four feet below the surface, the heavier nose cone pointing straight down at the ocean floor. Jonas was standing upright, his knees balancing on the shoulder harness, working on the battery in the rear of the sub. He was drenched in sweat, his breathing becoming increasingly difficult as his air supply diminished. Having located the disconnected electrical cables, he reattached them, bearing down with all his strength on the rusty wing nut in an attempt to tighten the connection with nothing but his fingers. The wing nut turned one revolution and stopped.

"That'll have to do," he grunted, twisting his body upside down, sliding back into the pilot's prone position. He felt the blood rush to his head. "Okay, baby, give daddy some juice."

The AG I flickered to life, blowing cool air on his face from its ventilation system. He pushed forward on the joystick, leveling out the sub, hovering it along the surface.

He looked around.

The *Kiku* was gone. To his right he saw the *Magnate*, listing but still afloat.

And then he spotted the flotilla.

*   *   *

Having remained in the waters adjacent to the Tanaka Lagoon, Andre Dupont and several dozen other boaters had looked on in horror as the Megalodon rose from the sea to wreak havoc among their unfortunate comrades. Even at a distance of a half-mile, the size and ferocity of the monster shocked the camera buffs.

The nature of the event had changed: This was no longer a game, people were dying!

A common thought passed through the group: Remaining in the water meant they too could be eaten! Forgetting about their ports of origin, the boaters swung their craft around and raced to the closest beach, a stretch of sand separating the lagoon's arena wall and the ocean.

The exodus left the fishing trawler as the only remaining boat near the lagoon. Etienne walked over to the rail and nudged Dupont. "Andre, the captain agreed to keep us in the shallows."

Dupont continued to look through his binoculars. "He's not going to beach the boat, like the others?"

Etienne smiled. "Captain says he just painted the keel, doesn't want to scratch it up. Still, how long should we remain? It's not safe."

Dupont looked at his assistant. "Those people out there, they are all going to die. I think we should do something."

"Captain says the coast guard is on the way."

"Etienne!" Dupont pointed to the south where the *Kiku*'s two lifeboats were making a run for the beach.

*   *   *

Jonas accelerated to thirty knots, holding his depth steady at twenty feet. Moments later, he came within view of the massacre.

Three smaller speedboats were in the process of descending to their final resting places, their fiberglass hulls torn apart. Jonas surfaced, afraid of what he was about to see.

The flotilla, once twenty strong, now consisted of a maze of floating fiberglass and the remains of cabins, decks, and broken hulls. Jonas counted eight fishing boats that appeared intact, their decks overloaded with panicked civilians. A coast guard rescue chopper hovered overhead, raising a hysterical woman in a harness. Those remaining on board seemed to be yelling, pushing each other in an attempt to be next.

Where was the Megalodon?

Jonas descended to thirty feet, circling the area. Visibility was poor, debris everywhere. He felt his heart pounding, his head moving rapidly in every possible direction.

Then he spotted the caudal fin.

The female was moving quickly away from Jonas, her tail disappearing into the gray mist. He verified her course on his instrument panel.

She was heading toward land.

*   *   *

The two lifeboats were less than a half-mile from the shoreline when the alabaster dorsal fin sliced in front of the lead boat and submerged, sending waves of panic among the *Kiku*'s crew.

Barre signaled to the other boat's helmsman to separate.

*   *   *

One hundred and eighty feet below the boats, the female circled, confused. Her senses had registered one prey, now there were two. She rose to attack the closest outboard.

Terry and DeMarco never saw the shark rise, only an explosion of bright blue sky, followed by bodies, then icy-cold water as their world spun like a gyroscope and then submerged, their lifeboat flipping on top of them.

Twelve heads broke the surface. Twelve pairs of hands reached for the capsized hull, its fragmented wooden hull glistening in the fading sun.

Twelve beating hearts . . . twelve dinner bells.

The albino dorsal fin circled slowly, its owner sizing up her next meal. The female rolled on her side, moving lazily just below the surface. The creature's sheer mass pulled the capsized lifeboat and its crew, its caudal fin slapping the surface, the crew's hearts jumping with each echoing clap. Water streamed into her open mouth, creating a gully as she moved nearer.

One of the men panicked and swam away.

The monster altered course, her streamlined body moving in quickly behind him.

Terry gasped, too petrified to scream as she watched the man struggle in the Megalodon's riptide. He kicked against the current, stroking with all his might, screaming as he glanced over his shoulder and saw the open mouth—

—just before he slid backwards down its gullet.

"Oh, God. . . oh my God," cried Adashek.

Like drowning rats, the surviving eleven tried to claw their way higher onto the capsized lifeboat.

Adashek grabbed onto the invested outboard engine, pulling himself higher. DeMarco's fingers were raw and bleeding, gripping the wooden hull. He knew he couldn't hang on, knew it didn't matter if he could. The hunter circled slowly, her undertow tugging them once more. This time DeMarco didn't fight it. He thought of his wife—she'd be waiting in the parking lot for him. He had promised her this would be his last voyage. She hadn't believed him.

Terry saw DeMarco drift away. "Al! Al, swim!" She pushed away from the boat, paddling lightly in his direction. Reaching him, she grabbed his arm from behind, pulling him toward her.

"No! Leave me! I can't take it anymore!"

The Meg moved toward them, again on its flank, content to consume her meal one at a time.

Terry fought to catch a breath. Twenty feet from the monster's snout, she could see the peppered-black ampullae of Lorenzini . . . the rows of teeth . . . the human flesh still caught between several fangs.

Terry and DeMarco kicked wildly as the jaws opened wider to accommodate its prey, pink gums exposed, serrated teeth reaching for them—

Six hundred and fifty pounds of submersible and pilot leapt out of the sea, the AG I momentarily blotting out the sun before smashing down hard upon the exposed upper jaw of the Megalodon. The triangular head lifted straight out of the water, blood oozing from its grapefruit-sized left nostril.

The AG I circled past the snapping jaws and dove.

Like a mad bull, the Megalodon plunged below the waves to give chase.

Jonas stole a quick glance over his shoulder, confirmed he was being chased, and pushed down on the joystick, whipping the *Abyss Glider* hard to port.

Despite his top speed the Meg was still gaining. *Where to go? Lead her away from Terry, away from the others.* He felt a bump from behind as the Meg rammed his tail fin. He plunged the ship deep, then banked a hard starboard roll and shot to the surface.

The AG I flew out of the water like a flying fish—

—the leaping Megalodon right behind it, its jaws snapping empty air.

Jonas's starboard midwing sliced through the surf, the sub righting itself underwater, heading deep.

The predator flopped back into the ocean, its thunderous splash rivaling that of the largest humpback whale.

Jonas pushed down on the joystick—

Nothing! *The landing must have jarred the battery cable loose again.*

Desperate, he twisted his upper body around, feeling for the loose connection, and quickly slammed it home.

The power engaged, but Jonas had no time. Extending his legs, he kicked his bare left foot against one joystick, pressing his right down against the other.

The submersible jumped, milliseconds ahead of the ten-foot snapping jaws, the passing caudal fin slapping hard against the Lexan nose cone, nearly shattering it.

In one motion he twisted back around in the tight capsule, praying the battery connection would hold.

The Megalodon was upon him again, snapping at his tail assembly. Jonas whipped the sub to port—

—as a red flicker beckoned from his control panel. The batteries were dying!

Jonas spun the submersible around in a tight circle . . . *where was the Meg?* Unable to locate the shark he slowed, registering the rumble of a heavy engine approaching in the distance.

*   *   *

It took Andre Dupont ten minutes to convince the captain of the fishing trawler that his institute would pay for any damages to his vessel. A wad of cash from Etienne sealed the deal, sending the boat racing to rescue the lifeboat's eleven survivors.

Terry Tanaka was pulled on board. She tried to stand, then simply collapsed on deck. Adashek vomited from the stress. DeMarco and several other shipmates fell to their knees, all thanking their maker for sparing their lives.

Twenty-five feet away, the Megalodon grasped the capsized lifeboat in its hyperextended jaws and shook the wooden hull into kindling.

On the opposite side of trawler, the tail assembly of Jonas's powerless submersible bobbed to the surface like a cork.

Jonas kicked at the batteries, but he knew it was hopeless. The voltmeter read zero. The heavier Lexan nose cone settled deeper in the water, Jonas hanging head down in the pilot's harness, reliving a nightmarish déjà vu.

It was eerily quiet, save for the sound of water lapping at the sub. Jonas peered into the gray mist beneath him, the blood pounding in his temples, his hands trembling.

"Get out . . . get out of the sub, J.T.! Do it! Move!" But he couldn't move . . . too afraid, all he could do was stare at the flickering beams of sunlight filtering below.

The female was wary. She had been circling below, sensing her challenger was wounded, waiting for it to die. Now it was time to feed.

She ascended slowly, rising through the gray curtains of light that could no longer harm her, her great caudal fin beating harder as she rose, her jaws agape, opening and closing, nostrils flaring, searching for a scent.

At four hundred feet Jonas saw her. The white face, the satanic grin. It was seven years ago and he was back on the *Seacliff* . . . only this was different, this time there was no retreat, no escape. *I'm going to die*, he thought.

Strangely, he felt no fear.

And then Masao's words came back to him. "If you know the enemy and know yourself, you need not fear the result of a hundred battles."

"I know my enemy," he said aloud, the monster whipping itself into a frenzy as it drove harder toward the surface.

Seventy feet . . .

Jonas reached forward with his right hand, grasped the lever, turning it counterclockwise.

Forty feet.

The mouth opened.

Jonas forced deep breaths.

Twenty feet! The jaws were now fully hyperextended!

Jonas screamed involuntarily, pulling the lever toward him. Hydrogen fuel ignited, transforming the AG I into a rocket, blasting it straight down through the open jaws of the Megalodon.

The black opening jumped at Jonas, the glider shuddering as its wings shredded, the pod shooting on through the open gullet, past cartilaginous ribs before slamming into gelid blackness.

Jonas lay unconscious, suspended from his shoulder harness.

He had entered the gates of hell.

HELL

The Megalodon exploded from the Pacific, its caudal fin nearly clearing the water. For a frozen moment, the thirty-ton monster hung in space like a marlin, then plunged back into its liquid realm, mouth open, dying to quench the fire that burned within.

The Meg's digestive system was relatively short. After food entered its stomach, it traveled through the duodenum, the beginning of the small intestine. Located inside the duodenum was a series of folds—the spiral valve. Similar in shape to a corkscrew, the spiral valve rotated within the Meg's small intestine like a Slinky, providing additional absorption area for the shark to maximize the nutrients of its meal. But the shape of the organ also served another purpose, providing the creature with a means of regurgitating items that could not be properly digested. It is a violent act, so powerful it actually turns the stomach inside out so that it protrudes from the shark's mouth like a pinkish balloon.

The capsulelike remains of the *Abyss Glider* were wreaking havoc within the female's stomach. Circling rapidly in 600 feet of water, the Meg's jaws heaved open in a sudden spasm, its insides attempting to vomit the eight-foot capsule from its gullet.

* * *

Jonas was slammed back into consciousness, the escape pod heaving in darkness, flipping over again and again as the Megalodon's involuntary muscles attempted to regurgitate the capsule back out through its mouth. But the opening was too narrow, the glider's remains unable to align correctly with the orifice. After a dozen attempts, the spasming spiral valve resettled, and the escape pod settled within its alien, pitch black confines.

Jonas hyperventilated. His hands felt for the toggle switch activating the sub's small backup generator, powering the life-support system and emergency lights. He flipped every switch until—

—an exterior light activated, revealing blistering pink insides and swirling brownish objects. Thick, hot, fist-sized chunks of mutilated whale blubber slapped across the acrylic cone. Jonas felt queasy, but couldn't stop himself from looking. He could discern the remains of a porpoise's head, a sneaker, several pieces of wood, and then something that made him gag.

It was a human head, the face—badly burned from stomach acid but still recognizable . . . Danielson!

Jonas gurgled, his scream cut off by the rising vomit. The walls closed in upon him, and he convulsed in fear. The sub shifted hard to one side, rolling with the gaping stomach, sloshing the remains of Taylor's former commanding officer out of sight as the host hurled itself in and out of the ocean, thrashing in agony.

*   *   *

Andre Dupont sat on deck, catching his breath, watching in amazement and fear as the greatest creature ever to inhabit the oceans spasmed out of control. Terry stood, her legs quivering, tears streaming down her cheeks. She had seen the fuel ignite, knew what Jonas had done. At that moment, she realized how deep her feelings were for him.

Leon Barre was arguing with the fishing trawler's owner, warning him that the boat's engines would attract the monster. The older man swore at Barre, swore at Dupont, but decided it might be best to cut the motor.

* * *

Jonas shook uncontrollably, unable to catch a breath, his nerves trembling amid horrific carnage the likes of which could not be imagined. This was claustrophobia, this was hell.

"Stop it! You're alive! Find a way out!"

He forced his mind to reason. *There are two ways out, the way you came in, and . . . and—*

"I can kill it."

It was a statement of fact, a rational thought declared in an irrational setting. "I can kill it." He said it over and over again, convincing himself, building courage, allowing the plan to germinate.

Then he felt it, the reverberation of a pulse, the beating of the monster's heart.

"It's close! It has to be close! Find a way! Tear it out!"

A calm resolve began to settle over Jonas. He had a plan—a ray of hope . . . one shot at escaping, one Lotto chance at surviving an impossible circumstance, but it was there, and it was more than Maggie had, more than Danielson.

Rolling onto his side, he located the small storage compartment below his seat cushion and removed the flashlight, dive mask, and the small pony bottle of air. He made sure the oxygen flowed. Satisfied, he searched for the underwater knife.

It was gone. Now what? How could he possibly cut through the thick muscular tissue of the Meg's stomach lining? Desperate, he felt around the capsule, his fingers settling on the fossilized Meg tooth.

The irony was not lost on him. He smiled. *An eye for an eye . . .*

Jonas secured the small cylinder of air around his head with Velcro straps and fixed the mask to his face, breathing through the regulator.

He was ready.

Flipping around, he unscrewed the escape hatch in the sub's tail. The rubber housing lost its suction with a hiss as he pushed the circular door open. A thick liquid, hot to the touch, oozed into the sub. He poked his head out of the open hatch, shining the flashlight into the darkness.

The mini-sub was wedged tightly in a confined chamber of muscle, its walls constantly moving, churning debris in a caustic atmosphere of humidity, burning excretions, and seawater. The digestive organ protested his presence, high-pitched gurgling noises alternating with a series of low, resonating growls. Beneath it all, the constant thumpa-thumpa of the Megalodon's heart vibrated through Jonas's body.

With no discernible top or bottom, the stomach simply appeared to be a pocket of continually collapsing and expanding muscle. Jonas crawled out of the glider, feeling the submersible shift position as he did so. His right foot touched the stomach lining, giving him the sensation of stepping on a surface of molten putty. A thick liquid oozed from pores in the stomach muscle, squishing between his toes and scalding his feet.

Without warning, the stomach bulged beneath him, the entire compartment rolling 270 degrees. Both his feet slipped out from under him, tossing him blindly onto his back. He could feel the heat of the mucus lining attacking his wet suit. Gagging, he rolled over on all fours and crawled on his hands and knees on the uneven, thickly muscled surface.

His exposed flesh began to burn, and the change in temperature started fogging his mask. Holding his breath, he rose to his knees, removed the mask, and spit inside, rubbing the glass clear. He gagged at the acidic smell, which began to burn his eyes.

Jonas sucked hard on the regulator, returning the mask to his face. Yes, that was better. *Stay calm, breathe slowly*, he coached himself. *Find the cardiac chamber. Feel and listen!*

The stomach shifted again, the *Abyss Glider* rolling at him, driving him down as the Megalodon surfaced. He slid on his belly, his legs suctioned down a two-foot gap leading into the intestines, his upper body following fast!

His head disappeared!

An arm lunged out of the hole, his hand gripping the fossilized tooth, plunging it into the stomach lining like a pickax.

Jonas pulled himself from the hole as the stomach rolled again, a wave of hot refuse washing over him. The mini-sub pinned him to the stomach lining. He held on for dear life as the Meg rose again.

On all fours he registered the sensation of his knees reverberating. Holding the tooth in one hand, the precious flashlight in the other, he drove the serrated edge into the stomach lining, using it like a saw. The thick fibrous tissue began splitting and bleeding, but it was slow work, like cutting through raw meat with a butter knife. Jonas pressed his weight behind each cut, tracing a four-foot-long incision into the thick tissue, rubbing the edges of the blade against the resilient muscle.

*   *   *

With his left hand, Bud Harris flipped the toggle switch, restarting the *Magnate*'s pumps. In his right hand was the gun, cocked and pointed at Mac's head.

"You're activating the pumps?" asked Mac. "You'll attract the Meg."

"I want to attract the Meg. Now move!" Bud pushed the barrel of the gun to the back of Mac's neck, forcing him up the steps and back out to the main deck.

The late afternoon sun beat down on the rapidly sinking yacht.

"That monster destroyed my life, took the one person I truly cared for," said Bud. "It continues to haunt me, preventing me from sleeping, preventing me from living. And you?" Bud pushed his face next to Mac's. "You had to interfere, had to play the hero."

Bud stepped back, motioning for Mac to walk toward the starboard rail. "Go ahead."

"Go ahead and what?" Mac listened for the coast-guard copter, trying to stall.

Bud fired the Magnum, blowing a three-inch hole in the deck. "You wanted to save this monster, now you can feed him." He fired again, this time nicking Mac in his right calf muscle. Mac collapsed onto one leg, blood oozing from the wound.

"The next shot will be at your stomach, so I suggest you jump now."

Mac moved to the rail, climbing over. "This is called murder. You know what they do with murderers?" Mac eased himself into the ocean.

Bud watched him tread water, moving away from the *Magnate*. "This is California. Murder and getting convicted of murder are two different things."

* * *

The female's inflamed stomach was convulsing in involuntary spasmodic contractions along her belly. Agitated, she attacked every motion that attracted her senses, a passing school of fish, sand from the driving current—

The vibrations sent ripples coursing across her lateral line. Accelerating within the thermocline, the female homed in on the hull of the *Magnate* and rammed it, opening a massive fourteen-foot gash along the stern.

Within seconds the yacht began spinning as the flood waters pulled it into the deep.

Bud stood in the bow, holding onto the mahogany rail with one hand, using Mac as target practice with the other. He laughed, amused until the yacht heaved beneath him and the deck started spinning.

The dorsal fin circled, the shark's senses more attuned to the dying *Magnate* than Mac.

Bud aimed at the towering fin and fired, blasting two bloody holes into the albino hide.

The last shot he saved for himself.

As Mac watched, Bud shoved the gun into his mouth and pulled the trigger, blasting the back of his head open like a watermelon.

*   *   *

Through Dupont's binoculars, Leon Barre watched the dorsal fin circle the *Magnate*, three hundred yards away. "Now, Captain, we should go now!"

The trawler's twin engines growled to life, the race on.

The female whipped her head around, her instincts gone mad. She accelerated in pursuit.

*   *   *

Jonas was exhausted, frightened, and running low on air. Whale blubber and other debris were piling up all around him, making him queasy. He refused to look, afraid to see what, or who, it might be.

The tooth finally sliced through the six-inch-thick lining, and Jonas pushed his head and arms through the slit. Having exited the stomach, he found himself in a totally different environment.

The cardiac chamber was a fleshy crawl space no more than a foot wide. Jonas squeezed his body prone into the space, wedging his back against a layer of striated muscle. It gave. Feeling the steady vibrations, he inched his way toward the source, one hand holding the flashlight, the other gripping the tooth.

The bass drum pounded in his brain, its reverberations seeping into his being. He felt the massive organ before he saw it—a throbbing five-foot rounded mass of muscle, enveloped by thick cords of blood vessels.

* * *

The fishing trawler was within two hundred yards of the beach when the Megalodon rammed its keel from below, the impact crushing the twin engines' drive shafts and nearly flipping the boat on its side.

The deck tilted wildly, the force of the collision tossing DeMarco, Terry, and four crewmen over the side into the sea.

The Megalodon went deep, circling below its wounded prey, the icy depths flowing through her open mouth, soothing the burning sensation within her gullet as she prepared to attack once more.

* * *

Jonas wrapped his body around the throbbing heart, his left hand gripping a thick root of blood vessels feeding the four-chambered muscle. His right hand stabbed and sliced blindly in the dark confines, hot liquid gushing everywhere.

*   *   *

Terry surfaced, shocked to see the trawler drifting away from her. Exhausted, it was all she could do just to stay afloat.

The crew yelled at her to swim.

*   *   *

Circling in fifteen hundred feet of water, the female sensed her prey struggling along the surface. She rose once more to feed.

*   *   *

Jonas hacked at the aorta in the pitch black, no longer caring if he lived or died, intent only on sending his monster back into extinction.

A sudden jolt of terror overcame Terry and she swam.

The Meg passed through curtains of warm light, following them up.

DeMarco pleaded for Terry to swim faster!

The Meg opened its jaws, then hyperextended them wider—

Two hundred feet.

Andre Dupont saw the luminescent glow. "Oh dear God—"

One hundred feet.

The female's upper jaw, teeth, gums, and connective tissue emerged from under the snout, projecting forward and away from the skull. The eyes, blind, rolled protectively back in the creature's head. The Meg would consume its prey in one gargantuan bite.

Fifty feet.

Terry reached the boat! Strained to grab DeMarco's hand—

—unable to reach it!

*   *   *

Jonas Taylor could not maintain a grip on the slippery cords. From the shifting angle of the cardiac chamber, he knew the Meg was rising to attack. He thought of Terry.

Anger and adrenaline coursed through his muscles. Wrapping the crook of his left arm around the bundle of cords, he braced his bare feet against the soft tissues of the inner chamber walls and pulled the beating heart downward with all his might. With one powerful slash, he cut deep into the exposed cords with the tooth, severing the organ from its blood supply!

*   *   *

Twelve feet from the surface, its upper jaw locked in hyperextension, the Megalodon slowed. Its nocturnal eyes bulged, its muscles frozen. The only movement came from the powerless caudal fin, which twitched involuntarily.

In total darkness, Jonas lay on his back, covered in hot blood that continued drenching him in buckets. Against his heaving chest lay the detached heart of the 62,000-pound Megalodon. He struggled to breathe from the regulator, hyperventilating from his effort. The drums had stopped, but the claustrophobic chamber was flooding with blood.

Jonas wriggled out from beneath the massive organ, and slid back down the tight walls of the cardiac chamber. His fingers felt something hard, yes, the light. He wiped the lens but the beam was barely perceptible. Feeling around in the near-darkness, he groped blindly for the incision he had made in the stomach.

*   *   *

Terry Tanaka had expected to die. When death did not come, she opened her eyes. The Megalodon's mouth hung open below her . . . the shark sinking! Blood surfaced in gouts, pooling around Terry's lower body.

"Terry, grab the rope," said DeMarco.

"Al, I'm okay. Throw me a mask!"

"Terry!"

"Just do it!"

Dupont grabbed a snorkel and mask and tossed them to her. She pulled the mask over her head, positioned the mouthpiece, and peered below. Through the scarlet-tinted brine, Terry saw a river of blood pouring out of the Megalodon's mouth as it continued to sink. The caudal fin had stopped moving.

*   *   *

Waves of panic rushed over Jonas as he lost all orientation in the darkness. Frustrated, he screamed into the dying pony bottle's regulator—

—his right leg pushing through the stomach incision. He pushed his head inside, flopping forward. *Where was the AG I?*

The Megalodon was angled upright, the lining of its internal anatomy too slippery to climb. Jonas lost his balance and fell into a mass of debris piled at the lower end of the stomach. His head struck something solid—the tail section of the *Glider*.

The exterior light from the AG I cast an eerie luminescent glow in the stomach, revealing the effects of its dying host. The muscular lining no longer convulsed. The undigested contents of the intestines were backing up into the stomach and seeping into a pool, actually raising the nose cone of the submersible. Jonas looked up. Sixteen feet above the stomach entrance, seawater poured into the esophagus, the only possible way out.

Jonas relocated the tail section, now sinking beneath three feet of deformed, half-digested whale blubber. He dug with his arms, scooping a hole in the refuse. His hands found the outer hatch and yanked it open. Slick with the Meg's blood, he slid through the opening, then reached back and secured the hatch.

Standing upright in the eight-foot-long capsule, he felt for the controls that would ignite the hydrogen fuel, praying there was enough left to free himself from his purgatory.

Turning the handle counterclockwise, he pulled.

The remains of the hydrogen ignited, propelling the pod upward along the stomach lining like a rocket scaling a wall. Jonas gripped the joystick as the nose of the AG I shot through the water-filled esophagus, revealing open jaws and a beautiful blue exit into the Pacific!

WHUMMMMP!

The AG I slammed to a halt, the pod wedged upright, caught along the sharp points of the Megalodon's upper and lower rows of teeth.

The carcass continued to sink, taking Jonas with it.

"No! No way!" Jonas launched his frame against the interior of the sub, inching the vessel out of the death-grip—

—each jolt driving the points of the shark's teeth deeper into the Lexan surface.

He hit it again and again, beads of water striking his forehead, as water pressure building in his ears as the pod inched its way toward—

Freedom!

With a last terrible scrape of dental bone on bulletproof plastic, the escape pod popped free from the death grip of the Megalodon and rose like a helium balloon toward the surface.

Jonas breathed. He laughed. He prayed Terry was still alive.

Then he saw the spreading cracks, seawater seeping through the damaged shell of the escape pod.

*   *   *

Mac could swim no farther. Unable to catch his breath, his legs numb, he sensed the creature circling, felt the current generated by its mass before actually spotting the three-foot triangular dorsal fin.

"A great white? Get lost you midget." The caudal fin of the thirteen-foot predator slashed back and forth along the surface, circling him, the shark's nostrils guided to Mac's bleeding leg.

"All right God, here's the deal. You let me escape the Grim Reaper this time, and I promise not to violate most of the commandments."

The shark went deep.

"Okay, all of them, all of them!"

Mac jumped as the harness fell next to him. He looked up, shocked to see the coast-guard rescue chopper.

He slipped one arm into the harness and frantically signaled to the crew to pull him out of the water. The conical head of the shark rose out of the sea just as he was yanked upward.

Mac looked up at the silhouette of the rescue chopper, a smile on his face, tears welling in his eyes. "Well, what do you know . . . rescued by the good ol' U.S. Navy. Saving my sorry ass after all these years." He shook his head. "Lord, you do have a sense of humor after all."

*   *   *

The Lexan cylinder slowed as it took on water, the integrity of the escape pod in serious jeopardy. At five hundred feet, what had been a tiny crack suddenly spider-webbed above Jonas's head. Physically and mentally drained, he could only watch as the cracks began circling the circumference of the cylinder.

Below, the satanic face of the Megalodon continued sinking into the canyon, trailing a river of blood. Jonas watched until the glow diminished, then disappeared entirely into darkness. He had escaped certain death twice, but to survive this day, he needed one more miracle.

Pressure. Air. Pressure and air. The all-consuming mantra entered his mind. Jonas knew nitrogen bubbles were beginning to form in his blood stream.

Four hundred feet. A fine spray of water soaked the interior of the pod. When the crack completed the circumference, the integrity of the structure would collapse under the tremendous pressures.

He tried to prepare himself.

At three hundred feet, the torpedo-shaped pod began vibrating.

I'm too deep . . .

*   *   *

"Terry, get out of the damn water now!" screamed DeMarco.

Terry ignored him, her face down in the water, breathing through the snorkel. The Megalodon was dead, that she knew. But her heart told her that Jonas had survived. She watched as the white glow disappeared.

Andre Dupont sat on the transom as Leon Barre and the trawler's captain disassembled one of the engines. Andre felt dazed and depressed. All his efforts to save the creature—the lobbying, the expense—all for naught. The greatest predator of all time . . . lost.

"I could have died today," he whispered to himself. "For what? To save my killer? What would the society tell my wife and children? 'Ah, Marie, you should be a proud widow. Andre died in the most noble of fashions, giving his life to feed an endangered species.'"

Dupont stood, stretching his sore back. The setting sun still shone strong enough to warm his skin. He watched the golden-yellow beam blaze a path from the horizon across the dark Pacific to the trawler. That was when he sighted the fin.

"Hey! Quickly . . . get the girl out of the water!"

The bone-chilling Pacific poured onto Jonas's head, washing away the Meg's blood. The additional weight had slowed his ascent to a crawl. Jonas shivered in his wet suit. He was afraid to move. He glanced at the depth gauge: two hundred feet.

The pod stopped moving. It began to sink.

Wedging his back against the leather pad, Jonas kicked at the glass.

The pod cracked open, releasing him to the sea.

*   *   *

The three-foot fin circled the fishing trawler. Eleven men as one screamed for Terry to get out of the water.

"That's a great white," yelled Wade Maller. "Terry, it's homing in on the blood!"

The trawler's captain went below and returned with a shotgun. The dorsal fin circled the girl. The captain took aim.

Terry disappeared below the waves.

The shark followed.

*   *   *

Jonas's muscles felt like lead in the freezing seawater, his ears ringing, crushed behind more than four atmospheres of pressure. His nose began bleeding, his legs aching as he scissor-kicked, toward a surface too far away.

One hundred feet.

So deep . . .

Eighty feet.

It wasn't his body anymore.

Don't . . . stop . . .

At fifty-eight feet Jonas saw a heavenly light, the periphery of his vision clouded by darkness.

At thirty-three feet, he blacked out.

Jonas felt nothing. He was flying, moving toward the light without his body, no more pain, no more fear.

I'm in heaven.

*   *   *

Terry grabbed Jonas's wrist as his body began slipping back into the abyss. She kicked hard, pulling water with her left hand. She felt the shark circling. She swam harder.

As her face broke the surface, Terry pulled Jonas's head free of the ocean. He was blue, no sign of breathing. She saw the dorsal fin surface eight feet away, accelerating toward her as the triangular snout broke the water.

The fishing net arced through the air, its lead weights dropping it around and beneath the predator. The creature twisted, attempting to escape, but the captain of the trawler had pulled the net taut. The shark was trapped.

Terry pulled Jonas to the boat. A dozen hands dragged them on board. DeMarco wrapped him in blankets, then verified a weak pulse.

Terry pushed DeMarco aside and began mouth-to-mouth.

A minute passed.

She pressed both palms to Jonas's belly, expelling water from his mouth, and began again.

Another minute passed.

Jonas coughed up a mouthful of water. Terry and DeMarco rolled him onto his side, allowing him to expel the seawater and vomit. She massaged his neck. "My God . . . Are you okay?"

"Just . . . a bad case of indigestion."

She laughed and leaned in closer. "Groucho, Chico, Zeppo, and Gummo, but Harpo was always my favorite."

Jonas smiled. "Bora Bora, huh? Do they have nice hospital facilities?"

"Some of the best." She rubbed his back.

Exhausted, Jonas squinted against the golden dusk.

"Try not to move," she said, stroking his hair. "The coast guard's on its way. They're going to tow us into the lagoon. We have a recompression chamber on site at the Institute." She smiled at him, tears in her eyes.

Jonas looked at her beautiful face, grinning through the pain. *I am in heaven.*

*　　　*　　　*

The shark thrashed back and forth within the fishing net, five feet below the surface, unable to free itself. Andre Dupont followed the captain throughout the boat, attempting to reason with him.

"Captain, you can't kill it," yelled Dupont. "It's a protected species!"

"Look at my boat. She's busted up. I'll kill this fish, stuff it, and sell it to some tourist from New York for twenty thousand. You gonna give me that much, Frenchy?"

Dupont rolled his eyes. "Harm that shark, and you're going to prison!"

The captain's response was interrupted by the blare of the coast guard's horn.

*   *   *

A crewman aboard the coast guard cutter tossed a towline to the disabled fishing trawler. Leon Barre attached it to the ship's bow. Within seconds, the line went taut, and the trawler was dragged into the Tanaka Lagoon.

Behind the trawler's transom, the two-thousand-pound predator continued thrashing within the net.

The massive doors separating the Monterey Bay Sanctuary from the lagoon had been left open for the *Kiku*. The cutter entered the canal.

*   *   *

Jonas was leaning against the transom when the sharp pains struck his elbows. Within seconds, every joint was on fire, stabbing pains running throughout his body.

Terry grabbed him. "What is it?"

"Bends. How much farther?"

They swung south into the main tank of the lagoon, the coast guard towing the fishing trawler toward the eastern bleachers where a physician and nurse were waiting.

"Almost there. Lean against the transom. Try to hold on."

The pain increased; he was dizzy, nauseated. His joints felt as if the Megalodon's teeth were biting down. Opening his eyes, he focused on the great white being towed along the port side of the stern.

Masao Tanaka was waiting by the bleachers, his head heavily bandaged. Mac was there, too, a female paramedic tending to his leg while he flirted.

Terry saw her father and ran to the bow. She waved.

Tears of joy flowed down Masao's cheeks as he waved back.

*　　　*　　　*

Jonas doubled over in pain, he could feel himself losing consciousness. He tried to focus on the predator in the water. She was struggling fiercely, twisting within the confines of the fishing net. Her albino hide cast a soft glow in the growing dusk.

For a brief moment, man and beast made eye contact. The creature's eyes were blue-gray. Jonas stared incredulously at the baby Megalodon. He closed his eyes and smiled.

And then the pain became overwhelming and the submersible pilot lost consciousness as the physician and two paramedics loaded him onto the gurney.

The MEG
series continues in
THE TRENCH (part 2)
and
MEG: PRIMAL WATERS
(part 3).

To contact the author, receive free monthly updates,
or to enter contests to become characters in his
novels, go to
www.SteveAlten.com

ATTENTION SECONDARY SCHOOL TEACHERS

MEG is part of *Adopt-An-Author*, an innovative nationwide non-profit program gaining attention among educators for its success in motivating tens of thousands of reluctant secondary school students to read. The program combines fast-paced thrillers with an interactive website AND direct contact with the author. All teachers receive curriculum materials and posters for their classrooms. The program is FREE to all secondary school teachers and librarians.

Volume discounts are available to participating schools through Tsunami Books.

For more information and to register for Adopt-An-Author, go to www.AdoptAnAuthor.com

New from Tsunami Books:

a 1500 year old legend . . .
One man's nightmare.

The LOCH

by
Steve Alten

Special Sneak Peek

PROLOGUE

Moray Firth
Scottish Highlands
25 September 1330

THE DEEP BLUE WATERS of the Moray Firth crashed violently against the jagged shoreline below. William Calder, second Thane of Cawdor, stood on an outcropping of rock just beyond the point where the boiling North Sea met the mouth of the River Ness. Looking to the south, he could just make out the single-sheeted Spanish galley. The tall ship had been in port since dawn, its crew exchanging silver pieces for wool and cod.

Calder's daughter, Helen, joined him on the lookout. "Ye're needed. A wounded man's come ashore, a soldier. He's demandin' tae see a Templar."

*   *   *

The young man had been left on a grassy knoll. His face was pale and unshaven, his blue-gray eyes glassy with fever. His battle dress, composed of chain mail, was stained crimson along the left quadrant of his stomach. A long sword lay by his side, its blade smeared in blood.

A silver casket, the size of a small melon, hung from his unshaven neck by a gold chain.

William Calder stood over the soldier, joined by two more of his clan. "Who are ye, laddie?"

"I need tae speak wi' a Templar."

"Ye'll speak tae no one 'til ye've dealt wi' me. In whit battle did ye receive yer wounds?"

"Tebas de Ardales."

"An' who did ye fight under?"

"Sir James the Good."

"The Black Douglas?" Calder turned to his men. "Fetch a physician and be quick. Tell him we may need a chirurgeon as well."

"Yes, m'lord." The two men hurried off.

"Why dae ye seek the Templar, laddie?"

The soldier forced his eyes open against the fever. "Only the Templar can be trusted tae guard my keep."

"Is that so?" Calder bent to remove the prized object resting upon the man's chest piece—the soldier's sword raising quickly to kiss Calder's throat. "I'm sorry, m'lord, but I wis instructed tae relinquish this only tae a Templar."

*   *   *

The sun was late in the summer sky by the time Thomas MacDonald arrived at William Calder's home. More Viking than Celt, the burly elder possessed thick auburn-red hair and a matted matching beard. Draped across his broad shoulders was a white tunic, emblazoned with four scarlet equilateral triangles, their points meeting in the center to form a cross.

MacDonald entered without knocking. "A'right, William Calder, why have ye summoned me frae Morayshire?"

Calder pointed to the young soldier, whose wounded left side was being bandaged by a physician. "The laddie claims tae have fought under the Black Douglas. Says he traveled frae Spain tae seek the Templar."

MacDonald approached. "I'm o' the Order, laddie. Who are ye?"

"Adam Wallace. My faither wis Sir Richard Wallace o' Riccarton."

Both men's eyebrows raised. "Ye're kin tae Sir William?"

"He wis my first cousin, my faither his uncle. I still carry William's sword in battle."

Calder examined the offered blade, sixty-six inches from point to pommel. "I dinnae see any markings on the hilt that designate this tae be Sir William's."

MacDonald nodded. "William aye kept it clean. A fine sword it is, fit for an Archangel tae wield, yet light in his terrible hand. " He pointed to the silver casket. "Tell me how ye came by this?"

"I served under Sir William Keith for jist under a year, ever since the Bruce fell tae leprosy. Oor king had aye wished tae take part in the crusades against the Saracens, but kent he wis dyin'. He asked for the contents o' this casket tae be buried in the Church o' the Holy Sepulchre in Jerusalem. The Black Douglas wis tae lead the mission, joined by Sir William Sinclair, Sir Keith, an' mysel'."

"Go on."

"When we arrived in Spain, Alfonso XI of Castile and Leon . . . he convinced Sir James tae join his vanguard against Osmyn, the Moorish governor of Grenada. The Black Douglas agreed, an' we set off on the twenty-fifth of March, that is, all but Sir William Keith, who had injured his arm frae a fa' an' couldnae fight."

"Whit happened?"

"The battle went badly. The Black Douglas wis deceived by a feint, an' the Moors' cavalry broke through oor ranks. It happened so fast, bodies an' blood everywhere, that I could scarcely react. I saw Sir William Sinclair fa' doon, followed by the Black Douglas. An' then a sword caught my flank, an' I fell.

"When next I awoke, it wis dark. My nostrils were fu' o' blood, an' my left side burned. It wis a' I could dae tae regain my feet beneath the bodies. I wanted tae flee, but first I had tae find the Black Douglas. By the half-moon's light, I searched one corpse tae the next 'till I located his body, guardin' the Bruce's casket even in death. By then, the dawn had arrived an' Sir Keith wi' it. He dressed my wounds, but fearful o' another Islamic attack, suggested we separate. I wis tae return tae Scotland, then make my way to Threave Castle, stronghold o' Archibald the Grim, Sir James's son. Sir Keith wis tae return tae the Lowlands an' Melrose Abbey wi' the casket."

"But yer plans changed, I see."

"Aye. On the eve o' oor sail, Sir Keith took sick wi' dropsy. Fearful o' his condition, I decided it best if the casket remained wi' me and too' it frae him."

Calder pulled MacDonald aside. "Do ye believe him?"

"Aye."

"But why does he seek a Templar?"

"Bruce wis a Mason, born intae the Order. The contents o' the casket belong tae Scotland. It represents nothin' less than oor freedom."

MacDonald turned back toward Adam. "Ye were right tae come here, laddie. Whit lies within that silver container's far ower important tae leave in any abbey. There's a cave, a day's walk frae here, known only tae the Templar. If Cooncil agrees, then I'll take the casket there and—"

"No ye willnae!" Adam interrupted. "The coven's between the Bruce an' the Wallace Clan. Direct me, an' I shall take it there mysel'."

"Dinnae be a fool, ye dinnae ken whit ye're sayin'. The cave I've in mind leads tae Hell, guarded by the De'il's ain minions."

"I'm no' feart."

"Aye, but ye will be, Adam Wallace. An' it's a fear ye'll carry wi' ye 'til the end o' yer days."

CHAPTER 1

Sargasso Sea, Atlantic Ocean
887 miles due east of Miami Beach

THE SARGASSO SEA is a two-million-square-mile expanse of warm water, adrift in the middle of the Atlantic Ocean. An oasis of calm that borders no coastline, the sea is littered with sargassum, a thick seaweed that once fooled Christopher Columbus into believing he was close to land.

The Sargasso is constantly moving, its location determined by the North Equatorial and Gulf Stream currents, as well as those of the Antilles, Canary, and Caribbean. These interlocking forces stabilize the sea like the eye of a great hurricane, while causing its waters to rotate clockwise. As a result, things that enter the Sargasso are gradually drawn toward its center like a giant shower drain, where they eventually sink to the bottom, or, in the case of oil, form thick tar balls and float. There is a great deal of oil in the Sargasso, and with each new spill the problem grows worse, affecting all the sea creatures that inhabit the region.

The Sargasso marks the beginning of my tale and its end, and perhaps that is fitting, for all things birthed in this mysterious body of water eventually return here to die, or so I have learned.

If each of us has his or her own Sargasso, then mine was the Highlands of Scotland. I was born in the village of Drumnadrochit, seven months and twenty-five years ago, give or take a few days. My mother, Andrea, was American, a quiet soul who came to the United Kingdom on holiday and stayed nine years in a bad marriage. My father, Angus Wallace, the cause of its termination, was a brute of a man, possessing jet-black hair and the piercing blue eyes of the Gael, the wile of a Scot, and the temperament of a Viking. An only child, I took my father's looks and, thankfully, my mother's disposition.

Angus's claim to fame was that his paternal ancestors were descendants of the great William Wallace himself, a name I doubt most non-Britons would have recognized until Mel Gibson portrayed him in the movie, Braveheart. As a child, I often asked Angus to prove we were kin of the great Sir William Wallace, but he'd merely tap his chest and say, "Listen, runt, some things ye jist feel. When ye become a real man, ye'll ken whit I mean."

I grew to calling my father Angus and he called me his "runt" and neither was meant as an endearing term. Born with a mild case of hypotonia, my muscles were too weak to allow for normal development, and it would be two years (to my father's embarrassment) before I had the strength to walk. By the time I was five I could run like a deer, but being smaller than my burly, big-boned Highland peers, I was always picked on. Weekly contests between hamlets on the football pitch (rugby field) were nightmares. Being fleet of foot meant I had to carry the ball, and I'd often find myself in a scrum beneath boys twice my size. While I lay bleeding and broken on the battlefield, my inebriated father would prance about the sidelines, howling with the rest of his drunken cronies, wondering why the gods had cursed him with such a runt for a son.

According to the child-rearing philosophy of Angus Wallace, tough love was always best in raising a boy. Life was hard, and so childhood had to be hard, or the seedling would rot before it grew. It was the way Angus's father had raised him, and his father's father before that. And if the seedling was a runt, then the soil had to be tilled twice as hard.

But the line between tough love and abuse is often blurred by alcohol, and it was when Angus was inebriated that I feared him most.

His final lesson of my childhood left a lasting impression.

It happened a week before my ninth birthday. Angus, sporting a whisky buzz, led me to the banks of Aldourie Castle, a three-century-old chateau that loomed over the misty black waters of Loch Ness. "Now pay attention, runt, for it's time I telt ye o' the Wallace curse. My faither, yer grandfaither, Logan Wallace, he died in these very waters when I wis aboot yer age. An awfy gale hit the Glen, an' his boat flipped. Everyone says he drooned, but I ken better, see. 'Twis the monster that got him, an' ye best be warned, for—"

"Monster? Are ye talkin' aboot Nessie?" I asked, pie-eyed.

"Nessie? Nessie's folklore. I'm speakin' o' a curse wrought by nature, a curse that's haunted the Wallace men since the passin' o' Robert the Bruce."

"I dinnae understand."

Growing angry, he dragged me awkwardly to the edge of Aldourie Pier. "Look doon, laddie. Look doon intae the Loch an' tell me whit ye see?"

I leaned out carefully over the edge, my heart pattering in my bony chest. "I dinnae see anythin', the water's too black."

"Aye, but if yer eyes could penetrate the depths, ye'd see intae the dragon's lair. The de'il lurks doon there, but it can sense oor presence, it can smell the fear in oor blood. By day the Loch's ours, for the beast prefers the depths, but God help ye at night when she rises tae feed."

"If the monster's real, then I'll rig a lure an' bring her up."

"Is that so? An' who be ye? Wiser men have tried an' failed, an' looked foolish in their efforts, whilst a bigger price wis paid by those drowned who ventured out oot night."

"Ye're jist tryin' tae scare me. I'm no' feart o' a myth."

"Tough words. Very well, runt, show me how brave ye are. Dive in. Go on, laddie, go for a swim and let her get a good whiff o' ye."

He pushed me toward the edge and I gagged at his breath, but held tight to his belt buckle.

"Jist as I thought."

Frightened, I pried myself loose and ran from the pier, the tears streaming down my cheeks.

"Ye think I'm hard on ye, laddie? Well, life's hard, an' I'm nothin' compared tae that monster. Ye best pay attention, for the curse skips every other generation, which means ye're marked. That dragon lurks in the shadow o' yer soul, and one day ye'll cross paths. Then what will ye dae? Will ye stand and fight like a warrior, like brave Sir William an' his kin, or will ye cower an' run, lettin' the dragon haunt ye for the rest o' yer days?"

*　　*　　*

Leaning out over the starboard rail, I searched for my reflection in the Sargasso's glassy surface.

Seventeen years had passed since my father's "dragon" lecture, seventeen long years since my mother had divorced him and moved us to New York. In that time I had lost my accent and learned that my father was right, that I was indeed haunted by a dragon, only his name was Angus Wallace.

Arriving in a foreign land is never easy for a boy, and the physical and psychological baggage I carried from my childhood left me fodder for the bullies of my new school. At least in Drumnadrochit I had allies like my pal, True MacDonald, but here I was all alone, a fish out of water, and there were many a dark day that I seriously considered ending my life.

And then I met Mr. Tkalec.

Joe Tkalec was our middle school's science teacher, a kind Croatian man with rectangular glasses, a quick wit, and a love for poetry. Seeing that the "Scottish weirdo" was being picked on unmercifully, Mr. Tkalec took me under his wing, allowing me special classroom privileges like caring for his lab animals, small deeds that helped nurture my self-image. After school, I'd ride my bike over to Mr. Tkalec's home, which contained a vast collection of books.

"Zachary, the human mind is the instrument that determines how far we'll go in life. There's only one way to develop the mind and that's to read. My library's yours, select any book and take it home, but return only after you've finished it."

The first volume I chose was the oldest book in his collection, *The Origins of an Evolutionist*, my eyes drawn by the author's name, Alfred Russel Wallace.

Born in 1823, Alfred Wallace was a brilliant British evolutionist, geographer, anthropologist, and theorist, often referred to as Charles Darwin's right-hand man, though their ideas were not always in step. In his biography, Alfred mentioned that he too was a direct descendant of William Wallace, making us kin, and that he also suffered childhood scars brought about by an overbearing father.

The thought of being related to Alfred Wallace instantly changed the way I perceived myself, and his words regarding adaptation and survival put wind in my fallen sails.

"... *we have here an acting cause to account for that balance so often observed in Nature—a deficiency in one set of organs always being compensated by an increased development of some others . . ."*

My own obstinate father, a man who had never finished grammar school, had labeled me weak, his incessant badgering (I need tae make ye a man, Zachary) fostering a negative self-image. Yet here was my great-uncle Alfred, a brilliant man of science, telling me that if my physique made me vulnerable, then another attribute could be trained to compensate.

That attribute would be my intellect.

My appetite for academics and the sciences became voracious. Within months I established myself as the top student in my class, by the end of the school year, I was offered the chance to skip the next grade. Mr. Tkalec continued feeding me information, while his roommate, a retired semipro football player named Troy, taught me to hone my body into something more formidable to my growing list of oppressors.

For the first time in my life, I felt a sense of pride. At Troy's urging, I tried out for freshman football. Aided by my tutor's coaching and a talent for alluding defenders (acquired, no doubt, on the pitch back in Drumnadrochit) I rose quickly through the ranks, and by the end of my sophomore year, I found myself the starting tailback for our varsity football team.

Born under the shadow of a Neanderthal, I had evolved into *Homo sapiens*, and I refused to look back.

Mr. Tkalec remained my mentor until I graduated, helping me secure an academic scholarship at

Princeton. Respecting my privacy, he seldom broached subjects concerning my father, though he once told me that Angus's dragon story was simply a metaphor for the challenges that each of us must face in life. "Let your anger go, Zack, you're not hurting anyone but yourself."

Gradually I did release my contempt for Angus, but unbeknownst to both Mr. Tkalec and myself, there was still a part of my childhood that remained buried in the shadows of my soul, something my subconscious mind refused to acknowledge.

Angus had labeled it a dragon.

If so, the Sargasso was about to set it free.

*   *   *

The afternoon haze seemed endless, the air lifeless, the Sargasso as calm as the Dead Sea. It was my third day aboard the *Manhattanville*, a 162-foot research vessel designed for deep-sea diving operations. The forward half of the boat, four decks high, held working laboratories and accommodations for a dozen crew members, six technicians, and twenty-four scientists. The aft deck, flat and open, was equipped with a twenty-one-ton A-frame PVS crane system, capable of launching and retrieving the boat's small fleet of remotely operated vehicles (ROVs) and its primary piece of exploration equipment, the *Massett-6*, a vessel designed specifically for bathymetric and bottom profiling.

It was aboard the *Massett-6* in this dreadful sea that I hoped to set my own reputation beside that of my great Uncle Alfred.

Our three-day voyage had delivered us to the approximate center of the Sargasso. Clumps of golden brown seaweed mixed with black tar balls washed gently against our boat, staining its gleaming white hull a chewing tobacco brown as we waited for sunset, our first scheduled dive.

Were there dragons waiting for me in the depths? Ancient mariners once swore as much. The Sargasso was considered treacherous, filled with sea serpents and killer weeds that could entwine a ship's keel and drag it under. Superstition? No doubt, but as in all legend, there runs a vein of truth. Embellishments of eye-witnessed accounts become lore over time, and the myth surrounding the Sargasso was no different.

The real danger lies in the sea's unusual weather. The area is almost devoid of wind, and many a sailor who once entered these waters in tall sailing ships never found their way out.

As our vessel was steel, powered by twin diesel engines and a 465-horsepower bow thruster, I had little reason to worry.

Ah, how the seeds of cockiness blossom when soiled in ignorance.

While fate's clouds gathered ominously on my horizon, all my metallic-blue eyes perceived were fair skies. Still young at twenty-five, I had already earned a bachelor's and master's degree from Princeton and a doctorate from the University of California at San Deigo, and three of my papers on cetacean communication had recently been published in *Nature* and *Science*. I had been invited to sit on the boards of several prominent oceanographic councils, and, while teaching at Florida Atlantic University, I had invented an underwater acoustics device—a device responsible for this very voyage of discovery, accompanied by a film crew shooting a documentary sponsored by none other than *National Geographic Explorer*.

By society's definition, I was a success, always planning my work, working my plan, my career the only life I ever wanted. Was I happy? Admittedly, my emotional barometer may have been a bit off-kilter. I was pursuing my dreams, and that made me happy, yet it always seemed like there was a dark cloud hanging over head. My fiancée, Lisa, a "sunny" undergrad at FAU, claimed I had a "restless soul," attributing my demeanor to being too tightly wound.

"Loosen up, Zack. You think way too much, it's why you get so many migraines. Cut loose once in a while, get high on life instead of always analyzing it. All this left-brain thinking is a turnoff."

I tried "turning off," but found myself too much of a control freak to let myself go.

One person whose left brain had stopped functioning long ago was David James Caldwell II. As I quickly learned, the head of FAU's oceanography department was a self-promoting hack who had maneuvered his way into a position of tenure based solely on his ability to market the achievements of his staff. Six years my superior, with four years less schooling, David nevertheless presented himself to our sponsors as if he were my mentor, me, *his* protégé. "Gentlemen, members of the board, with my help, Zachary Wallace could become this generation's Jacques Cousteau."

David had arranged our journey, but it was my invention that made it all possible—a cephalopod lure, designed to attract the ocean's most elusive predator, *Architeuthis dux,* the giant squid.

Our first dive was scheduled for nine o'clock that night, still a good three hours away. The sun was just beginning to set as I stood alone in the bow, staring at endless sea, when my solitude was shattered by David, Cody Saults, our documentary's director, his cameraman and wife, and the team's sound person.

"There's my boy," David announced. "Hey, Zack, we've been looking all over the ship for you. Since we still have light, Cody and I thought we'd get some of the background stuff out of the way. Okay by you?"

Cody and I? Now he was executive producer?

"Whatever you'd like, Mr. Saults."

The cameraman, a good-natured soul named Hank Griffeth, set up his tripod while his wife, Cindy, miked me for sound. Cindy wore a leopard bikini that accentuated her cleavage, and it was all I could do to keep from sneaking a peek.

Just using the right side of my brain, Lisa . . .

Cody chirped on endlessly, forcing me to refocus. ". . . anyway, I'll ask you and David a few questions off-camera. Back in the studio, our editors will dub in Patrick Stewart's voice over mine. Got it?"

"I like Patrick Stewart. Will I get to meet him?"

"No, now pay attention. Viewers want to know what makes young Einsteins like you and David tick. So when I ask you about—"

"Please don't call me that."

Cody smiled his Hollywood grin. "Listen kid, humble's great, but you and Dr. Caldwell are the reason we're floating in this festering, godforsaken swamp. So if I tell you you're a young Einstein, you're a young Einstein, got it?"

David, a man sporting an IQ seventy points lower than the deceased Princeton professor, slapped me playfully across the shoulder blades. "Just roll with it, kid."

"We're ready here," Hank announced, looking through his rubber eyepiece. "You've got about fifteen minutes of good light left."

"Okay boys, keep looking out to sea, nice and casual . . . and we're rolling. So Zack, let's start with you. Tell us what led you to invent this acoustic thingama-jiggy."

I focused on the horizon as instructed, the sun splashing gold on my tanned complexion. "Well, I've spent most of the last two years studying cetacean echolocation. Echolocation is created by an acoustic organ, unique in dolphins and whales, that provides them with an ultrasonic vision of their environment. For example, when a sperm whale clicks, or echolocates, the sound waves bounce off objects, sending back audio frequency pictures of the mammal's surroundings."

"Like sonar?"

"Yes, only far more advanced. For instance, when a dolphin echolocates a shark, it not only sees its environment, but it can actually peer into the shark's belly to determine if it's hungry. Sort of like having a built-in ultrasound. These clicks also function as a form of communication among other members of the cetacean species, who can tap into the audio transmission spectrum, using it as a form of language.

"Using underwater microphones, I've been able to create a library of echolocation clicks. By chance, I discovered that certain sperm whale recordings, taken during deep hunting dives, stimulated our resident squid population to feed."

"That's right," David blurted out, interrupting me. "Squid, intelligent creatures in their own right, often feed on the scraps left behind by sperm whales. By using the sperm whales' feeding frequency, we were able to entice squid to the microphone, creating, in essence, a cephalopod lure."

"Amazing," Cody replied. "But fellows, gaining the attention of a four-foot squid is one thing, how do you think this device will work in attracting a giant squid? I mean, you're talking about a deep-sea creature, sixty feet in length, that's never been seen alive."

"They're still cephalopods," David answered, intent on taking over the interview. "While it's true we've never seen a living specimen, we know from carcasses that have washed ashore and by remains found in the bellies of sperm whales that the animals' anatomies are similar to those of their smaller cousins."

"Fantastic. David, why don't you give us a quick rundown of this first dive."

I held my tongue, my wounded ego seething.

"Our cephalopod lure's been attached to the retractable arm of the submersible. Our goal is to descend to thirty-three hundred feet, entice a giant squid up from the abyss, then capture it on film. Because *Architeuthis* prefers the very deep waters, deeper than our submersible can go, we're waiting until dark to begin our expedition, hoping the creatures will ascend with nightfall, following the food chain's nocturnal migration into the shallows."

"Explain that last bit. What do you mean by nocturnal migration?"

"Why don't I let Dr. Wallace take over," David offered, bailing out before he had to tax his left brain.

I inhaled a few temper-reducing breaths. "Giant squids inhabit an area known as the mid-water realm, by definition, the largest continuous living space on Earth. While photosynthesis initiates food chains among the surface layers of the ocean, in the mid-water realm, the primary source of nutrients come from phytoplankton, microscopic plants. Mid-water creatures live in absolute darkness, but once the sun sets, they rise en masse to graze on the phytoplankton, a nightly event that's been described as the largest single migration of living organisms on the planet."

"Great stuff, great stuff. Hank, how's the light?"

"Fifteen minutes, give or take."

"Let's keep moving, getting more into the personal. Zack, tell us about yourself. Dr. Caldwell tells me you're an American citizen, originally from Scotland."

"Yes. I grew up in the Scottish Highlands, in a small village called Drumnadrochit."

"That's at the head of Urquhart Bay, on Loch Ness," David chimed in.

"Really?"

"My mother's American," I said, the red flags waving in my brain. "My parents met while she was on holiday. We moved to New York when I was nine."

With a brazen leer, David leaned forward, mimicking a Scots accent, "Dr. Wallace is neglecting the time he spent as a wee laddie, hangin' oot wi' visitin' teams o' Nessie hunters, aren't ye, Dr. Wallace?"

I shot David a look that would boil flesh.

The director naturally jumped on his lead. "So it was actually the legend of the Loch Ness Monster that stoked your love of science. Fascinating."

And there it was, the dreaded "M" word. Loch Ness was synonymous with Monster, and Monster meant Nessie, a cryptozoologist's dream, a marine biologist's nightmare. Nessie was "fringe" science, an industry of folklore, created by tourism and fast-talkers like my father.

Being associated with Nessie had destroyed many a scientist's career, most notably Dr. Denys Tucker, of the British Museum of Natural History. Dr. Tucker had held his post for eleven years, and, at one time, had been considered the foremost authority on eels ... until he hinted to the press that he was interested in launching an investigation into the Loch Ness Monster.

A short time later he was dismissed, his career as a scientist all but over.

Being linked to Loch Ness on a *National Geographic* special could destroy my reputation as a serious scientist, but it was already too late. David had led me to the dogshit, and, as my mother would say, I had "stepped in it." Now the goal was to keep from dragging it all over the carpet.

"Let me be clear here," I proclaimed, my booming voice threatening Hank's wife's microphone, "I was never actually one of those 'Nessie' hunters."

"Ah, but you've always had an interest in Loch Ness, haven't you?" David crowed, still pushing the angle.

He was like a horny high school boy, refusing to give up after his date said she wasn't in the mood. I turned to face him, catching the full rays of the setting sun square in my eyes—a fatal mistake for a migraine sufferer.

"Loch Ness is a unique place, Dr. Caldwell," I retorted, "but not everyone who visits comes looking for monsters. As a boy, I met many serious environmentalists who were there strictly to investigate the Loch's algae content, or its peat, or its incredible depths. They were naturalists, like my great ancestor, Alfred Russel Wallace. You see, despite all this nonsense about legendary water beasts, the Loch remains a magnificent body of water, unique in its—"

"But most of these teams came searching for Nessie, am I right?"

I glanced in the direction of David's boyish face, with its bleached-blond mustache and matching Moe Howard bangs, but all I could see were spots, purple demons that blinded my vision.

Migraine . . .

My skin tingled at the thought. I knew I needed to pop a *Zomig* before the brain storm moved into its more painful stages, yet on I babbled, trying desperately to salvage the interview and possibly, my career.

"Well, David, it's not like you can escape it. They've turned Nessie into an industry over there, haven't they?"

"And have you ever spotted the monster?"

I wanted to choke him right on-camera. I wanted to rip the shell necklace from his paisley Hawaiian shirt and crush his puny neck in my bare hands, but my left brain, stubborn as always, refused to relinquish control. "Excuse me, Dr. Caldwell, I thought we were here to discuss giant squids?"

David pushed on. "Stay with me, kid, I'm going somewhere with this. Have you ever spotted the monster?"

I forced a laugh, my right eye beginning to throb. "Look, I don't know about you, *Dr. Caldwell*, but I'm a marine biologist. We're supposed to leave the myth chasing to the crypto guys."

"Ah, but you see, that's exactly my point. It wasn't long ago that these giant squids were considered more myth than science. The legend of the Scylla in the *Odyssey*, the monster in Tennyson's poem, 'The Kraken.' As a young boy growing up so close to Loch Ness, surely you must have been influenced by the greatest legend of them all?"

Cody Saults was loving it, while tropical storm David, located in the latitude of my right eye, was increasing into a hurricane.

". . . maybe hunting for Nessie as a child became the foundation for your research into locating the elusive giant squid. I'm not trying to put words in your mouth, but—"

"Butts are for crapping, Dr. Caldwell, and so's everything that follows! Nessie's crap, too. It's nothing but a nonsensical legend embellished to increase Highland tourism. I'm not a travel agent, I'm a scientist in search of a real sea creature, not some Scottish fabrication. Now if you two will excuse me, I need to use the head."

Without waiting, I pushed past David and the director and entered the ship's infrastructure, in desperate search of the nearest bathroom. The purple spots were gone, the eye pain already intensifying. The next phase would be vomiting—brain-rattling, vein-popping vomiting. This would be followed by weakness and pain and more vomiting, and eventually, if I didn't put a bullet through my skull, I'd mercifully pass out.

It was misery, which is why, like all migraine suf-
ferers, I tried to avoid things that set me off: direct
lighting, excessive caffeine, and the stress that, to me,
revolved around the taboo subject of my childhood.

My stomach was already gurgling, the pain in my
eye crippling as I hurried past lab doors and state-
rooms. Ducking inside the nearest bathroom, I locked
the door, knelt by the toilet, shoved a sacrificial digit
down my throat, and puked.

The intestinal tremor released my lunch, threatening to implode the blood vessels leading to my brain.
It continued on, until my stomach was empty, my will
to live sapped.

For several moments I remained there, my head balanced on the cool, bacteria-laced rim of the toilet.

Maybe Lisa was right. Maybe I did need to loosen up.

*   *   *

It was dark by the time I emerged on deck, my long
brown hair matted to my forehead, my blue eyes glassy
and bloodshot. The migraine had left me weak and
shaky, and I'd have preferred to remain in bed, but it
was nearly time to descend, and I knew David would
grab my spot aboard the sub in a New York minute if
I waited any longer.

A blood-red patch of light revealed all that was
left of the western horizon, the sweltering heat of
day yielding to the coolness of night. Inhaling several
deep lungfuls of fresh air, I made my way aft to the
stern, now a hub of activity. The ship's lights were
on, creating a theater by which four technicians and

a half dozen scientists completed their final check on the *Massett-6*, the twenty-seven-foot-long submersible now suspended four feet off the deck like a giant alien insect.

Able to explore depths down to thirty-five hundred feet, the *Massett-6* was a three-man deep-sea sub that consisted of an acrylic glasslike observation bubble, mounted to a rectangular-shaped aluminum chamber, its walls five inches thick. Running beneath the submersible was an exterior platform and skid that supported flotation tanks, hoses, recording devices, gas cylinders containing oxygen and air, primary and secondary batteries, a series of collection baskets, arc lights, a hydraulic manipulator arm, and nine 100-pound thrusters.

I caught David leaning against the sub, hastily pulling on a blue and gold jumpsuit—*my* jumpsuit—when he saw me approach. "Zack? Where've you been? We, uh, we didn't think you were going to make it."

"Nice try. Now take off my jumpsuit, I'm fine."

"You look pale."

"I said I'm fine, no thanks to you. What was all that horseshit about Loch Ness? You trying to discredit me on national TV?"

"Of course not. We're a team, remember? I just thought it made for a great angle. *Discovery Channel* loves that mysterious stuff, we can pitch them next."

"Forget it. I've worked way too hard to destroy my reputation with this nonsense. Now, for the last time, get your scrawny butt outta my jumpsuit."

"We're ready here," announced Ace Futrell, our mission coordinator. "Mr. Wallace, if you'd care to grace us with your presence."

The cameras rolled. David, back to playing the dutiful mentor, animated a few last-minute instructions to me as I slid my feet into the jumpsuit. "Remember, kid, this is our big chance, it's our show. Work the audience. Relate to them. Get 'em on your side."

"Chill out, David. This isn't an infomercial."

The hatch of the *Massett-6* was located beneath the submersible's aft observation compartment behind the main battery assembly. Kneeling below the sub, I poked my head and shoulders into the opening and climbed up.

The vehicle's interior was a cross between a helicopter cockpit and an FBI surveillance van. The claustrophobic aluminum chamber was crammed with video monitors, life-support equipment, carbon dioxide scrubbers, and gas analyzers, along with myriad pipes and pressurized hoses. Conversely, the forward compartment was a two-seat acrylic bubble that offered panoramic views of the sub's surroundings.

Taking my assigned place up front in the copilot's seat, I tightened the shoulder harness, then inspected the controls of my sonic lure, which had been jury-rigged to the console on my right. Everything seemed stat. Looking above my head out of the bubble, I watched as a technician double-checked the lure's underwater speaker, now attached to the vessel's exterior tow hook.

Donald Lacombe, the sub's pilot, joined me in the cockpit, wasting little time in establishing who was boss. "All right, boy genius, here's the drill. Keep your keister in your seat and don't touch anything without being told. *Capische?*"

"Aye, aye, sir."

"And nobody likes a smart-ass. You're in my vessel now, blah blah blah blah blah." Tuning him out, I turned to watch Hank Griffeth as he climbed awkwardly into the aft compartment. A crewman handed him up his camera, then sealed the rear hatch.

The radio squawked. "Control to *Six*, prepare to launch."

Lacombe spoke into his headset, clearly in his element. "Roger that, Ace, prepare to launch."

Moments later, the A-frame's crane activated, and the submersible rose away from the deck, extending twenty feet beyond the stern. The *Manhattanville's* keel lights illuminated, creating an azure patch in the otherwise dark, glassy surface, and we were lowered into the sea.

For the next ten minutes, divers circled our sub, detaching its harness and rechecking hoses and equipment. Lacombe kept busy, completing his checklist with Ace Futrell aboard the research ship, while Donald showed me photos of his children.

"So when will you and this fiancée of yours start having kids? Nothing like a few rug rats running around to make a house a home."

No problem havin' children, runt. The Wallace curse skips every other generation.

"Zack?"

"Huh?" I shook my head, the lingering ache of the migraine scattering my estranged father's words. "Sorry. No kids, at least not for a while. Too much work to do."

I returned my attention to the control panel, forcing my thoughts back to to our voyage. Descending thousands of feet into the ocean depths was similar to flying. One is always aware of the danger, yet comforted in the knowledge that the majority of planes land safely, just as most subs return to the surface. I had been in a submersible twice before, but this voyage was different, meant to attract one of the most dangerous, if least understood, predators in the sea.

My heart pounded with excitement, the adrenaline escorting Angus's words from my thoughts.

Ace Futrell's commands filtered over the radio. "Control to *Six*, you are clear to submerge. Bon voyage, and good hunting."

"Roger that, Control. See you in the morning."

Lacombe activated the ballast controls, allowing seawater to enter the pressurized tanks beneath the sub. Weighed down, the neutrally buoyant *Massett-6* began to sink, trailing a stream of silvery air bubbles.

The pilot checked his instruments, activated his sonar, engaged his thrusters, then turned to me. "Hey, rookie, ever been in one of these submersibles?"

"Twice, but the missions were only two hours long. Nothing like this."

"Then we'll keep it simple. Batteries and air scrubbers'll allow us to stay below up to eighteen hours, but maneuverability's the pits. Top speed's one knot, best depth's thirty-five hundred feet. We drop too far below that, and the hull will crush like a soda can. Pressure will pop your head like a grape."

I acknowledged the pilot's attempt to put me in my place, countering with my own. "Know much about giant squids? This vessel's twenty-seven feet. The creature we're after is more than twice its size—forty to fifty feet—weighing in excess of a ton. Once we make contact with one of these monsters, be sure to follow my exact instructions."

It's okay to use the "M" word when attempting to intimidate.

Lacombe shrugged it off, but I could tell he was weighing my words. "Three hundred feet," he called out to Hank, who was already filming. "Activating exterior lights."

The twin beams lanced through the black sea, turning it a Mediterranean blue.

And what a spectacle it was, like being in a giant fishbowl in the middle of the greatest aquarium on Earth. I gawked for a full ten minutes before turning to face the camera, doing my best Carl Sagan impression.

"We're leaving the surface waters now, approaching what many biologists call the 'twilight zone.' As we move deeper, we'll be able to see how the creatures that inhabit these mid-water zones have adapted to life in the constant darkness."

Lacombe pointed, refusing to be upstaged. "Looks like we've got our first visitor."

A bizarre jellylike giant with a pulsating bell-shaped head drifted past the cockpit, the creature's transparent forty-five-foot-long body set aglow in our artificial lights.

"That's a siphonophore," I stated, fully immersed in lecture mode. "Its body's made up of millions of stinger cells that trail through the sea like a net as it searches for food."

Next to arrive were a half dozen piranha-sized fish, with bulbous eyes and terrifying fangs. As they turned, their flat bodies reflected silvery-blue in the sub's beams.

"These are hatchet fish," I went on. "Their bodies contain light-producing photo-phores which countershade their silhouettes, allowing them to blend with the twilight sea. In these dark waters, it's essential to see but not be seen. As we move deeper, we'll find more creatures who rely on bioluminescence not only to camouflage themselves, but to attract prey."

Jellyfish of all sizes and shapes drifted silently past the cockpit, their transparent bodies glowing a deep red in the sub's lights. "Pilot, would you shut down the lights a moment?"

He shot me a perturbed look, then reluctantly powered off the beams.

We were surrounded by the silence of utter blackness.

"Watch," I whispered.

A sudden flash appeared in the distance, followed by a dozen more, and suddenly the sea was alive with a pyrotechnic display of bioluminescence as a thousand neon blue lightbulbs flashed randomly in the darkness.

"Amazing," Hank muttered, continuing to film. "It's like these fish are communicating."

"Communicating and hunting," I agreed. "Nature always finds a way to adapt, even in the harshest environments."

"Two thousand feet," the pilot announced.

An adult gulper eel slithered by, its mouth nearly unhinging as it engulfed an unsuspecting fish. All in all, I couldn't have asked for a better performance.

But the best was yet to come.

It was getting noticeably colder in the cabin, so I zipped up my jumpsuit, too full of pride to ask the pilot to raise the heat.

Hank repositioned his camera, then reviewed the list of prompts Cody Saults had given him. "Okay, Zack, tell us about the giant squid. I read where you think it might actually be a mutation?"

"It's just a theory."

"Sounds interesting, give us a rundown. Wait . . . give me a second to re-focus. Okay, go ahead."

"Mutations happen all the time in nature. They can be caused by radiation, or spontaneously, or sometimes by the organism itself as a form of adaptation to changes within its environment. Most mutations are neutral, meaning they have no effect upon the organism. Some, however, can be very beneficial or very harmful, depending upon the environment and circumstance.

"Mutations that affect the future of a particular species are heritable changes in particular sequences of nucleotides. Without these mutations, evolution as we know it wouldn't be possible. For instance, the accidents, errors, and lucky circumstances that caused humans to evolve from lower primates were all mutations. Some mutations lead to dead ends, or extinction of the species. Neanderthal, for instance, was a dead-end mutation. Other mutations can alter the size of a particular genus, creating a new species altogether.

"In the case of *Architeuthis dux*, here we have a cephalopod, a member of the family *teuthid*, yet this particular offshoot has evolved into the largest invertebrate on the planet. Is it a mutation? Most certainly. The question is, why did it mutate in the first place? Perhaps as a defense mechanism against huge predators like the sperm whale. Was it a successful mutation or a dead end? Since we know so little about the creatures, it's impossible to say. Then again, who's to say *Homo sapiens* will be a success?"

The pilot rolled his eyes at my philosophical whims. "We just passed twenty-three hundred feet. Isn't it time you activated that device of yours?"

"Oh, yeah." Reaching to my right, I powered up the lure, sending a series of pulsating clicks chirping through the timeless sea.

I sat back, heart pounding with excitement, waiting for my "dragon" to appear.

* * *

"Yo, Jacques Cousteau Junior, it's been six hours. What happened to your giant octopus?"

I looked up at the pilot from behind my copy of *Popular Science*. "I don't know. There's no telling what kind of range the lure has, or whether a squid's even in the area."

The pilot returned to his game of solitaire. "Not exactly the answer *National Geographic*'ll want to hear."

"Hey, this is science," I snapped. "Nature works on her own schedule." I looked around at the black sea. "How deep are we anyway?"

"Twenty-seven hundred feet."

"Christ, we're not deep enough! I specifically asked for thirty-three hundred feet. Giant squids prefer the cold. We need to be deeper, below the thermocline, or we're just wasting our time."

Lacombe's expression soured, knowing I had him by the short and curlies. "*Six* to Control. Ace, the kid wants me to descend to thirty-three hundred feet."

"Stand by, *Six*." A long silence, followed by the expected answer.

"Permission granted."

* * *

A half mile to the south and eleven hundred fathoms below, the monster remained dead still in the silence and darkness. Fifty-nine feet of mantle and tentacles were condensed within a crevice of rock, its 1,900-pound body ready to uncoil like the spring on a mousetrap.

The carnivore scanned the depths with its two amber eyes, each as large as dinner plates. As intelligent as it was large, it could sense everything within its environment.

* * *

The female angler fish swam slowly past the outcropping of rock, dangling her own lure, a long spine tipped with a bioluminous bait. Attached to the underside of the female, wagging like a second tail were the remains of her smaller mate. In an unusual adaptation of sexual dimorphism, the male angler had ended its existence by biting into the body of the female, his mouth eventually fusing with her skin until the two bloodstreams had connected as one. Over time, the male would degenerate, losing his eyes and internal organs, becoming a permanent parasite, totally dependent upon the female for food.

Feeding for two, the female maneuvered her glowing lure closer to the outcropping of rock.

Whap!

Lashing through the darkness like a bungee cord, one of the squid's eighteen-foot feeder tentacles grasped the female angler within its leaf-shaped pad, piercing the stunned fish with an assortment of hooks protruding from its deadly rows of suckers. Drawing its prey toward its mouth, the hunter's parrotlike beak quickly crushed the meat into digestible chunks, its tongue guiding the morsels down its throat, the meat actually passing through its brain on its way to its stomach.

Architeuthis dux pushed its twelve-foot torpedo-shaped head out of its craggy habitat, then swallowed the remains of the angler fish in one gulp.

The giant squid was still hungry, its appetite having been teased over the last eight hours by the sonic lure. Though tempted to rise and feed on what it perceived as the remains of a sperm whale kill, the immense cephalopod had remained below, refusing to venture into the warmer surface waters.

Now, as it finished off the remains of its snack, it detected the enticing presence moving closer, entering the cooler depths.

Hunger overruled caution. Drawing its eight arms free of the fissure, it pushed away from the rocky bottom and rose, its anvil-shaped tail fin propelling it through the darkness, its movements alerting *another* species in the Sargasso food chain to its presence.

*   *   *

Blip.

Blip . . . blip . . . blip . . .

Donald Lacombe stared at the sonar, playing up the drama for the camera. "It's a biologic, and it's big, headed right for us. Fifteen hundred feet and closing."

"Are we in any danger?" I asked, suddenly feeling vulnerable.

"I don't know, you're the marine biologist. Nine hundred feet. Stand by, it's slowing. Maybe it's checking us out?"

"It doesn't like the bright lights," I countered. "Switch to red lights only."

The pilot adjusted the outer beams, rotating the lenses to their less-brilliant red filters. "That did it, it's coming like a demon now. Three hundred feet. Two hundred. Better hold on!"

Seconds passed, and then the *Massett-6* shuddered, rolling hard to starboard as the unseen beast latched on to our main battery and sled.

My heart pounded, then I nearly jumped out of my shoes when the padded sucker, as wide as a catcher's mitt, snaked its way across the outside of our protective bubble.

Eight more tentacles joined in the dance, each appendage as thick as a fire hose, all moving independently from its still unseen owner.

Even the pilot was impressed. "Jeez–us, you actually did it! And will you look at the size of those tentacles? He must be a monster."

"She," I corrected. "Females grow much larger than males, and this monster's definitely a female."

Ah, the "M" word again. If only I had known . . .

The pilot flicked the toggle switch on his radio. "*Six* to Control, break out the bubbly, Ace, we've made contact."

We could hear clapping coming from the control room.

"We're getting the feed. Congratulations, partner," David broke in over the radio, "we did it."

"Yeah, *we*," I mumbled.

The sound of wrenching aluminum caused me to jump. "What was—"

"Stand by." Lacombe seemed genuinely concerned, and that worried me. At three thousand feet, water pressure is a hundred times greater than at the surface, meaning even the slightest breach in our hull would kill us in a matter of seconds.

What if she tears loose a plate? What if she breaks open a seal?

The thought of drowning sent waves of panic crawling through my belly.

"Hey!" Hank aimed his camera at one of the video monitors. The grainy gray picture revealed an impossibly large tubular body and the edge of one gruesome eye, as massive as an adult human's head. Several of the squid's tentacles were tugging at the sealed lid on one of the collection baskets.

"She's only after the fish," I declared, praying I was right. The creature tore the lid off the steel basket as if it were a child's toy, releasing 200 pounds of salmon to the sea.

As we watched, one of the two longer feeding tentacles deftly corralled a fish, while the others resealed the collection basket, preventing more fish from drifting away.

The pilot shook his head, amazed. "Now that's impressive."

"Yes," I agreed, trying to mask my concern. "Her brain's large and complex, with a highly developed nervous system."

"Control to *Six*." This time it was the surface ship's radioman who sounded urgent.

Lacombe and I looked at one another. "*Six* here, go ahead, Control."

"We've detected something new on sonar. Multiple contacts, definitely biologics, not a squid, and like nothing we've ever heard. Depth's seven thousand feet, range two miles. Whatever they are, they've just adjusted their course and are ascending, heading in your direction. Feeding the acoustics to you now. Dr. Caldwell seems to think it's just a school of fish, but we're officially recommending you surface immediately, do you concur?"

Lacombe turned the volume up on his sonar so Hank and I could listen.

Blee-bloop . . . Blee-bloop . . . Blee-bloop . . . Blee-bloop . . .

The pilot looked at me, waiting for a verdict.

"Way too loud to be a school of fish," I whispered, my mind racing to identify the vaguely familiar pattern. "Sounds almost like an amphibious air cavity."

"Must be a whale," offered Hank.

"At seven thousand feet? Not even a sperm whale can dive that deep." I plugged my own headset into the console to listen privately.

Blee-bloop . . . Blee-bloop . . . Blee-bloop . . .

It was a freakish sound, almost like a water jug expelling its contents.

And suddenly my brain kicked into gear. "I don't believe it," I whispered. "It's the *Bloop*."

"What the hell's a Bloop?"

"We don't know."

"What do you mean you don't know?" the pilot shot back. "You just called it a Bloop."

"That's the name the Navy assigned it. All we know is what they're not. They're not whales, because of the extreme depths, and they're not sharks or giant squids, because neither species possesses gas-filled sacs to make noises this loud."

"Are they dangerous?" Hank asked. "Will they attack?"

"I don't know, but I sure as hell don't want to find out this deep."

Lacombe got the message. "*Six* to Control, we're out of here." Grabbing his control stick, he activated the thrusters, adjusting the submersible's fairwater planes.

We began rising, crawling at a snail's pace.

"Look!" yelled Hank. The giant squid had abandoned the catch basket and was now scampering up the bubble, its tentacles wrapping around the cockpit glass, blocking much of our view. "She knows it's out there, too."

"What scares a giant squid?" I wondered aloud, then grabbed my arm rests as the submersible was jolted beneath us and the sound of twisting metal echoed throughout the compartment.

Lacombe swore as he scanned his control panel. "It's your damn octopus. It's wedging itself beneath the manipulator arm."

"She's frightened."

"Yeah, well so am I. That sound you're hearing is our oxygen and air storage tanks being pried away from the sub's sled. We lose that and the *Massett-6* becomes an anchor." The pilot repositioned his headset as he dialed up more pressure into the ballast tanks. "*Six* to Control, we've got an emergency—"

Another jolt cut him off, followed by an explosion that rattled our bones and released an avalanche of bubbles. Thunder roared in our ears as the sea quaked around us. Red warning lights flashed across Lacombe's control panel like a Christmas display, and the once cocky pilot suddenly looked very pale. "*Six*, we just lost primary and secondary ballast tanks. Internal hydraulic system is off-line. Propulsion system's failing—"

And then, my lovelies, the *Massett-6* began falling.

It fell slowly, tail first, but it was worse than any thrill ride I'd ever been on. Metal groaned and plates shook, and my hair seemed to stand on end, rustling against the back of my chair.

The rest of me just felt numb.

The pilot glanced in my direction, his expression confirming our death sentence.

Ace Futrell's voice over the radio sent a glimmer of hope. "Control to *Six*, hang in there, guys, we're readying an ROV with a tow line. What's your depth?"

Lacombe's perspiring face glistened in the control panel's translucent light. "Three-three-six-four feet, dropping fifty feet a minute. Better get that ROV down here quick!"

I felt helpless, like a passenger aboard an airliner that had just lost its engines, accompanied by an inner voice that refused to shut up. *What are you doing here? God, don't let me die . . . not yet, please. Lisa was right, I should've lived a little. Lord, get me out of this mess, and I swear, I'll—*

The sub rolled and rattled, shattering my repentance, and I fell back in my seat, my sweaty palms gripping the armrests, my eyes watching the depth gauge as I tensed for our one final, skull-crushing implosion.

"Jesus, there's something else out there!" Hank cried, pointing between the squid's thrashing tentacles.

I leaned forward. Several long, dark figures were circling us, stalking the squid. I could see shadows of movement, but before I could focus, our bubble became enshrouded in clouds of ink.

The Bloops were launching their attack.

Through my headphones, I could hear them as they tore into the giant squid, their sickening high-pitched growls, like hungry fox terriers, gnawing upon their prey's succulent flesh.

My mind abandoned me then. Too terrified to reason, I squeezed my eyes shut—and was suddenly hit with a subliminal image from my childhood.

Underwater.

Deathly cold.

The darkness—pierced by a funnel of heavenly light!

Get to the light . . . get to the light—

"The light!" Opening my eyes, I tossed aside my shoulder harness and twisted the knob on the control station panel, changing the arc lights from red back to normal.

The sea appeared again, and we could see the torn hydraulic hoses and the sub's mangled manipulator arm dangling from its ravaged perch, along with the severed remains of lifeless tentacles, all swirling in a pool of black soup.

"Control to *Six*. The ROV's in the water. Hang in there, Don, we're coming to get you."

"Huh?" Lacombe pulled himself away from the spectacle outside to check our depth. "Control, we just passed thirty-eight hundred feet. Put the pedal to the metal, Ace, we're living on borrowed time."

I was on my feet now, looking straight up through the bubble cockpit at a lone tentacle still wrapped around the sub's tow arm. The arm's death grip was preventing the rest of the dead squid's gushing mantle and head from releasing to the sea.

Lost in the moment, I stood and watched that lifeless appendage as it slowly unfurled. The remains of the giant squid's torpedo-shaped body released, drifting up and away, away from our light.

They were upon it in seconds, long brown forms darting in and out of the shadows, each maybe twenty to thirty feet in length, ravaging the carcass like a pack of starving wolves.

They were dark and fast and were too far away for me to identify, but their size and sheer voracity intensified my fear. I was witnessing a gruesome display of Mother Nature—it was pure animal instinct—and for a brief moment I felt relieved I'd be dead long before their voracious jaws ever tore into my flesh.

Craaaaack . . .

Death danced before me once more as the hairline fracture worked its way slowly, inch by crooked inch, across the acrylic bubble. The fear in my gut seemed to suck me in like a black hole.

Lacombe grabbed desperately for his radio. "Ace, where's that goddamn ROV?!"

"She just passed twenty-two hundred feet."

"Not good enough, Control, we're in serious trouble down here!"

I fell back in my chair again, then I was up on my feet, unable to sit, unable to keep still, the pressure building inside the cabin, building inside my skull, as the crack in the acrylic bubble continued spiderwebbing outward, and the depth gauge crept below 4,230 feet.

I closed my eyes, my breathing shallow, insane last thoughts creeping into my mind. I imagined David

Caldwell reading my eulogy at a grave site. ". . . sure, we'll miss him, but as the Beatles said, oh blah dee, oh blah da, life goes on . . . bra—"

Just when I thought things couldn't get worse, the Grim Reaper proved me wrong. With a sizzling hiss, the sub's batteries short-circuited, casting the three of us in a sudden, suffocating, claustrophobic darkness.

Panic seized me, sitting on my chest like an elephant. I gasped for air, I couldn't breathe!

Neon blue emergency lights flashed on as the blessed backup generator took over.

I wheezed an acidic-tasting breath, then another, as I watched the blue lights begin to dim.

"Just hang on, just hang on, we'll be all right." Lacombe was hyperventilating, clearly not believing his own lie.

The aft compartment's five-inch aluminum walls buckled in retort.

All of us were losing it, waiting our turn to die, but poor Hank couldn't take any more. Limbs shaking, his eyes insane with fear, he announced, "I gotta get out of here—" then lunged for the escape hatch.

Paralyzed, I could only watch the drama unfold as Donald Lacombe leaped into the rear compartment and tackled the cameraman, pinning him to the deck. "Kid, get back here and help me! Kid?"

But I was gone, my muscles frozen, my mind mesmerized, for staring at me from beyond the cockpit's cracking acrylic windshield was a pair of round, sinister, opaque eyes . . . cold and soulless, unthinking eyes of death . . . mythic and nightmarish, eyes that burn into a man's mind to haunt him the rest of his days . . . as final as a casket being lowered into the earth and as unfeeling as the maggots that reap upon the flesh.

It was death that stared at me, brain-splattering, final as final can be death—and I screamed like I've never screamed before, a bloodcurdling howl that halted Hank Griffeth in his delirium and sent Donald Lacombe scrambling back over his seat.

The dragon can sense yer fear, Zachary, he can smell it in yer blood.

"What? What did you see?"

I gasped, fighting for air to form the words, but the creature was gone, replaced by a blinking red light, now closing in the distance.

Lacombe pointed excitedly, "It's the ROV!"

The mini torpedo-shaped remotely operated vehicle homed in on the sonic distress beacon emanating from our tow hook. Within seconds, the end of the tow-cable was attached, the line instantly going taut.

Our submersible groaned and spun, then stopped sinking.

I closed my eyes and continued hyperventilating, still frightened beyond all reason.

"Control, we're attached, but the pressure's cracked the bubble. Take us up, Ace, fast and steady!"

"Roger that, Don. Stand by."

Tears of relief poured from my two companions' eyes as the crippled *Massett-6* rose. As for me, I could only stare at the depth gauge as I trembled, counting off seconds and feet as we climbed.

4,200 feet . . . 4,150 . . . 4,100 . . .

To my horror, the cracks in the acrylic bubble continued radiating outward, racing to complete the fracture.

3,800 feet . . . 3,700 . . . 3,600 . . .

My mind switched into left-brain mode, instantly calculating our constant rate of ascent against the pattern of cracks and declining water pressure squeezing against the glass.

No good, the glass won't hold . . . we need to climb faster!

A pipe burst overhead, spewing icy water all over my back. Leaping from my seat, I attacked the shut-off valve like a madman.

"Faster, Control, she's breaking up!"

3,150 . . . 3,100 . . . 3,050 . . .

The pipe leak sealed, I curled in a ball, allowing Hank to replace me up front.

2,800 feet . . . 2,700 . . . 2,600 . . .

The first droplets of seawater appeared along the cracks in the bubble. "Come on, baby," Lacombe chanted, "hold on . . . just a little bit longer."

1,800 feet . . . 1,700 . . . 1,600 . . .

We seemed to be rising faster now, the ebony sea melding around us into shades of gray, dawn's curtains filtering into the depths.

The pilot and cameraman giggled and slapped one another on the back.

Hyperventilating, I exhaled and inhaled, preparing my lungs for the rush of sea I prayed would never come.

"Thank you, Jesus, thank you," Hank whispered, crossing himself with one hand, wiping sweat and tears from his beet-red face with the other. "Praise God, we're saved."

"Told you we'd make it," Donald said, his cockiness returning with the light.

"My kids . . . I can't wait to hug them again."

What were they talking about? Didn't they realize we were

still too deep, still in danger?

"Hey, Zack, hand me my camera, we need to document our triumphant return."

Like a zombie, I reached to the deck and picked up the heavy piece of equipment, passing it forward, confused about why we were still alive.

See, you're not such a genius, you can be wrong. Now lighten up. As Lisa would say, enjoy the ride.

1,200 feet.

1,000 feet.

800 feet . . .

David's voice blared over the radio. "Dr. Wallace, you still with us?"

Hank swung his camera around, but I pushed the lens away.

"Dr. Wallace? Hello? Say something so we know you're alive."

"Fuck you."

600 feet . . . 520 feet . . . 440 feet . . .

The ocean melded from a deep purple into a royal blue as we passed the deepest depths a human had ever ventured on a single breath.

The second deepest point, only a few feet higher, had resulted in death.

365 feet . . .

Good . . . keep going, the water's weight subsiding every foot, the cracks slowing now.

310 feet.

I wiped away tears, my face breaking into a broad smile. Hank slapped me on the back and I giggled. *Maybe we were going to make it.*

"Control to *Six*, divers are in the water, standing by. Welcome back, team."

Lacombe winked at Hank. "Hey, Control, wait until you see what we've got on film."

Life is so fragile. One moment you're alive, the next, a semi-tractor trailer plows into you and it's all over, no warning, no final words or thoughts, everything gone.

At 233 feet, the bubble exploded inward, the Sargasso roaring through our sanctuary like a freight train, blinding us in its suffocating fury.

I saw the pilot's face explode like a ripe tomato as shards of acrylic glass riddled his harnessed body like machine gun fire. Hank appeared out of the corner of my eye, and then the Atlantic Ocean lifted me from my perch and bashed me sideways against the rear wall. Only the sudden change in pressure kept me conscious, squeezing my skull in its vise. Buried beneath this howling avalanche, I lashed out blindly in the darkness, my muscles lead, my hands groping . . . my mind recognizing the rear hatch even as it ordered my spent arms to turn its wheel.

I felt the surface ship's support cable *snap* beneath the weight of the sea. My hands held on desperately to the hatch as the freed submersible tumbled backward, falling once more toward the abyss.

The sudden loss of pressure tore at my eardrums.

And then, miraculously, the hatch yawned open.

My kids . . . I can't wait to hug them again . . .

Hank!

The left side of my brain screamed at me to get out, my chances of making it to the surface already less than 10 percent, but it was my right brain that took command, suddenly endowing me with the courage of Sir William Wallace himself.

I groped for Hank. Grabbed him from behind his shirt collar, then pushed his inert 195-pound body out the hatch, into the Sargasso's warm embrace.

A laborious twenty-five seconds had passed, and I was struggling to haul an unconscious man topside through 245 feet of water.

Get to the light . . .

I kicked and paddled, forcing myself into a cadence so as not to excessively burn away those precious molecules of air.

You'll never make it, not with Hank. Let him go, or you'll both drown.

But I didn't let go, not because I wanted to be a hero, not because I actually believed we would make it, but because, at that moment, I knew in my heart that his life was more important than mine.

My lungs seemed on fire, my beating heart the only sound I could hear.

Was I even making progress? My legs were lead ... were they even kicking?

Scenes from my adolescence flashed before my eyes. My inner voice took over the play-by-play: *This should be the last play, Princeton down by four. Here's the snap, the quarterback pitching to Wallace. He escapes one tackle, then another, and he's heading for daylight.*

The light ... so precious. Get to the light.

He's across mid-field ... he's at the forty ...

Get ... to ... the ... light ...

Wallace's at the thirty ... the twenty ...

The liiiiii ...

He's at the ten, with just one defender to beat ...

Shadows closed in on my peripheral vision. I saw death's dark hand reach for me ... reach for Hank.

Oh, no! Wallace's tackled at the goal line as time expires.

Out of air, out of strength, out of heartbeats, my willpower gone, I slipped out of my body, and drowned.

Again.

THE LOCH

On Sale Now